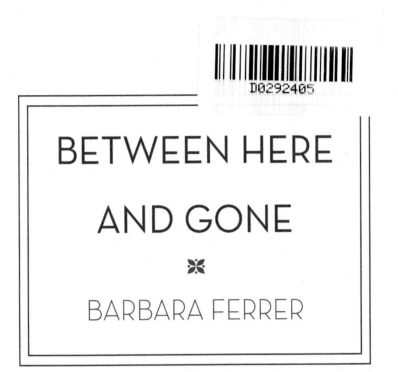

BETWEEN HERE AND GONE

BARBARA FERRER

DIVERSIONBOOKS

Also by Barbara Ferrer

Both Sides Now

Diversion Books
A Division of Diversion Publishing Corp.
443 Park Avenue South, Suite 1008
New York, New York 10016
www.DiversionBooks.com

For more information, email info@diversionbooks.com

First Diversion Books edition January 2016.
Print ISBN: 978-1-62681-713-5
eBook ISBN: 978-1-62681-712-8

For Nate and Abby—may your journeys take you far and wide, yet always bring you home. I love you both more than you know.

PROLOGUE

APRIL 1959

"Talia, I'm going to be sick."

"Oh, no. *Otra vez?* How can you even have anything left?"

But Carlito was already leaning against me, the harsh, dry rattle of his heaves contrasting with the sloppy wet sounds of the waves slapping against the sides of the boat. I fought to suppress my own gagging as bile soaked through my skirt, hot and acidic and smelling faintly, ridiculously, of *maduros*. Probably nothing more than a product of exhausted and overwrought imagination. Wistful memory of the final meal served at home before we left, colluding with the terrifying uncertainty of our future.

Nothing out of the ordinary.

Everything out of the ordinary.

None of the servants any the wiser that it would be the last time they'd be cooking for us, serving us, cleaning up after us.

Or maybe they'd known. No one could trust anyone else any longer. I wonder how many of them at least suspected? Might have been watching, waiting …

We should have just flown. We should have *left*—long before Papi made the decision. I *tried* telling them. I had desperately wanted to leave. Almost as much as I wanted to stay. Wanted things to be the way they'd been, childish pipe dream that it was. Wanted to curl up and die.

But Papi insisted that not only could we bring more on the boat, it would also serve us well in bringing extra money since we'd be leaving almost everything behind. What we still possessed was tied to the country in ways that would all too easily rouse suspicion if we tried to make substantial changes. Another reason we'd taken so long to leave. Gathering money and items in small increments, all very cloak and dagger in a way that might have been thrilling and exciting if not for the sheer terror overlaying every step or word.

Not that any of this was discussed directly with me. After all, I was just *la niña*—*la princessa*—no need to worry my precious little head with such trivialities.

What a joke.

Yet so typical that he'd still think of me in such a way. Attempting to keep me locked away and preserved in some airtight box despite all that had already happened. So willfully blind to the fact that I'd left innocence behind in one shattering moment weeks ago. How could he be so callous? Who knew? Perhaps it was for his own benefit. Protecting himself.

Mami and Abuela had always said it wasn't that the men in our lives didn't care or weren't aware. Just simply that they couldn't handle our pain. It overwhelmed them. So instead they focused on believing we were delicate flowers requiring protection. We allowed them the illusion. To protect *them*. And because it suited our purposes.

However, I didn't *want* to be strong. I didn't want to protect anyone. I wanted to howl and scratch and spit and rip flesh from bones and rail at the inhumane unfairness of it all.

Perhaps I was better at this pretending than even I had imagined. Because they—Papi, Mami, Abuela, Carlito—every one of them thought I was strong enough to cope.

Using a clean section of my skirt, I wiped Carlito's mouth, dabbed the perspiration off his sweet face, trapped in that shimmering moment somewhere between boy and man. *Pobrecito*—there was so much he'd be missing. So much he should be experiencing that wasn't this hell.

"Let me get you some water, *hermanito.*"

"Don't go." His voice cracked. Definitely more boy there, as his arms tightened around my waist—afraid I'd leave.

"But it'll make you feel better."

"It'll make me throw up again." Shades of a deeper tone. A surety. Almost against my will I smiled. So stubborn, my little brother. Since the cradle, no one had known him as well as he knew himself—or so he very firmly and vociferously believed.

However, this wasn't simply a matter of wanting to get him water—I also desperately wanted to change my clothes. Get out of this dress with its soaked, filthy skirt. Never mind that in sacrificing clothes in order to leave room for other items and the fact that this was far from the first time I'd held Carlito through a bout of nausea, I didn't have much left. At the very least, I could always borrow a pair of Carlito's pants and a shirt. Anything would be better than sitting for God only knew how much longer with sodden, smelly cotton clinging to my thighs. Perhaps if I'd still been wearing my girdle, I could have simply shimmied out of my dress and left myself in the equivalent of a bathing suit, but the torture device had long since been discarded—along with the gloves and stockings. It was simply too damp for that many layers of clothing. What could Mami have been thinking when she insisted we dress in our Sunday best—that we were going to wash ashore at a yacht club? It was absurd.

So many things—once considered of paramount importance—all of a sudden seemed absurd.

"Carlito, I have to change my clothes."

"Stay." A command, coming easily from the young prince accustomed to getting his way, yet easy for me to ignore. That is, until his gaze fixed itself on my face, his eyes enormous dark smudges in the pale oval of his face. An unnerving deception, since those eyes, in the light of day, were the same pale, brilliant green as Papi's. The "eyes of the San Martín men" as Abuelita proclaimed time and again from her spot of honor at the foot of the French mahogany table. But in the dark, the color was lost—overwhelmed by fear. Ignoring the wet and the stink and my own terror and fury, I gathered him close, my little brother, taller than me now, the future man of the family yet forever the baby, holding him as the yacht bobbed quietly along the waves. We were saving our last bit of gas, I knew. For those final crucial miles.

I closed my eyes and turned my face into the breeze drifting through the cabin's open door, breathing deeply. Sea air always helped. Always soothed. Even under these circumstances.

"Natalia—"

I blinked, not sure if I'd drifted or not. But I must have, because where before there had been nothing but infinite dark—

Lights.

Through the window—tiny pinpricks of light in the distance, piercing the black, *gracias a Dios.*

Finally.

Lights that appeared to be standing still, only their reflections bobbing and weaving the slightest bit on the dark water. Looking like fireflies. Difficult, but not impossible to catch.

Beneath the smooth leather soles of my shoes, I felt the engines rumble to life, the distant lights continuing to beckon, reaching out, guiding us in.

"We're here," Carlito whispered, struggling to sit straighter. "Natalia, we're here."

"*Yo sé,*" I whispered absently. But *where?*

My stare never strayed from the lights that drew closer, closer … so close I could practically touch them, then—gone, my hip stinging, fingers digging into the padded cushions of the bench as I struggled to regain my balance, to sit up, shaking my head to clear it of the buzzing whine.

"*Vamos, niños.*"

That came through loud and clear. I hadn't hit my head. But

it felt like it as I stared at Abuelita who was tugging at my arm with one hand, pushing Carlito toward the cabin door with the other. "*¡Ahora!*"

"But Abuelita—where?" Carlito was already on his feet, one hand blindly reaching out to help me up as he stared through the door at the lights.

"*Tírate*—into the water!" she ordered, pushing past us and onto the deck, unfolding the hinged wooden ladder bolted to the back of the boat. No. Just … no. That ladder—the center of each step worn several shades lighter—it was meant for sunny days and jumping into clear turquoise waters. Not desperate, nighttime tumbles into an inky, terrifying mystery.

"Your father hit something. He doesn't know what. It was too dark."

"Where is Papi—Mami? Why can't we use the life raft?" I tried to charge past my grandmother, trying to get to the cockpit, but she grabbed my shoulders, shaking me.

"*¡Bastante!* We can't fit everything we need into the life raft if we are all in there. Do not worry, they are coming and we are getting everything important, but you must go over the side and get to shore. *Now.*"

"Wait! I need to get—"

She held my arm in a death grip. "You can't."

"*No!*" I wrenched away from her, lurching back toward the cabin and finding myself unceremoniously yanked back, the seams of my dress digging painfully into the soft flesh beneath my arms as my grandmother's hold on the back of my dress tightened.

"Natalia, we do not have time." Spinning me around, she grasped my shoulders, her features softening for an instant. "He will get your things. *Te lo juro*, I'll make sure he gets everything."

"But—"

"*M'ijita*, when have I ever let you down?"

It was futile. If she had to push me over the side herself she would. Resigned, I nodded, my hand going to the front of my dress, feeling for my gold chain, tracing the outline of the small cross I'd worn since my Confirmation and the other, weightier pendant that had only recently joined it. I headed for the opening where Carlito waited, pale, yet clear-eyed and practically quivering with a palpable anticipation. A flash of irritation shot through me. The little idiot was actually *excited* about this turn of events.

But before I could take more than a step or two, my grandmother captured my arm once again. "Natalia, your shoes—*dejalos.*"

"What?" I glanced down, almost shocked to find them still on my feet. And all of a sudden, it seemed vital—the most important thing—to win one battle. Keep just one thing. "No—they're from Paris." Papi had bought them for me on our last trip—when we visited the Sorbonne and he'd told me I could go and I entertained visions of myself as Audrey Hepburn or Leslie Caron. Cavorting along the wide avenues and rues in my soft, black flats and capris and the slightly scratchy wool beret I'd bought from a street vendor on my final afternoon.

I'd had such dreams.

"*No importan.* Who cares where they came from? Leave them."

I could feel the fast, heavy throb of my pulse, right in the crook of my elbow, just below where her fingers curled, tight and cold. "We need to move quickly. Your father's not certain what damage the boat may have sustained. *Deja los jodido zapatos and vete. ¡Inmediatamente!*"

My mouth opened on a wordless scream at my grandmother's harsh shove, the rage that drove the urge to fight breaking free of the iron shackles with which I'd restrained it. My fists clenched—

"*No—*"

"*¡Ay!*" Her breath rushed out in one explosive huff. "Fine. Suit yourself. I have no time for this nonsense."

"But you're coming? All of you?" Carlito asked, grabbing my shoulders and turning me toward the opening in the rail.

"Yes, yes—I am going to help your parents. We'll be right behind you. You—" she pointed at Carlito, "take care of your sister."

My laugh came out so bitter and full of rage, it was a shock the gleaming brass railing didn't corrode in that instant.

"You're kidding." I laughed again. "He's a baby."

"I'm thirteen," he retorted from where he waited, poised to jump, no second thought about it. Further proof that he had no business taking care of anyone.

Be careful, hermanito. *Don't swim too far out.*

Why don't we play with the dominoes, Carlito? We'll make a design and I'll let you knock them down.

No ... no llores, m'ijito—don't cry. It's just an ice cream cone. Here, I'll share mine with you. I'll always share.

I took care of him.

"*Bueno, m'ija,* you're the one acting like a baby and wasting valuable time." Abuelita pointed a long elegant finger, ghostly white in the dim light, at the rail. "He's not."

Because now he thought this was some big adventure. That it was exciting, like those stupid movies he'd spent his Saturdays watching in the dark, butter-scented confines of *El Capitan.* He was practically bouncing up and down, waiting for me. Waiting to begin. My eyes stinging, I pushed past him and started down the steps.

"Your shoes, Talia," Carlito whispered as he started down after me, his feet slender and bare and white above my head.

"Shut up."

I paused on the final rung before the ladder descended into the water and reached down, slipping off one shoe, then the other. Holding the pair in one hand high above my head, I lowered myself the rest of the way, gasping as I began treading water. It wasn't cold—not really. I'd simply never gone swimming at night. Not in the ocean. Not fully clothed. Not like this—with this queer dread and its accompanying chill lapping at me more insistently than the waves.

It would be so easy to go limp—sink to the bottom.

But the lights ... they were there, getting closer, bit by bit. Even faster if I would truly swim. I was a strong swimmer. I could forget the shoes—it was stupid really. They were just shoes. My breath hitched in my chest, a serrated edge slicing from the base of my neck all the way down to my belly, cramping in hard knots. Who cared what they meant? Nothing really.

"What do you think lives in the water here? Do you think there might be sharks?"

"Shut *up*, Carlito."

"Maybe jellyfish. I bet there are jellyfish."

I didn't even know where we were and he was asking about sharks. Or jellyfish. Or—

I screamed as something brushed my leg, long and slow—a few feet in front of me, a dark form surfaced and I screamed again, one shoe dropping from nerveless fingers to land beside me with a quiet splash.

"Don't scare the sharks, *hermana*."

"*Carlito*—it's *not* funny. It's not a joke. Don't you understand? Don't you? Don't *you*?"

I kept saying it over and over, my shoulders burning from the strain, my lungs, my eyes, my legs, kicking and kicking—everything burning, water filling my nose, my ears, muffling the noises outside my head even as it made the sounds inside grow louder and louder—

Just let go … It would be so easy … Just let go … You know you want to …

"Stop—it's okay. You're here. You're safe."

I kicked some more, fighting the new pressure under my arms—shaking my head, long strands of hair whipping across my face and catching in my lashes and mouth.

"Stop, honey, you can stop, it's okay. It's okay."

I shook my head again, rubbed my face against my shoulder, felt the gritty rasp of wet sand scratching my skin as the disembodied voice floated above me.

"Do you understand me?"

Slowly, I blinked, eyes stinging as fresh saline from tears cleared away the salt from the ocean water.

"*Si*—" I shook my head again. "Yes. I understand." My voice emerged thin and brittle, rising on each word as I looked around, frantic, desperately trying to focus. "My little brother—"

"He's fine, sweetheart." Hands, warm and secure, like Tata Sucre, my long-ago nanny, draped a blanket over my shoulders, then turned me gently, focusing the beam from her flashlight on Carlito, hunched over on his hands and knees, gasping as a man draped a blanket over his body, back to looking slender and delicate—the terrified glance he shot my way returning him to the boy I had always looked out for.

"*Ay, gracias a Dios—gracias madre santisima—gracias.*" Rough sand scraped the tender skin of palms and knees as I scrabbled across the short distance separating us. Fresh tears flooded my eyes as I felt his arms go around my neck, his thin chest heaving with sobs as our stealthy flight, the terrifying journey, and this final race toward our future finally caught up to him. Reflexively, I crossed myself once, then twice, feeling again for my chain, making certain it was still there, before stroking the seal smooth curve of his head, murmuring reassurances that everything was all right. We were all right. I would take care of him. Like always.

The voice beside me quietly said, "You were right, John." Then softer—"What's your name, honey?"

I went to clutch the edges of the blanket, pull it tighter around Carlito, startled at what I found in my hand.

"Natalia San Martín," I said softly, staring at the single black shoe, the leather soaked and dripping and ruined. "My name is Natalia San Martín. I'm ... from Havana."

It would be the last time I said that.

PART ONE

ONE

DECEMBER 1964

"*Downtown* ...

   "*Downtown* ...

   "*Downtown* ...*"*

   "*I'm Dan Daniels on WMCA, New York's station for all your favorite hits from today and tomorrow and that was 'Downtown,' the brand-new single from lovely songbird, Petula Clark, and our latest Good Guys Sure Shot. How's about a prediction that's one song that's gonna shoot straight to the top of the charts and have everyone dancing well into the New Year? Call in if you agree—or even if you don't. And we want you to tell us—after 'Auld Lang Syne' plays and the ball drops, what song are you going to be rockin' out to come New Year's Eve? Call and talk to me at PL5-9622.*

   "*But right now, let's take a trip down Memory Lane to February of this past year. Do you remember where you were when the lads from Liverpool debuted on Ed Sullivan with this song?*"

A moment later, the first, unmistakable notes of "All My Loving" rang out from the Philco perched in its spot on the shelf just above the big gas range, accompanied by an exuberant—and thankfully melodic—tenor.

Remy, Remy, Remy.

The incorrigible Creole chef was forever getting scolded for playing "that raucous children's music" in the kitchen as opposed to the jazz that customarily played in the dining room, but the scoldings had little effect. He'd merely flash his dimpled smile with the very white, slightly crooked teeth and begin murmuring endearments and apologies equally in rapid-fire French-English *patois*, charming anyone within earshot and causing Mrs. Mercier to tut and shake her head, throwing up her hands as she stalked off. And peace once again would reign in the kitchen. It helped, too, that everyone, including Remy, knew his worth. Barely thirty, he was a master of his craft, wooed by restaurants throughout the city, but unfailingly loyal to Mercier's—two facts of which Mrs. Mercier was well aware. Ultimately, if allowing him to play popular music in the kitchen stimulated the creative genius and kept him firmly planted in her kitchen, then popular music there would be.

A plate materialized at my elbow. "A *lagniappe*."

I stared at the line of crêpes, delicate gold on the outside, thick, pale cream dotted with bits of smoked salmon and tiny peas spilling from the ends.

"This would appear to be a good deal more than a little extra."

Blue eyes, so dark they almost appeared black, the illusion heightened by almost indecently thick lashes, stared unblinking— the expression in them not the slightest bit innocent. "It's not as if the ingredients aren't already here. Besides, you're my guinea pig for the filling. I blended ricotta into the béchamel. If it's good, I'll propose we add it to the Sunday brunch menu."

"Well, then, so long as it's in the pursuit of a noble cause."

"*Absolument, chère.*" A single black eyebrow rose as he glanced at the bowl before me. "What's wrong with the soup?"

"Nothing—as well you know. It's not like you to fish for compliments, Remy." Mostly because he didn't need to.

"Forget compliments—why ain't you barely touched it?"

"Because a customer came in who needed to be seated, so I've only just started," I explained, suppressing a sigh as the eyebrow lowered to meet its mate in a straight line.

"*You* were supposed to be on your break—" he spared a glance at the antique grandfather clock standing sentry on the landing leading up to the second floor offices, "ten minutes ago."

"It took but a moment." Honestly, he had the soul of a nervous auntie. If he got it into his head, he'd go scold the other hostess on duty and the poor girl was still new. She needed more experience before being faced with Remy in temperamental chef mode.

"Customer could have damn well waited. You act like we got but one hostess, *bebe*. Bad enough you wait to the end of your shifts to eat, now you lettin' your food go cold for no damn good reason."

I fought a smile. "If Mrs. Mercier heard you describing her valued customers as 'no damn good reason.'"

"*Pfft.*" He shrugged, clearly unconcerned. "Go on now, eat before it goes any colder." He turned and stalked back into the kitchen, the *swish* of the door swinging closed only just managing to muffle what I was quite certain was extremely colorful grumbling.

Generally, I wasn't prone to argument with Remy—even considering his old lady reprimands and barely-disguised ulterior motives. His ulterior motives smelled too heavenly for argument.

And *tasted* entirely too heavenly. Using the side of the fork, I separated another small piece and speared it on the tines as I opened my book to the saved page and resumed reading.

"That doesn't look like anything on the menu."

Surprised, I glanced up, fork halfway to my mouth. "It's not."

"Hm—if it tastes as good as it looks, perhaps it should be."

I carefully lowered the fork to the plate and set my book and napkin aside as I stood. "May I help you, Mr. Barnes? Was something not to your satisfaction?"

"No, no, please—" Before I'd fully slid from behind the secluded corner table where I habitually took my meals, he was already waving me back down. "May I?" he asked, gesturing at one of the free chairs.

"Of course."

Since one simply did not refuse a Barnes—not at Mercier's, given that the venerable old restaurant had served as something of a secondary office for the equally old New York publishing family for several generations—and considering that Gregory Barnes was the scion of his distinguished family, then refusal was even less of an option. So if it was the older man's desire to join me, then I would be gracious and accommodating, as nothing less would be expected or tolerated.

Every bit the gentleman, he waited for me to resume my seat before taking his, nodding at the waiter who materialized at his elbow. A moment later, a Scotch and bowl of Remy's secret recipe Creole-spiced almonds appeared.

"Damned lunch went so long it's practically cocktail hour anyway."

What, exactly, was one supposed to say to that? With no response immediately forthcoming, I settled for the polite smile and non-committal sound low in my throat—a modified, ladylike version of one Remy often used and that had served me rather well in the past. Not that Mr. Barnes seemed to expect a response, necessarily, his narrow blue gaze roving over my simple lunch setting and lingering on the book I'd placed facedown at his approach.

"Those aren't in the translation."

Delivered in cultured, well-bred tones with a hint of a question, but for the most part, definitive. I glanced down at the cover. "How did you know?" There was nothing there to even indicate what the book was other than the remnants of what had once been a gold-embossed "Guy de Maupassant."

His fingers drifted over the worn edge of the faded red cloth cover. "I'd love to claim tremendous powers of clairvoyance," he finally admitted with a self-deprecating smile. "However, it's more a simple case of observation coupled with an educated guess. I know someone who has a copy that's near identical to this one. It happens to be in French."

The way his fingertips continued to gently stroke the book's cover clearly asked—in response, I nodded, watching as he took the book and began leafing through the pages, careful to hold my place with a finger. "By whatever means you used, Mr. Barnes, as you can see, you guessed correctly."

I rolled the edge of my napkin between my fingers, forcing them still only when Mr. Barnes' gaze flickered from the book to my hand.

"Please don't let me keep you from your meal. Remy would never forgive me."

"I—" I was hungry. And this was my break. The only time I'd have to myself again until late tonight. I didn't want to be rude— couldn't *afford* to be rude—but still, this was my time. Mine.

With a deep breath, I replaced the napkin in my lap and lifted the abandoned bite of crêpe to my mouth, chewing carefully while watching Mr. Barnes from beneath my lashes.

"*The Necklace*," he murmured quietly, flipping back to the page he'd been holding. "It's quite the story. So much in so little."

"He was a master of the form." The words were out before I could stop myself. I quickly separated another piece of crêpe and shoved it in my mouth in as ladylike a fashion as I could manage. Before I gave away anything else.

"Indeed." Drawing a slim silver case from the inside pocket of his jacket, he extracted a small card, using it to carefully mark the page before he closed the book and placed it between us on the table. Picking up his Scotch, he leaned back in his chair as if he had all day. Uncomfortable with someone simply watching me eat, I set my fork on my plate and pushed it slightly to one side before picking up my water glass.

"Wine?" Again, Gregory Barnes surprised me. Treating me almost like ... well, if not a social equal, then at the very least a respected guest. But that was backwards. Here, *he* was the guest. And while once upon a time I might have been his social equal, those days were very long gone and it could only serve me well to remember that.

"Thank you, sir, but—"

"I asked Marguerite if you were still on the clock," he

interrupted, bringing a more immediate worry to mind. Why had he been discussing me with Mrs. Mercier? "She told me that without fail, you save your meal break for the very end of your shift. Ergo, technically, you're no longer on the clock." With another one of those subtle gestures with which men in power seemed to be singularly gifted, he waved the waiter over and murmured, "Pinot gris for the young lady," while I was still trying to formulate a polite refusal. Especially given the glance the waiter shot my way. He was going to have to work on his discretion, that one. I could only hope he wouldn't immediately go play town crier in the kitchen, but I knew better.

"Seriously, Natalie, please eat. If I imagine that Remy wouldn't forgive me, then I *know* Marguerite would have my hide if she thought I was keeping you from your meal. She's liable to sign me up for a dish-washing stint." He waited until the waiter deposited the small goblet by my elbow and melted into the shadows that blanketed the restaurant in this quiet time as afternoon blended into evening. Defeated, I lifted my goblet and touched it to his already raised glass, the light chime continuing to ring as I took a sip, holding it on my tongue.

Oh my. Oh … *my*. My entire body felt as if it was sighing in pleasure. Just this once couldn't hurt, could it?

"Why in French?"

I was beginning to get the distinct impression that Mr. Barnes' mind was akin to a firefly, the lightning-quick manner in which it flitted from question to question. However, I also had the distinct impression that there was a rather deliberate method behind the seeming randomness. And that he wouldn't let go until he got the answers he sought. After all, one did not become the scion of a successful family without a certain tenacity, no?

"There's a certain rhythm to the romance languages." Resigned to the conversation, resigned to this whole … whatever this was, I pulled my plate close and resumed eating. "And a purity of thought and intent when a story is told in its native language that I feel is often lost within translation. To me, there's no way you can truly grasp the author's meaning—the vision he was trying to convey, when you're reading it ..." I paused, momentarily struggling for the words. "Secondhand, I suppose would be the best way to express it."

"Interesting insight."

And there it was left, with not a one of the barrage of questions for which I'd steeled myself. After all, how many restaurant hostesses, no matter how cultured the restaurant, spent their breaks reading French short stories? Then again, how many patrons of such restaurants even bothered noticing the hostesses at all, let alone what they were reading? One of the reasons I'd always felt safe doing so. However, all Mr. Barnes did was take another sip of his Scotch and leisurely pick through the almonds in the bowl, popping the occasional nut into his mouth as I finished my meal.

I did have a brief moment of wondering if I'd revealed too much. But it was just as quickly dismissed. What possible harm could come from his knowing I read fluent French?

"Don't you like the wine? I'm sorry—I should have asked. My wife says I don't know when to leave the boss persona behind and behave like a normal human."

I stared into the shimmering pale gold depths of my nearly full glass and relaxed marginally. "No sir, the wine is wonderful." I took another sip, simply because to not, would be an insult to both Mr. Barnes and the wine. "It's just I can't afford to indulge overmuch. I may be off the clock here, but I do have another job."

"Now?" He pushed back his sleeve and glanced down at his watch, while I fought back an unexpected pang at the sight of the mellow gold and cream-colored face of the Patek Phillipe. A near-twin to Papi's. The one he'd worn every day I could remember until ... he didn't any longer.

"But it's going on five."

"Which means I run the risk of being late if I don't get going. If you'll excuse me—"

"Of course." Automatically, he rose as I did. Taking my dishes, I went into the kitchen, where I left them beside the washing station with a murmured thanks before going to collect my belongings. On my way back from the employees' coat closet, I paused by the break room where Remy sat alone, staring off into space as he smoked. A rarity—to see him so still, head tilted back, eyes nearly closed, aromatic smoke cloaking him in a filmy gray veil. An amorphous wall that few dared breach. I dared, because I knew he didn't mind if it was me. However, in deference to his stillness, I kept my voice soft.

"Thank you again for the crêpes, Remy. They were wonderful."

His head inclined slightly. "You'll tell me more what you thought?"

"*Absolument.* Tomorrow. I promise."

Another nod, then casually, still staring off into a distance only he could see, asked, "What'd Greg Barnes want with you?"

If I was one of the few who could disturb Remy during a break, then he was one of the few who'd dare ask anything so personal. As well as being one of the even fewer to whom I'd give any answer beyond a mind your business stare.

"I have no idea. Asked about the book I was reading."

"Plying you with wine just to ask about some book?" The corner of Remy's mouth twitched as he brought the cigarette up and took another leisurely drag. "That's a new approach."

I suppressed a sigh as I fumbled with the pins to my hat. "Honestly, Remy—just because you're utterly debauched doesn't mean the rest of the world is." I closed the distance between us and leaned down to drop a quick kiss on each shadowed cheek. "*À bientôt.*"

"*À bientôt, chère.* You behave now, you hear?"

"As if I know any other way to be. Besides, how much trouble could I possibly get in between now and tomorrow?"

"You should let me show you someday." Dimples flashed in the grin that Mrs. Mercier likened to the devil's own. "You off uptown?"

"Last time before the holidays."

"Well, you take care when you head back home. People like to go crazy, this time of year."

"Speaking from experience, Remy?"

That disgusted noise rumbled low in his throat as he stood and put a hand to my back, shooing me out the door. "Get on with you, girl. And be careful."

Smiling, I returned to the near-deserted dining room, where I found Mr. Barnes leaning against the brass-railed bar near the front door, wearing a black topcoat and appearing as if he was also finally leaving as well.

"Where are you headed?"

Why?

But I merely replied, "Uptown."

"Pleasant coincidence. I'll give you a lift."

I tugged on my black gloves, lacing my fingers together and pushing until the soft leather molded itself to my skin. "Mr. Barnes, truly, that's not necessary—"

He took my coat from the stool on which I'd draped it and held it open. "I interrupted your meal and played Twenty Questions when I'm sure you would much rather have been reading and relishing some downtime. If I'd had any idea you had another job to get to, I would have never—"

"Sir, really—"

"Natalie, grant me this small favor, please? Ease my conscience. If I go home feeling guilty about having potentially made you late, especially with the weather worsening, and my wife picks up on it, then I'll have to confess all and risk never hearing the end of it." His voice rose slightly in pitch. "How on *earth* could you jeopardize that girl's job, Greg? Don't you understand that other people have lives that don't operate by the same rules as yours, you overprivileged nitwit?"

I smothered a laugh into my gloved fist. "Your wife would say that to you? Those exact words?"

"Oh no." He smiled, years and end-of-the-day weariness falling away. "That's the censored version. Her actual words would be far more … colorful."

This time, my laugh escaped freely. "She sounds—"

"Headstrong?" he broke in, his smile broadening a notch.

I lowered my head to fasten the large jet buttons on my coat.

"Actually, I was going to say interesting."

"She has to be both, marrying into and staying one step ahead of my family. Not to mention, run a household, raise three sons, and deal with me."

The fond, exasperated manner in which he spoke of family struck another unexpected pang, this one sharp enough to leave behind a physical ache.

"So please—" He held the door—and my gaze. "It would honestly be a favor."

Years of being schooled in precisely the right thing to do and say asserted themselves, much as they had at so many crucial times before. Shoving the ache of memory deep to the recesses of my brain where all the others lived, I nodded and said, "Of course. Thank you very much."

"No—thank you." He gestured toward the long, black Lincoln at the curb, a driver standing beside the open back door. Once ensconced inside, Mr. Barnes turned to me. "Where to?"

"Upper East Side. Concord School." I didn't bother with a street address. People of Gregory Barnes' stature knew precisely where Concord was. Even mere peons knew where Concord was. An athletic powerhouse of a private school housed in elegant brick buildings cloaked in ivy and old money.

I waited for him to pass the information to the driver, then answered what was likely to be his inevitable question. "I tutor. English literature and French."

Mostly.

He settled back into the leather seat and regarded me.

"They must pay rather well if you're willing to trek all the way up there, especially on a miserable day like today."

"When you're on your own, every little bit helps." I turned my head just far enough to study the icy rain sticking to the car window and the streets beyond. That made the Tuesday afternoon rush hour traffic even slower than usual and the commuters, rushing along, bags and briefcases held over their heads, even more visibly foul-tempered than usual. Closing my eyes, I shut it all out and took a deep breath—leather and tobacco and memories wrapping around me. Even if the lingering chill of my skin and the scent of damp wool painted them with a slightly different hue it nevertheless allowed me to pretend—for just these few moments—that that wasn't my world out there. That my world was fine wine and private cars and polite, educated gentlemen. It would be a memory to hold onto. Good timing. Some of the other memories, they'd begun fading to the point where they felt more like ephemeral wisps of a dream. Snippets of fantasy.

"Natalie—we're here."

"*Ay*—" I caught myself, almost too late. "Oh no, I'm so sorry. I'm so, so sorry." At least I'd been leaning against the window and not Mr. Barnes. *What* was I thinking? What would Mrs. Mercier think if this ever got back to her? I couldn't risk anything that might cause me to lose Mercier's. I should have just gone home. I could always find another tutoring job. I hoped. "Please forgive me, Mr. Barnes."

"Okay, first off—" The hand on my shoulder went from the gentle touch that had woken me, to a firmer hold, demanding attention. "I'm the first to appreciate professionalism, but I've known you since the first day you began working at Mercier's. I think we've progressed beyond Mr. Barnes, don't you? Call me Greg."

"But Mrs. Mercier—"

"Has known me since God was a boy. And knows I don't give a damn for formality. When you're working, I'll understand the need for professional courtesy, but otherwise, it's Greg."

Nice man, but clearly out of his mind. Because there was no way. I simply couldn't. But I also knew arguing would be a waste of time. Not that he gave me opportunity.

"Second. You're clearly exhausted." His hand moved from my shoulder to my chin, tilting my head back while his other hand reached up and turned on the domed ceiling light. His brows drew together. "Clearly." Releasing my chin, he flicked the light off, the sudden darkness doing little to obscure his frown. I could practically feel it across the seat. "I know Darby Carmichael. Do you want me to call—"

"No sir, Mr. Bar—Greg," I stammered. "Really, I'm fine." No, I really wasn't, the customary dread making its appearance, right on time, the sight of the distinctive wrought iron scrolls of the gates ringing the campus' perimeter bringing on the vague beginnings of nausea. However, I did not need him calling the headmaster. It was a day. Just like any other.

"I don't know why I dozed off, I'm terribly sorry. Perhaps I'm coming down with something—"

"Then I definitely should call. Darby's only a terror to the boys—otherwise he's rather humane and would certainly understand if one of his tutors was under the weather."

"Please. Don't." Fully awake now, I was able to assume my usual calm impassiveness. "I'll be fine and I really do need to meet with this student. It's disgraceful how little he knows and with his finals a week away."

Greg released a long sigh. "I've had many an acquaintance who went here. Unless things have experienced a seismic shift, there's not much would surprise me about a Concord student's academic prowess—or lack thereof."

Stepping from the car, he extended his hand. "You promise you're fine?"

"Yes." During my impromptu nap, the rain had become snow, flakes peppering Greg's sandy hair and black coat and stinging my eyes.

"Will you be all right getting home?"

"I'll be all right. I promise. Only the one student tonight, then I'll be on my way home before it even grows too late."

"All right then." From years of practice, I could easily translate his expression and body language. He was leaving; he wasn't happy about it, because to his mind, the situation wasn't satisfactorily under control, but what else could he legitimately do in this situation? His wife really did have her hands full with him.

With a wave, I headed up the brick walk to the scrolled gate. After exchanging a quick pleasantry with the gateman, I turned back to wave once again, knowing Greg would still be standing there, waiting until he saw me safely through. I took steadying breaths as I approached the library. Hopefully, my student would be here, would be prepared to study, and I could make a relatively quick session of it.

Wishful thinking, but it's what I held onto—what kept me coming back. That hopefully, one time—just once—it would be different. As I signed in at the desk, the pale Columbia student who served as the evening librarian handed me a key.

"Study room three. He's already there."

"Thank you."

As our gazes met during the perfunctory exchange, I caught the look in his eye—I wasn't quite sure if it was pitying, mocking, or some combination thereof. Truthfully? It wasn't as if analyzing would make any difference so why concern myself with it? Climbing the wide marble stairs, I made my way around the bronze-railed rotunda and entered the room where I found my student—a junior basketball player the team couldn't afford to lose, or so I'd been told—sitting in a chair, endless gray flannel-covered legs ending in burnished loafers propped on the table in front of him as he skimmed through *The Grapes of Wrath*.

"Hello, um …" I glanced down at the piece of paper I'd fished from my coat pocket. "Derek? I'm Natalie. Your tutor."

"Yeah, I figured." The legs swung down and the book landed on the floor.

I forced a laugh even as my stomach clenched and bright lights streaked across my vision, threatening my equilibrium. "Ready to be quizzed already?"

"No." Standing, he crossed to the door and pulled the privacy blind down over the window and turned the deadbolt. "Ready for you to be of service though."

TWO

He smiled and ran a hand over dark, close-cropped hair, exuding a palpable sense of casual confidence—an attitude he'd done *nothing* to earn—that started a familiar burn, deep within my chest. No matter what his athletic gifts or his family's background—there was no way he'd earned the right to that smug, overbearing countenance at—what? Sixteen? Seventeen, at best? God, but I despised that attitude. I despised all of it.

The bit of Pollyanna that refused to die tried appealing to the shred of human decency I hoped lurked somewhere in him. "Derek—"

"Coach has had us on a short leash. It's been a hell of a dry spell. You'll be a good girl, right? For me ..." he cajoled in silky tones far beyond his years. "Uh, what's your name again?"

I'm sure he thought his smile was charming. And he had that odd, grating way of speaking—as if he had marbles in his cheeks. Gritting my teeth for a brief, painful moment, I tried again, ignoring his request for my name. Not as if he'd remember it. "But—your test. You have to pass—"

Dark eyes rolled as he yanked the navy blue pullover with its embroidered school crest over his head. "Yeah, yeah... Dust Bowl, Depression, poor people, Tom Joad. All that crap. I'll pass. You'll make sure of it—" He paused with his hand on his fly. "But afterwards. I can swear I won't be any good otherwise," he drawled, the threat implicit.

No choice. As usual, no damned choice.

Admittedly, I could make the choice to walk away. But it would spell the end of this job as definitively as not giving in to this spoiled brat would. And while in those rare glib, optimistic moments, I told myself I could get another tutoring job with little effort, the simple fact of the matter was there was no real way. Not one of this magnitude.

Once upon a time, my great-grandmother had had a Japanese puzzle box sitting on a table in her parlor: smooth, deceptive, red and black lacquer with many moves and only one sure way to solve the dilemma. It felt very much like this.

"You don't have to take the dress off." I felt the mass of him hovering just behind me. Turning my head slightly, I glimpsed his fly gaping open, the fabric of his boxers tented.

"Yes, I do." I forced my voice to remain cool and steady as I slid the zipper down the side of my favorite black wool sheath and pulled it off along with my slip, carefully laying both over a chair, shivering as the sudden chill raised gooseflesh on my bare arms and along my back.

"Oh man." He took a step closer, the heat of his body invasive. "Oh man... Leave the girdle on. And the bra."

My eyes closed at the feel of his breath, damp gusts that made my skin crawl. "Do you—" I swallowed hard as his hand grazed my hip. "Have anything?"

"What?" His voice was thick and stupid—a slow wet noise beside my ear.

"Never mind." I pulled my handbag—always kept within easy reach for just this purpose—close and removed my cosmetics bag. Unzipping it, I pulled out a small, square packet that I handed back to him.

"I don't want to wear this."

The whine told me I had as much of an upper hand as I was going to get. Without a word, I reached for my dress.

"Wait—wait." His voice remained petulant, but with a definite note of surrender. "Okay, fine."

Paper tore behind me as I closed my eyes and breathed deep. Large as he was, he could have easily overpowered me. They so rarely did, however. While the outward trappings may have been those of full grown men, they were little boys, really. Easily reaching a point where they were so eager to get what they wanted they'd do whatever was required. It was the one tiny advantage I maintained.

"Bend over." A large clammy hand pushed between my shoulder blades until my cheek rested on the pale wood surface. This close, if I opened my eyes, I knew I would see years' worth of gouges and ink stains and youthful declarations of loathing and infatuation and lust. If I opened them.

I never did anymore.

One hand tight on my hip, he used the other to manipulate himself, shoving aside the modesty panel between my legs and pushing. And pushing again, his grunts overriding the quiet whimpers I muffled further by biting into my palm; shoving until I could feel the metal teeth of his zipper digging into my thighs, snagging the tops of my stockings.

"Yes," he groaned against my shoulder, his hands rubbing in rough circles over the tight black nylon and lace encasing my hips and buttocks. "Oh yeah." Groans devolved into a high-pitched whine as he began moving in short, jerky thrusts, his hands rubbing, snapping at my garters, rubbing some more. "Yes, tell me I'm good … tell me I'm a good boy—tell *me*." The fact that he kept shoving further in, that his hands pressed down on my shoulders, forcing my head to remain down meant he neither needed nor expected a response. Thank God.

It burned, the physical violation—the humiliation hot and acid in my chest as his thrusts grew faster and harder, my pelvis slamming into the table's edge with painful intensity. There would be visible reminders—would be more difficult to block this one. And then he was gone, blessed relief and cool air washing over my heated skin until seconds later, I heard him grunt again and felt heat soaking into the fabric across my backside, another hot splash along my spine.

"So pretty. So fucking pretty." Then his hands again, rubbing, massaging the sticky, wet mess into my skin, my undergarments, the damp heel of his palm grinding between my legs, his fingers probing, and I couldn't even protest this new, this … unspeakable violation. I wanted to. I wanted to stand up and say *enough*. But I was just too tired.

An hour later, I returned the study room key to the librarian, not caring if it was pity or mockery that I saw in his eyes as I met his gaze. One simply did what one had to. That knowledge is what made it possible to ignore the residue that had nylon clinging to my skin; that kept me from wincing with every step at the burn between my thighs as I said my goodnights to the gateman.

It was only once I was clear of the gate and in the shadows beyond the lamps lining the walkway, that I finally allowed my head to drop, keeping it resolutely lowered the entire subway ride home, refusing to meet anyone's eyes.

Grateful beyond belief that Helen was on another one of her endless dates, I went through the ritual of undressing and taking a cursory hot shower, wincing at the sting as I carefully washed between my legs, douching just to make doubly certain all traces of him were gone. Tightly wrapped in my heaviest robe, I moved on to the clothes. The lingerie had to be washed, of course, and one stocking was ruined, the teeth from the little idiot's zipper having created a wide ladder run that couldn't easily be mended. This was precisely why I continued to use stockings when everyone else was moving to the more convenient pantyhose. Not that such details were ever liable to come up in polite conversation.

Spot cleaning and a light spritz of diluted Jean Naté would ensure I could wear my dress at least once more before a trip to the cleaner's—distasteful perhaps, but when every penny counted, one did what was necessary.

After preparing a pot of tea, I sat at our battered dinette and wrote the check for my share of the rent, blowing on the paper until the ink was dry. Buying those few extra moments as I sipped tea and watched the still-alien snow drift and swirl past the window. Finally, I picked up my pen once more and with the penmanship perfected under the watchful eyes of the nuns, wrote out the amount for my one other large monthly expense.

Just as carefully, I addressed an envelope, affixed a stamp, and slipped the check inside, wrapped in a plain sheet of white stationary. No note, or salutation. None was really needed. Or wanted if I had to hazard a guess.

A shrill ring echoed throughout the apartment, its immediate, demanding call cutting off memory before it had opportunity to take root. Thank God. Even if it was no doubt for Helen—another one of her many paramours. The idiots often had no concept of time or propriety, calling at all hours, expecting her to be available and all too often, she complied, hurriedly throwing on a dress and applying a quick slash of Cherries in the Snow before some young man would appear at the door, reeking of whisky and smoke and sometimes, expensive perfume. No wonder the girl had yet to "land one of those yummy dishes," as she referred to the bevy of young professionals. She had no sense of playing hard to get.

"Because really, why should they pay for a hamburger if they're getting steak for free?" I muttered as I pushed myself away from the table. Cradling my teacup, allowing its warmth to bleed into my skin, I took my time about strolling into the living room, hoping whoever was on the other end of the ringing phone would give up since I wasn't quite in the mood to insist that no, I had no idea where Helen was or with whom or when, or even if, she'd be back this evening. Well, I wasn't quite so indiscreet as to include that last bit, but there were times it had been tempting. Finally, on the seventh ring, I gave up and picked up the receiver.

"Hello?"

"There you are. You just now getting home?"

I smiled at the familiar kitchen sounds in the background. "I've been home for a bit, Remy. I was just having some tea."

"Didn't get too wet in this mess I hope?"

I flinched at the unwitting reminder. "Only a little, but I took a hot bath the minute I got home."

"I'm about done here—you want I should bring you by some more soup? I got some pecan pie leftover, too."

"You don't need to go to any trouble on my account."

Even with the muzziness crackling along the connection due to the bad weather, his short explosion of breath carried clearly. "If it was, I wouldn't offer *chère*."

"Really, you—"

"I'll be there shortly."

He hung up without saying goodbye. He never did, not that it bothered me. Wasn't a word I was overly fond of either. Setting my battered espresso maker on the range, I went into my room, donning a heavy flannel nightgown before belting my robe once again. I grimaced at the image in the mirror as I brushed out my still-damp hair and worked it into a braid. Like I was one to scold Helen, even if silently, about propriety, given I couldn't even be bothered to fully dress for a male guest. But it was Remy.

A single sharp knock sounded just as the espresso maker emitted its final gentle burbles. After rapidly winding an elastic around the end of my braid, I opened the door.

"I brought a sandwich, too," he said as he dropped a quick, snow-chilled kiss to each cheek. "Made it with some of the peppered steak I had leftover. Tell you what, I'm so hungry I'm 'bout ready to gnaw my own arm off. Felt like everyone and their mama came in tonight—didn't have half a second to scratch my watch or wind my behind." Moving as easily around my tiny kitchen as he did the larger space at Mercier's, he pulled a saucepan down from the shelf above the small range, lighting the burner and pouring the soup from a thermos. "Coffee smells wonderful *bebe*—you got some milk? I got a taste for an *au lait*."

I smiled as I locked the door behind him and followed him into the kitchen, discreetly sliding the white envelope from the table and into my pocket. "I'll get it."

"Never you mind." He waved me toward the table, reaching into the battered Frigidaire for the bottle. "No room for both of us to be moving around here. You just sit there and tell me about your evening. How was this one?"

"As stupid as all the others." I suppressed a shudder as I sank back into my chair.

He snorted as he selected a smaller saucepan for the milk. "I swear, I don't know how you put up with them. Lord knows, you're some kind of saint."

My answering snort *almost* escaped, only just turning into a short laugh at the last possible moment. "I hardly think so. So—" I propped my elbows on the table, watching him work. "Were there any interesting demands tonight? Any visitors of note?"

"Just some crazy woman wanted me to make her crawfish étouffée. When Becca told her they wasn't in season yet, she asked well, couldn't I just make it without the mudbugs?"

As we laughed, comfort settled over my shoulders, ever so slightly loosening those tight knots that held my muscles captive on nights like tonight.

But perhaps … not tonight.

THREE

DECEMBER 1960

"The hell I will."

The crack of skin against skin echoed throughout our small kitchen. My fists clenched, I stared at my mother through vision blurred by tears. Anger? Shock? Pain? Who knew. And how they didn't fall, I had no idea.

"*Habla con respeto.*"

"Tell me why I should." I refused to speak in Spanish. It would be seen as a sign of acquiescence and I didn't want to give even the slightest indication they might win this battle.

"Because it's the way of things. You will respect your family's wishes and you'll do as you're told."

"Somewhere along the line, Mamá, you seem to have forgotten I'm no longer a child."

"So long as you live under our roof, you *are* our child and you'll behave in a manner befitting your heritage." She gestured with hands no longer soft and white and delicate, since the task of keeping the house now fell primarily on her shoulders. Even rough and reddened, their beauty was still readily apparent, long and aristocratic, her diamond wedding rings, which Papi had refused to allow her to part with, glittering in the harsh overhead lights.

"What heritage? We have no such thing here." Not without effort I unclenched my fists, tried to relax and get her to at least *see*, for God's sake. "All we are now are working class people, like thousands of others, trying to survive. I know how it bothers you, that Carlito has to attend Columbus on scholarship, but remember, it is *my* paycheck that helps make up the difference in tuition and keeps him from suffering the burden of hand-me-down uniforms and secondhand shoes. For us to have the occasional steak, instead of *picadillo* yet again. Does none of that earn me at least a modicum of honor or respect as an adult or the right to make my own decisions about *my* life? What there is of it?"

Mami shook her head, the light catching the silver-white strands scattered through her dark curls. Strands that had multiplied to the point where it was almost an equal distribution between silver and dark. A stark realization that hit with such suddenness, it left me more than a bit lightheaded.

"Do not make the mistake of thinking I don't understand how difficult this has been for you, *m'ija*, but really, in the end, how is what we're asking you to do so very different from what you'd planned for your life?" She looked around at the worn pots and pans, the battered stove and refrigerator that had come to us thirdhand—or perhaps it had been fourth—at the curtains that remained limp because gently starched window coverings now fell under the aegis of frivolous nicety rather than absolute necessity, and shaking her head, added with a resigned sigh, "*Bueno*, if things were normal."

And still … even with that acknowledgment—the closest she'd come yet to admitting out loud that our lives were irrevocably altered from what they'd been—that she could still expect this of me? After everything that had happened? Cuban women were known for their solid and clear-headed pragmatism, but this was utterly beyond the pale. Did she not understand how much I still hurt?

"How can you even say that? To *me*? It's not at all the same. There's no possible way it could be. Can't you see, Mamá—things *aren't* normal. There is no such thing here—not the way you want it to be." I slammed my palms down on the worn yellow Formica of the kitchen table. "It's not about *what* I planned. It's …" I shook my head, trying to free it of the images, swallowing past the heavy beating of my heart that overwhelmed my chest—constricted my throat until it felt as if it was lined with sandpaper. "If only … if we'd—" I gave up, sinking into the nearest chair and squeezing my eyes shut—*trying* to forget.

Knowing it was impossible.

"It's true you're an adult, Natalia." Abuelita's agreeable voice prompted me to open my eyes. As she approached, her expression was calm … pleasant. Too pleasant. "After all, you're nineteen and as you say, a valuable contributor to the household. So as such, I will speak to you as an adult." As I held my breath, she drove the knife in the final inch. "It's been nearly two years. No one is asking you to forget, but don't you think it is time you stopped daydreaming like a little girl and wishing for things that will never be?"

My jaw clenched for a long painful moment, streaks of light crossing my vision in a blinding flash. "I might say the same for you," I finally ground out. "For all of you."

Silence reigned in the kitchen then, the only sounds the gentle bubbling of the pot of *frijoles negros* cooking away on the stove and the faint rise and fall of voices coming from the small television in the living room where Papi and Carlito were staying out of it. Far better and easier for them to let the women deal with the issue of my future while they kept their attention resolutely focused on the flickering images of Beaver and Wally and their idealized American lives with their perfect lawns and pristine homes and crises that could be solved with reasonable, measured conversation, and in less than half an hour, to boot.

Difficult to believe we all lived in the same country.

Mounting tension combined with the heavy silence as Abuelita crossed the kitchen to stand beside my mother. Individually, they were formidable enough, even now, but the two together? They were banking on that, I knew. That in presenting a unified front, they would be able to counter any argument I might use, any objection I might raise.

Except—

Even they could not counter the reality of what our lives had become. No matter how hard they tried to pretend otherwise. More importantly, they had no way of knowing how I truly felt. They had absolutely no way of knowing what lay beyond the shell of what I presented to the world. How I fought to keep the rage banked so that I could function. Each day, forcing myself to feel less and less because numb had to be a better alternative than helpless fury eating one away from the inside.

"It has been nearly two years," I said softly, my fingers tracing the futuristic silver designs adorning the tabletop. "Nearly two years since that bastard stole the island. Since—" I stopped, swallowed hard against the tears, because if I started now, I might never stop.

"Since then, *nothing* is the same, but still, you all insist on pretending everything is all right when it's so obviously not. Papi working as a clerk in a law office. You down on your knees scrubbing the toilets. Abuelita having to cook every single day." My gaze rose from the table, meeting each of theirs in turn, silently daring them to contradict me. "Tell me, how is my marrying some boy whose family is in our same situation going to change any of that? Furthermore, how could you even begin to imagine I would even consider such a thing?"

Their faces remained calm and implacable. Finally Mamá said, "There comes a time you have to accept certain things, Natalia. It is insurance. The same way that our collective sacrifices so that Carlito can obtain the same education he would have had at home is insurance." She took a deep breath and smiled faintly, as if it were all settled. "When we return—"

"*Nothing* will be the same." To my own ears my voice sounded disembodied, each word drenched in anguish. "Why do you refuse to accept that?" Were they really that far into a fantasy land? Peter

Pan had had a better grasp on reality than my family and all of their friends. "You are all positively drunk on this idea that we'll be able to return and pick up our lives precisely where we left off. But no matter how many plans Papi and his cronies hatch over cigars and Sunday barbeques, or how many candles you and Abuelita light after Mass, it will never, ever be the same. Why is that so difficult for you to comprehend?"

I stared from face to face—Mami and Abuelita; Papi and Carlito, who'd finally been moved to join us, drawn, no doubt, by the fact that my rising voice was in all likelihood obliterating the polite, neutral tones of Mr. and Mrs. Cleaver who would never dream of raising their voices. They had no reason to do so. Nothing in their placid, black and white American lives to feel such passion and drama over.

Nothing—*nothing*—like what I'd left behind.

I missed it all so much. The vibrant colors and warm winds rustling the leaves of the ancient oaks shading the Prado. The waves rushing in with a dull roar until they crashed up against the Malecon, a fine spray creating a translucent curtain through which I looked out over sky and water that went on forever. Breathing in salt air, suffused with the sense of well-being that had once been my everyday existence. The way that food had tasted more complex and intense, how my clothes, those linens and cottons that were as fine and light as air, had brushed in an almost sensual manner against my skin. How past, present, and future could be rolled together and savored in one lingering kiss from a beautiful young man. A kiss that had tasted of forever.

That tangible sense of promise that the whole world had been spread out before me, waiting—that even if I left Cuba to explore that world, Cuba would be there, waiting with her open arms and passionate embrace.

Never.

Never again.

Even before we left, my beautiful island had been irrevocably altered. Now, it was ... unspeakable.

The latest news to reach us was that our house in Miramar had been "reclaimed for the people." And promptly turned into apartments for high ranking members of the Party. It would have been bad enough, this idea that some random stranger was in my childhood room, lying in my bed with its soft sheets and rifling through my clothes. Pawing through my things—the photographs and journals with all the hopes and dreams of the innocent girl I'd been carefully inscribed between the covers—those things, real and intangible, I'd been forced to leave behind. But that it was those heartless, filthy bastards with all that blood on their hands was abhorrent on a level I couldn't even begin to express.

"Even if the opportunity comes to return to Cuba, it will never be the same again."

"You don't know what you're saying, *niña*."

I stared at my mother before allowing my gaze to touch on Abuelita and Papi, lingering the longest on Carlito—swallowing hard as our gazes met, watching light gradually dawn in the depths of those striking pale green eyes. A smile forced its way out even as my heart felt like it was breaking. "Oh yes I do. I don't ever want to go back. I can't."

• • •

I sat straight up in bed, shivering, the covers in a tangle around my ankles. Despite the midnight chill in the room, I was sweating, my flannel nightgown sticking in damp patches to my shoulders and back. Standing on shaky legs, I grabbed the blanket and draped it around my shoulders as I went to stand by the window. I leaned my forehead against the chilled glass, welcoming the cold against my overheated skin as my shallow gasps created misty, irregular circles of condensation.

It had been too much to hope that Remy's unexpected visit, full of good food and laughter would be enough to keep the dreams at bay. Like clockwork, every time I wrote one of those checks I'd relive that final evening. How I'd gazed into each face by turn and understood with utter certainty they weren't prepared to relinquish their dream, any more than I was prepared to embrace it. We were at cross-purposes, my family and I, and I couldn't bear to keep playing out this drama, over and over, until they broke me. Because that's what it would have taken.

So I'd left. That very night. But I hadn't left them behind. Not in the ways that mattered to them. Despite the fact that I never once heard a word in response to the checks I sent, I continued to send them every month. Something I *had* to do. If only for Carlito. I wanted him to at least have a piece of our former life—in the ways that would benefit him the most—and I knew that without the financial contribution I provided, that would have been close to impossible. But he deserved at least that much for all he'd left behind. For all he'd never be able to reclaim—or claim, for that matter—even if he wasn't fully aware of that just yet.

Most of all, I wanted him to have the tools with which to forge his own identity. His own future.

And if in turn, the price for *my* freedom was to mentally revisit that scene, month after month, well then, that was a cross I could bear.

FOUR

"Natalie, good to see you."

The sudden rush of frigid air was almost immediately swallowed by the dry heat emanating from the massive cast-iron woodstove. The old thing had stood sentry in the corner of the foyer for nearly a century—since the days of red velvet-flocked wallpaper and ornate lamps, their beaded shades casting mysterious shadows throughout the rooms. Back then, lush Oriental rugs had lain scattered haphazardly across the black and white marble tiles—warming the floors while the lovely multihued ladies imported from the original Mercier stomping grounds of New Orleans reclined prettily on brocaded sofas and chairs. There, they'd gossip and read and tat lace and do needlework, passing the time until their respectable beaus could slip away from their Gilded Age balls and fragile wives.

Those men, they would arrive at the brick and wrought-iron fronted Gramercy townhome for their nighttime visits, relaxing in the easy, Southern-drenched hospitality that first generation of Merciers had raised to an art form that they offered along with good drinks and even better food, providing a safe, discreet environment in which the men who served as starchy pillars of society during the day could shed the strictures that came from living within such a highly constrained caste system. In so many integral ways Mercier's mission hadn't changed since its earliest inception—providing food, drink, and discretion, whether it was for the city's power brokers or couples in search of the perfect romantic dinner. More than reason enough for Mrs. Mercier to refuse to get rid of the old stove, no matter how much the busboys complained about having to clean it and keep it stocked with wood. She insisted it was a good luck charm—a symbol of Mercier's beginnings—and that it would be bad luck to get rid of it before it was ready to go. When it fell apart or ceased working otherwise, she'd get rid of it then, but not a stone cold moment before.

"Mr. Barnes, what a lovely surprise. Good afternoon, gentlemen." I smiled and nodded at his two companions.

"I apologize for just dropping in. This is kind of an impromptu meeting—any possibility you have space for three? Just for cocktails."

"Of course. Right this way." Shifting the reservation time for a new customer to a slightly later spot in the log, I wrote Gregory Barnes' name above it, then turned to lead him and his guests to a high-backed corner booth near the front windows flanked by potted palms, a spot both visible and private. As they seated themselves, one of them, a tall, younger man with that same air of quiet power as Mr. Barnes, nodded at me with a polite smile while the other, a more visibly loud sort, taking up space not so much in size, but rather more in how he held himself and moved, not-so-inadvertently brushed a hand against my backside as he seated himself.

Taking an unobtrusive step to one side, I subtly turned away from him as I asked, "Your usual, Mr. Barnes?" waiting for his nod. Turning my attention to the other men, "Gentlemen, if I may take your drink orders, I'll have them taken care of right away."

"You can take care of me any way you want, honey." The loud man winked and laughed, the sound discordant and jarring.

So, so predictable, these types of men. At least the other two looked disgusted with their companion, expected from Mr. Barnes, since he'd never been anything less than a perfect gentleman, but the added apologetic smile from his younger companion was surprising enough that I found myself returning it with a small one of my own.

As a busboy arrived at the table with a pitcher of ice water and Mr. Barnes' usual bowl of spiced almonds, I made my way to the bar where I passed on the orders for a martini, extra dry, three olives, and a Johnnie Walker and soda in addition to Mr. Barnes' preferred Macallan. Brought by him each year from Scotland and kept in a locked display behind the bar with an engraved brass nameplate identifying the owner of the locker's contents. One of the perks of being a regular at Mercier's—ensuring that a favored customer's preferred drink was always available.

I turned away from the bar and glanced down at my watch, surprised to discover it was already past six—I wasn't particularly hungry, but I knew if I didn't take my break before I left for the evening, Remy was liable to tattle on me to Mrs. Mercier.

"Ah, just in time," the devil himself cheerfully proclaimed, holding up a silver dome-covered plate as I entered the kitchen. "Now, don't look at me like that," he added, half plaintive, half cajoling. "It's nothing more than a simple grilled cheese and *pomme frites*, *chère*."

I crossed my arms. "Made with?"

A rare wash of scarlet momentarily overtook his olive complexion as he set the plate on the stainless steel counter. "Roblochon and Emmental on brioche."

In a rush, my dormant appetite came to life and I tried not to drool noticeably. Or smile. "And?"

"Come on, *petit*, why you spoilin' for a fight?"

"I'm not," I insisted. "I think it only fair I know what I'm your guinea pig for today."

"I infused the oil with fresh garlic before I fried the potatoes," he confessed. "Then I sprinkled more cheese over them and popped them under the broiler. It can be a casual item for the luncheon menu or I can play with it further, make it a gratin Savoyard for dinner."

"More a lunch item, wouldn't you think?" I selected a crystal goblet and filled it with ice. "The ladies will never want to leave their dinner reeking of even the merest hint of garlic whereas for most men, it wouldn't matter in the slightest."

"Eh, you're right, of course," he agreed with a laugh that faded to a wry half-smile. "Not that I mean to imply in any way that you're not a lady, *chère*. You know if anythin' I think you're twice the lady than half them rich bitches darken our doors," he finished with an indignant sniff.

As he ranted, I finally allowed myself the smile I'd been holding back. "It's all right, Remy. It would only matter if I had anywhere to be after work tonight."

A full ring of white surrounded the deep blue irises. "No date?" I filled the goblet with the house specialty sweet tea. "No."

"On a Friday."

"Which means both my favorite bookstore and coffee shop are open late."

He leveled a dark glare at me from beneath the floppy brim of his chef's toque. "It's not natural, Natalie." Annoyance colored my name with even more lilt than usual. "You're what—twenty-two? Twenty-three? You should be out, tryin' on all them boys who ain't worthy of you until you find the one who is before you settle down and have yourself your own sweet *bebes*. Not livin' the life of a widow woman three times your age."

"Oh, Remy." The smile held even as I fought back the old, once too-familiar pain, hot and needle-sharp. "What's natural, really? Juggling three mistresses?"

Glowering shifted to a satisfied Cheshire-cat smirk. "It is if you're an Abelard man."

"And *laissez le bon temps rouler*?" I teased, relieved to feel the pain receding.

Putting the fingertips of one hand to his lips, he kissed them. "You got it." He put the still-warm plate in my hand and held the kitchen door open. "Now go eat. And tell me what you think of the potatoes."

"*Mais oui.*" I kissed both cheeks and headed for my usual secluded corner table, grateful to find the restaurant close to deserted as expected, save for the few early cocktail guests, like Mr. Barnes and his party. I would have time enough to enjoy my meal before the Friday night dinner crowds descended with the added benefit of avoiding the rush hour commute on my way home. Amazing how one learned to savor the small gifts. Especially when accompanied by a heavenly bite of warm, melted cheese on rich, buttery bread.

"De Maupassant last week, now Parker. Is it that you're particularly fond of short works or are you on a jag?"

It took a moment for the words to penetrate, another for their meaning to crystallize in my brain, and still another before I glanced up at Greg Barnes, meeting his gaze. His undeniably curious gaze.

"I suppose you could say I'm partial to short works right now. Perhaps a bit easier to set aside if the moment demands." I took the small card—the business card he'd given me the week before, I idly noted—and marked my page. "I'm not certain, however, that Dottie would care much for interruption." I smiled as I traced Dorothy Parker's name, the black slashes against the sepia cover every bit as bold as the author's wit.

"Back in the day, Dottie reveled in *being* the interruption."

"You *know* her?"

"Mostly by reputation." He braced his hands on the back of the empty chair opposite mine. "A handful of memorable cocktail parties where I was more observer than anything else, too young and far too intimidated by the formidable Mrs. Parker to do little more than watch in awe as she shredded any hapless fool who happened to cross her into very precise, very bloody ribbons."

"How delicious," I murmured, more to myself, as I stroked the cover once again, my finger catching on one worn, bent edge.

"I'm sure Dottie thought so." Straightening, he crossed his arms and smiled down at me. "Are you tutoring this evening?"

"No—never on Fridays." Relaxing against the padded back of my chair with a sigh, I was able to return his smile. Even allowed myself the luxury of releasing a lovely, slow breath. "And since finals are over at Concord, I'm at liberty until next semester. So I currently have nothing more pressing on my schedule beyond dinner and browsing bookstore shelves."

"Christmas shopping?"

It took more effort than I might have expected to keep the smile fixed. "Well, perhaps some." Helen wasn't much of a reader, but she was nevertheless easily appeased. A lovely engraved lighter or even a box of imported truffles would suit her fine. However, perhaps I would slip into the consignment store next door to the bookstore and indulge in a rare splurge. Something just for me that was frivolous and purely, unabashedly pretty. Or not. While I needed at least one new dress to be able to wear to work and while it *could* be pretty—one had to make allowances, after all because it was those little things that kept the dull reality of life at bay—frivolous was not so much an option. So no doubt, another basic black it would be.

Regardless of what the season brought, in whatever form, I could definitely be assured it would be a far cry from the glittering gifts and endless rounds of parties that would always culminate in the expansive Noche Buena celebrations that were a hallmark of my childhood. In my mind's eye, I could still picture our house, the Italian crystal chandeliers blazing warm light through every window as cars lined the brick-paved circular driveway, waiting to drop off beautifully dressed families, most related to us in some fashion, some business or political acquaintances, and all of them wanting to share this beautiful, blessed night with the San Martíns.

There would be cocktails and toasts galore, deep into the evening until finally, we were called to the feast, the centerpiece of which were always the *lechóns* that Coquita's staff had tended throughout the day, the pigs roasting slowly in the backyard pits, lined with banana leaves, the scent as tantalizing as a beautiful woman. The whole pigs would be carried out and placed on their own table, crispy brown skins glistening and fragrant with the garlic, cumin, and imported Spanish olive oil of the *mojo* and hiding deliciously tender, succulent meat. In the kitchen, the counters would practically be groaning under the weight of the platters holding all the gastronomic accoutrements that comprised a proper Cuban Christmas Eve dinner.

Even now, I could envision the scene, down to the most minute detail. The vast, sprawling blue and white-tiled courtyard, with its elaborately set tables. Towering palms and oaks and immaculately manicured hedges interspersed with multi-hued hibiscus, pink oleander, and fragrant night-blooming jasmine surrounding the perimeter while the multileveled flower-shaped fountain dominated the center, the sound of cascading water providing an elegant counterpoint to the strolling musicians and animated lilt of conversation. From the smaller adjoining courtyard would come the occasional squeals of the little children as they were entertained by the hired clowns and magicians. The Waterford crystal would chime like delicate church bells in multiple toasts to our continued health and good fortune as breezes tinged with the fresh scent of the sea caressed shoulders and necks left bare because we *could* in the decadent, balmy late-December air. No cold, numbing winds or harsh, stinging snow to contend with—not for us.

I could still recall those Christmas cards Papi would receive from business acquaintances in the States and Europe with their snowy scenes depicted in shades of white and silver and pale blue and that, to me, had always appeared so pallid. So ... boring. My numerous cousins would pore over them, exclaiming over their beauty and exoticism, but this fascination for what was deemed a "traditional" Christmas had always escaped me. How could Christmas be anything but warmth and color and vibrantly, shockingly alive? Those winter scenes, filled with snow and bare-limbed trees and lengthy shadows—as a child, they'd felt so desolate and lonely. And as I'd grown older and learned about the cycle of seasons, more and more, they seemed to represent death. A shroud for a world that required rejuvenation, whereas the paradise where *I* lived was in a constant state of renewal, never allowing itself to fall into such a state.

The ignorance—and hubris—of youth, I suppose. A dangerous, disheartening combination.

"Well, I won't keep you—however, I did want to extend an invitation on my wife's behalf before you left for the evening."

Half-lost in memories of ghosts of Christmases past, Greg Barnes' words emerged as little more than gibberish.

"I beg your pardon?"

Carefully, he slid a stiff cream-colored envelope beneath the hand still resting on the volume of Parker, slowly obliterating her name beneath a wash of fine, heavy linen.

I made no motion, save to move my hand far enough to stare at the inscription—and yes, there it was, my name, written in an elegant, feminine script.

"It's for a holiday party. Nothing overwhelming, I promise—

mostly for my benefit since Constance swears that anything over twenty guests leaves me hiding in my study," he said with a self-deprecating laugh. "Anyhow, it's for a week from tomorrow and Constance and I both hope you'll be able to attend. I've told her about you and she's absolutely dying to speak to another woman with tastes in literature that go beyond *Vogue* and *True Confessions.*"

"Surely she can do far better than me."

As heat from the impetuous words suffused my skin, Greg Barnes' thoughtful gaze studied me for a long moment. "No, I don't think so," he finally said, his tone no less authoritative than usual and certainly no less kind, but with an unexpected … gentleness? So unexpected, I felt a surprising prickle at the backs of my eyes. "Please, Natalie, do consider attending."

"I usually work …" I began, but temptation swept over me in a powerful rush, rendering the words weak and ineffective. Like the wine last week, it was a taste of what had once been mine. Already my mind was categorically sorting through my closet, wondering if there was anything even remotely appropriate lurking in the depths and just as quickly dismissing everything as completely wrong. While a trip to Saks or Bendel's was supremely tempting, the more practical aspect of my nature immediately reasserted itself, sternly scolding that yes, something new was in order, but it would have to be new only to me.

"I hardly think Marguerite would begrudge you one Saturday evening off." Stated with a definitive edge to the words and a slight smile that had an answering one tugging at the corners of my mouth.

"You've already asked her."

His smile grew broader. "When I delivered her invitation."

"Of course." There was no use even putting up token resistance. Not with Mrs. Mercier in on it. Why they had singled me out for this, I wasn't at all sure, but at this point, I had neither energy nor inclination to question too closely. It was too dreary a time of year and I'd been feeling the loneliness of my self-inflicted isolation more keenly than ever before.

Forget wanting this. Deep down in a place I rarely acknowledged, I needed this. I needed a moment to remember who I'd been.

FIVE

NEW YEAR'S EVE 1958

"*Oye,* Nicolito, shh ..."

"You worry too much, Natalia. No one's going to bother us here."

"You really imagine we're the only ones with this idea?" I pushed at his dinner-jacketed chest, as if to put some respectable distance between us, but not really. Even though it wasn't cold, the damp breeze coming off the ocean reached even the vine-shrouded pergola tucked away in a far corner of his family's expansive Varadero Beach property, making me grateful for his body's warmth. As if sensing my thoughts, he pulled me closer, drawing my hands beneath his jacket until they rested against the strong length of his back.

"No, not the only ones, not by a long shot, Talia. But who would dare bother us here? This has been our spot forever."

His hands caressed my shoulders, fingertips teasing along my collarbone in a way that left me breathless while his words conjured images of the ghosts of our younger selves. Cavorting across the rolling lawns and along the stone pathways or slinking along the walls of the kitchen, pestering the staff as we'd been wont to do. Many years on, we no longer lurked in the kitchen, hoping for one of the tolerant cooks or maids to give us a sweet *pastelito* or a bowl of fresh, hot *mariquita* chips before shooing us off, but instead preferred huddling together in the cool, leafy alcove we'd stumbled across one blistering summer day around the same time we'd discovered that we liked each other as far more than childhood playmates and friends.

I could hardly recall a time when we hadn't been together. In some way.

"I can't believe you're really going to Paris."

He looked so crestfallen, I drew my hands from his back and raised them to his face, one thumb rubbing at the two small lines between his fine, black brows. He was so beautiful, my Nicolito. Always had been—inside and out.

"Please don't look like that. We've already survived your being in Miami the last two years." Ever since Batista ordered the University closed because of those idiot student protests and he'd had to find alternate means by which to finish his degree. So horribly unfair, but we *had* survived and grown closer for all that. It made the child in me want to stick my tongue out at the fools who would try to keep us apart.

"It was ninety miles and a quick plane trip, Talia. You're hardly going to able to come home almost every weekend."

"No—" I said slowly. He was right and admittedly, it was the one aspect dulling my joy. "But we will have every holiday break and the summers. I'll visit you or we can both come home or we can even travel. See the world together. Wouldn't that be exciting?"

"With the *dueña* your parents would insist on hovering over us the entire time?" His eyebrows rose. "Exciting isn't exactly the word that comes to mind, *mi amor*."

"You know what I mean." I delivered a light smack to his arm. "We'll find a way. You know I can't be away from you for too long."

"Then why go?" His hands were restless, stroking my shoulders, dropping to my waist, then rising again to stroke along the length of my arms before taking my hands in his and lowering them to our sides, gripping them tight. "It's not as if I don't want you to continue your education. There are schools in the United States every bit the equal of the Sorbonne. Maybe even better."

"But they're not Paris. And Paris is what I've wanted since I was five." A powerful dream, borne from a childhood infatuation with *Madeline*, nurtured by subsequent books and photographs, and finally cemented with a trip that showed Paris was everything I had imagined and more. Impossible to set aside—even for Nicolito. Nothing could usurp his place in my heart—could derail the future we knew lay ahead of us—however, neither could I deny the restless insistence that kept whispering I had to do this. That if I tasted and experienced and spent some time with myself—a privilege I'd never before been granted—it would make everything else so much better and richer. I'd told Nicolito all of this. And I knew he understood. But I also knew how he was feeling. How I'd felt when he had to leave for Florida two years earlier.

"I know how hard this is, but this is something I *have* to do. It's the one choice I can make for myself before we're together for always."

"I would never try to stop you from making your own choices." His thumbs traced light, restless patterns along mine. "I'm just being selfish—wanting you with me as well."

"I *am* with you. I have been since our first sand castle." Almost without thinking, I added, "You could come to Paris, too. Go to law school there." And even as much as that seemed like the perfect solution—as much as I wanted to be with Nicolito—a small, dark part of me was rebelling. Wanted to have this one thing, just for myself. Just this once. I hated the thought of being so far from him and I didn't want anyone else. Ever. But I wanted Paris for myself.

But even as the silent war raged inside me, he was shaking his head, sending relief chasing after hope and rebellion and making me drop my gaze, hoping the shadows would mask the conflict I was certain was reflected in my eyes.

"I don't have your gift with languages. English, yes, but I would never be able to handle the demands of law school in French. But you know, there are other alternatives…"

I jerked my head up, fighting the shadows to search his face, fresh hope flaring.

"England? Are you thinking of England?"

He couldn't be. For so long his dream had been the Ivy League. Harvard and Yale and of course, Columbia, since it was in New York, with its skyscrapers and brash attitude that had captured his imagination every bit as much as Paris's quaint buildings and cool elegance had captured mine. To hear that he was willing to give up his dream of New York and the prestige of an Ivy League law school in order to be closer to me?

"I was saving it as a surprise until I knew for certain." A self-satisfied smile crept across his face. "How does the University of London sound?"

"London," I breathed out on a long sigh, desperately trying to envision the map and attempting to recall the distances. Almost immediately giving up because all that mattered was that it was *London*. A world closer than New Haven or Boston or New York. And I would still have Paris. For me. "I almost can't believe it. But are you certain? Absolutely certain? I don't want to keep you from your dreams any more than you would keep me from mine."

I continued to search his face, looking for signs of any disappointment, any doubt, and finding nothing but a smile and a hopeful expression.

"You're my dream, Talia. New York will be there after law school. We can live there for a few years—I can practice international law, you can become a world-renowned author, and then we can return home in triumph." His grin broadened as he condensed the many dreams and desires we'd shared into one simple goal that suddenly seemed both real and attainable. "What's important for now, however, is that we'll be closer. Not quite ninety miles, but so much better than an entire ocean, don't you think?"

I released his hands to once again slide my arms around his

waist. Leaning my head on his shoulder, I reached up to press a kiss against the sharp, defined line of his jaw, tasting the bitter, citrusy tang of his aftershave. "*Dios mío*, Nicolito, that's just made my New Year. You and I, together in Europe."

"Nico."

Slowly, I drew back, just far enough to look up into his face, seeing even in the shadows, the glint of humor in those deep brown eyes and the way the corners of his mouth twitched.

"What?"

"Or Nicolas—whichever you prefer, but not Nicolito. I'm not that little boy anymore, Natalia. And you are no longer that little girl. It's not only the New Year but it's also time for a new phase of our lives."

My heartbeat thundered in my ears as he reached into his jacket pocket with one hand as the other drew my left hand from around his waist. I couldn't even bring myself to look down, keeping my gaze firmly fixed on his face—the beautiful, dear face that I'd watched evolve from boyish softness to determined young man. This had been assumed between us for a very long time—since the days our mothers would tease us for being such an inseparable pair as children, to some time in the last few years, where we'd gradually seen each other in the light of growing adulthood. Where each separation had become more difficult yet made each reunion that much sweeter. Where we'd tentatively explored those new aspects of our relationship—the soft, tender, increasingly heated moments that no longer allowed for teasing from the families and rather, shifted to a quiet anticipation coupled with the occasional warning from everyone from our mothers to not embarrass them, *por favor*, to the priests and the nuns, admonishing us to be *careful* and remember that we were God's children first.

"I spoke with your father earlier today. I believe he was actually hoping that I'd be able to convince you to get married this spring or summer, before I started law school, so that we could be settled and on our way out of the country." His expression grew somber as he gazed down at me. "Especially with things the way they are."

It did seem as if you couldn't pass a radio these days without hearing at least a snatch of Fidel's crackly pirate broadcasts from the Sierra Maestra or coming across the old people discussing his latest fiery rhetoric and the vicious fighting going on in the outer provinces. Discussions that would fall ominously silent the moment my brother or I walked into a room, the radio stations abruptly changed. But *mira*, this was Cuba. When had things ever been settled? Political turmoil was almost as much a national sport as *béisbol*. Someone was always trying to overthrow someone else.

"Do you really think it could be a problem?" I wanted my adventure, true, but I wanted the things I held most dear, my family and my home, to remain the same. To be there at the end of the day.

"I don't know."

He lifted his head, glanced around quickly and when he spoke, his voice was even softer than before. "Before, it's always been a case of favors exchanged and money promised and our lives and businesses could go on as before, but listening to our fathers and my *tíos*, they honestly feel there is something different about Fidel. Something compelling. So many think he's some sort of savior."

I couldn't deny the truth of his words. From the little I'd seen and heard, *el comandante* definitely seemed cut from a different cloth—his vision for Cuba clear and unwavering and fervent and definitely contagious among the masses. All of them. For the first time, I felt a hint of fear, twisting low in my stomach.

"Do you want to get married right away, then?"

"Only if you'd want to. And I know you don't. Not yet." His smile was so understanding, I felt a twinge of guilt pricking my conscience. "We don't have to be married for me to take care of you, Natalia—the way I always have. So I told him we could wait—I may want your heart and your promise, but otherwise, there's no need to rush. I wasn't wrong to say that, was I?" His hand trembled slightly over mine, hiding what I knew rested on the third finger, as if he was waiting for my assurance.

"You are my most precious gift." I lifted my right hand to his face, my fingertips tracing the outline of his full lips, up along his cheekbones, the feathery tips of his lower lashes teasing my skin. "I love you so much, my Nicolas."

He turned his head, his lips brushing against my palm as he murmured, "So that's a yes?"

"You know it's been yes since I was three." As he lifted my other hand to his lips, I finally caught my first glimpse of the ring he'd placed there—a brilliant antique diamond I recognized as having belonged to his grandmother. As multifaceted and beautiful as the future he was promising me.

"I know I shouldn't ask this." Both of his hands had moved to frame my face, his fingers tangling in the loose waves of my hair, styled so that it brushed my shoulders, just like Elizabeth Taylor's in *Giant*. "It's completely inappropriate and God knows it's a sin but you're so beautiful and I've wanted you for so long—"

"Shh …" I put my fingers to his lips. "How could it possibly be a sin for us?"

"But we will have the rest of our lives." Yet with each word, he drew me closer still, his hands stroking agitated circles low on my back until nothing remained between us beyond layers of fabric and heat and perhaps the merest breath of air.

"We also have tonight. Like you said—a new year and a new phase of our lives, Nicolas. We deserve to celebrate it. Together."

"Natalia—"

• • •

"Natalie—"

I glanced up from the compact's small, round mirror to find Mrs. Mercier regarding me with an amused expression. "Darlin', I doubt any nose could shine quite so much."

"I—" Had been drifting. Again. A far too frequent occurrence of late. The nightmares were one thing—an expected burden to be endured, but these daydreams were of another ilk altogether. Memories, not often indulged, had been fighting their way to the surface, crowding each other in their eagerness to catch me unawares—leave me shaken. Like now, where I was gripping the compact so tightly, I could feel the metal edge cutting into my gloved hand, and still, the tremors continued, just beneath the skin, leaving behind a prickly, brittle feeling. As if the slightest touch would cause me to shatter.

"You look lovely." Mrs. Mercier gently snapped the compact closed. "Besides, we're here."

Here, of course, being Greg and Constance Barnes' apartment at which the elevator had arrived during the time I'd ostensibly been powdering my nose. As we stepped from the elevator and into a large, marble-floored foyer, I murmured, "It was very kind of the Barnes to send their car for us—not to mention the invitation. At least where I'm concerned."

Mrs. Mercier paused on the elevator's threshold. "They're an unusual couple, Greg and Constance. Utterly without pretension, which is rare. Doubly so when you take into consideration their backgrounds."

"Indeed," I replied, looking away and busying myself with slipping the compact into my black satin evening clutch. It wasn't that I didn't believe Mrs. Mercier or respect her opinion, but more that in my own experience, lacking in pretension came in two primary flavors—that which was genuine and that which was studied. Usually, the latter was reasonably easy to spot, what with its shiny uniformity, the lack of nuance, but there were always some who were capable of making it appear natural. Until I could ascertain for myself where the Barneses fell, I would do well to remain on guard. The last thing I needed—or would stand for—was to feel like someone's pet project for the holidays.

But then again—why else would I be here? I couldn't deny that even amidst my growing excitement for the impending evening that one question had hovered around the edges of my mind. Muffled, perhaps, but nevertheless insistent, like a distant drumbeat. Why? Why invite someone like me? To be the poor young lady on whom the wealthy benefactor had taken pity for some mysterious reason? Introducing her to a world beyond all her imaginings?

The longer I stood there, the more the mellow light given off by the antique light fixtures faded, the soft shadows they cast appearing to grow deeper, swallowing the cream-colored walls until I felt smothered, surrounded the way I'd been by that ink dark, midnight water, my lungs burning as I fought to get to shore. To the unimaginable life I now claimed as my own. I no longer belonged here—in places like this. I needed to get out.

Needed to escape—

Needed—

"Ladies, your coats?"

My surroundings swept around me with an almost audible rush and settled themselves back into the warmly lit, luxurious foyer where Mrs. Mercier and a uniformed maid stood poised beside the door to a coat room, both gazing at me with expectant smiles. With the discipline honed over the past several years, I steadied my breathing and schooled my features into a carefully neutral expression as I began working at the three oversized rhinestone buttons securing my coat. As I slipped it off my shoulders, Mrs. Mercier said in the genteel drawl maintained with twice-yearly visits back to New Orleans, "I know I already said it, but truly, that is a stunning ensemble, Natalie."

I glanced up, unable, not to mention unwilling, to restrain my pleased smile. "Thank you."

Even though the Pauline Trigére coat and dress were hardly the pretty-yet-practical I'd walked into the consignment store determined to find. Clearly, my subconscious had other ideas. Or perhaps it was simply echoes of my past that had drawn me toward a mannequin modeling the vibrant turquoise wool coat with the rhinestones scattered across the shoulders and bodice draped over a lush velvet dress, its folds the exact color of white sand beaches tinged with the faintest hint of rose. Together, they brought to mind that precise moment when the sun rose above the horizon, brightening sky and water from nighttime darkness and teasing the beach with that same, exact rosy hue, the palm trees casting their delicate shadows while the gentle breezes wove through the fronds, accenting the rush of the incoming surf.

In the store, at that moment, that was as practical as I needed to be.

And yet, I could still stand here and be honestly mystified as to why the memories had seemed so much more vivid and insistent of late. It was difficult to determine whether I was a special brand of masochist or merely a fool.

Now, I could only send up a fervent prayer that the ensemble hadn't once belonged to one of tonight's guests—or if it had, that they wouldn't have the poor taste to say anything. For a fleeting moment I desperately wished I'd stuck to my original plan of the classic anonymity of the little black dress. What could I have been thinking, choosing such a distinctive dress and coat? However, catching a glimpse of myself in the elevator door's mirrored surface, brushing a fingertip along the sparkling aurora borealis crystals of my earrings, I recanted the thought. Staring into the wavy, slightly distorted reflection was like staring into a portal—a crack in time— and wasn't that just what I'd wanted? To shed that anonymity with which I'd cloaked myself. To remember who I'd been, if only for a few hours?

Yes, I would have to imagine that special brand of masochist was definitely winning out over mere fool. Suppressing a sigh, I turned away from the girl I'd been and peeled off my gloves, tucking them into a pocket of the coat.

"You know ..." Once again, I glanced up to find Mrs. Mercier studying me with a narrow-eyed stare—somewhat akin to the expression she'd wear when weighing the merits of various cuts of meat on delivery day. "I do love seeing your hair down like this. Allows the light to pull out all this lovely auburn. Altogether you look *trés elegant* and if you'll forgive my saying so, younger. It's nice to see you like this, *petit.*"

I felt a blush rising from the dramatic portrait neckline framing my shoulders as Mrs. Mercier took my coat and handed it off along with her own full-length silver fox to the maid with an absent thank you and proceeded to fuss about me like a mother hen, brushing an errant strand of hair into place among the loose, side-parted waves before she tucked my arm in hers and led the way through the ornate double doors, already standing open, the muted, polite sounds of conversation and tinkling crystal beckoning me into the unknown, yet oh, so familiar.

Rarely had I ever been so terrified.

SIX

"Natalie and Marguerite—finally."

Mrs. Mercier turned an immaculately powdered cheek to accept Mr. Barnes' welcoming kiss. "What's this finally, Gregory? If we're later than you expected, perhaps you should have sent your car earlier."

"Touché." He laughed then turned to take my hand in his. "I'm guessing midtown was a problem?"

"Does a bear shit in the woods?"

The colorful retort, delivered in an unexpectedly patrician tone had Mrs. Mercier laughing outright while Greg Barnes merely shook his head with a rueful smile.

"Impeccable timing as always, darling. Saving me from own lack of social graces."

"With respect to social graces, *I'm* the one swearing like a sailor, but honestly, Greg, while stating the obvious as a form of chitchat may be de rigueur for you, especially given some of the thickheaded louts you work with, you know the inanity of it drives me thoroughly insane."

"And why, exactly, do you think I prefer staying home on weekends as opposed to going the theatre and cocktail party route?" While Greg's tone was martini dry, the look in his eyes as the tall, patrician woman slowly approached was warm and undeniably loving—almost making me feel as if I was intruding on a private moment.

"Point made." She inclined her head slightly in acknowledgment. "Now, going back to your lack of social graces, you haven't even introduced us yet."

"You've hardly given me the opportunity to say hello, let alone perform introductions, now, have you?"

As he protested, Constance Barnes made some dismissive noise low in her throat while taking my hand from his and enfolding it between both of hers, her grasp as warm as her smile. Actually, that was my first—and somehow, I knew it would be my lasting— impression of her. The all-encompassing sense of warmth, from her smile, to the bright brown eyes that creased at the corners to the way she leaned in, quickly kissing both cheeks, before taking a step back, grasping both hands and holding them out to either side as she looked me up and down. Admittedly, I was glad for the opportunity to do the same, taking in the smooth blonde French twist, the elegant scoop-necked hostess gown of pale blue and chocolate brown satin, the simple engagement ring and wedding band that along with creamy pearl stud earrings were the only jewelry she wore. There were those who would compare the unfussy demeanor Constance Barnes presented in contrast to her lavish surroundings and feel the two didn't jibe. However, I found it an intriguing contrast, especially considering that really, it wasn't that unlikely a contrast. No—everything about this woman spoke to the highest of quality, just exhibited with exceptional taste and restraint. This was not someone who felt a need to prove anything.

Despite my earlier promise to stay at a remove, I couldn't help but warm to the older woman, returning her smile.

"You must be the lovely Natalie my husband has gone on and on about although I must say, I'm not at all certain he came close to doing you justice. Shame on you, Greg," she chided her husband.

"My apologies, darling. Natalie." He nodded at both of us in turn while I allowed myself yet another smile. As a child I'd hated being fussed over and petted and showed off—trotted before the adults, academic achievements extolled to a chorus of "oohs" and "ahhs" and "*¡que preciosa!*" Perhaps made to recite a little poem or play a ditty on the piano or perform a dance, solemn in sparkling cupcake pink tulle and soft-soled slippers, before being shepherded off with the rest of the children for the remainder of the evening.

Tonight, however, the fussing had a comforting, familiar feel to it, even if I had no real idea why Greg Barnes would be praising me to his wife to the point where she would seem genuinely anxious to meet me.

"Welcome to our home, my dear. I'm so pleased you could join us this evening."

"Thank you so much for having me, Mrs. Barnes."

"Constance, please." She gently drew me to her side and tucked my hand into the crook of her elbow, much like Mrs. Mercier had. With her free hand, she resumed her grasp on the arm crutch that had remained attached by a cuff just below her elbow when she'd taken my hand in both of hers moments before. Odd, how something that should have been so obvious, had in reality been so unobtrusive. Perhaps it had something to do with how her movements, while slow, were still so graceful and regal it had taken a discreet second glance to ascertain that yes, I really had seen it.

"Polio when I was fifteen," she tossed off matter-of-factly as we fell into step behind Greg and Mrs. Mercier.

Well then, perhaps not as discreet as I had thought. "Oh, I'm—"

"Oh, don't bother apologizing, dear. You weren't in the slightest bit obvious. I just prefer to get it out of the way so we can get on to far more interesting things." Said with a smile that was so genuine and filled with good humor, it soothed the slight flush of embarrassment before it even had opportunity to fully manifest.

"Ultimately I was one of the lucky ones," she elaborated as we entered yet another stunning, high-ceilinged room. "After all was said and done, all I had to learn to cope with was a mostly useless leg and a future husband."

"Really?" I studied Greg Barnes as he smoothly drew Mrs. Mercier into one of the several small clusters of guests scattered throughout the room, the volume rising with a chorus of "hello darlings" and "you look smashing," followed by a burst of laughter at some quip or another.

"Oh yes." She smiled as her gaze followed him to the long marble-topped credenza that was serving as the evening's bar. "I was a junior counselor at the same summer camp where he was a dashing senior counselor, flirting madly with each other, when that blasted virus decided to take a crack at me. Once I was no longer contagious, he visited every single day despite the fact that his mother was vehemently opposed. My mother-in-law never quite forgave me for that," she added with a wicked grin. Settling herself in a chair she gestured I should take the one opposite. "For nearly a year, Greg would come by, rucksack stuffed full of books that he'd nicked from the library at the publishing house and we'd talk for hours about what I'd read, what he'd read, what we liked or disliked, the why of it. Even during physical therapy, there he was, walking alongside, pushing me to move *and* think at the same time. He'd even argue with me—can you imagine?" she said with another laugh and glance at her approaching husband. "The utter crust of the man. But he refused to allow either brain or body to atrophy."

"Telling tales out of school again, Connie?" he asked as he offered her a martini.

"Just that while you may be a brilliant publisher, you still can't pick a tie to save your life and you leave your socks on the floor," she teased.

"Well, there go my chances at making a favorable impression on a guest—however, it doesn't mean I won't try." He handed me a Waterford goblet, the pale gold wine making the sharp-edged crystal facets shoot off brilliant, rainbow-hued sparks. And I knew, even before I took a sip—

"Pinot gris?"

"You never did have enough to fully appreciate it that day." He lifted his own cut-crystal tumbler of Scotch. "Cheers, ladies, and happy holidays."

As Constance and Greg touched glasses, I murmured *"Salut,"* my throat clenching tight on the end of the word, making it come out far more clipped than it should. Oh God. Oh no. Oh *no*. Granted, it was only one word, an innocuous word among this cosmopolitan crowd, but still—

Much as I might wish it weren't so, I couldn't prevent the occasional thought that flitted through my mind in my native language. The dreams—those perhaps were a given. And foolishly, I continued to read in it, unwilling to give up that connection, but speaking it? Not so much as a word had passed my lips in more than three years. Not since I left Miami. I'd had to. Imposing that sort of discipline had been a necessity. As a manner of not only burying my background but also declaring my independence, I wanted nothing more than to become just another American girl, speaking nothing but English, all traces of an accent eradicated thanks to sheer will and repeated viewings of films starring the likes of Katharine Hepburn and Elizabeth Taylor.

But the honest truth of the matter was not speaking Spanish kept the demons at bay. Actually tasting the words on my lips and tongue, feeling the gentle vibrations of the rolling Rs and the soft, sensuality of the speech cadences was simply too much to bear. Too many memories echoing in the sound of my own voice. Better still to not allow it at all. Ever.

Luckily, however, my *faux pas* seemed to have passed unnoticed, lost amidst the clink of glasses, Bing Crosby's soothing croon, and wisps of cigarette smoke. Constance, as Greg had predicted, asked what I was currently reading and we set off on a compare and contrast of Wharton and Fitzgerald that continued on throughout the lavish dinner.

"You see, what I find most remarkable, Natalie, is how each of them became renowned for exemplifying a distinct era of Old New York."

"Yes, but as distinct as each of those eras was, as marked by the accepted behaviors, what I find fascinating are the commonalities.

How in both, there was this contradiction of the rigidness of social mores and castes versus the excesses of the times."

"Very true." A delighted grin revealed two tiny crescent-shaped dimples in Constance's otherwise smooth skin. "So either Scott was a bit more Victorian than he might have wanted to admit or Edith's High Victorian New York a bit more licentious."

I smiled as I took another sip of the excellent red Constance had had served with the main course. She was truly a formidable woman, overseeing the dinner from her place at the head of the table while she maintained our conversation and made sure that everyone seated near her was comfortable and had everything they wanted. The warmth of familiarity blended with the warmth from the wine to run through my veins in a heady cocktail.

"Well, I think perhaps the more fair assessment is that Fitzgerald wrote of his time, whereas Wharton wrote of a time past, viewing it through the scrim of her experiences. The elapsed years had to have colored her memories and views to a certain degree and allowed her to see a licentiousness she might not have recognized as a sheltered young woman, don't you think?"

"Another astute observation." With a subtle gesture, Constance indicated to a nearby maid that she should check the water glasses as conversation continued to ebb and flow, topics ranging from the most difficult tickets to get on Broadway to the recent presidential elections to which matron had worn the most appalling gown to the opening gala for the New York City Ballet's *Nutcracker* at the new State Theater at Lincoln Center, and what seemed to be every parent's current complaint: those long-haired boys from Liverpool and the disturbing influence they were having on their daughters.

So different—yet so similar.

"It really *was* the most astounding thing." The voice rang out, not so much strident as commanding; enough that the rest of the conversations gradually fell silent, all attention focused on the far end of the table.

"What was?" Greg leaned back in his chair, not at the head of the table, opposite Constance, as one might have expected, but rather, dead center on one of the long sides.

"You would know, Gregory, if you bothered to go to church."

"I go, Aunt Agatha. Easter and Christmas—the rest is between the gentleman and myself." Greg lifted his wine glass toward the older woman occupying the traditional seat of honor and took a drink as he cast a quick glance and wry smile heavenward.

"Nothing shy of blasphemy, my boy. It's a wonder you haven't been excommunicated."

"Well, it's not for lack of trying."

"Insolent." Punctuated with an impatient shake that threatened her towering silver bouffant. "No doubt then, you'll find nothing wrong."

"With what?" Greg's voice remained infinitely patient, yet from my vantage point, I could see the corner of his mouth twitching, ever so slightly.

"With the utter downfall of the Church as we know it. Advent indeed," the older woman sniffed, pulling a large lace-trimmed square from the depths of a black velvet sleeve. "It's a sign, I tell you," she continued, pointing with the hand holding the handkerchief. "That they chose that day."

"I know I'm going to be sorry I asked, but what *are* you talking about Ag?"

"At Mass—on the First Sunday of Advent, the priest, he … he faced us. And recited parts of the liturgy in English!" The older woman's face suffused with color as her voice rose in outrage with each word. "And do *not* call me Ag, Gregory."

As Greg murmured a decidedly not contrite, "Sorry, Aunt Agatha," another man chimed in from the far end of the table.

"I was reading about it in the *Times*. One of the first results of the Vatican Council—a move to make the Church more of the people."

"It's a disgrace, I tell you." Aunt Agatha again sniffed into her handkerchief as she took a sip of water, her color restored to something much closer to normal. While she seemed to be a bit of a dramatic sort, she at least didn't appear to be of the ilk to stage a theatrical faint, sliding boneless from chair to floor in hopes of precipitating a family panic. I knew the type all too well.

"Making the church of the people is peanuts, all things considered. From what I understand, one of the most highly charged topics is the proposed commission to consider birth control as part of the council."

"Gregory Barnes, we're at the dinner table and you knew exactly what I was talking about all along, didn't you?"

The subtle quirk played about his mouth again, the cat, toying with its prey. "Actually, Aunt Agatha, I didn't know precisely what you were talking about, with respect to Mass, but I'm not a complete Luddite. I do keep up. In the interests of intellectual curiosity, of course."

Poor Aunt Agatha was liable to have a stroke right there if Greg didn't let up on his teasing. However, it appeared the lady had more backbone than the fragile façade might indicate.

"It is not intellectual curiosity, it's the Church. It doesn't need to be *of* the people—it just needs to be. And it most certainly does *not* have to change. Not like this."

"But—that's not right either."

The room grew silent as all eyes turned ... toward me. The sudden shock of recognition had my fingers curling around the stem of my wineglass tightening, then relaxing as Constance's hand brushed over mine. "What do you mean, Natalie?"

"I—"

Just in time, I caught myself and started to change whatever inanity I'd been about to blurt out to a polite, innocuous, "—nothing." But that long-denied part of me—the same part that had compelled me to buy the wholly impractical dress and wear my hair down—made me pause and reconsider.

Yes, "nothing" was my standard reply—the mantra which ruled my existence. *Nothing ... it's nothing.* Blend in, say no more than necessary, do as little as possible to distinguish myself, give no hint as to who I'd been. However, in this warm room, glowing with the light from dozens of tall tapers set in silver candelabras soft with the patina of time—buzzing with the conversation and intellectual stimulation I'd lacked for so long—I wanted *so* badly to speak.

Another part of me, slipping free of its restrictions.

Taking a deep breath I began slowly, measuring each word carefully. "It's just that with … theology. Or any ideology, really, shouldn't it be somewhat subject to the times? To allow for personal interpretation? Otherwise, how can it evolve in a manner that's congruent with not only its time, but its people?"

"One might argue that the Church is there to guide—Natalie, is it? Not to be subject to our whims and fancies." The statement, issued more as a gentle challenge rather than as a rebuke came from the man who'd first mentioned the Vatican council.

"Yes, but—" I pushed my plate to the side, leaning forward on the table to better face my challenger. "To force any group to subject themselves so wholly to a single, unwavering belief with no room for interpretation or challenge, it … it—" I faltered, searching for the right words.

"Would invite totalitarian rule."

"Yes." Relieved, I nodded at Greg. "Exactly." Because really, "allows a madman freedom to take everything you hold dear," was most assuredly not the right choice for this particular discussion, making little sense to these people.

"Nonsense." Aunt Agatha bit the word off as if was a sour wedge of lemon. "That's not the Church—that's Communism."

"Yes," I breathed far more quietly, looking away from the table at large and down into my wine glass. "Exactly."

"You argue like a Jesuit, Natalie."

My gaze rose to meet Greg's. "I'll take that as a compliment." Nico had been taught by the Jesuits at Belén. Could carry an argument for days.

"It's meant as one." With a wink, he turned to placate Aunt Agatha who was still spluttering about Communists and what did that have to do with birth control and really, Gregory, it was rather in poor taste and quite possibly heresy, to be discussing such things at the dinner table. As various other conversations resumed, I toyed once again with the stem of my wine glass, more than content for the moment to sit quietly, both exhilarated and exhausted from my rare moment in the spotlight.

"No, he's got a new tutor, and I tell you, it's working miracles. The changes in him in this last term alone, are nothing short of remarkable. It's as if he's gone from boy to man, almost overnight."

"Natalie? You've gone absolutely white as a sheet, dear. Are you all right?"

Once again, the table gradually grew silent as my worst nightmares came true, the insistent drum at the back of my mind now berating me, steadily and with increasing fervor, what a tremendous error of judgment this whole night had been. What a fool *I* had been, to think I could recapture a hint of my past without my present intruding and making itself shockingly, painfully known.

But *how* known? No one had given any indication that they recognized me or my name, other than Constance.

"I-I'm … fine." Just trying to remember how to breathe. Reaching for reserves of discipline and calm much in the same way I reached for my water goblet and took a careful sip, trying desperately to steady the nerves that had my pulse beating wildly at the base of my throat, making it difficult to swallow. *Dios mío*, what if this woman's son was—what if he—

"So, Farraday's proven to be more of a challenge than Ryan expected then, Faye?" Greg's voice, light, conversational, immediately drew attention away from me.

Farraday.

Not Concord. Farraday. Tony prep school in rural Massachusetts. Not the Upper East Side. Stepping stone for privileged young men—those future doctors and politicians and captains of industry. A school much like Concord. Too much. But *not*. As the realizations tumbled one, after the other, fighting to be heard over the roaring of blood in my ears, I stole a glance at Greg, ostensibly absorbed in the woman's accounts of her son's exploits, yet for just a split second, our gazes met and I experienced the most uncanny sensation of having been rescued. Again. Which, in this case, was absurd.

"Are you certain you're all right, dear?"

"Y-yes, Truly." Never mind that my heart was continuing to beat a rapid, painful tattoo against my ribcage. "I-I think I just overindulged a bit in the wine." I laughed, mildly surprised at how carefree it came out sounding. "I'd best stop before it leads to my embarrassing myself further. Or a hangover." Using a corner of my napkin, I dabbed at my upper lip, the gentle rasp of the linen against the sensitive skin serving as an anchor, centering my focus. Loosely fold the cloth into a long triangle, set it alongside my plate—little rituals, learned a lifetime ago, helping to keep me grounded and not from dissolving into a mass of hysteria.

"Perhaps splashing some cool water on your face?"

I stared at Constance, her face wavering gently in my field of vision, the words seeming to come from a distance.

"I think … yes, that might be a good idea." My words sounded even more distant and hollow than Constance's.

"Or would you prefer to lie down? You're certainly welcome to use the study or perhaps one of the boys' rooms—"

"No—" I took a deep breath, marveled at how cold my fingertips felt against my cheeks. "Honestly, Constance—it's nothing a splash of water won't fix."

"If you're sure," she conceded, her fine, light brows not relaxing from the frown into which they'd drawn. "Florence—" She gestured to one of the nearby maids. "Please show Miss Martin to the restroom attached to Greg Junior's bedroom," she instructed quietly, her gaze shifting to meet mine as I stood and moved to follow the patiently waiting maid. "In case you change your mind and want to lie down for a moment."

What I wanted was to disappear. Right then and there. I wanted nothing more than to have a hole open up and swallow me and these ridiculous delusions that I could recapture a moment of my past. Better still, that some time warp would magically appear to transport me back, oh … a week or so, before my carefully ordered world had begun tilting sideways.

"But you can't. And the sooner you accept that, the better off we'll all be, Natalia."

Wonderful. I was now reduced to scolding myself in a mirror. And referring to myself in the plural. Turning the elegant brass handle with a vicious twist, I sent water cascading into the bathroom sink. Without hesitation, I plunged my hands and wrists beneath the icy stream, shivering as the tingling sensations traveled across my palms and up my arms. Mesmerized, I watched the patterns the water made as it streamed over my hands, their skin gradually turning pink, pinker still, then finally a bright, vibrant red, a color of feeling. Which made the fact that my hands were now completely numb, oddly amusing. Removing them from the water, I flexed the fingers a few times, prompting the blood to begin flowing again, then adjusted the water to a gentler stream. Cupping my hands, I splashed my cheeks, once, twice—again and again until the feverish, overheated feeling was gone. Yet, when I lifted my face to stare into the mirror I noted how my cheeks remained flushed, my pupils glittering and enlarged to where nothing but a slight trace of dark green iris was visible.

With a sigh, I turned the water off and reached for one of the neatly folded hand towels left beside the sink by the helpful Florence, as she'd asked once again if there was anything she could get me, a "bicarb or maybe some hot ginger water." Cures she said her mama had sworn were the only remedy for her daddy's hangovers. I'd had to summon every ounce of autocratic insistence that just a few splashes of water and I'd be perfectly all right, before she would leave, skepticism still clearly written across her features.

Right as rain, chère. I could hear Remy's voice echoing as I shook the towel open and held it against my face. Moments passed, my fingertips pressing the plush terrycloth harder and harder into my eyelids until miniscule red dots danced and chased each other across the blackness.

No, Remy. Not right as rain. There simply wasn't enough water in the world.

But I'd do my best.

Setting aside the towel, I turned my attention to repairing the damage—at least that of the external variety. Thankfully I'd thought to stop by the coat closet and retrieve my evening bag, so I was able to line and lipstick and powder my face into some semblance of normality. A few runs of the comb through my hair disguised the random damp strands and by some miracle, my dress had escaped unscathed from my reckless splashing. Ultimately, no one looking at me would be able to see anything amiss. Good thing most people never bothered to look beyond the surface.

I snorted lightly at my repaired reflection—if revisiting my former life, however tangentially, was enough to render me even more cynical than usual, it would no doubt be in my best interests to refrain. Another valuable lesson learned.

While I could have exited the bathroom through the door that led directly into the hallway, I instead chose to wander through the adjacent bedroom. Such a boy's room, with its felt school and team banners tacked to the wall alongside photographs of lithe-limbed young women and boys, arms slung around bare, tanned shoulders, brilliant, carefree smiles aimed toward the waiting camera. The books competing for shelf space with trophies, a well-worn ball cap carelessly tossed over one gold, upthrust arm. What would it be like, I wondered idly, to take Constance's invitation and lie down on that neatly made bed with the plaid coverlet and plump pillows and the blanket folded at the foot? To sink into the darkness of this spacious room that was easily half as large as my current apartment and not wake up until sunlight streamed through the windows that looked out over the expanse of Central Park.

"Plenty of water—" said a smooth Gregory Peck-like baritone behind me, "—and two aspirin right before bedtime."

I spun, banging my shoulder against the doorframe, clutching for it at the same time as a large hand grasped my elbow. After the shock and disorientation passed, I recognized him as another guest, one who'd been seated farther down, beside Greg. Although there was something else, something terribly familiar, that I couldn't quite place. But now was not the time to try to figure such a thing out, not with him still standing before me, clearly waiting—

"I beg your pardon?" I finally stammered, easing back a step so I could look up at him.

"Plenty of water and two aspirin right before bedtime are the best cure for any potential hangovers. Most useful thing I ever learned at Farraday." A smile, fleeting and again, teasing the edges of memory with its familiarity, crossed his face. "Definitely came in handy during subsequent collegiate bacchanals."

"I—thank you?" I groaned inwardly at the wholly ridiculous response, but at a loss as to what else I could possibly say. Luckily, it seemed as if nothing more was required.

"You're welcome. And I apologize for having startled you. But I saw you leave the table looking unwell and when I asked Constance if you were all right, she expressed her concern that you weren't, despite your insistence to the contrary, so I offered to come check on you." The fleeting smile had completely disappeared, leaving his expression somewhat somber, the austere lines completely at odds with the large, heavy-lidded hazel eyes set beneath sandy brows, varying shades of green and gold and amber vying for dominance in the soft light from the hall sconces. Faun's eyes, I thought irrationally—or maybe entirely rationally given his advice and references to bacchanals. Eyes that studied me with an almost uncomfortable intensity.

Managing a smile, I said, "I appreciate your concern Mr—"

"Roemer." His hand slid from my elbow to my hand, taking it in a formal grasp. "John Roemer. Although most people just call me Jack."

"Well, then … Jack." The harsh, clipped name felt foreign and odd on my lips, the more old-fashioned, formal John appearing to suit him better and clearly, this whole evening was taking a toll, given the fanciful imagery and assumptions with respect to a complete stranger's name. And eyes. "I do appreciate your concern, but as you can see, I'm fine." I pulled my hand from his grasp, breathing an internal sigh of relief as it slid free with no resistance, no motion on his part to hold on. "We should probably return to the dining room—I'd like to set Constance's mind at ease—"

"Actually, one of the reasons I offered to check on you was because she was in the process of shooing everyone to the living room for dessert and coffee."

"Oh. Well, then, thank you. Again." And could I sound any more inane?

Nodding, he fell into step beside me, hands in his pockets. "Are you really all right?"

A sidelong glance revealed that maddeningly familiar half smile had returned to his face. "Truly, I'm fine—" I glanced again, trying to remain subtle, but there was simply something about him… Tall, broad-shouldered and stocky, though not in a soft, self-satisfied way. More … solid. Older than me, at least thirty and … and …who *was* he? I felt as if I should know, familiarity teasing me with gossamer lightness, there and gone.

"I'm telling you, this is not the time."

"Connie—"

"Did you not see her face?"

"Of course I did. Which is precisely *why* it's the time. It needs to stop. We can't let her go back."

"Oh Greg—so intent on saving the world. Or at the very least, helpless young women."

"You were never helpless, Connie. And neither is she. But this situation—it's not right. I don't know how someone like her found herself in such circumstances, but it's going to crush her if it's allowed to continue. We can make it stop."

The voices, quiet yet urgent, drifted through the cracked-open pocket doors to my left, setting all my senses on high alert. Chancing another glance at Jack Roemer, I found him studying me once again with that quietly intense gaze, as if deliberating. Then, just as I decided it best to simply continue on to the living room … perhaps better still, make my excuses, claim illness, leave all of this behind, Jack discreetly knocked on the door, then slid it open further, revealing what appeared to be an immense study, all dark paneled wood and shelves filled to the brim and beyond with books. A massive partner's desk, papers strewn across the vast surface, occupied one end of the long room, an elaborately carved fireplace the other, the details sharp and magnified, much like the moment itself. It was before the fireplace that Connie and Greg stood, silhouetted in the glow, their bodies creating shadows that angled up the walls and crept along the ceiling, dark, flickering apparitions, bearing down on us where we stood.

My gaze darted around the room, settling on Connie and Greg, who'd turned to face us, then Jack, back to them, again to Jack, who was making a motion as if to put a hand to my back, to urge me through the doors, push me into this new unknown. Gasping, I shrank back against the opposite doorjamb, pain shooting up my hand as a nail tore, my fingers cramping as they dug into the wood, shaking my head, each breath shallower than the last. All I wanted was to leave, because this was not right. At all. But at the same time, what was left of my rational mind argued, what could possibly happen here? There was a party going on, for God's sake—nearly two dozen people in this apartment.

Yes, a party. People who'd been drinking all evening, who might not even notice that two guests and both of their hosts had gone missing.

Yet what could possibly happen in a library? In a room meant for study. For knowledge. For learning.

With people nearby. Plenty of people.

Certainly they would hear. Someone would notice something. Hear something. They wouldn't let anything happen. Would they?

Would they?

Would *they*?

Around me, the world wavered ... then steadied for a brief, hopeful instant before wavering again ... fading, then—

Black.

SEVEN

"I think she's coming around."

The first slow blink was just enough to bring me out of the darkness. A gradual return to awareness, surroundings sharpening, beginning with the hypnotic dance of flames, red and orange tinged with nebulous black edges. When I closed my eyes again, it was the sharp snap as wood collapsed that held my attention, followed by the distinctive, smoky aroma, teasing the inside of my nostrils. Familiar, comforting sounds and scents, allowing me to imagine I was at Mercier's, the old woodstove standing sentry. Other than blinking, I remained very still, taking in dark wood gleaming in the mellow light from the fire and the Tiffany lamps standing sentry at either end of the mantle, the antiqued brass bases appearing to wind and twist upwards as if trying to capture the brilliant blue and green dragonflies ringing the shades.

Maybe if I lay perfectly still—played dead for long enough—the soft voices rumbling nearby would leave. Then I could get up and run. Run far away and pretend that none of this had happened. Whatever "this" was.

At the same time, however, I couldn't lie here forever. And whatever awaited me beyond the curtain of full consciousness couldn't possibly be any worse than anything I'd faced in the past.

But I would start slowly.

Tentatively opening and closing one hand, the tips of my fingers encountered what felt like the edges of a small pillow, scratchy wool, nubby with embroidery, tucked beneath my neck. By contrast, softness lay beneath the palm of my other hand—my dress—the velvet almost obscenely lush and rich in comparison to the sharp throbbing at the tip of my ring finger.

That's what anchored me. Allowed me to understand this really wasn't some bizarre nightmare. That pain simply felt too real. As did the soft caress along my hair, brushing it away from my face, while what felt like a cool cloth was placed across my forehead.

"Natalie?"

It was good that Constance's was the first face I saw. Her soft brown eyes, brimming with kindness and concern as she leaned forward from the chair set close beside the sofa I lay on, just far enough behind my head I hadn't noticed her in the initial perusal of my surroundings.

"What happened?" The words emerged on a thin whisper. Weak. *No, no, no* ... I needed to be strong. To regain control, at least of myself.

"Shh ... just lie there for another moment."

I struggled to an elbow, the damp cloth falling from my forehead unheeded as the world spun briefly before righting itself. "What happened?" Still lacking the weight and conviction I would prefer, but at least I didn't sound as if I was on the verge of sliding back into nothingness.

She sighed and reached down to the floor to retrieve the washcloth. "Spectacularly poor timing, my dear, and I can't begin to apologize enough for that." My gaze followed her long fingers as they smoothed over the fabric, folding it back along damp creases, although her gaze never left my face. She did not, however, offer anything more. If I wanted to know, I would have to ask. At the very least, I could read that much in her troubled expression. She would give no more than I wanted. If I wanted, I could get up and leave, no further questions asked.

But no questions answered either. And therein lay my choice. That I had questions, of that there was no doubt. But did I want them answered? It would be far less troublesome to allow them to die in this quiet room.

"Timing about what, Constance?"

"Are you sure you want to know?"

I looked up at Greg who'd appeared at the opposite end of the sofa, maintaining a safe distance even as he extended his hand, a cut crystal snifter half-filled with amber liquid.

Struggling to a fully seated position, I took a moment to consider. It couldn't have been stated any more baldly—that whatever I wanted to know had the potential to upset me further. Silently, I held out my hand, trembling only slightly, wincing as I noted the ragged nail edge, torn down below the quick. When Greg placed the snifter in my hand, he did so carefully, waiting until he was certain my hold was secure before withdrawing. He glanced from me to the far end of the sofa, eyebrows raised. Feeling slightly foolish at granting the man permission in his own home, I nodded, then took a sip of the brandy, wincing again as the liquor burned a trail down my throat and settled into a glow in my stomach.

"We have a proposition for you."

The sip I'd just taken erupted into a cough as Constance snapped, "Jack, I adore you as much as if you were one of my own sons, but for the love of all that's holy, keep still until you're needed."

Jerking my head in the direction Constance was glaring, I discovered Jack Roemer directly behind me, hovering almost, like those dark shadows had appeared to just before I—

"Natalie—"

My head jerked again, a puppet, my body's movements dictated by the whims of others, this time toward Greg.

"It's honestly not as dire and dramatic as all this might lead you to believe."

No? But I remained silent, taking another small, measured sip of brandy.

"Jack's right that we do have a proposition for you—a project that's had me at wit's end for well over a year. Involving my goddaughter—" He selected a framed photograph from the nearby end table that he offered much in the same way as he'd offered the brandy, steady and careful.

I took the photograph, studying the black and white image of a hauntingly beautiful woman, the elegant head with its heavy chignon turned in a three-quarters profile pose, an obvious attempt at Grace Kelly iciness. However, the sidelong glance from beneath delicately arched brows and thick lashes was so full of inherent heat and sensuality, it rendered the image a study of vivid contrasts.

"Ava began as a model before moving to Los Angeles at the invitation of a producer to become an actress. She's enjoyed a reasonable amount of success but not as much more than the ubiquitous beautiful girl or second or third ingénue. She has, however, cultivated quite the notorious reputation." His eyes narrowed on my face as I glanced from the photograph to him. "None of this rings a bell, does it?"

"Should it?"

"Ava is a fairly well-known debutante from a very old money New York family." Constance took up the mantle of explanation. "She's always been a bit of a wild child—an unrepentant attention-seeker. Modeling, acting, impulsive marriages and divorces—scandalous affairs or wild dances on a table at the Cocoanut Grove." She lifted a resigned shoulder. "The type of attention doesn't matter much so long as Hedda or Army notices and favors her with a mention in their columns. Which of course, leaves her well-bred family practically breathing fire in their disapproval." One eyebrow rose. "They're of the ilk to value discretion above all else while discretion isn't even in Ava's repertoire."

My head was throbbing with too much liquor combined with the sudden onslaught of information. Confusing information, but at the same time, like so much else this evening, familiar. I'd known of girls just like this back in Havana. Girls from good families who were nevertheless the object of many whispers—called "fast" by the boys and "trouble" by the nuns and "whores" by the *tías*. The epitome of what we were not supposed to be. I forced the little voice whispering I had no room to judge because I'd become just that, to the back of my mind. For one thing, it was not a status to which I'd ever aspired and for another, those girls—much like this Ava—had at least appeared to be having fun, even if it wasn't *my* idea of fun.

"All right," I said carefully.

Greg leaned forward, matching my pose on the edge of the sofa. "Ava's going to be turning thirty in the coming year and as such, has decided the time is ripe for her to write an autobiography. Especially since word's come out that Liz Taylor's working on hers."

Dumbfounded, I blurted, "But … Elizabeth Taylor is the most famous woman in the world."

"You say that as if it should matter," Jack commented drily from the position he'd assumed leaning against the mantle. "At least to Ava." He smiled, but beneath the humor, I sensed a thread of something darker.

"I agree that on the surface it's blatantly ridiculous," Constance added, "but truth is, Ava, even in her limited fashion, carries a good deal of notoriety. Perhaps not to the extent of Liz Taylor, but then again, who does? However, Ava's still managed to maintain a regular presence in the gossip columns with her various shenanigans. Couple that with her roots in a venerable old New York family filled with high-powered businessmen and politicians and philanthropists and that has fiercely guarded its privacy throughout its existence and it adds up to irresistible fodder for most any publisher—especially the ones lacking a certain measure of ethics." She spared the photograph another glance and sighed.

"But while she may be vain and reckless and rather more full of herself than she has any right to be, there is still something rather … fragile, I suppose, that invites protection. Which is why we've put such effort into finding the right person to—"

"Indulge her whims?"

Constance's mouth briefly tightened. "Yes, Jack. It is in all likelihood a momentary whim. And for all we know, tomorrow she may change her mind about the whole thing and find something else on which to focus. However, until she does, you cannot argue that we are in the best position to do preemptive damage control."

As Jack expelled an impatient breath and turned to pour himself another drink, Greg settled himself more comfortably on the sofa and met my gaze. "Look, I'll cut to the chase. Would you be interested in submitting a writing proposal in consideration for becoming Ava's ghostwriter?"

A log snapped and a shower of sparks, much like fireworks, fanned behind the wrought iron grate, brilliant shades of red and orange and gold briefly illuminating the sitting area, throwing everything beyond it into even deeper shadow.

"*What?* Why? I mean, why me, of all people?" The words followed, each faster than the one that came before, in my mind appearing almost as if they were running, tumbling after each other in a merry chase, much in the way as this whole thing was beginning to feel.

"Because I've gone through more than half a dozen of the best ghostwriters in the business and all of them, for whatever reasons, have failed to meet with Ava's approval. Or she's run them off with her impossible behavior. Or, as with the last one, seduced him and suddenly, he was far less interested in writing." He snorted. "So I've decided to take a different approach—try a female ghostwriter. It at least eliminates the danger of seduction."

"I … but…" I stammered, trying to absorb and understand precisely what it was Greg was suggesting. "You don't even know if I can write."

"Natalie …" Greg's smile was one of contrasts for as much as it was gentle, it still had an unmistakably predatory edge to it. The businessman I'd first come to know breaking the surface. "Anyone as widely read, as passionate and eloquent as you are about literature— surely it's not an unimaginable stretch."

"The ability from one hardly translates to the other," I pointed out, finally feeling myself on firmer ground. "Well read, yes, but other than that, nothing more than a restaurant hostess and part-time tutor."

"Let's just say gut instinct suggested there was a bit more to you than that." He shrugged. "And my gut has rarely led me astray."

"And in this case, was spot on and led us to some fascinating discoveries."

The firmer ground I'd briefly imagined myself on shifted

precipitously as I stared at Jack.

"Graduated from high school at sixteen—won a sought-after acceptance to the Sorbonne—" A quiet thump drew my attention to the marble surface of the coffee table on which now rested a dark green cloth-bound volume I'd never expected to see again. "Gifted enough to have had her first collection of short works published prior to turning seventeen. I'll admit, I was doubtful, but Greg's gut was dead right—you know how to write. And quite well, if what I read is any indication, Natalia."

Silence, pregnant with shock, enveloped the room as the person I'd once been at long last fully exploded into being after hovering about the edges all evening—set free by the casual utterance of the name by which I hadn't been addressed in years.

"Jesus *Christ*, Jack."

"Jack, you promised."

Greg and Constance's chorused shock was punctuated by the muffled thud of the snifter slipping from my fingers to land on the Oriental carpet. The smoky, sweet smell of brandy wafted up, burning my sinuses as I stared, open-mouthed. Standing in front of the fireplace, his face a shifting assembly of sharp planes and shadows, like a Picasso come to life, Jack Roemer became the menacing silhouette I'd feared from the moment he'd slid open the doors to this room.

"I didn't so much promise as I respected your wishes for as long as I could, Constance. But really, what's to be gained by pussyfooting around? She wants to know why. It's been clearly established that she's not stupid."

"There's pussyfooting and there's an ambush."

"Oh, come on. Ambush is a bit strong don't you think?"

"I most certainly do *not*. You were hardly raised in a barn, Jack. You *know* her history."

"Yes, I do. And I imagine she can handle this just fine once she gets over the initial shock of having her charade exposed."

I sat there, fighting off another wave of lightheadedness as the two of them volleyed back and forth like finalists at Wimbledon with me as the unwitting ball. Finally, Jack turned to me. "I'm here because I'm Ava's attorney and the administrator of her affairs. Perhaps of greater relevance, I'm also her cousin. And while she is without a doubt flighty and impulsive and has driven me mad throughout most of our lives, I stand firmly with Greg and Constance when it comes to protecting her. And by extension, my family. Which means a thorough investigation of *any* individual who could potentially get close."

I could feel my jaw working, a faint popping sensation as it opened and closed as if desperately trying to remember how to form words. Any words. In any language.

"I know it must seem like a healthy dose of paranoia—but it's one I'm sure you understand. How you can never be too careful." His eyes narrowed, the intensity of his gaze closing the distance between us until I felt as if he were physically hovering over me. "Compared to the others, you did present something of a challenge—initially easy enough for our investigators to track back to when you became a citizen and legally changed your name. Even back to when you first arrived in the country. However, anything before that became … difficult. But with the means at our disposal, not impossible."

How could a smile possibly be so cool and somber? The tone of voice so easy and measured and almost … *kind*—yet menacing, for all that?

"What … exactly—" I swallowed hard, my fingers curling into the edges of the leather cushions. "What do you know?"

"Everything we needed." He circled the coffee table to perch on the edge, the fine wool of his trousers brushing my skirt. "Natalia San Martín—Havana, Cuba. Only daughter of the head of one of the oldest and wealthiest families on the island. Immensely strong and deep ties to the country, yet with an unusual history of remaining classically apolitical. Ultimately, that's what proved their undoing, wasn't it?" Again, not sounding completely unkind or unsympathetic. But any faint hope that he'd leave it there quickly dissipated as he continued reciting moments from my history as if they were facts memorized for a test. "After disappearing from the island in 1959, your immediate family resurfaced in Miami, where you lived with them until you came to New York. By yourself. And since then, you've been completely on your own—four years where you've divided your time between working as a hostess at Mercier's and as a tutor at Concord."

Did he? Really? In the midst of that matter-of-fact litany, did he actually pause—just slightly? Was I imagining that his gaze narrowed again, as if searching my face for my reaction? Or was it simply panic on my part?

"Your father has a law degree from the University of Havana, but is of course unable to use it here. He *could* return to school and take the bar in this country, but that would require both time and money—two resources he no longer has. So he clerks at a law office while your mother and grandmother run a small business making dresses for baptisms and First Communions and some sort of elaborate birthday parties—"

"*Quinceañeras,*" I offered dully as he paused to search for the word. And they had? When had they done this? And I couldn't imagine Papi having approved of Mami and Abuelita working in any capacity, but then again, when the two of them got an idea in their head, there was no stopping them. Still ... I'd had no idea.

This ... man. This stranger. Knew more about my family than I did.

"Your parents and grandmother and younger brother are all still in Miami and like clockwork, shortly after the fifteenth of every month, money arrives—from you. Money that allowed your mother and grandmother to start their business and that helps to send your brother to one of the best parochial schools in Miami, yet beyond that monthly check, you maintain no other contact with them. As far as we can tell, haven't had any in the four years you've been gone." The austere lines almost appeared to relax as his brows drew together. "The one mystery we've been unable to resolve," he finished on an even softer voice. "Why, exactly, that is."

And in the scheme of things, of very little importance, otherwise, they would have worked harder to resolve it or more likely, I wouldn't be here at all. My voice as soft as his, I said, "If you know everything, then you've already surmised a theory, yes?"

It was the look in his eyes, more so than the slow nod, that affirmed yes, he knew everything. Everything he thought was important.

"And you'd be wrong. Not that it matters."

I blindly reached down and groped for my shoes, discovering them along with my bag. Constance's concerned "Natalie?" was overridden by Greg's quiet "Leave her be, Connie," as I slipped my pumps on and stood, gathering enough resolve to render Jack Roemer frozen, hand extended, attempting to offer assistance.

"I'll be leaving now." Arms crossed over my midsection, I backed slowly from the seating area. "I—" Started to say thank you, but realized how utterly outrageous and inappropriate and wrong it would be. There was nothing to thank here. Not with Constance's worried gaze following me. With Greg closing his eyes in what appeared to be regret. And Jack—I couldn't bear to look at him again. How *dare* he? No matter who he thought he was. Or his cousin was. Or who he *thought* I was.

"Please let Mrs. Mercier know I've left." And no matter how hard I tried to have the words come out powerful and strong—to have my persona reassert itself into the cool competent Natalie—it was the voice of the frightened girl, Natalia, that emerged.

"Natalie, at least allow us a few moments to call the car to take you home. Or ask the doorman to hail a taxi—"

"*No*—" I skittered away from Greg's plea, my arms unfolding from around my body to reach back for the door, my hands blindly scrabbling for the brass handle that would slide it open, provide freedom. "I don't need a ride. I don't need your charity." The door shuddered as it slammed into its pocket frame.

"I don't need anything. Do you understand me? I will *never* need anything from any of you."

EIGHT

"Natalie?"

Time had completely slipped away while I'd walked. I'd managed to escape the apartment undetected for the most part—nothing more than a quizzical glance from the maid manning the coat check. Leaving the building behind with every intention of going home. I think. Or whatever it was that passed for home. But then, rather than hail one of the many cabs that streamed past, or descend into the steaming, claustrophobic confines of the subway, I'd simply continued walking, weaving in and out of the weekend revelers, out celebrating the holiday season. Ignoring the cat calls and the invitations from outside the bars to join them for a drink. I'd just kept my head down and weaved and pushed through the small knots of people, the couples, the others who were as alone as I was. Along Central Park West, around Columbus Circle, down Broadway and into the seedy bustle of Times Square with its honking horns and too-bright lights and jaded regulars lurking in shadowy doorways—a place where any whim could be indulged if only for the right price.

It was as if I was seeing it through the glass of the globes I'd adored as a child, except I was the one trapped inside, sparkling snow falling about my shoulders, reflecting the lights. Like a dream, I walked through it all, protected by the translucent walls of my bubble, the sights blurred and distorted, sounds muffled into an indistinct rumble.

I continued to meander down Broadway, no longer even bothering to pretend I had any real destination in mind, simply allowing myself to be pushed along by the cold wind and stinging snow blowing down the street, pausing for a breath when the wind did, stamping pins and needles from my feet and legs and watching the clouds of my breath dissipate into the frigid night air before the wind decided it was time for me to resume my aimless journey. It was during one such pause that I found myself in front of Macy's, the windows brilliantly dressed in holiday splendor meant to evoke this year's theme: Santa Claus in a multitude of different guises.

There was, of course, the traditional Santa in full *Miracle on 34th Street* mode, a dark-haired little girl perched on his lap and whispering secrets. The Cowboy Santa holding the reins of a bucking bronco with a delighted little boy perched in front of him. Then there was the Rock-and-Roll Santa in a red lamé jacket and piled high pompadour with sideburns as he strummed his guitar, a pose that a decade earlier would have been considered scandalous, but was today, endearingly anachronistic.

Despite the wind picking up, insisting I should *go*, I stood riveted in front of the final window, unable to move, even if I'd wanted to. All I could do was stare at the Santa in his old-fashioned candy-cane striped bathing suit and sunglasses, languidly reclining in a chaise lounge beneath an umbrella. Positioned beneath a glorious smiling sun, the chaise was surrounded with sparkling sand and potted palms and flowers, while a photo backdrop of endless white beach and turquoise waters completed the optical illusion of a tropical paradise. And all I could do was laugh. Peal after peal, until I slumped against the window, my breath leaving smears of condensation on the pristine glass.

Dios mío de mi alma—the irony. All this shiny, tropical splendor, as foreign and incongruous here, with cold and snow and traffic streaming past as those cool silver and blue winter-scene Christmas cards had been in the brilliant warmth of my home, all those years ago.

It didn't make sense. None of it.

Spinning away from the window, I continued along 34th, still walking aimlessly, it seemed, but after a few blocks I paused again, leaning my head back, back, still farther back, wavering off-balance, my gaze following the Empire State Building's sleek, endless lines, as far as I could see, the skewed perspective leaving me dizzy and disoriented.

The entire time I'd lived in New York, I'd not been here. It was too iconic, far too much a symbol of the city Nicolas had so loved. Easier for me to reduce New York to the immediate—the dirty, crowded streets and faceless, anonymous strangers streaming in and out of claustrophobic offices and apartment buildings. To make it as indistinct as any other large city. That other New York— the beautiful one of shining skyscrapers and glittering lights—that had been the fantasy. Nico's dream. I understood that. And stayed as far away from it as humanly possible. My demons may have driven me to this godforsaken city, but they did *not* have agency over the entirety of my heart.

At least, until tonight.

Paying my fee and following the guide's bored instructions to a cordoned line, I waited my turn to ride the elevator to the 86th floor, and the expansive observation deck. And even here—surrounded by the excited chatter of tourists and the quiet murmurs of lovers— with the unending panorama of the city stretched before me— Even *here*, I couldn't completely shed the near overwhelming sense of isolation. Perhaps it simply wasn't possible any longer.

The city lights appeared to wink as they merged with the gently falling snow, a riotous sea of color and pattern, undulating to the rhythm of the streets far below and tempting me with whispered promises.

Just one step.

All it would take was one step out onto its vast expanse, then I, too, could reach up and touch the heavens.

That if I did, I could be with the one person who'd always known me.

Those poor lovers and tourists—with their confused expressions and the expletives and shouts they hurled after me as I pushed past, heart pounding in my mad dash for the elevator, squeezing through the rapidly closing doors, reluctant to wait even the few minutes it would take for the next one to arrive. Ignoring the startled faces and less-than-subtle whispers of *drugs* or *drunk*—shrinking back into a corner and praying that the damned thing would get to the lobby. Just get to the lobby, *please*.

Through the doors and out onto the street and running, running… Horns and shouts hardly registering, icy splashes from cars speeding through puddles barely eliciting a gasp as I paused on street corners, attempting to get my bearings before taking off again. My once-lovely satin pumps, never meant for this sort of panicked flight, skidded on slick, frozen patches and sank into wet piles of slush as my gloved fingers grabbed onto iron banisters, parking meters, jutting bricks, anything that might propel me forward, including, in one tire-squealing moment, the hood of a taxi, my heart pounding in my ears as I stood, illuminated in the headlights like the star of some horribly surreal show. Through the grimy expanse of windshield, I watched the agitated motions of the driver's hands, and the way his mouth worked—was it in fear or anger?—before limping off, thigh hot and throbbing, blindly turning corners, relying on instinct, because I'd only been here a handful of times and never for anything like this and please be home, *por favor, por favor, por favor*, be home—

The soles of my shoes scrambling for purchase on the stone steps, numb fingers pulling open the exterior door, then still more steps, the marble worn smooth over the decades, each step echoing briefly before being drowned out by the next one. My fist, mimicking the desperate sound, pounding on the solid wood door, forehead propped on my upraised arm, unwilling to face the possibility that no one might be home. That I'd be left alone—

I didn't want to be alone. Not tonight. Not again.

"*Natalie?*"

I clung to the door jamb, grateful to the point of tears that he was here.

"*Chère*, what are you doin' here—what's happened? Girl, look at me—c'mon now, talk to me *bebe*, you hurt?"

And as I stood there, teeth chattering, unable to answer or even to take the single step necessary to cross the threshold—to complete my impromptu journey—Remy took charge. Thank God, because I simply couldn't. Cradled in his arms like a baby, I dropped my head to his shoulder as he drew me from the shadowed hall into the light and warmth of his apartment.

"You sit right there and don't move."

He eased down onto the sofa still holding me, as I clung to him like a limpet, afraid to let go, even for a second. Afraid if I did, he'd dissipate and I'd realize I had done nothing more than conjure an elaborate vision out of sheer desperation.

"It's okay, *chère*," he crooned. "I'll be right back. I'm not goin' anywhere, I promise." With a gentle touch, he pushed lank, ragged strands of hair from my face, tilting my chin up just far enough for my gaze to meet his. "Just give me a minute, that's all."

After he shifted me more fully onto the sofa, rather than turn to walk away, he chose instead to retreat, nodding slowly all the while as if in reassurance, his gaze steady, holding mine the entire way until he disappeared into his kitchen with a final nod to just hold on. Just another minute longer. The minute he vanished, I drew my frozen, aching legs up, curling in on myself. Dropping my forehead to the back of the sofa, I allowed the soft velvet of the throw draped across the streamlined leather surface to cradle my throbbing head and absorb the occasional tear.

"C'mon, *bebe*, drink. Then we'll get you into a hot bath."

I lifted my head, my nose twitching at the steam curling up from the mug Remy held. "No more alcohol," I croaked. Even though the promise of a soothing drink was so very tempting, my throat feeling as if it was on fire—as if I'd been screaming and railing for real instead of simply from inside my own head.

"It's not alcohol, it's a toddy."

Unbelievably, I managed a laugh. Rusty and pained, but a laugh nevertheless. Because this was Remy and this was at least in part *why* I'd come here, after all. Right?

"I've had your toddies."

"Hush you," he scolded, bringing the mug to my lips. "I can tell you don't need any more liquor. You smell like my granddaddy's still. This is mostly cider with some fresh orange and just a splash of rum to warm you up from the inside. Now drink. Then that bath for your outsides." As I took a careful sip, he resumed brushing my hair back from my face, mock-grumbling, "I don't know why you always spoilin' for a fight, *chère*. Always givin' me a hard time."

With each sip, each teasing admonition to drink up because it was nectar of the gods, and his *grandmére* swore by it, if with a bit more rum, you understand, I relaxed a bit more, breathed easier, as if I'd managed to escape this … *thing* that had been attempting to capture me. And the fact that he wasn't questioning or probing for explanations—that he was just unequivocally wrapping me in care and protection even if it wasn't something I'd ever requested of him before—allowed a measure of warmth to seep back in that had nothing to do with the hot cider.

"Remy, what's going on? Who's that?"

Holding the mug steady, Remy calmly responded, "A friend, Penelope." Sparing scarcely a glance toward the open doorway where the Bridget Bardot blonde posed, tousle-haired and sleepy-eyed, the barely buttoned men's shirt she wore exposing endless legs, shadowy cleavage, and the fact that she was nude beneath the fine white fabric. As nude as Remy presumably was beneath the robe I was only now realizing was what he wore.

It was as if her sudden appearance served as a signal, alerting me to the rest of my surroundings beyond the immediate. Nina Simone, rich and throaty, streaming from the gleaming wood and chrome console stereo, the remnants of what had been an intimate dinner on the café table. The distinctive aroma of melting wax from candles burning low wrapping the room in cashmere sensuality while the various items of clothing strewn across the floor paved a clear trail toward the doorway where the woman still waited.

"I knew you were a faithless bastard, but two women in one night is low, even for you," she snapped in clipped English tones.

"Now that's some high opinion of my manhood," he replied with that all-too-familiar edge of laughter. "Even if it's not altogether wrong. But really, *chère*, you think I would've gone to all this effort if

I'd been expecting to entertain a second lady tonight? I already told you—she's a friend." He shifted slightly, pointedly turning his back to her, while I couldn't seem to stop staring. Why on earth had he opened the door? I didn't belong here any more than I'd belonged at that ridiculous dinner party. God, but I was a *fool*.

"Stop it."

I stared at Remy, the pressure of his hand on my shoulder keeping me pinned to the sofa.

Panicked, I glanced from his set expression to Penelope, whose anger practically shimmered about her. "Of course," she said, nodding slowly, "a *friend*."

"Yes." His shoulder lifted in a typically Remy shrug. "And—?"

"It's rather one thing to know about your other birds in the abstract, but to be slapped in the face with it like this? Cheap sewer rat."

As the slam of the bedroom door echoed throughout the apartment, Remy raised an eyebrow. "Sewer rat? I take offense to that. I'm no dirty sewer rat. Louisiana swamp rat, now that's another thing altogether. Can't say I could've argued overmuch with that."

"Oh, Remy," I finally managed, my hands fisting in the damp folds of my skirt, my thumbnail picking restlessly at the dirty snow and slush marring the once-pristine velvet. "I'm so sorry. I should never have come."

"Hush," he repeated as he lifted my chin and brought the mug to my lips once more. "Of course you should. And she should act with the sense God gave a goat. She and I have always had an understanding. Convenient for her as for me, so don't you trouble yourself a minute over this." He resumed stroking my hair as I took careful sips, each swallow more pained and difficult and just shy of choking. It wasn't fair—it wasn't. I just wanted … wanted…

What did I want? What was I *supposed* to want? I'd known these things, once upon a time.

Putting the now-empty mug on the coffee table, he immediately gathered me close again. "You think I don't see how hard you try not to rely on anyone else? How you hate takin' anything that might be considered charity?" His voice floated above my head, accent even more pronounced and lilting than usual. "My mama didn't raise no fool, *chère*. If you're here, it's because something's happened *and* you finally trust me. Far as I'm concerned, that trumps all else— even spectacular blondes."

He rocked me back and forth, humming along with the music, lulling me into a drowsy sense of security interrupted only by the bedroom door opening once again to reveal Penelope, now fully dressed in a crisp stewardess uniform, hair neatly wound into a twist beneath a navy pillbox. The heels of her stilettos punctuated each step with a sharp click as she followed the trail of clothes across the wood floor, flinging the occasional piece into a leather flight bag. She paused behind the sofa, indecently sheer black lace dangling from one hand, her narrow-eyed gaze raking over us.

"You should be bloody ashamed of yourself." Stuffing the lingerie into the bag, she stormed toward the door, pausing only just long enough to snatch a dark coat from the curlicued wrought iron stand from which it had been hanging.

"I ain't never done nothin' to you to be ashamed for, *chère* and you'll be feeling mighty foolish you thought otherwise when you're back in your right head."

"I meant about *her*." She thrust her arms into the coat. "She's an infant—totally in over her head with you."

"What you think you know and what's truth are worlds apart, so you'd best mind your business." Remy's voice never changed tone or volume—yet something unmistakably harder had crept in. "Such a shame, *chérie*. I liked you well enough, but God don't like ugly."

She paused in the midst of pulling on leather gloves. "Y'know, just because you're fabulous in the kitchen and in bed doesn't make you any less of a miserable wanker." Picking up her bag, she stood there a moment longer, tense and wide-legged. "Well? No pithy Creole retort?"

With smooth, unhurried elegance, he rose and strolled to the front door, opening it with a small flourish. "*Laissez le bonne temps roulez?*"

The sharp sound of a slap was followed by the door slamming

hard enough to cause the record to skid and skip halfway into the next song. After making certain the locks were turned then casually straightening a framed picture left skewed by Penelope's dramatic exit, Remy finally turned to face me, our gazes meeting, the silence between us stretching thin until it finally broke into an enormous wave of laughter. Laughter that had me clutching my sides and wiping tears away although I had absolutely no business laughing. Not with what I'd just done.

"Remy—"

"Forget it." He returned to stand in front of the sofa, smiling and far more relaxed than I would have expected, given the circumstances and the livid red mark decorating his cheek. "It was nearing the end of its time anyhow. She just wanted to be the one to do it, on her terms." One eyebrow rose. "I suspect she wanted one last night if only so I'd be left well aware of what I was losing and really, who was I to deny her the pleasure?"

"Or yourself."

"I'm an Abelard man." He shrugged, thoroughly unconcerned. "She's just peeved it didn't unfold according to her plan of making sweet, sweet love before leaving me at the very least marginally devastated by her departure. A role I would have played, along with a nice touch of regretful understanding. Now, however, she has to deal with the unhappy realization that life does go on—at least for me." White teeth and dimples flashed in a brief, unapologetic grin, then faded as he pulled me up and led me, unresisting, down a short hallway.

A quick glance as we passed by the open bedroom door revealed the bed, sheets tangled, dents in the pillows, a rich red paisley throw spilling from the foot and puddling on the wood floor. It was a scene both luxurious and primal, the overall effect hitting hard and low, threatening everything I'd consumed this evening.

"You been in these clothes too long." I blinked back sudden tears at the anger in his voice. Through a shimmering veil I watched him drop to a knee and slip off the ruined shoes. "Goin' more pale by the second—" Whatever else he was grumbling in his familiar *patois* was lost amidst the sounds of the taps squealing as they were spun open and the rush of water splashing against the porcelain surface of the claw foot tub.

"C'mon, *chère*—let's get this off." He gently grasped under my elbows and drew me closer, pushing damp turquoise wool from my shoulders, still murmuring. "Damn, I'm some kind of fool, not getting it off you right quick. Thing's wet clear through. It's all right … shh … it's all right—" Long-fingered hands stroked up and down my arms, a calming motion, meant to soothe the sudden tension that stiffened me into immobility as I stared at the hair-dusted vee of skin left exposed by the deep burgundy silk lapels of his robe, bringing to mind the throw on the bed, the draperies cocooning the windows. How was it I'd never known that Remy liked red so very much?

So much I didn't know.

I could feel his gaze on the top of my bowed head. "You don't have to say a thing, Natalie. You don't owe anyone anything. Not a damn thing." Carefully, he turned me away—as he did, I caught a brief glimpse of my face in the medicine chest mirror, a washed-out oval with dark, bruised splotches where my eyes should be. I couldn't even claim the look in them was lost because the overwhelming impression was that there simply wasn't anything there.

"I'm gonna unzip this pretty dress, help you with anythin' else you need, then leave you to take your bath," he said, his voice dropping back to its lilting croon. The slow rasp of the zipper's metal teeth parting took on an almost hypnotic sound, the air teasing the skin above the strapless long line brassiere delicate and refreshing. "Do you want me to get this for you?"

Remy's fingertips brushed—hesitantly, it felt—against the skin between my shoulder blades, just above the first hook. Probably assumed I had finally reached my limit in accepting assistance. Or was trying to be a gentleman, because no matter how much he teased or protested otherwise, Remy, was at heart, very much a gentleman.

Turning my head slightly, I took as deep a breath as the constricting garment would allow. "Yes, please."

Again, there was a pause, a sense of hesitation, then I felt the first hook release, then the next, and the next, each one allowing breath to flow a bit more freely, the humid air bathing skin left irritated and hot from its many hours of constriction.

"*Merde.*" A fleeting touch brushed against my back before it moved to my chin, turning my head a bit farther, just enough for his gaze to meet mine. "There are oils and such in a basket by the tub I keep handy for … guests." He lifted an eyebrow, an obvious attempt at his usual teasing banter that was completely undone by the fierce red suffusing his olive-hued skin. A rare blush I only caught the merest glimpse of before I reached up with both hands and pulled his head down to mine, capturing and swallowing the soft, surprised noise that tried to escape.

Oh God.

Oh … *God.*

Panic nearly overwhelmed the desire driving me to do this. I didn't know what to do. I didn't know how to do this. I hadn't done this in so very long. Not since Nico. Those … boys. I'd never permitted them that. Not that they were ever interested in more than nominal fashion in anything above my neck, so deterring them had been surprisingly easy. And that's when I understood how this one act of what I'd always thought of as defiance had been more about self-preservation. Retaining a piece of myself, however small.

Unfortunately, it also made for a clumsy meeting of mouths—lips sliding wet and awkward, the surreal dull pain of teeth bumping together, scraping delicate skin. No, no, *no*—I so wanted this to be an act I could execute with the smooth perfection of a movie kiss—so desperately wanted it to be good. But the harder I tried, the worse it got, my nose colliding against Remy's, arms trapped into immobility by my dress.

As his hands covered mine, I leaned in further, tried to deepen the kiss, make it better, anything to keep him from pulling away and I couldn't … I needed …

"Shh … Natalie. Let me …"

In less than a breath, he'd turned me fully into him, one hand firm between my shoulders, the other sliding into my hair, his thumb teasing the surprisingly sensitive skin in front of my ear. This time, our mouths met smoothly, effortlessly, our bodies drawn flush against each other, Remy molding my body to his, supporting my weight.

Oh, yes.

Yes.

This was what it was supposed to feel like.

I'd forgotten.

And felt tears, hot and accusatory, that I'd forced myself to forget.

I sank further into Remy, into the rediscovery of this odd, strange, thrilling, incredibly intimate act. The sensation of stubble abrading skin, the subtle pain feeding growing arousal. The way lips, tongue, and teeth were no longer separate entities or impediments, but worked together in concert, taking what was offered, inviting me to explore in my own right. To relearn not only the sensations but the tastes. Those remnants of spices and wine and something vanilla-sweet and further back, the faint, bitter tang of tobacco, creating layers and texture. Demanding that I delve deeper, take more, until finally, a small pause, a measure of physical distance as Remy drew back, a mere heartbeat of space, close enough so our breaths still mingled as if continuing the caress.

"We both know I'm no one's idea of a gentleman, but one thing I don't do is take advantage of damsels in distress."

A damsel? How could he possibly think that? Couldn't he see? All the stains? The hands that had probed and grasped and touched with no purpose other than to take and to please themselves? Couldn't he see how I'd allowed that to happen? Damsel? No. Not for a very long time.

"I'm hardly anyone's idea of a damsel."

Grabbing his hands, I drew them between us, brazenly placing them over my breasts. With the stiff boning and the closeness of our bodies still holding my dress in place, his hands cupped mostly fabric; however, the longer we stood there, the more pliant his fingers became, a soft, "Lord, Natalie," escaping between shallow breaths as his hands shifted. His fingers brushed against bare skin, stroking the upper slopes of my breasts and dipping beneath the fabric, molding and caressing, his touch gentle, but with an underlying tension and impatience. Emotions I was overjoyed to recognize, that fed my own, making my stomach clench with desire even as I closed my eyes in gratitude. I could feel this. I *wanted* to feel.

"Remy," I breathed out on a sigh as his head lowered, his mouth finding that incredibly sensitive spot where neck and shoulder met as his hands moved to curl around the edges of my bodice. Tension balanced on a razor's edge for an achingly long moment before he murmured something unintelligible against my skin as he released the fabric. One finger rested at the base of my throat, right in the hollow where my pulse beat, erratic, but strong and growing more rapid the longer we stood there. Could he feel it? How much I wanted this?

He lifted his head, his hand returning to my back and resuming a slow stroking motion. A touch to ease and calm, not seduce. Those intensely dark blue eyes scrutinized me so long and so intently, the individual colors began revealing themselves—shades of indigo and navy and sapphire and pewter. Utterly masking whatever he might be thinking. An open book, Remy, until you looked into his eyes. I began to fidget, despite the soothing nature of his caresses, wondering what, exactly, he was looking for. What he might be seeing.

"You are absolutely a damsel and don't you dare ever let anyone say otherwise."

Tears clogged my throat as I sensed the one anchor, the one bit of comfort I'd felt in so very long drawing away. His hands returned to the edges of my bodice, carefully lifting the shoulders of my dress up, ensuring that it wouldn't fall away as he moved to spin the taps on the tub closed. Between the steam in the room and the tears threatening my vision, he took on the blurred nebulous edges of a ghost as he moved around, draping a clean washcloth along the edge of the tub, making certain shampoo and soap and towels were all within easy reach before pulling me close again. Warm and undeniably real, one hand closed around mine as the other pointed at the back of the door where a heavy, white terry robe hung on a hook.

"Don't no one use it but me," he said quietly, holding tight to my hand, as if afraid I might disappear otherwise. "You want me to make you something to eat? An omelet or some toast, maybe?"

Silently, I shook my head, unable to look at him.

"*Bebe*—" Fingertips brushed against my cheek with a delicate, feather light touch. "You don't want this to happen—not really. Not now. God knows, I want to and if it was simply a question of you bein' innocent—" He leaned in closer, his voice resonating low, like a tuning fork struck right beside my ear. "Believe me, the devil's sittin' right on my shoulder, urging me to take and it wouldn't be the first time I listened and not thought twice afterwards. But this ain't about you being innocent. Whatever happened tonight—whatever brought you to this place—if we did this, you'd hate yourself afterwards and we can't have that." Both hands moved to frame my face, tilting my head up. "I can't have that."

Stunned, I searched his face for the lie. The false assurances offered in order to keep me from completely shattering, leaving him to pick up still more pieces when it wasn't a task he'd ever asked for in the first place. Instead, I was met with a slow smile, one tinged with a hint of something more—something indefinable.

"You're pretty, you're smart, you laugh at my jokes, and you try all my cooking experiments. I told you—my mama didn't raise no fool." The smile faded. "I recognize demons when I see them, Natalie. And I won't take advantage of yours."

How transparent had I been? All this time I'd been so certain— Had *everyone* seen that I wasn't what I tried so hard to be? And if they had … if that surprisingly fragile exterior had been so completely torn away … where to go? What to do?

"Remy, may I tell you something?"

"Of course."

One small thing. It's not as if it wasn't already out there, this piece of my previous life intersecting with the life I'd so painstakingly built. Instinctively I knew I could either take the effort to mend the breach, pretend it had never happened—or find a way for the two worlds to coexist.

The choice, I knew, would be simple if I truly loved the life I currently inhabited.

So then—one small step, to see how it felt, wouldn't hurt, would it?

"Natalie's not my name. I mean, it is, but not really."

Though his eyes widened slightly, he remained silent, his thumb stroking across the back of my hand. The slow, rhythmic drag of skin against skin served to keep me in this life as I drew my former existence out a bit further from the shadows.

"My name—my real name—it's actually … Natalia." It tripped off my tongue, the normally mellifluous cadence of the syllables stilted and broken from lack of use.

"Natalia." Remy quietly repeated before leaning down and touching his mouth to mine. "I do believe it suits you, *chère*. Suits you just right."

HOLIDAYS OVER–BACK TO REALITY

GAY TALESE
THE NEW YORK TIMES
JANUARY 4, 1965

NINE

Entering Mercier's kitchen was akin to entering another world. One where the aromas of chicory-spiked coffee and the house gumbo and butter melting over crusty, fresh-baked bread combined into a mélange so rich and heady, it created an ambience where time and season had little meaning. In this one small corner of New York, it wasn't a blustery, frigid January afternoon. It was coffee and sugar-dusted beignets on a Garden District balcony shaded by ancient oaks draped in lacy Spanish moss. It was a leisurely evening stroll along the Mississippi and the joyful noise of the jazz clubs on Bourbon Street and the frenetic intensity of Mardi Gras. In here, it was always spring in New Orleans.

It was no wonder, really, that I spent more time here than I did in my own apartment.

Comfortably perched on a stool, I studied the movement of Remy's elegant long-fingered hands as he deftly chopped celery, bell pepper, and onion for "trinity," the Creole version of *mirepoix*. Generally a job for one of the *sous* chefs, but one he enjoyed doing himself, pace of the day permitting. It was a joy, really, watching him do these little tasks, the ones where he didn't even have to focus and could just retreat into himself. He was most open then, his face revealing a myriad of thoughts. What they were, exactly, remained a mystery to everyone but him, although some gestures provided small clues, like the subtle pursing of his lips when he was deep in thought, or the slightly unfocused, faraway expression in his eyes when he was standing at the stove and breathing deep.

"Helen got married."

"Who?"

"My roommate."

He spared me a sidelong glance, though his blade never ceased its hypnotic tattoo against the maple cutting board. "The one who's always out on a date?"

"One and the same."

"Wouldn't have thought she bumped uglies with any one fool enough to get a proposal."

"Bumped uglies?"

Half-moons of onion, sliced so thin as to almost be transparent, fell away from his blade—subtle mocking smiles that said far more than words could.

"All right, so perhaps you have a point," I said, finally giving in to a laugh. "But in a shocking twist, he's not one of the local offerings. Rather, it's her hometown sweetheart. From South Dakota. Came all the way out here to propose on New Year's Eve." Selecting a celery stalk that had yet to meet its fate, I drizzled it with a thin stream of rich green olive oil. "You know, we've lived together nearly four years and I had no idea she was even from South Dakota?" I crunched into the celery, savoring the bitter greenness mingling with the mellow oil.

"I didn't know *anyone* was actually from South Dakota—or at least, who'd admit to it."

"Be nice."

"Come now, you know that's not a condition I ever lay claim to, *chère*." The hiss and pop of the chopped vegetables meeting hot oil seeming to corroborate his offhand statement. "So," he added with a grin and raised-eyebrow glance as he added a heaping pile of minced garlic to the sauté pan, "does this mean you'll be needin' a new roommate?"

"Honestly, Remy." Incorrigible to the end. But despite any claims to the contrary, a very nice man. So much better than he'd ever admit to being.

He'd refused to let me go home, that night I'd landed on his doorstep. Simply bundled me into his bed in his take charge, bossy manner, while he kept vigil on the couch—an arrangement that lasted close to a week with the unsurprising onset of a miserable cold leaving me unable to protest even if I'd wanted to. For once, I simply gave into my body's demands, drifting in and out of sleep with no thought to schedules or whether it was night or day—lost in dreams of Nico and tropical paradises with snow falling among the palm fronds. Running after him, desperately trying to catch him before he disappeared into a mist that I'd fight through, only to find myself back on the windswept deck of the Empire State Building ... waiting, sometimes falling, sometimes floating—sometimes coming face to face with Jack Roemer and Greg Barnes morphed into angels of the stern warrior variety the nuns had used to instill fear in us as children. Because it would have been far too easy to have Botticelli's cherubic angels fluttering harmlessly about in my subconscious.

Regardless of the nature of the dreams, however, I'd always wake to find Remy beside me, holding a glass of water to my lips, murmuring comforting words until I was soothed back to a calmer sleep.

But past that week, he surprised—and shamed me a bit—by never once referring to what had happened. Not even in a teasing manner. Which wasn't to say his behavior toward me wasn't altered, but only in the subtlest, most delicate of ways. A lingering touch or his dark, all-too-seeing gaze studying me an extra moment longer as he presented me with one of his never ending cooking experiments. While the after-hours visits to my apartment remained the occasional occurrence they'd always been, they were now supplemented with coffees and walks around Gramercy Park and an almost nightly phone call, never lengthy but enough to bring a sense of comfort and peace that had long been lacking.

"Truthfully, I don't want a new roommate. I saw Helen so infrequently, it was almost like living alone. I don't want to potentially wind up with some eighteen-year-old, fresh off the bus, expecting to become best friends and do each other's hair and gossip about boys."

"You say that as if it's a bad thing."

I wrinkled my nose. "Can you really see me that way?" Even when I had been of an age to enjoy that sort of thing, it hadn't been my preferred mode of entertainment. Books and dreaming and Nico. That had more than filled my world.

"No," he admitted as he lowered the flame beneath the pan. "Never really have struck me as that kind of flighty. So you gonna stay in your place by yourself, then?"

I shook my head. "I need to look for something new. I hardly need a two bedroom apartment for myself."

Even if both bedrooms together amounted to the size of my girlhood closet. But beyond not needing the rooms, I wouldn't be able to continue to afford it—not with my expenses. Luckily, there was a constant overturn of studios and small one bedrooms within the Village as people arrived, trying to find their version of the New York dream and just as quickly departed, the reality all too often failing to meet the expectations. Much better to arrive with no expectations. Far less opportunity for disillusionment. But for my purposes, fortunate, since it meant finding a new apartment wouldn't prove to be too difficult—a gift for which I was grateful. I had a genuine fondness for my eccentric dowager of a neighborhood with its chess players in the Square and old Italian men arguing on stoops. Where denim-clad long-haired boys and girls walked hand-in-hand past earnest college students handing out flyers for one protest or another and mothers watched their children play while they gossiped on park benches. As alive at night as during the day, with laughter and folk music and impassioned poetry and fragrant smoke drifting in equal measures from the open doors of the clubs on humid summer nights. The changes going on in the rest of the world reflected in those few blocks.

If Mercier's reflected balmy decadence, then the Village was a slice of bohemian Europe. A psychology degree was hardly required to understand how each fed a distinct piece of my soul. Or to recognize both locations as intrinsically New York, yet out of step with the image the rest of the world had of this too-large, too-hard city.

Remy glanced up from giving the sautéing vegetables another stir.

"Seriously, *bebe*, if you need somewhere to stay until you find a new place, you're more than welcome. No ulterior motives."

"No? You're losing your touch, Remy."

"I'm not sayin' one or two might not cross my mind," he shot back. "I'm only human. And I don't know why you're forever spoilin' for a fight." Amidst a grumbling stream of *patois*, he clapped the lid back on the pot and removed the sharpening steel from the woodblock. Over the whine of steel against steel he repeated, "Seriously—my door's always open."

I waited until he replaced the knife in the block before touching my hand to his back. "I know that." Hoping he understood how it would be such a monumentally bad idea. Too many memories and emotions. One desperate moment still hovering entirely too close to the surface.

"Lord, but you're a stubborn thing," he grumbled, moving on to the next knife, the blade dissolving into a silver blur.

He understood. Didn't mean he agreed. But he understood—at least, as well as he was able.

In the foyer, I made certain all was in order at the curved French West Indies table—another elegant leftover from Mercier's early days—that served as the reception desk as a busboy gave the brass handles on the massive wood and leaded glass doors a final polish. Mrs. Mercier, regal in a suit of deep rose brocade, made one final, assessing circuit around the dining room before inclining her head at the busboy who, having waited for her signal, turned the locks, and with that, our day was officially underway. Busy, as always. Far too busy to allow one to think much—the blessing of this job.

"Hello Natalie."

Surprised, I glanced up at the clock—one-thirty, right on time. My shock came more from how quickly two hours had elapsed than from the man who stood before me. An eventuality I'd been prepared for.

"Good afternoon, Mr. Barnes, how are you today?" Each word came out easy and measured, just as it had the dozens of times practiced before my bathroom mirror. No nerves, no anger. Just calm, cool Natalie. The one thing weighing on my mind. What would he say? What would he do? And how would *I* react, practice notwithstanding? First thing every day, I would check the register, breathing a momentary sigh of relief each time I didn't see his name neatly inscribed in the big leather book, only to have that relief chased off by tension. His name would be there at some point. Or worse still, he would just drop in, as he'd so often done before. The only question was when. At least the fates had seen fit to grant me this one small favor in the form of a reservation. So I'd had time to prepare.

"Quite well, thank you. And you?" And since, as usual, he was accompanied by business associates, that was the most he would say—something we both understood and which allowed me to muster a polite smile as I checked his name off on the register and collected leather-bound menus.

"Very well, sir. Thank you." Everything so very normal and routine. Even my polite smile had a natural feel as I waited for them to check their coats and hats before leading them to their table, placing the menus atop the plates, allowing them to seat themselves before taking drink orders. Nothing at all out of the ordinary. Unless, of course, you took into account the fact that beyond that brief welcoming smile—a gesture where I stared as much past him as at him—I hadn't been able to bring myself to fully meet Gregory Barnes' gaze. And I wouldn't. To face the knowledge and pity that I knew had to live in that concerned blue gaze would require more than I was capable of.

Luckily, the table was where my duties ended and luckier still,

Mr. Barnes didn't seek me out, as I'd feared he might. Even his departure, when he might have been able to beg an extra moment for conversation, passed uneventfully enough, punctuated only by an almost imperceptible pause in the open doorway—just long enough for him to glance over his shoulder and tip his hat before disappearing into the snow swirling beyond the threshold.

And finally, I was able to breathe. To just … sit, eyes closed and fingers pressed against throbbing temples. Inhaling deeply of the unique combination of sharp cold outside air meeting the humid, fragrant air inside. One clearing the senses, the other providing a sense of comfort.

"I'm breaking a promise to my wife doing this."

My eyes snapped open as a lungful of the cold air that had followed Greg Barnes back inside knifed through my chest.

"I swore to her I'd leave this alone, that if you came to us, it was one thing, but that it was better to leave it—and you—alone." He propped his hands on the desk and leaning down, said very quietly, "The offer is still open and I'd like you to consider it. I honestly think you're the right person for this and that it would be good for you—and perhaps even Ava."

Panicked, I turned my head from side to side, praying no one lurked within hearing distance. "How *dare* you." My jaw clenched, tiny muscles cramping. "After what you people did—"

"I know." He straightened and took a deep breath. "I know that right now, it seems unpardonable and you know, I can't say I disagree."

"You know *nothing*. Now please—leave me alone." The words feeling like ground glass lodged deep in my throat.

Greg nodded slowly, the brim of his hat casting shadows across his face. "I'm so sorry."

He was. Only a fool could have missed the true regret. But I didn't care. What they'd done— Night after night of waking up, surrounded by paper thin walls and memories so horrific, I couldn't even scream my way out, just relive them, over and over, until there was nothing left except a tangle of sheets and cold sweat.

And now—after steeling myself for this encounter, imagining it successfully navigated, only to have it revealed as nothing more than a flimsy charade.

No. Greg Barnes could be sorry until the gates of hell iced over for all I cared.

"Gregory—I thought you'd left."

"And I thought you'd gone upstairs to cook the books."

"Really, Greg." Mrs. Mercier sniffed as she descended the last few steps of the gently curving staircase leading to the second floor. "You know I have a firm of lovely high-priced accountants to 'cook the books' as you so inelegantly put it."

"And I know you don't trust them worth a damn, so you feel compelled to go over their work with a fine-toothed comb and your own formidable skills."

"Well, have to keep them honest, otherwise, they're liable to rob the widow woman blind."

"They'd be fools to even think to attempt it."

"True."

She hadn't heard. That was all I could think, as she turned her gaze on me. She hadn't heard me being impossibly rude to one of our best customers—to an old family friend. Even if the rudeness was warranted and I had no doubt that Greg would defend it as a fully justifiable reaction on my part, but without context, how could Mrs. Mercier possibly understand? And how could I even begin to explain? But I wouldn't have to because she hadn't heard. *Gracias a Dios*, because I couldn't lose this. Not Mercier's. Not on top of everything else.

"Natalie, darlin'—you're looking absolutely peaked."

I groped for something to say, but my tongue felt thick and unresponsive.

"She was just saying she'd skipped breakfast and was wondering what Remy might have in store for her today," Greg inserted smoothly, his expression as placid and guileless as an altar boy's.

"Skipping meals? You tryin' to catch your death again? Go on, now, take your break."

"But—"

"Right now, child. I know you like to wait until the end of your shift, but what good is that going to do if you're going to fall over in a dead faint before then? Go on now—" She made a shooing motion with one hand as the other tugged on the carved back of my chair. "Get Remy to dish you up some of the jambalaya. And the rice pudding—you need something to stick to you."

"I'm not—"

"Hush."

Part of me wanted to argue—to hold fast, refuse to give into weakness.

The sane part was unspeakably grateful at being granted permission to escape. I pushed myself away from the table and walked slowly toward the kitchen, slow enough that I was able to hear Mrs. Mercier's biting, "Good thing I've known you practically since the cradle, Gregory, and know Constance as well as I do. Otherwise, I'd be damned suspicious. I know you don't think me stupid enough to have failed to notice what's been going on."

By the time I reached the kitchen, I could barely breathe. Weaving my way through the bodies going about their work, I came up behind Remy, clutching his arm, unmindful of the sizzling sauté pan he was shaking over the flame.

"Do you have a cigarette?"

His head whipped around, eyes narrow. "You don't smoke."

"Dammit, Remy, do you have a cigarette or not?"

Sighing, he reached into his trousers pocket and pulled out a battered box of Lucky Strikes and a silver lighter. Snatching them from his hand, anxious to go, I nevertheless hesitated … unsure where—

"Oh for God's sake."

Fingers closed hard around my wrist as he tugged me into the break room. "Y'all get out. Now." His voice held the familiar commanding edge that brooked no argument. "'Cause God knows, no one needs to see this," he muttered beneath the annoyed scraping of chairs against tile. A pair of waitresses and a busboy, I registered in the one glance I risked taking, looking justifiably annoyed at being rousted early from their breaks but I couldn't be bothered to care. Right now, all I cared about was the salvation this cigarette promised. Everyone was so happy when they were smoking—a soothing ritual and that's all I wanted. Just a little bit of calm and happy and soothing. Drinking during working hours was out of the question, so the cigarette it would have to be if only I could … could only …

"Jesus *Christ.*"

Again, Remy's hand grasped my wrist as with the other, he snatched the lighter from my shaking hand, a flame appearing at the tip of the cigarette. One deep, desperate inhale and I immediately doubled over, choking and gasping and fighting the urge to vomit.

I remained that way, even after the coughing subsided and the nausea passed—bent over, blinking back the tears that I was going to swear had to do with the smoke stinging my eyes. Finally, I straightened and faced Remy as he leaned against the wall, narrow-eyed gaze focused on the glowing tip of my abandoned cigarette as he exhaled a narrow stream of smoke.

"Wanna tell me what that was all about?"

"No." The only response, really, since there was no point in lying and saying it was nothing. And no point in trying to explain the entire, disastrous mess—there simply wasn't enough time even if I wanted to. I smoothed my hands along the sides of my skirt, tensing to still the tremors that beat a subtle tattoo against my thighs.

Calmly, he reached over to a nearby table and crushed the cigarette out in the small glass ashtray. "Lord, it's hard, not knowin' what it is you need."

"I know, Remy, but I can't. Not yet."

"I don't know what to do then."

"Why do you have to do anything? Can't it just be …" I searched for the right words. Normal would be a laughable choice. "The way it's been? The way it … is?"

"Tell me, *chère,* how's that workin' out for you?" His drawl thickened, equal parts rebuke and caress. "Thing is, you *want* help— you're just so out of practice askin', you got no idea how. With me, though, you don't have to ask—I'm here, ready to give you what I've got. But you got to at least give me somewhere to start."

"What happened to I didn't owe anyone anything? Are you somehow exempt from that?"

His mouth compressed—clearly not liking how I'd thrown his words back at him. Too bad.

He prowled the room's perimeter—each dark glare making me feel as if he *had* to keep moving, keep his hands jammed deep in his pockets, otherwise, he was likely to grab me by the shoulders and shake the truth out of me. A guess reinforced by the slam of his open palm against the door—the sharp ricochet making me flinch.

"You know what's like to drive me insane? How you got this idea in your head you're the only person in the world with secrets. I told you—I *know*. I know how they bring the demons out to wreak havoc with your soul."

Dios mío—I was so unbelievably sick and tired of these recent assumptions by people that they knew me—they had some idea about me and what drove me or tormented me. Why couldn't they just leave me alone? Leave this alone?

"You have *no* idea what's going on in my soul."

"I think a week listenin' to you cry like a lost baby in your sleep suggests maybe I do." Then he smiled. The loveliest, yet most enigmatic smile I'd ever seen from him. Bastard.

Anything else he might have added, however, was eclipsed by a sudden, insistent pounding on the door, a disembodied voice calling Remy's name and asking what the hell was he doing, orders were staring to back up, they needed him out there, *now*.

With one swift motion, he leaned forward and grasped my elbows, pulling me close. "One of these days, girl, I swear I'm gonna take you home, set your pretty behind down on my couch, and take the time for us to reveal *all* our secrets."

I shivered as his lips brushed against my ear, the edges of his teeth grazing along the rim, the tip of his tongue soothing the faint sting. Contrasts—so many contrasts. The different faces we presented to our various worlds. To the different people in them.

To ourselves.

Random, absurd thoughts—tumbling through my head, inviting me to study them, one by one, because really, they were fascinating, before coming to a screeching halt as Remy's hands dropped to my hips and drew me flush against him.

He breathed in my slow sigh as his lips met mine, his mouth shaping a single word. A word felt rather than heard. That granted access to the dark, hidden parts of my soul I'd so tentatively begun to reveal to him. Sinking into a chair, I watched through the open door as he returned to the kitchen, immediately reverting to the Remy I knew so well. Who controlled the kitchen with smiles and *patois* and played the radio far too loud as he created magic, while I remained behind, the taste and feel of his final word lingering on my mouth.

Natalia.

He hadn't said it since the night I revealed it to him. He hadn't needed to. To the rest of the world I firmly remained Natalie, but Natalia was something quiet and secret, much in the way the Remy from that night—a Remy I instinctively understood very few people were privy to—remained between us. Those two private beings meeting within the prolonged glances and subtle touches. Yet he'd chosen to bring it into the open now. Here. And again, my past self and the self I'd created over the last several years inched closer together, leaving me with the inescapable sense that a full-scale collision loomed on the horizon. Was it avoidable? Of course. I could just start over.

But was I willing to keep paying that price?

TEN

Hours later, I trudged up the brick walk toward Concord's library. Of all the places I did not want to be right now, this easily topped the list. All afternoon—with Greg Barnes' apologies echoing in my mind and Mrs. Mercier's speculative gaze resting on me at odd moments. With every silent, accusatory glance from Remy—defenses already dangerously battered were further chipped away. More than once throughout the afternoon, I'd lifted the receiver, even once going so far as to dial the main office, to make my excuses, beg off. I even entertained the idea of simply not showing up for my appointed tutoring session—ever. But in the end, duty and responsibility won out and I'd very carefully replaced the receiver in its cradle, the tinny voice on the other end repeating, "Hello? Concord School, may I help you? Hello? Is anyone there?"

At least today, there was no question of there being anything more than tutoring. My scheduled student was a freshman—those babies—still learning the ins and outs of this odd society. I liked freshmen—while they might have heard rumors, while they might stare as we thumbed through the pages of Melville or Hemingway, they were still entirely too terrified to try anything.

Still—

I stared up at the lights ringing the curved second floor of the library, caught sight of the occasional shadows passing by windows I knew from uncomfortable experience were wavy with age and the miniscule bubbles peppering the panes of leaded glass.

Dios mío, but I didn't want to be here.

I had never wanted my past to catch up to me. I'd done so much to try to suppress it since there was no point in dwelling, certainly no going back and frankly, I had no desire to be that girl again. But yet this person, standing frozen on the walk, wasn't someone I'd ever intended to be. And I didn't want to be her anymore.

After tonight, I'd find a different second job. I'd take this last paycheck, because I needed it. For a new apartment. And I was due to send money to Miami.

Why?

My fists clenched inside my coat pockets, the question echoing. *Why?*

They had their own business.

And I'd heard nothing. I always made sure to put my return address on the envelopes—they could have sent something, even if it was only an impersonal flyer advertising their business. But they hadn't. I had no idea how long they'd had this business—had no idea how successful they were. They just continued to take the money I sent without ever once saying a single word—about anything. *Nada.*

Did they even need me any longer?

Staring down, I watched as my feet, almost of their own volition, turned, took careful steps on the cleared walkway, avoiding icy patches, counting bricks, because I knew, from previous nights, previous walks, that there were one hundred and thirty-seven rows of bricks between the library steps and the wrought iron gate bordering the campus.

Forty-two ... forty-three ... forty-four ...

How long have they been doing this? How many times have I come here when it was no longer necessary?

Fifty-six ... fifty-seven ...

"Wrong direction."

Hands gripped my shoulders, forcing me to look up. Because this day couldn't get any worse. Derek. My previous ... student. A face I'd hoped not to see again for a long time. If ever.

"Let go."

"I told you—you're going the wrong way. And I thought you were supposed to be so smart."

I struggled to free myself, my gloves slipping on the leather sleeves of his varsity jacket, unable to find purchase. "I quit."

"There's a laugh." He turned me back toward the library, his hold painful even through the many layers I wore. "Girls like you don't quit. We get tired of you."

"Let go of me—" I grunted, wincing at the icy air knifing through my lungs, bringing tears to my eyes and making it impossible to draw a full breath. "Damn you, let go or I swear, I'll scream for the watchman."

"He won't come." His smile was thin-lipped and calculating. "Look, you want to quit after tonight, that's fine. I could give less of a shit. There'll be another one just like you inside a week. But I can't disappoint my little brother—he's been looking forward to this since I promised him at Christmas."

I stared blankly, certain that I wasn't hearing right.

"Freshman—" He shrugged and continued in a conversational tone, as if this was all perfectly normal. "Hasn't had a woman yet. Can't go into spring formal season without experience." His grip tightened as he frog marched me up the steps to the doors. "Plus he really does have a test next week on Gatsby if you want to pretend you're actually useful for anything else." With his free hand, he swept one of the doors open in a courtly, gentlemanly gesture that the mocking smile made an absolute joke of. As we stood in a circle of lamplight, his eyes roved over me, no smile to be found there. Just—that hateful sense of entitlement and a, oh … oh God, no.

"Besides, I've always wondered what it would be like to share. Can kill two birds with one stone—show my baby brother the ropes and try something new all at the same time." His hand dropped down, caressing my buttocks in rough circles that brought our earlier encounter rushing back in a sickeningly vivid series of images. Bent over the rough wood table, his body probing and pushing and violating.

No … No *por Dios de mi alma…* No.

No more.

Blindly, I kicked, feeling the pointed toe of my pump connect with something—just solidly enough or surprising enough to produce a muffled curse and a slight loosening of his grip. Enough ... it was just enough... Pulling free, I stumbled down the steps, crying out as a blinding pain shot from my scalp and down my spine. The world blurring then jerking to a stop as another jarring pain shot along my jaw.

"Bitch." My head snapped to one side, then the other, the pain from the blows blending into one nauseating morass. "Fucking bitch."

Screaming, I swung wildly, aiming toward the snarl dominating a face I knew so many girls would be taken in by in the future, the looks and the false charm and the money, most of all the stupid money ... never knowing, not realizing until it was too late what it could cost them—

A blurred arc of lights gave way to black, moonless sky before my view was obliterated, wet cold soaking my back, icy shards scraping along my cheek as I choked on a mouthful of snow, felt it clump in my eyelashes as I turned my head at the last possible second. *No. No. No.* Hearing the panicked cries in my head before realizing that it wasn't just in my head, that I was actually saying it aloud. *No.* They'd taken everything else—but he could *not* have this.

And the more he struggled to turn my face back, for some reason determined to take this one last thing from me, the more I squirmed and fought, cold snaking between my thighs as my coat and skirt rode higher up my legs, freeing them until I was finally able to draw a knee up, hard and vicious—every ounce of frustration and rage and hate suppressed for too long behind the blow.

His scream barely registered over the harsh gasps roaring through my ears, the pounding of my heart against my ribs.

"*Hijo de puta*," I spat, struggling to my feet as he wheezed and writhed in the snow, knees drawn nearly to his chest. "Come near me again and I swear, I will cut your balls off and feed them to the pigeons in Central Park."

I left him there, tears freezing on his cheeks as I stumbled down the walk toward the main entrance where the watchman waited, gate already open.

"He paid you."

He nodded. "Told me under no circumstances was I to unlock the gate for you until he gave the okay. To stop you if you tried to leave. To forget anything I might see or hear," he explained softly. "But if I'd known he was gonna hurt you—"

"How much?"

He hesitated. "Three hundred." More words following in a rush— "I need the money so bad. I got kids at home—another on the way."

I held up a hand, stopping the flood of excuses. "What did you *think* he was going to do?"

I was angry, but curiously not so much as I might have expected. After all, I knew better than anyone how acts that at one time might have been considered unthinkable became excusable out of a sense of desperation. Any anger I felt was more because the *only* person I'd ever consciously harmed was myself. Yet the rest of the world seemed to take that as license to do what they would with me.

Why?

"I'm sorry. I'm so sorry. It's just … I'd hear the boys talk and I knew what they did. What … you … I thought—"

"That it was nothing less than what I deserved because I was just a whore?"

"I—" His voice was hoarse, struggling for the words to speak what was written all over his face, beneath the pity and genuine remorse.

"It's not as if you were completely wrong." Swallowing hard because after all of this, I'd be damned if I would cry. Not now. "But it's not anything I ever intended to … I never wanted—" I could hear the pitch of my voice changing as my sinuses filled, resolve failing.

"You should go. If he comes back, it won't be alone."

I glanced over my shoulder, heart sinking as I saw the indentations in the snowbank, the dark patches where the struggle had worn pristine drifts down to dead grass and dirt. But Derek nowhere in sight. For the moment.

Lifting his fingers to his mouth, the gateman released a piercing whistle, a taxi appearing at the curb as if by magic.

"I can't afford this." Although it was so very tempting to duck into the dim recesses that beckoned—sink into cracked vinyl and lay my throbbing cheek against the cold glass. To ride in anonymous darkness and not have lights illuminating me in all my battered, disheveled shame at every stop.

"Let me." Putting several bills in my palm he folded my fingers over them. "As penance goes, it's not that much."

It wasn't until the taxi had come to a stop in front of my apartment building that I unclenched my fist—and discovered far more than cab fare. Several twenties, and I knew without counting that it would add up to three hundred dollars—or at least, close to it.

Leaving the driver with a generous tip, I slowly climbed the three flights of stairs to my apartment, wincing only slightly at the muffled thumps and gasps and moans coming from Helen's room. Only one more day. She was leaving tomorrow, happily married and looking westward to her future and I would no longer have to be faced with all of the hopeful, expectation that had replaced the air of quiet desperation that had been wearing away the edges of late, draping her in a dull veil. It said something horrible about me as a human that on some level, I'd been reassured by her weariness—felt less alone. Only difference between us is she'd actually come to New York with the highest of expectations.

Quietly I closed the door to my room, unwilling to alert the lovers to my presence, I shrugged my coat off as I reached into my closet for a hanger, desperately clinging to routine, and trying to ignore the incessant throbbing of my face and the way my scalp ached—the faint coppery tang that remained in my mouth, no matter how many times I swallowed.

Coat and hanger slipped from my fingers as I dropped to my knees. Bracing my hands on my thighs, I gasped for air, trying to suck in enough to steady my breathing … just like that long ago night, emerging exhausted from the water, trying to get my bearings. Fighting the lightheadedness, I pitched forward, blindly rooting around in the darkest corner, behind the shoe boxes and milk crates of books I couldn't bear to part with, until finally, I unearthed the large wooden cigar box. I lifted it into my lap, smooth and satiny with age, the elaborate gilt lettering nearly worn away, my fingers tracing the remembered inscription, skimming along the edges and rubbing the corners. No matter how much time elapsed, it always came back with no effort. A remembered dance, a ritual once performed so often, it had become as automatic and integral as breathing.

Carefully easing the top open, I tucked the remainder of the money into a corner. I wasn't sure what I'd do with it. Common sense dictated I should keep it, that I needed it. *Por todo los santos*, I *deserved* it. But at the same time, it was blood money and I wasn't sure I wanted it anywhere near me. Perhaps better to return it to the gateman. Let him live with the consequences.

A question for another day. Right now—I couldn't think. I couldn't…

My fingers toyed with the various items in the box, picking each up in turn. The shell, found on a childhood adventure along the beach, the exterior worn as smooth as the box, only the faintest of indentations remaining to mark where spirals had once cut deeply into its surface. Turning it over, however, revealed how the inside had remained vivid, corals and pinks shading to creamy white, carrying a trace aroma of its former ocean home. A red ribbon, snatched from my hair during my tenth birthday party, produced, faded and frayed, from the pocket of a tuxedo and returned with a shy apology during the first dance of my *quinceañera* ball. A postcard with a picture of a bridge along the Seine on one side, a hurriedly scribbled *te quiero*, on the other.

A bent, salt-stiffened, grayed scrap of leather that I'd refused to leave behind so very long ago. That had represented so much to that young, idealistic girl and ultimately, meant nothing. Such a stupid, naïve girl she'd been.

From its hiding place deep in the toe of the black flat, I removed a small folded square of ivory satin. Gently drawing the edges back, I gradually revealed the platinum and diamond ring—every bit as sparkling and beautiful and full of promise as the night I'd received it. I slipped it on my finger, clenching my fist to keep it from sliding off because it no longer fit the way it once had.

Very slowly I curled onto my side, the box and all its treasures held close.

• • •

I stood before the imposing glass doors, makeup carefully applied, hair pinned in a neat twist, and dressed in a midnight blue silk shantung suit normally reserved for only the most special of occasions, alternating glances between the card in my white-gloved hand to the gargoyles doggedly guarding the Fifth Avenue behemoth. The lingering hesitation that had the uniformed doorman eyeing me curiously stemmed less from reluctance than from the knowledge that crossing that threshold was as much symbolic as it was literal.

One way or another, everything would be different if I chose to walk into this building.

Then again, everything was already different, wasn't it?

"You lost, miss?"

I took a final look at the gargoyle closest to me, oddly reassured by its homely, grinning visage.

"Actually, no, I'm not." With a deep breath, I stepped into the marble-floored lobby and crossed to the vast elevator bank. When the doors finally slid open on my desired floor, I strode past the startled, impossibly young receptionist, ignoring the string of questions, delivered in an increasingly panicked voice—did I have an appointment, who was I looking for exactly, and really, if I would just give her a moment she could help me...

"Miss ... *Miss*—"

"I'm here." With a final glance at the discreet nameplate beside the door, I turned the knob and walked into Greg Barnes' office, the young woman tagging close behind, the stream of questions now a stream of apologies.

"I'm so sorry, Mr. Barnes. She wouldn't say who she was, just barged on in here. I know I should have called security first, but I didn't know what she wanted or who she was looking for, and Lorraine wasn't at her desk to stop her from coming in to bother you—"

Greg's face was impassive, revealing nothing, his gaze never leaving my face as he addressed the young woman. "It's fine, Rosemary. She's a family friend. You can go."

"Thank you, sir." As the door closed with a quiet click behind the visibly relieved girl, Greg rose from behind his desk and came to stand in front of me, his face losing its mask of calm as close up, he could see what the makeup couldn't fully hide.

As his hand rose, as if to touch—to see if it was real—I flinched, unable to help myself. Hand falling helplessly to his side, he asked, "Natalie, what the hell happened? Who did this?"

Rather than answer I moved past him, away from that probing gaze with all its questions, to stand in front of the enormous picture window overlooking Fifth.

"Natalie?"

Staring out at the blinding cloudless blue of the sky, I asked the question that had tormented me for a month—that had kept me awake all of the night before, cold and aching everywhere.

"Why?"

ELEVEN

So many ways in which that could have been answered. Which was why, of course, he didn't.

Common sense would dictate that I was merely asking why he'd singled me out for the ghostwriting project. After all, everything had seemingly snowballed from that one simple query. But that would have been naïve, no? And naïve was the last thing anyone would accuse Greg of being.

So I was willing to wait, first while he made the call out to his secretary, for tea and coffee and who knows what all else. Then there were the few minutes where he oh, so politely excused himself, which led to the shock of seeing Constance Barnes, slowly making her way across the office to sit beside me on the sofa.

"Were you not aware I work here as well?"

No. Although not surprising. Clearly an intelligent woman, more than capable of holding her own, and she and Greg—a team, in all ways. Perfect sense.

"Keeps me out of trouble." She attempted a smile—something reassuring and warm, but the small vertical lines between fine, blonde brows belied her concern. "Greg hoped that with me here, perhaps you'd feel a little less ganged up on." Her worried gaze searched my face, smile fading as she took in the bruises and light abrasions I'd done my best to mask. "However, I'd understand completely if you would prefer to speak with him privately." Punctuated with a pointed look toward the doorway through which Greg's secretary was wheeling a beverage cart, Jack Roemer close on her heels.

She was the only one who ever offered alternatives. Who, that night, had been the only one taking into consideration that I might not be ready to have my past revealed. Not then, or maybe ever. "Please stay."

She nodded and patted my hand, her eyes widening a fraction before her gaze flickered down, taking in the details. "This is lovely." She lifted my hand, gently tilting it from side to side, taking in the fine Victorian-style workmanship with the delicate scrolls engraved on the band winding their way up to a brilliant solitaire—the same ring that had once been a long-ago gift from Nico's grandfather to his grandmother.

"My family wanted me to get married again." I stared down at my ring, held firmly in place with the layers of adhesive tape I'd wound around the underside of the band, creating a makeshift guard. Raising my gaze, I focused on Constance—pretended she was the only one in the room. It was easier to tell the story that way. To say out loud these things I'd never before revealed. "They didn't understand ... they thought it had been long enough, but I couldn't. That's when I left."

"Again?" I looked over to where Jack Roemer leaned against Greg's desk, eyebrows raised. "That would mean—"

"That I was already married." I broke in. "Yes." Drawing my hand away from Constance's I reached into my handbag, retrieving a folded sheet of paper that I held out, indicating with a nod that he should take it. He or anyone else could contradict me until they were blue in the face. As far as I was concerned, I'd been married—and had the proof. Hidden first in the lining of my suitcase, then buried at the bottom of the cigar box. I'd protected this sheet of parchment every bit as fiercely as my ring.

"It's a church certificate—saying you and Nicolas de Betancourt were married. My men found the announcement of your engagement, but ... married? We found no evidence—"

"So ... what? If your people didn't find it, it doesn't count? You can go to hell." I almost laughed at the expression of shock that flashed across Jack's face before it was replaced by his habitually neutral expression. But it was enough. He was beginning to understand how very little he did know.

"I'm not sure how well it would stand up legally, not that there's anything to legally defend. However, in the eyes of God, and as far as Nico and I were concerned, we were married. Not long after Castro took over." I answered the unspoken question reflected in Constance's eyes. "At first, Father José didn't want to perform the ceremony. Without our parents, without the banns or Pre-Cana, but Nico—he knew. He understood how everything had changed irrevocably. How there was no time for any of the niceties and he wanted to be sure I was protected." My gaze shifted to the windows, seeking solace in the endless blue expanse of sky stretching above the buildings. None to be found unfortunately.

"It was important for us to be married. In retrospect, maybe it seems silly—what difference could having that piece of paper possibly have made? But at the time, it seemed like the most important thing in the world to do. Like the only thing we could do."

Constance's voice was extraordinarily gentle as she asked, "What happened?"

I took a shaky breath, held it for a moment. "I'm sure you know he died."

I sensed, more than actually saw, her nodding, since I'd shifted my focus from the window to Jack, whose face revealed nothing other than yes—he knew Nico had died. "Do you know how?" I asked softly, waiting for him to shake his head. I knew they didn't know. The *Revolución*—they had a way of keeping these types of details quiet unless it suited their purposes.

"While I think both our families wanted to hope that things wouldn't change any more than they had in the past, everything was going so completely insane, it was foolish to imagine they wouldn't. So as a precaution plans were made for Nico and I to fly to Miami as soon as possible, taking Carlito with us. We'd be married again in a civil ceremony, as soon as possible, just so there were no loose ends."

"But then he died."

"Was killed, Jack." I responded to his raised eyebrow with a small, humorless smile. "Come now, surely you'd guessed?" Ever so slowly—reluctantly, even—that eyebrow lowered. "I was there.

Days before we were to leave, he was killed—by his own cousin. Lazaro—who'd left university to join Fidel's thugs, taken in by all the pretty, idealistic words of creating some utopian society. The idiot." They had all been idiots—these well-bred children who'd never worked a day in their lives, sending home photos of themselves clad in army fatigues and boots, pointing their pistols and rifles at imagined enemies.

"Then he appeared at the house one morning with a jeep full of his fellow comrades, all of them spouting the propaganda they'd swallowed along with their cheap rum and the smoke from all of those campfires. Told us to get out of the house. It was no longer ours, but belonged to the people. To Cuba." I twisted the ring around on my finger, around and around, the sharp edges of the tape digging into my skin, until my hand was captured in a firm grip—Constance, nodding her head, saying it was all right, I could keep going, she was right there, holding on.

"He ... shot Nicolas—" My voice broke, then I shook my head, determined to say it, because they'd wanted to know the whole thing—all those damned missing pieces. And because I wanted someone, *anyone*, to know just how brave my Nico had been. "He shot him because Nico was trying to get him to see reason. Trying to get him to understand how completely insane this was. Did he really understand what he was doing? That it didn't have to be this way. And when he realized that there was no longer any reaching Lazaro, he tried to get an extra day—just one day—for their grandmother to have in the house in which she'd been born. To gather a few things. But Lazaro didn't care. Right there, in the living room where we all played together as children, he shot Nico, in front of his family. For treason against the people, he said. First his chest, then ... then ..."

I struggled to breathe, my vision graying out as the images replayed themselves in my head—images I'd fought so hard to keep buried.

"Another shot ... between his legs." Bile flooded my mouth in an acid rush before I swallowed it back. "He said ... he ... said he wanted to make absolutely certain there was no possibility of any more devils being born that could weaken the new Cuba. The free Cuba. And he laughed while Nico screamed." Haunting screams that I would never forget.

I spoke faster, ignoring Constance's gasp and Greg's muffled "*Jesus.*" From Jack, nothing as he continued holding my gaze, expression inscrutable. "I don't know what they did up in those mountains—before they came parading into Havana like some damned conquering heroes. They weren't heroes, they were animals. *Ese hijo de puta*, he just laughed and laughed as one of his bastard friends held me back—wouldn't even let me hold Nico as he slipped away. He—" I turned to Constance, my voice rising in pitch even as it dropped to a whisper. "He was so frightened—all he wanted was for me to hold him and I couldn't. I *couldn't*."

I doubled over, fighting the urge to vomit as the sheer helplessness overtook me as violently as if the whole nightmare was happening all over again. It might have only been moments, perhaps more, as Constance rubbed small circles between my shoulder blades with one hand, the other, cool and smooth, holding my forehead as she quietly ordered Greg to fetch a wastebasket and pour a glass of water. Time moved around me while I remained trapped, staring into Nico's eyes as the light gradually dimmed, his final words not even a whisper, but a mere movement of his lips, meant only for me.

"He ... made Nico's father drag him out to the street in front of the house and ordered me and his mother and grandmother to get on our knees and clean up the blood. Wouldn't allow the servants to help. People who'd known Nicolas since he was a baby, who were crying and sick right along with us. Told them it was their first step toward freedom. To see their oppressors finally spill blood for Cuba. Do you know what a body looks like after it's been scavenged, Jack?" I asked, my voice sounding dreamy and distant—a graceful, disconnected specter weaving around the frozen tension holding my body completely still. I straightened far enough to look into his face. "Picked over and ravaged?"

I was momentarily shocked as he slowly nodded, a haunted expression darkening his eyes, his knuckles white as they gripped the desk's edges.

In any other moment, I'd doubt him. Suspect him of lying because how could he possibly? But that slow nod spoke of an unflinching honesty I couldn't deny. Nor could I deny that same emotion reflected in his eyes as his gaze never left mine, rendering us the only two in the room for the span of those few seconds.

"I'll never forget what that looked like." I put my free hand to my stomach, trying to settle the nausea that continued to roil, slow and acidic. "Now you see why, when my parents suggested I marry again, I wasn't exactly … enthusiastic? I'd lost Nico—how could I be expected to replace him? And for the reasons they put forth? It was unthinkable.

"I know they honestly had only good intentions. They no doubt felt it the best way for me to recover. But to them, recovery included not simply an advantageous marriage but the expectation of a return to Cuba."

I shook my head, recalling once again the blank looks on my family's faces that last night. The sheer lack of comprehension. "While as far as I was concerned—that whole world—that life—it died along with Nico. So I left. And came here. He always wanted to live in New York." My breath shuddered out on an enormous sigh—almost done.

"But I never wanted to abandon my family. I wanted to help them—help my brother."

I could still see him, that sweet, slender boy whose head I'd cradled in my lap—the young man I'd left behind, pale green eyes flashing with anger and confusion as I'd argued with Mami that last night, sequestered within the walls of his own self-centeredness as only an adolescent boy could be. Then … a gradual understanding dawning. Which was why, late that night as I'd left, I'd found him huddled on the couch, waiting. Why I'd hugged him, the promise implicit in my embrace that I'd always, always take care of him, to the best of my ability.

Perhaps it was unrealistic, perhaps he'd already moved beyond this and I hadn't realized, but my instinct had been to protect—to allow him be a boy, for just a while longer. He had so little that resembled the life we'd been forced to leave behind. I wanted to give him something—*anything*—that might allow him opportunity to become the man he was meant to be.

"I could have sold my ring, I suppose." Pulling my hand free from Constance's, I resumed twisting it on my finger, studying the way the brilliant rose-cut captured the sunlight streaming into the office. "I went so far as to take it to a diamond merchant, but in the end, I couldn't. If I lost this too, it would make it all seem too much like a dream. As if it had never existed. So instead, I answered the ad to tutor at Concord. I suppose what happened afterwards—it was a product of my own pride and selfishness."

For the first time during my story, I looked Greg directly in the eye. "You realized what was going on, didn't you? The day you dropped me off."

He sighed. "I suspected as much. There have been rumors for years."

"The first time it happened, I was ... outraged. Sick. Violated ... shamed ... every reaction you could imagine. That boy—he ... held me down. Took what he wanted. As if it was his right. And I was *so* angry. I threatened to report him. He told me to go ahead. Which should have been my first sign, really. Stupid me—" A laugh escaped, as I recalled huddling in the hard wooden chair, rearranging my clothes with shaking hands and trying not to vomit at the feel of wetness between my legs. "After all I'd seen and experienced, that I was still capable of the illusion that the world was fair—or that at least here, it would be different. When I went to the athletic director the next day, his first words, before I even said anything, was that it would be a waste of my time to go to the police. The young man in question was from a quality family, attended a quality school, and who was I again?"

My fingers stilled on the ring. "I think that was when I truly understood. My family, who I was ... who I'd *been*—meant nothing. Natalia San Martín de Betancourt was dead." I paused, allowed the taste of the name to linger, before slowly shaking my head, the illusion disappearing. "I was just any girl. Eminently dispensable."

"And yet you returned to the school, time and again."

My chest burned at the implied accusation in Jack's question. Standing there in front of the beverage cart, methodically stirring a spoon in a fine china cup, immaculate in his sharply creased navy flannel suit as if his quiet confession and the torment in his eyes had never existed. Or at least, ceased to matter. In that moment I hated him every bit as much as I hated Lazaro and that athletic director and that first boy and all the boys since.

"For the money, of course," I snapped. "It's what you've already assumed, after all." Restless, I pushed myself from the sofa, focusing on the artwork on the walls, on the view out the window, on everything but the flat monotone of my voice.

"Despite the insults and warnings, I still had every intention of going to the police, even if it amounted to little more than a futile gesture. But that's when he slid a check across the desk. Hush money—payment for services rendered, I wasn't sure exactly what it was for and in that moment, I didn't care. That check was for more than my father earned in a *month*." I came to a halt in front of the window but instead of staring out, turned to face into the office, welcoming the feel of cold glass against my back.

Keeping my stare firmly fixed downward, at the play of my foot as I crossed one ankle over the other, I quietly said, "The old me would have torn it up. Thrown it in his face for the insult it was. But my *God*, to be able to send money like that home. To these fools, it was a pittance—" I exhaled slowly, seeing not the carpet the pointed toe of my pump played through, but the wide, elaborately tiled hallways of our house, lined with feathery palms, the walls hung with family portraits and fine art dating back a hundred years. "Once upon a time it would have been as much play money to me as it clearly was to them, but now? It was enough to help give Carlito, in particular, something of the life we'd left behind. But I can't do it anymore. I ... can't."

"Sweet God, Natalie."

I mustered a smile as I lifted my head and met Greg's horrified, yet undeniably sympathetic gaze. Not entirely reassured, I looked harder ... but no. No disgust. *Gracias a Dios.* It so easily could have been. I saw it in my own reflection after all—all too often. Through the telltale tightening of my throat I said, "I desperately want something different. Something like what you've offered has long been beyond my wildest imaginings. However, do you still think I'm the right person to do this?"

"You might be the only one who can."

Shocked, I stared at Jack. No horror or sympathy or pity or anything in his gaze. Wait. Not entirely true. The longer our gazes held, the more I could detect ... weariness. Echoed in the subtle slump of his shoulders.

He did not want to do this. But he would. Because he felt he must.

The door clicked quietly behind him as he turned and left, leaving me feeling more unsettled and uncomfortable than if he'd punctuated his departure with a dramatic slam. Something to express all the anger and sadness he was clearly so practiced at holding in and masking. I did *not* want to have anything in common with this man. Didn't want to feel a shred of sympathy. After all, had he? Going through my past and ripping off the layers with which I'd tried to protect myself?

No. I didn't care what torments might drive him. I would not.

"Birds of a feather, the two of you." Greg joined me at the window, shaking his head at the closed door. "He takes his self-appointed responsibilities as family protector pretty seriously."

"You don't think it foolish? That I was so worried about Carlito—wanting the best for him? He left so much behind—his entire childhood, really."

"Not foolish, no. He's your brother, you were even charged with his protection. For all intents and purposes, you had a charmed and enviable upbringing and you feel more than a little guilty that he only experienced a fraction of that." He regarded me with his frank gaze, the light coming in from outside reflecting off his eyes, turning them opaque. Eerily like images I'd seen of the inside of a glacier, those brilliant, unearthly shades of blue. "But let me ask you something, Natalia—how old is he now?"

"How … old? Well … he's—"

Stunned, I looked from Greg to Constance, to any and everything within the office's confines, reluctant to consider … trying to find anything else on which to focus but the obvious. My gaze finally ended its restless wandering on a framed photograph hanging on the wall—a stark outline of a mountain, illuminated by the impossibly bright moon hovering high above. The longer I stared, the more the mountain appeared to take on the shape of a head in profile, reclined as if asleep, the moon appearing to take on the role of the proverbial light bulb snapping on overhead. Clearly, my subconscious was going to force me to acknowledge the obvious.

My boy child of a brother—pesky, always tagging along, wanting to be part of every adventure, clinging to me during that horrific voyage in the dark, teasing me about sharks on the interminable swim. As if gazing into a mirror to the past, I could clearly see the tender, vulnerable curve of his back as he choked up seawater, fingers digging into the sand of our new home.

He was nineteen now.

"But … he was the baby." I shook my head, attempting to dispel the images that were beginning to emerge—Carlito's face filling out, growing shadowed with a dark beard, the shoulders and chest broadening into those of a young man. Images superimposing themselves over the boy who'd been my shadow. No longer a boy. A man.

And I had no idea who he was.

"I always took care … watched out for …" I dropped my face to my hands, the heels of my palms pressing hard against my eyes, trying to dismiss the inevitable.

"Whatever debt you felt you owed, I imagine you've more than paid it—don't you?"

Silence fell over the room as Greg allowed me to absorb his words. Consider his question and what, exactly, it meant.

Carlito was now a man. Older now than I'd been when I married and imagined myself a woman. The same age as when I first arrived in New York. Mami and Abuela had their own business. Did they need me for *anything*? Had I finally outlived my usefulness? But fast on the heels of the self-pity, a second thought emerged. A brighter thought, casting illumination over the jumbled muddle of my emotions much in the way the moon in that lovely photograph cast its light over the mountainscape, exposing trails and niches and ledges from which one could survey the landscape. Areas that had all previously been shrouded in darkness.

For the first time, I could allow myself to see alternatives. Make choices based solely in what I wanted. What might be best for me.

If they no longer needed me, I was … free.

TWELVE

"You're angry."

For as incredibly loud and chaotic as the kitchen was at any given moment, even during this ostensibly quiet time prior to opening, it was amazing how Remy's refusal to speak created a vacuum of silence that completely overrode all other extraneous noise. The hush felt so heavy and overwhelming, we might as well have been alone in a church.

"Remy, please say something."

"Like what?"

"Like … you're pleased for me?"

Another silence—this one coupled with a dark, narrow-eyed stare. That should have been enough of a sign for me to leave well enough alone. Let him have some time. Wait until after work. Yet, perversely, I felt the need to press ahead, try to get him to acknowledge this was a good thing. Get this difficult hurdle over and done with because I'd know—it would be difficult. Perhaps that's why I'd done it here. Safety in numbers, both in people and distractions that wouldn't exist in either his apartment or mine.

Coward.

"You're fixin' to go clear across the country, to spend God knows how long following around some faded cotillion belle you don't know from Adam, pretending her life's important. And I'm supposed to be happy about this, why?"

"Aren't you the one who's harped over and over how I need more than this place? Needed to get out more, see more people?" The last delivered with a wholly unintended edge.

"You're no fool, *chère* and don't be thinkin' I am, either." He returned to his prep station, hands moving across the counter, wiping a fresh coat of oil across the maple wood block, arranging and rearranging bowls and pans and tools, lining them up with a surgeon's care and precision. He drew a knife from the wood block, appeared to study it, replaced it, methodically repeating the process with each knife. "You know damn well I said most of that before ..."

Pulling the final knife free, he slowly turned it over in his hand, eyebrows drawn into a straight line. Over and over, he turned it in his hand, a fingertip running along the sharp, sensual curve of the blade, before he finally slammed it back into the block with a vicious jab that was enough to shake the entire counter and drop an actual, palpable quiet over the kitchen.

Ignoring the stares and whispers that swelled in the wake of the momentary silence, I grabbed Remy's arm and dragged him to the break room where the busboys taking a few minutes before the day got underway rolled their eyes at our appearance.

"Yeah, we know. Beat it," one of them said with an exasperated sigh, as they stabbed cigarettes into ashtrays, empty Coca-Cola bottles rattling as they tossed them into the wastebasket. "What's going on with you two anyway?" he groused, accompanied by a sly, annoying wink, obviously already having drawn his own conclusions.

As the door closed behind them, I turned to Remy. "That's a fair question, don't you think?"

Snatching the chef's toque from his head, he shoved a hand through his hair, leaving it standing in unruly black spikes. "I don't know exactly," he finally admitted. "But I do know we ain't gonna be able to figure it out with you all the way out in California."

"Being offered this job is a once in a lifetime chance—an incredible opportunity." I repeated everything I'd already told him in our hushed corner of the kitchen. Gave him the same reassurances. "And I'm coming back."

My one stipulation—if a leave of absence wasn't acceptable to Mrs. Mercier, then I wouldn't take the job. Perhaps on the surface working as a hostess at Mercier's was nothing more than a job, one that undoubtedly paled beside the opportunity that Greg Barnes offered. However, this place—these people—were the closest thing to a home and family as I'd had since I'd come to this country. No matter what I might have thought, I couldn't do it—leave them behind. Leave another life behind. I was done running.

"Why do you have to go in the first place? Why can't the rich girl come here if she's so hellbent on having you write about her?"

"She doesn't feel as if I'd get a sense of the 'real her' if we were here. Her life and her work—such as it is—are in Los Angeles."

Scattered within the stream of disgusted *patois*, I caught variations on "spoiled" and "entitled" and "ridiculous" along with a few other less than flattering terms. Honestly, I couldn't say I completely blamed him. I had also assumed I'd be staying in New York. Had thought, given my relative inexperience, that Greg or Constance would insist on overseeing the project.

And while in no way would I ever consider New York my dream city, it was at the very least a known quantity. For better or worse, I'd made a life here. Plus—my family. They knew I was here. If they ever … needed me. Or simply wanted to find me.

And now, Remy.

But at the same time, the more I considered it, the more appealing it seemed, this idea of California. Obviously, it wasn't Paris—wasn't even close—but perhaps that was a good thing. The time for that particular dream had long since passed. And the lure of somewhere with no history—no dreams or nightmares attached—was undeniably tempting. Even if only for a brief interlude.

"I'll return."

Nothing. My words might as well have disappeared into a void for all the response they garnered.

"I promise." The only sign he was even paying attention was the increasingly agitated drumming of his fingers against the soda cooler. Finally, the drumming gave way to the sound of coins dropping into the machine, the blast of frigid air as he opened the door, the clink of glass as he pulled one free. Little, mindless tasks, allowing him the freedom to lose himself in his thoughts, his face revealing so much—especially when one knew what to look for. The subtle twitching of the muscles at the corners of his eyes, tiny crescents appearing at the corners of his mouth, the blinking of his eyes growing slower, as if searching for answers—or simply perhaps calm—within those brief moments of darkness.

"I ..." The muscles of his throat worked as he swallowed. "I don't think you should go."

"Remy—"

His mouth compressed, the crescents deepening. His thumb rubbed the bottle's ridged surface, methodically tracing each letter. "I don't want you to go," he said, his voice flat and devoid of its usual lilt.

I twisted my hands in my skirt. "Why?"

"Why?" His knuckles turned white as his hold on the soda bottle tightened. "I already told you—neither of us is a fool and I won't treat you like one."

"I'm not trying to play the fool." I looked away, unable to meet his steady gaze. "I don't know enough of ... this. To understand why."

With Nico, it had had a sense of predetermination—of destiny. It had been gentle and lovely and absolutely inevitable. Befitting the well-bred girl I'd been once upon a time, schooled by the nuns in manners and modest behavior and piety, and by Mami and Abuela on how to dress beautifully, how to cook and run a household, and host anything from a family beach barbeque to formal party for a hundred. Without ever straying into the vulgar, they—the nuns, Mami, Abuela—made certain I was taught all the different ways to keep your man from wandering and if he did, how to turn a blind eye, because *ay m'ijita*, that was simply how men were. Except Nico would never have behaved in such a way. I knew if I said it, however, I would have simply been met with those looks suggesting I knew nothing of human behavior and *real* life.

Of course, these days, I knew far more of real life. A life the likes of which they could never have imagined.

However, Remy was a different beast altogether—fitting within no parameters, playing by no rules with which I was familiar. With him, I didn't know *anything*. Didn't know what constituted right or proper or if those words even held meaning.

"Understanding's different, *chère*." The words were achingly soft, spinning a web that drew me closer. "I don't understand any better than you do. But it's not about understanding—it's about knowing and way down deep, you know."

Each breath came slower, grew more shallow, ink black dots floating in my vision, an oddly monochromatic kaleidoscope.

Taking pity on me, he finally said it. Finally put into words what had been between us since that night. "I want more than a body in my bed whose name I'm not going to remember the next day. For the first time, *chère*, I *need* … more. With you. So please … don't leave." The gauntlet thrown. It was up to me to acknowledge it—to respond in kind, if indeed, I felt the same way.

Yes.

God, yes. I wanted … *so* much. All he'd said and more. And it terrified me, given I'd never expected to feel anything like this again. However, despite those feelings—or perhaps because of them—

"I have to." I tried to make my words as gentle as possible. Tried to put every ounce of emotion I had into them, hoping he would understand. "I can't just … just give myself over to you without—"

"You were damn willing to give yourself up before." Color streaked across his cheekbones, sudden and fierce in its intensity. "Practically beggin' for it."

"Remy, please don't—"

Glass shattered, liquid exploding and foaming across the table's surface. "A thousand times I've told myself I should've just taken you that night. Fucked you good and proper and gotten you out of my system. A thousand times I've told myself I should've never let you get under my skin to start with."

Pulling open the door, he shoved his way through the small crowd gathered outside. As the distinctive slam of the outside door to the alley echoed through the kitchen, the heads that had turned to follow his progress swiveled back, one by one, marionettes on strings, their expressions ranging from speculative to appalled to sympathetic to outright leers. Heat once again flooded my face as I stood rooted to the floor, tempted to go after Remy. Terrified of what might happen if I did.

I should never have pushed. Should have let him have time. Because now there were emotions and intents and desires aired, and made more real and I had *no* idea what to do.

Into that stunned, indecisive silence, Mrs. Mercier's cultured drawl flowed like a soothing balm.

"All right now, y'all. Get on back to work. We've only got thirty minutes before the doors open. Charles, be ready to take lead on the line if Remy doesn't return directly."

Her gaze surveying the room's interior, she disappeared, reappearing moments later bearing a large water-filled bowl and several clean dishtowels. With a stern glare that sent the few remaining stragglers scurrying off, she firmly closed the door. Setting the bowl on one of the chairs, she dipped a dishtowel into the water, wringing it out.

"Our Remy, he's a difficult man at the best of times, no? An absolute trial at the worst and near impossible when he's scared."

I spared her a glance as I tossed larger pieces of glass into the wastebasket.

"Oh yes, *petit*—you've got our boy terrified something fierce. And looks like hurt, too. You'll have to tread carefully." Folding the damp dishtowel, she ran it across the surface of the table in brisk, efficient strokes, soaking up the worst of the soda spill along with the pieces of glass too small for me to get by hand. "That is, if it matters." Not one to be bothered with the subtlety of a sidelong glance she simply moved around the table until we were face to face.

"Oh, of course it does—" She shook the towel over the wastebasket, tiny bits of glass showering the metal interior with a satisfied sound that matched her Cheshire cat smile. "It's written all over your face."

I sank into a chair, weary beyond all measure. "I don't know what to do."

"Tread carefully," she repeated. She cupped my chin in a soft, manicured hand. "Remy doesn't trust or care easily. Not with the life he's led. It's too difficult for him. Too painful."

In spite of the tone of her words and the fear and trepidation churning in my stomach, I managed a small laugh—managed to cut it off before it developed into the sob I felt threatening. "Is there anyone's secrets you don't know?"

"Huey Long." She sighed. "The things that man must've taken to his grave." Her expression softened. "However, despite how it must appear, Natalie, I truly don't make a habit of poking into people's business. It's simply Remy's from my neck of the woods—I know what he comes from. I'll admit, he's prideful to a ridiculous degree, but strange as it may sound, it's saved him, time and again. It does, however, make things considerably more difficult for you."

At a time when the last thing I wanted was complications. All I wanted right now was this opportunity. To reach out and grab this moment for myself. And regardless of how much I needed to do this, he knew I would have returned. I promised.

A icy sense of *déjà vu* shuddered down my spine—this moment eerily reminiscent of another. Another promise to return, another plea to take a chance and do something different. Something unique.

Rising from the chair, I backed away, rubbing my fingertips across my forehead. The sickly sweet smell of the Coke clinging to my hands sent a fresh wave of nausea coursing through me. So similar—this scene—and so different. No choices would be made for me here. No accommodations to whims and tender feelings. I'd be making the choices and I had to be prepared to deal with the consequences.

Drained, I sagged against the wall. "God, what a mess."

"Well, no matter what Remy thinks, you've got to do what's best for you, child. Whether it ultimately involves him, only you and he know that." Grasping my shoulders, she pulled me upright, tucked a stray lock of hair back into my chignon. "He's contrary and difficult, but trust me when I say that at heart, he's a good, *good* man. And he deserves something good in his life. Something true."

Finally. Something that wasn't a secret. I knew he was a good man. But was he the right man? Right now? What was I willing to do to find out?

"Natalie?"

I met Mrs. Mercier's piercing gaze.

"Only you can decide if he's worth the effort, *petit*."

. . .

I'd ignored the heart-shaped cookies and the cupcakes with their little plastic Cupids perched atop swirls of red and pink frosting that signaled Valentine's was only days away. Passed over the cakes and pies that were too much, that were intended for parties or families. In the end, my lengthy perusal of Mama Zanardi's overflowing bakery cases yielded the perfect choice: two simple, rustic cannoli, plump with the luxurious ricotta cheese filling that was rich without being overly sweet, outsides studded, jewel-like with pale green pistachios. Carefully packed into a small white box by Mama Zanardi herself, tied with gold string, and handed over accompanied by a broad smile and a wink because in four years of visiting my neighborhood bakery, I'd never once bought two of anything.

The wavy-glassed mirror hanging in the building's narrow entryway was by no means ideal, but illuminated by the muted light from the single shaded lamp, it was enough. I was able to apply one final coat of lipstick and smooth my hair, falling loose in rare freedom, down my back. I was able to see well enough to note the high color in my cheeks and the glittering, slightly unfocused gaze staring back from the mirror. Taking the most recent of what had been innumerable deep breaths, I tightened my hold on the small white box and began the climb to Remy's apartment, praying that the day he'd had to himself would allow him to listen without all the fear and anger as an obstacle.

Once in front of his door, I paused again, unbuttoning my coat and smoothing my hand over the deep red sweater and ivory slacks. Another impulsive buy—wholly impractical and utterly necessary—giving myself the oft-denied pleasure of dressing to not only show myself off to advantage but to please someone else. Knowing I'd be facing him at home, I wanted no evidence of the real world Natalie. Tonight, with Remy, I wanted to be Natalia.

I knocked on the door, my heart pounding as I waited, fidgeting with the bow on the box. *Please … be home.* I wasn't sure I'd have the courage to attempt this again. I began to knock again but just as my knuckles grazed the wood, the door opened.

Madre santisima.

He leaned against the jamb, clad only in a pair of white pants, light gauzy things, reminiscent of the type the *guajiro* musicians would wear as they played for locals and tourists alike at Varadero. For the briefest moment, I wasn't standing in a dark, chilly hallway, but rather on the beach in a thatched-roofed pavilion, open to sea breezes, sand gritty beneath the bare soles of my feet. A memory as powerful as an ache swept through me. I could *feel* the insistent rhythms of the *sons* and rumbas from the band conspiring with the pounding of the surf, urging me to move shoulders, hips, feet, in joyous, sensual dances—a publicly accepted form of sexual expression and lovemaking. One of which we partook, at every opportunity.

Back then, I never looked twice if a man wasn't wearing a shirt. It was Cuba—the beach—where a fully-dressed man was the oddity. Here, though, in these close confines, there was something uncomfortably indecent about the fact that those lightweight pants were the only thing Remy wore—clearly evidenced by the soft light illuminating him from behind, exposing normally hidden planes and contours, the barely opaque layer of fabric more teasing invitation than modest cover. He leaned in the doorway, goblet of red wine carelessly dangling from one hand, the other tracing the dark hair disappearing into the low-slung waistband in slow, hypnotic rhythm. A rhythm matched by his gaze as it ranged over me, each slow blink appearing to take in new details, filing them away.

"You look very pretty, *chère.*" The words emerged slower than usual, his drawl thick and laced with cane syrup. "This all for me?"

"Yes."

His chest rose and fell. "Gotta say, your timing's impeccable."

My gaze followed the path of the goblet to his lips, the play of the muscles in his throat as he drained the wine. The way the tip of his tongue emerged so very slowly fascinated me, the manner in which it deliberately captured a stray drop lingering in the corner of his mouth easily the most sensual thing I'd ever witnessed in my entire life. The whole brief interlude so riveting, I completely missed that at some point, he'd fully opened the door.

He stepped aside in silent invitation, I thought, but really, simply revealing what lay beyond the threshold—the pale gleam of a long leg crooked along the sofa's edge, a tousle of hair, gilt against dark leather, the gentle rise and fall of a chest as bare as his. For a brief hysterical moment I thought perhaps it was Penelope, the erstwhile stewardess paramour, but no—this was a different one. Unlike that night, however, I got no immediate sense of familiarity, that there had been a slow, unhurried seduction. No candles burning or music playing or evidence of a carefully prepared meal—just clothes scattered haphazardly across the floor, door to his bedroom firmly closed. I wasn't sure if that was supposed to make me feel better—or worse.

"You do like your blondes," I finally uttered on a weak, high-pitched laugh. Another breathy laugh—a wheeze, really—escaping as I realized I was making an effort to keep my voice soft so as not to wake the other woman.

One shoulder rose as he lit a cigarette, inhaling deeply. "They're interchangeable." He lazily blew smoke rings that shimmied and danced through the space between us, expanding, almost as if they meant to reach out and try to capture me, before dissipating into an amorphous gray mist that eventually disappeared—nothing but illusion.

"Shame you went to such trouble, *bebe*." He captured a lock of my hair, twisting it around his finger, using it to draw me closer. As his hand brushed my cheek, I caught the mingled aromas of tobacco and alcohol, of cheap perfume and something musky—familiar, yet not.

I jerked my head back, blinking away sudden tears as the hair that didn't easily slide from his grasp pulled free, the strands remaining tangled around his finger. "Why? *Dios mío de mi alma*, Remy *¿porque ahora? ¿Por qué usted insistió en captura de mi corazón si todo lo que iba a hacer es dejarlo partío?*" Defying years of discipline and practice, my words emerged exactly as I thought them, the idea that he might not understand barely registering. Except, how could he not? The hurt I was feeling—that had to transcend stupid words. Stupid language.

Yet, he wouldn't answer, damn him. Wouldn't react. Just stood there, staring down at his thumb methodically rubbing over the long strands of my hair, twisting them into a loose coil. Finally, he looked up, lines I'd never before seen rendering his face into an unrecognizable mask.

It wasn't until I got home that I realized I still clutched the crumpled remains of the small white bakery box, bits of crushed pastry shell and pistachios and ricotta filling running over and staining the surface of my gloves, ruining the leather.

No matter.

I wouldn't need them for the foreseeable future.

PART TWO

THIRTEEN

I stretched, luxuriating in the sensation of smooth cotton and down pillows and liquid sun. Another languorous stretch, my slowly waking senses searching for the expected. The musky aromas and tastes of two intertwined bodies. The feel of skin against skin, one leg heavy across my thigh, hand curling over my hip, each gentle exhale bathing my skin in warmth, the dampness left behind cooling and raising gooseflesh. Marking me even in sleep.

One hand rested on the empty pillow beside me as a lone tear trickled across my temple and into my hair, trailing along the back of my ear like a whisper of a caress. It had been so much easier to bury the pain of missing Nico in the furthest recesses of my mind while I resided in my parents' shabby house in Miami or my thin-walled apartment in New York. When my bed more closely resembled that of a schoolgirl's or a monk's, narrow and cold, the sheets soft not because of their quality, but because they'd been washed to the point of threadbare.

In Natalie's world, Nico had never existed.

However, once again lying in a bed draped in fine linens? One so vast it seemed to mock how little space I occupied? I turned away, trying to block the emptiness and while what I faced was far from empty—breathtaking views of towering palms and blue skies framed by an elegantly wide window—it was every bit as lonely as the bed.

I stared out the window at the rich brown and green mountains, sharply etched despite the unshed tears blurring my vision. Close as an arm's length yet distant as the edge of the horizon. Another tear escaped, rolling across the bridge of my nose.

Oh Nico.

Closing my eyes, I drifted, caught somewhere between exhaustion and the odd awareness brought on by the strangeness of new surroundings. Memories, faded and crumbling around the edges from the passage of time, passed through my mind with the flickering sepia tones of an old newsreel while other memories— newer, saturated with color—fought their way to the forefront. Dark brown supplanted by impossibly deep blue, a young man's gentleness and consideration giving way to brashness and moodiness and a searing hurt that had led to harsh retaliation.

Why, Remy? Why?

And the worst part? No matter how angry, how certain that I was in the right in following this dream, I hadn't been able to forget how he'd looked that night. That haunted, drawn expression. For all his devil-may-care nonchalance, I couldn't help but feel he was as devastated by what he'd done as I was. But I might never know, since in the interminably long week that had followed that night—a week filled with plans and discussions and more plans that finally culminated with a late-night cross-country flight and a bleary-eyed, sunshine-drenched arrival—I simply hadn't had time to see him. Or the desire. So I told myself.

Over and over, throughout all the plans and travel, that was the refrain I repeated. The distance was for the best. From three thousand miles away he could be as difficult and prideful as he wanted, could bed as many blonde whores as he wanted. And I could scream and stomp as much as I wanted without a care for delicate male egos.

Throwing back the covers, I sat up, a soundless laugh emerging. Oh, if only it was that easy. I dragged my toes through the plush faded rose carpet. Remaining busy would no doubt help, beginning with familiarizing myself with my new surroundings.

Bathed and dressed and made up just enough to hide the past week's lack of sleep, I followed the maître d' through the main room of the venerable Polo Lounge and out to my requested table on the patio.

"Dining alone, miss?"

Offered with exquisite politesse as he assisted me into the chair and draped a snowy napkin across my lap, but still, in such a way that suggested it would be … surprising. Especially for the intensely romantic patio, with its twinkling lights draped through the tree branches overhead while candles spluttered in exotic storm lanterns placed on the small, intimate tables. Sunset hues of rose and indigo and purple saturated the sky, while the mountains and palm trees made their final dramatic stand in silhouette before succumbing to the oncoming night. Even the hotel's famous pink-hued Mediterranean exterior, made all the warmer by the mellow light pouring from the many windows, felt inescapably right to my senses.

The poor man had absolutely no way of understanding, but at this point, I didn't care if I had to dine surrounded by every lovesick couple in Beverly Hills staring moonily into each other's eyes—it would be well worth it. To be able to sit surrounded by an expanse unencumbered by skyscrapers. Where night draped over the world with the security of a comforting blanket and one could actually *see* the stars.

A peaceful spot where jazz played quietly in the background, without the discordant accompaniment of car horns and squealing tires and the shouts of harried pedestrians.

It was exactly what I needed.

But just as I began to respond that thank you, yes, I was perfectly content dining alone, a familiar Gregory Peck-baritone with its distinctive clipped accent replied, "No, Henry, as a matter of fact, the young lady will not be dining alone tonight."

And before I could utter so much as a "boo," Henry had murmured a quiet, "Very good, Mr. Roemer," gestured for a busboy to fill our water glasses, and melted away into the shadows.

He took his time about seating himself, settling into the chair not opposite as I might have expected, but rather, directly to my right, shaking his napkin over perfectly creased charcoal wool. "Hope you don't mind," he finally said, without interrupting his perusal of the wine and spirits list.

"Would it matter if I did?"

Now, he glanced up from the leather-bound folder, meeting my gaze.

"Of course it would. If you really objected, I'd move." Pausing, he cocked his head in the direction of the nearest vacant table. "Over there, at least."

He smiled. Not particularly large and not quite reaching his eyes which continued their somber regard. But definitely genuine.

The corners of my mouth twitched, in spite of myself. "It's tempting, you know."

"I know." He returned his attention to the wine list. "But what if I told you I hated dining alone?"

"I'd put it down to more manipulation." The shocking burst of good humor faded as quickly as it had appeared. "It's quite the skill you possess."

Once again, his head rose, the muted light from the candle echoing the shades of gold and amber in his eyes and bringing the green into stark relief. The faun's eyes. Mysterious, capricious creatures. How unwittingly right I'd been that first night.

"No one manipulated you into accepting the job, did they?"

No. But I kept that to myself. An unnecessary bit of discretion, since he obviously already knew the answer.

"Mr. Roemer—"

"Jack," he corrected almost off-handedly.

"Jack." Small enough concession to make if it might get me a direct answer. "What are you doing here?"

"Having dinner."

"Guilelessness really doesn't suit you."

One shoulder lifted. "Do you like the hotel?"

"It's lovely. Is that why you traveled three thousand miles? To see if I actually managed to get myself here without mishap?"

"Why would I worry about something like that?" he replied easily. "You're obviously quite capable."

"Yet here you are, checking up on me."

"For God's sake, don't be an idiot." Impatience sharpened his tone as he rose, picking up the pale green cardigan from where I'd draped it across the back of my chair. "It's only a fool who would leave you to beard the lioness in her den by yourself."

Blindly, I pushed my arms through the sleeves as he held the sweater open, resisting the urge to burrow into the sudden comfort. I hadn't realized how chilly the occasional breeze had become since the sun had sunk below the horizon, only a few purple and rose-hued streaks lingering in the distance, waving goodnight.

"No comment?" he asked as he carefully untwisted the collar and smoothed it—the gesture at odds with the slight mocking edge to his words.

"Too many and not a single one fit for public."

His hands stilled on my shoulders, yet I had the most uncanny sensation if I turned my face up to look, the smile would have finally reached his eyes. Before I could test my theory, however, a waiter appeared, charming smile and pad at the ready to take our drink orders.

"Drinks for you and the young lady, sir?"

"Natalie?" Jack deferred to me as he resumed his seat.

"An Old Fashioned. Please." I'd originally planned for nothing stronger than wine, but that was before Jack Roemer appeared out of nowhere.

"Martini, extra dry, three olives."

And of all the insignificant, absurd things in the world—

"You—"

One heavy brow rose. "I'm sorry?"

"I can't believe it took me so long to make the connection. It was *you*."

"If you say so, Natalie—or … will you be using Natalia now?"

That question—hearing *him*, of all people, say my real name so easily, as if he'd been granted the right—slipped through my bloodstream like quicksilver, a brief flash of anger suffusing my body with heat.

As I replayed that scene again—then once more, just to make absolutely certain—our drinks appeared. "Thank you," Jack murmured as the waiter set them in front of us and handed us menus, reciting the evening's specials before departing, leaving us in the care of the low hanging branches and the heavy moon that was beginning its rise.

The brush of Jack's arm against mine as he nudged my glass closer was little more than incidental, but it was enough to deliver me out of my own head. I took a deep breath and returned his silent toast before taking a sip of my drink with a nonchalance I wasn't quite feeling.

"You were at the restaurant—the day Greg invited me to the party. Inspecting me, like some cut of beef."

"Ah—that."

"Yes, that."

Jack shrugged. "The other gentleman, and I use the term loosely, was another ghostwriter under consideration for the project. Clearly unsuitable. The fact that you happened to be there was just—"

"Don't."

At least he had the good grace to nod—acknowledge that I'd guessed correctly. "All right—it *was* a logical case of killing two birds with one stone. I wanted a closer look at you and—" He paused, studying me over the rim of his glass. "If I may be frank?"

"You're asking permission now?" I made no effort to keep the venom from my voice.

Lowering his glass to the table, he stared down at the drink as if it were a mirror. Grimacing, as if not enjoying what he saw, he finally said, "I was honestly hoping to find something obviously objectionable about you. Anything I could use to buy more time." He laughed down into whatever he saw reflected back from the transparent surface. "The joke then, was of course on me. The more I learned about you, the more perfect you were."

"Why?"

"You're tough. Won't let her run you off. And you have a unique insight into the kind of life Ava comes from. You know our world. It's a valuable asset."

He offered the compliments and simple platitudes so smoothly. Too smoothly. Enough to confirm my suspicions that there was far more to it than that. I knew it. I took another sip, welcoming the harsh burn of the liquor. "More games. From the very beginning of this ... *farce*, I've been nothing more than a pawn, moved to and fro at your whims without any regard for what it might do to me." The fury began building again, slower and fueled by whisky.

"I know. And I'm sorry."

Sorry?

Men like Jack Roemer never apologized. For anything. Which begged even more questions and suspicions. And for what seemed like the hundredth time, I questioned the wisdom of having taken on this project. But now, I was well and truly in with no way of gracefully extricating myself. And truthfully, did I really want to? How could I consider giving up before I'd even begun? Especially when the only viable alternative was returning to New York and Mercier's. I couldn't. Not yet. And not simply because of pride. Or Remy.

Much as I hated to admit it, my curiosity—the thirst for adventure that had once fueled dreams of travel and education— had been reawakened. Perhaps in a more subdued fashion than what had existed in that giddy, hopeful girl, but undeniably there. Insistent enough to overcome memories of painful experience and very legitimate reservations.

"I hope you like steak."

I stirred from my contemplation of the bright red maraschino submerged amidst the dregs of my drink. "I beg your pardon?"

"The waiter was rather patiently waiting for you to tell him what you wanted for dinner, but you were off in another world. So I ordered for both of us—Chateaubriand and Caesar salad for two. Lobster bisque to start. A nice vintage Bordeaux."

"I don't understand you, Jack."

"How so?" After a subtle gesture requesting a fresh round of drinks, he settled himself in his chair, leaning back with the air unique to powerful men—the same air Greg Barnes possessed. Relaxed, yet fully aware of his surroundings. With his austere features and tawny hair combed close, following the elegant slope of his head, he took on the aura of a jungle cat, surveying his realm, those exotic eyes not missing a single detail. For the Jack Roemers of the world, the entire world *was* their realm.

"You give me seemingly kind advice on how to prevent a hangover all the while aware you're about to turn my world upside down. You give the go ahead that I should be given this project, yet you clearly hate me—"

"Not you," he broke in sharply. "Not at all. The situation, however…" He stared up into the branches extending over the table. A leafy canopy providing a sense of privacy. "I don't think I'm speaking too far out of turn if I say that Ava's …"

"Mercurial?" I guessed when he faltered, recalling how Greg and Constance had described her.

"Mercurial. Capricious. Either one works, really." His fingers toyed along the rim of his martini glass. "You're very astute."

"I've spent the better part of the last several years doing little more than observing people. I suppose that's also a trait that will be useful."

"It is a large part of what makes you so perfect for this. Maybe even more so than your upbringing."

"But Jack—why offer me, or anyone else for that matter, the job at all? Surely as her attorney and the administrator of her estate you have some power to put a stop to all of this."

God knows—if the job had never been offered, none of the

past two months' insanity would have ever occurred.

Yet if it hadn't …

If not forced into the light, my past would most assuredly have remained in the veils and curtains and half-truths in which I'd kept it so firmly shrouded. Had Jack not forced me to confront my past, I would have remained blissfully unaware of the changes to my family's circumstances—remained trapped between scarred wood tables and an anonymous parade of entitled young men for who knows how much longer.

"Technically, I have the legal power to put a stop to this, but again, you have to take into account all those capricious, mercurial qualities of Ava's. I call a halt to this without her okay and she's liable to run off to some unscrupulous bastard who'd make a sensationalistic hash of her story and put it in print faster than you can say Jack Sprat. Yes, we could eventually stop it but not before considerable damage was done. And *not* to the family, necessarily. Again, I don't think I'm speaking out of turn by saying that Ava—" He sighed. "She's her own worst enemy. By choosing to play the game her way, regardless of how much time it wastes for everyone, I maintain more control than if I exert actual control."

"Damned if you do and damned if you don't." I stirred the slush of ice cubes and alcohol in my glass with the pastel swizzle stick. "But me?"

A corner of his mouth twitched. "I at least trust you have a sense of integrity."

"How strange to hear you equate me with integrity. Especially with what you know of me."

He reached into the inside pocket of his jacket and withdrew a cigarette case. After I declined the silent offer, he lit one with a sleek silver lighter. The fine web of lines radiating from the corners of his eyes deepened as he exhaled a steady stream of smoke, blue-gray against the oncoming night. "Most of us, at some point or another, find ourselves in situations where we do the unthinkable," he said slowly. "From that standpoint, I understand you—better than you might ever begin to imagine."

Aside from a brief thinning of his mouth, his face revealed nothing more, schooled into carefully neutral lines. "This whole farce … it's been a year—a lifetime—of frustration that I took out, rather unfairly, on you. My behavior—how cavalierly I treated your personal history—was reprehensible."

I waited until the waiter had placed fresh drinks in front of us. "Did Constance make you promise to apologize?"

He regarded me steadily. "She didn't have to."

I so wanted to hate him. For everything that had transpired since the moment he walked into my life, I desperately wanted to hate him. But I wasn't entirely sure I could.

• • •

Past the salad and well into the chateaubriand and Bordeaux, the topics shifted subtly more toward the personal. Preferences and opinions on art and music and current events. He leaned toward Klee and O'Keeffe. I argued the merits of Seurat and Picasso. I declared Rachmaninoff ideal for rainy weekend mornings and the smoky longing of Ella for listening to in the dark and yes, I did like the Beatles a great deal. He insisted if I listened to jazz of any kind, then it was a moral imperative to broaden my horizons and include Mingus and Brubeck and Coltrane. He was currently enjoying Joan Baez and Bob Dylan—an unexpected admission, since the notion of a high-society WASP listening to folk and protest songs seemed incongruous at the very least.

Less surprising was his interest in the well-publicized space race. But rather than the cool intellectual discourse I would have expected from him, he instead leaned forward in his chair, propping his elbows on the fine white tablecloth with the earnest abandon of a schoolboy. His voice rose and fell as he discussed the Mercury and Gemini missions in more than casual detail, a wistful smile crossing his face as he quoted Kennedy's words on the importance of man eventually reaching the moon and what it meant to the world.

Curiouser and curiouser. And fascinating.

And in spite of the drama and sheer surreal nature of the circumstances that had brought me to this dimly lit patio on a mild February night, it was as normal an evening as I'd experienced in, well … years. A lovely, genuinely enjoyable evening.

As he poured the last of the wine, Jack casually mentioned, "Just so you know, while I have a few business matters that require my attention, my schedule is otherwise clear." Left unsaid was that he would be available for that first meeting with Ava, scheduled to take place in a few days' time after her current modeling assignment—a Palm Springs photo shoot for Harper's—concluded. That as promised, he'd not leave me to beard the lion in her own den comprised of one of the luxurious hotel bungalows.

Originally the plan had been for me to conduct the interviews at her Bel Air home, but that would now be impossible since it had recently been sold. The affair with the wealthy married Italian lover from whom the house had been a gift had run its beautiful tragic course—meaning the staunch Catholic wouldn't be divorcing his wife to become Ava's next matrimonial conquest. As such, he'd been summarily dismissed, and memories of the house's role as secluded love nest were simply too … *something*. No, it wouldn't do at all. Information Jack conveyed with a wry grin.

Lacking for anything else to say, I settled for, "Well, in that case, being so close will be … convenient."

"For Ava. As usual." In one smooth motion, he pushed his chair back and stood. "Care to dance?"

I stared at his outstretched hand. "Dance?"

"Yes. Acceptable form of social interaction between a man and a woman." He spared a glance at the couples swaying beneath the canopy of light strewn branches. "Seems like the thing to do."

What a volatile, maddening, undeniably fascinating man. One who, enjoyable evening notwithstanding, I wasn't even sure I liked very much. Slowly, I placed my hand in his and allowed him to lead me to a small cleared space in front of the dais from where a small combo had provided background music throughout the evening. For this set, they'd been joined by a winsome blonde singer clearly meant to draw the patrons out onto the floor. Silky smooth vocals skated through a serviceable rendition of "Girl From Ipanema" with no real smoke or edge, but somehow, the absence of such seemed unimportant in light of what I did have—fabric, lying warm and smooth beneath my palm, the breeze rustling the leaves of the tall, regal palms and the moon hanging low, as if keeping a watchful eye. All that was missing was the roar of crashing surf.

At my sigh, Jack pulled me fractionally closer, his hand splayed low on my back. Afraid he'd misinterpreted the longing that had been so apparent in that one long exhalation, I resisted, trying to subtly angle my body away, maintain distance. His hand tightening around mine, he lowered his head, his breath tickling the fine hairs along my temple. "It's not quite the same, is it?"

I wasn't compelled to question his intuition. Releasing another sigh, I relaxed back into the sway of the slow bossa nova. "No. But it is the closest I've been in a long time."

"Is that good or bad?"

After several heartbeats I answered, "I don't know."

The band segued to "Blue Gardenia," the cool blonde managing to deliver the lyrics of love and loss and broken-heartedness with a respectable amount of pathos.

"Such a mystery, Natalia."

With each step, each breath, calm drew me more closely into its embrace. A few more breaths, another verse of the song, and I was able to recognize that it came from feeling as if he was speaking to *me*. He used my real name not to taunt, but because that's who he saw me as. Not the façade I'd worn for so long. Yet I still felt compelled to threaten our fragile truce—to challenge him yet again.

"I don't know how you can say that. You know everything. Every dirty little secret."

"But don't you see?" He drew me another fraction closer, his voice floating above me. "Therein lies the real mystery."

FOURTEEN

If I'd imagined anything more would follow along the lines of that cryptic statement, I would have been disappointed. Rather, we simply finished our dinner with coffee and dessert and more conversation, retreating to the safe topics of weather and what I might do with the next few days.

"The usual sightseeing haunts, I suppose," I mused out loud as I stirred sugar into my coffee. "Seeing as I have the time. Grauman's and the stars on Hollywood Boulevard and definitely Griffith Park."

"I'll take you to that."

I stared over the delicate china rim of my cup.

"I love the Observatory. I go every time I'm in LA so I'd be going anyway. Unless it's an imposition." He paused, the sugar spoon poised above his own cup. "Would it be an imposition?"

"No, of course not." Which came as a bit of a surprise. It wouldn't be an imposition. If it was anything like tonight, it would be fun. Never mind that at the evening's outset I had considered his presence an imposition. One that had quickly disappeared. But why was he offering? His presence tonight I understood. Equal parts obligation and warning seasoned with a dash of reassurance. But to commit himself further begged further questioning. "Are you sure, Jack? It's lovely of you to offer, but it's not nece—"

"I'll take you."

Any further protest died a quick death at the look on his face. Half excited boy, half powerful man who got precisely what he wanted. He would take me himself and that was that. I wasn't quite sure whether to laugh or to find the nearest flowerpot to bash over that elegant head. Dealing with a man who inspired such contrary reactions was exhausting—even in limited doses.

But on the appointed day, he surprised me again by remaining on his best behavior—being the charming, easygoing Jack with whom I'd shared that first fleeting encounter. Before ... but no—I wouldn't think of that. Not today. Today was for simply being two people. Sightseeing. Being normal.

We strolled the grounds of the park as he pointed out sights from our hilltop perch and showed me how to look through the telescopes and peppered me with so many fascinating nuggets of information about the Observatory's history and exhibits that I finally had to hold my hand up like a police officer and call halt. Both of us laughing at his unbounded—and infectious—enthusiasm. And still another surprise, that after I begged for the break, he was perfectly content to be quiet. Allowing me to just take in the beauty of the day and absorb the various sounds that seemed as if they were coming from a distance. Birds chattering back and forth, the distant hum of cars winding their way up the road to the park, a conversation taking place mere feet away. Sitting on this hillside felt like being on top of the world but in a far more natural way, a safer way, than that horrifying platform atop the Empire State Building. I shuddered, remembering how naked I'd felt, frigid winds swirling, with their taunting calls to draw me out into nothingness.

As if sensing the change in my mood, Jack asked, "Ready to go?"

"I am tired." But since he'd been the perfect escort, polite and deferential to my desires, I felt compelled to add, "But we can stay if you have more you'd like to see."

Another one of the open and unmistakably pleased smiles that had been commonplace today crossed his face, softening the patrician lines. "We can always come back. If you want."

We. Casual error or deliberate choice? Jack didn't strike me as the type to be given to casual errors—or invitations. We began walking along the path to the parking lot. "Jack?"

"Hm?"

"Thank you."

He nodded but remained silent until we'd reached the car—even then, he never spoke, but merely hummed along with the radio, the melodies combining with the rush of the wind and providing pleasant accompaniment down the twisting, hilly roads to the hotel.

Just inside the lobby doors, Jack paused, gesturing toward the concierge's desk. "Ava should have checked in by now. I'll call and see if she wants to meet for drinks later. Just for a half hour or so, let you two become acquainted before getting down to brass tacks tomorrow."

I pressed a hand to my stomach, suddenly wishing I hadn't yielded to Jack's insistence and indulged in the ice cream cone. Or the hot dog. Or any food, really. "That sounds … fine."

Straight white teeth flashed in a smile as much reassuring as it was slightly mocking. "Relax, Natalia. It's just drinks. Ava doesn't bite over drinks. And if she does, rest assured, I'm fairly certain she's up to date on her shots."

I nodded and resisted the urge to look around for the nearest flowerpot. "Well then—"

"No, wait." His smile broadened into the boyish grin that had appeared with increasing frequency throughout our day together. "This should only take a moment. We'll go up together." God, but the man could be charming, even when he wasn't visibly trying. I allowed him to lead me to a seat on one of the lobby's tufted circular benches where I leaned my head against the high back and allowed my gaze to play out over the scene spread before me. One of elegance and leisurely grace—underscored by quiet conversations and soft piano music and the high-pitched tinkling of glasses drifting from the adjacent lounge as the cocktail hour got underway.

"Are you certain? No word?" I twisted around on the bench, watching Jack as he paced, the whitening of his knuckles clearly visible as he gripped the phone's sleek ivory receiver. "No … no. Thank you. I'll be in contact as soon as I hear something."

While clearly agitated, it was an eerily controlled agitation, his steps slow and measured, his words losing the relaxed edge which had laced them throughout the course of the day, the syllables growing more crisp and uniform as his well-bred WASP accent reemerged. Only the sharp ricochet of the receiver as it was forcefully returned to the cradle indicated just how truly angry he was. I sat frozen, only my fingers moving, carefully pleating my skirt, over and over, as he approached.

"Ava hasn't checked in."

"Is it really that bad?" I offered, tentative in deference to the anger that vibrated more strongly the closer he came. "Perhaps she was detained."

"Or perhaps she's merely toying with us. She never showed up at the Palm Springs shoot either."

"Oh."

A derisive quirk of an eyebrow accompanied his, "Yes, oh." He dropped to the seat beside me, an explosive sigh escaping. "Damn her." He shoved a hand through his hair, further disheveling locks that had been at the mercy of the Jaguar convertible he'd somehow procured for today's adventure. Declaring California sightseeing *needed* to be open air to make it complete. Another utterly boyish moment thoroughly at odds with the starchy New York high-society side of him.

"She's letting us know how unhappy she is."

"With?"

It was merely a breath—a heartbeat of hesitation—but it was enough. "She was unhappy with our decision to hire a female ghostwriter."

"I see." My fingers resumed pleating the fabric of my skirt into tight folds. "Were you planning on telling me? Or was it simply going to be a pleasant surprise?"

Dull red splotched the fair skin exposed by the open collar of his shirt, his shoulders twitching beneath the light blue knit fabric as if sunburned. His restless gaze traversed the lobby, as if hoping his cousin would somehow miraculously pop out from behind one of the immense potted palms or whip off a scarf and sunglasses used as a disguise from behind which she could watch Jack squirm, the victim of an elaborate hoax.

No such luck. While there were any number of glamorous young women in oversized sunglasses and Pucci scarves, languorously posing throughout the lobby and hoping to be noticed, not a one was Ava Roemer. Short of actually rising to go check every face hidden behind a magazine or investigate every shadowed corner, Jack was left with no choice but to face me.

"I'd hoped that by meeting you—casually, over drinks with me, she'd relax," he confessed. "That she'd see there was nothing to worry about. I honestly saw no need to tell you."

"Lovely." One hand moved to the looped handles of my straw handbag, ready and wanting ... oh, so badly—

"Natalia—"

I forced my grip to relax, to release the bag. Forced myself to not drop my hands to my lap and immediately burrow them within the already wrinkled depths of my skirt. But with nothing to hold on to, I felt weightless, lacking any sort of anchor. My gaze found and focused on the chandelier suspended high above my head.

"You've got every right to be angry." Even at his touch on my shoulder—the awkward fidgeting as he adjusted the collar of my sweater and revealed more than I'm sure he intended—I refused to look at him. "However, in the interests of efficiency, do you think you could be angry at me in my suite?"

Even the somewhat startling request didn't interrupt my intense scrutiny of the frosted crystal petals of the domed chandelier. Lalique? Once upon a time I would have known at a single glance. What a stupid thing to know with such certainty.

"I want to give you an explanation, but I also have to track down Ava. For that I need to be near a phone. We could order room service."

"You think I'm so easily enticed?" I asked more of the chandelier. As if it would act as some sort of crystal ball, telling me what to do. Which direction I should take. Sadly, it revealed no pearls of wisdom, leaving me to rely on Jack's response and my own instincts.

"Only if you need a drink as badly as I do."

In the elevator, he met my gaze in the mirrored walls. "Look at the bright side. I'll probably be so preoccupied, I won't notice when you lace my cocktail with rat poison."

Maddening, maddening man. "I suggest you not give me any ideas."

Unfortunately, while drinks and hors d'oeuvres were accomplished easily enough, little in the way of explanations were managed, since the phone began ringing from nearly the moment we crossed the threshold into Jack's lavish suite. With nothing else to do, I sat on a chaise on the terrace, bare feet tucked beneath me as I sipped wine and watched as Jack paced back and forth as far as the phone's cord would allow. There were calls to lawyers and loyal family retainers and a brief conversation with one Dante Campisi—Las Vegas hotelier and Ava's second husband, I recalled—someone with whom she'd clearly maintained some sort of relationship. At least, enough for Jack to contact him. Oddly enough, however, no apparent effort on Jack's part to contact Ava's parents or any other family member as far as I could tell. More to file away for future reference.

As the sun was just beginning to edge its way toward the western horizon Jack appeared in the terrace doorway. "We found her."

I swung my feet to the floor, toes instinctively curling against the cold tile. "Where?"

"Malibu." He turned and stalked back into the suite, making a beeline for the bar. Following, I watched as he poured a hefty measure of bourbon.

"Malibu?" I parroted stupidly.

"Yes and don't ask why because I haven't the faintest goddamned idea." He tossed back the whole of the drink in one impatient swallow. "Come on. I've already called for the car." Setting aside the glass, he reached for my wrist, eyes widening as he felt my resistance.

"Natalia, come on. I don't have patience for any more games."

Oh, he had to be rattled. For a man as intelligent and deliberate as Jack Roemer to use that term so carelessly with *me*? I yanked my arm free. "I'll be damned if I go any further without some idea of what I'm getting into, which I'm starting to get the impression is a great deal more than anyone has let on."

His eyes narrowed. "It's complicated."

"I have time." I sat at the edge of a whitewashed cane chair upholstered in a vibrant tropical print. Very deliberately, I crossed my ankles and tucked them to the side, primly smoothing my skirt over my knees and laying my folded hands in my lap with studied casualness.

He shoved his hands into his pockets, mouth tightening into a tense line. "It goes beyond mercurial, you know. Fact of the matter is, Ava's ... different."

I nodded. "The question is what kind of different?"

The sleek brass clock mounted on the wall marked each passing second with a rhythmic ticking. An insistent heartbeat, as if the room itself was holding its breath—waiting. Into the silence, the clink of a melting ice cube collapsing in Jack's abandoned glass resonated with a gentle chime.

"Initially I felt it best that Ava meet you, have an opportunity to become comfortable with you. Now, however, I think it would be more to your benefit. That you deserve the right to make the choice." Taking his verbal cues from the room's serene atmosphere, Jack's words came out measured, but gentle. No trace of the upper-crust WASP—just a man. A very tired man. "It's one thing to pick up impressions from dry facts on paper or based on what we might say about her, but another altogether to experience it. Afterwards, if you want to walk away, you're free to do so, no questions asked and with full compensation for the project. You've earned at least that much for—" He hesitated, then added softly, "Everything."

It was his tone, more than the words themselves, that had me nodding slowly and following him down to the already waiting Jaguar. Even though he hadn't really answered my question.

We made the near hour-long drive in silence, welcome especially after we turned onto the Pacific Coast Highway and I was gifted with my first sight of the ocean, the lowering sun bathing the view in a shimmering gold and white veil. More welcome than the view, however, was the smell. Oh, that *smell*. Clean salt and brine and sheer freedom. Filling me with a renewed sense of determination. In exchange for this? I could put up with a great deal.

"There—" I tugged at his sleeve as I pointed with the hand holding the paper on which he'd scrawled the address and directions. "Hidden Cove Road."

"Hidden Cove. Hiding in plain goddamned sight. I swear to God, she does this just to try me." He flicked the burned down stub of his cigarette over the window's edge before wrenching the wheel to the left, veering off onto the nearly hidden side road, small rocks spitting up beneath the tires and rattling against the Jaguar's glossy red finish as he caught the edge of the asphalt.

"Jack, slow down, please." His fingers tightened around the polished wood of the steering wheel as if he wanted nothing more than to pretend he hadn't heard me. Wanted nothing more than to turn around, floor the accelerator, and leave this quiet shaded street and whatever might be waiting far behind. But he did as I asked, slowing enough to allow me to read the elegantly scripted numbers on the stone pillars standing sentry along the roadside.

"There it is."

He turned, the crunch of the tires slowly rolling over gravel unnervingly loud as the path sloped sharply into a densely wooded ravine. Only the occasional weak shaft of light penetrated the sudden twilight, a taunting hint that something real *might* exist at the end of the journey. Despite the numbers on the pillars and the obviously well-tended driveway with its deliberately casual wildflower border, my palms grew damp.

"You don't think this is some kind of joke, do you?"

"It would hardly be the first time." He slowed further, pulling his sunglasses off in order to better see.

No ... I did *not* like the way this felt. My heart raced, my breath catching in rapid shallow gasps at the sensation of forging through darkness with no idea what lay on the other side. My fingernails dug into the edges of the seat as I fought the memories.

Just as I was about to suggest that we leave, that we get out *now* rather than venture further into the nerve-wracking dark, the trees broke to reveal a clearing flooded with light, the path widening into a neat oval drive crowned with the most perfect house I'd ever seen. Or rather, I reconsidered as we emerged from the car, not a house. A fantasy.

Weathered stone and bleached rough-hewn wood gave the impression that it had emerged, bit by bit, from its quiet surroundings while behind the house the ocean stretched in wild, vivid contrast. Jack and I stood transfixed, watching the white-capped waves roar in before suddenly disappearing with a crash and hiss, the occasional fine mist springing up over the cliff's edge, sparkling against the burnt orange horizon.

It was a scene from a fairy tale.

So of course it seemed perfectly natural that when Jack pushed at the oversized bronze door it swung easily inward—just as in those fairy tales, the innocents unwittingly lured into a trap.

"Ava, where the hell are you?"

"Oh, good, you made it. Come on down." The voice drifted from the open stairwell leading to a lower level. Lacking a banister or any visible means of support, the stairway appeared to be nothing more than wide, irregular planks floating in space, prompting Jack to grasp my elbow, the two of us instinctively drawing closer together as we took those first tentative steps.

"Jesus ..."

I silently echoed Jack's low-voiced exclamation as we descended. Clearly, this immense glass-walled room stretching the width of the house served as the main living area. While the exterior of the house was evocative of its surroundings, the interior reflected a coolly elegant tropical paradise—filled with flowering plants and glossy wood ceremonial masks and batik wall hangings, brilliant against the white walls. Sleek metal and teak furniture with white canvas cushions clustered in cozy groupings, their creamy expanses interrupted only by the occasional matching throw pillow. But luxurious and dramatic as the décor was, it faded against the room's shimmering centerpiece: a spectacular indoor pool. Framed by a towering rock waterfall and the wide glass wall, it fooled the eye into imagining it an extension of the outdoors, the ocean rushing into a pristine, isolated lagoon. And rising from the depths like Venus emerging from the sea, a fully nude Ava Roemer Elias Campisi McLaughlin, every bit as exquisite as Botticelli's creation.

"Hello, darling." She spared a quick, raised-eyebrow glance past his shoulder. "And how nice—you brought a guest. Not your usual type, though, is she?"

Too late I became aware of the disheveled waves of hair tumbling around my shoulders and the sting of windburn on my cheeks. I fought the impulse to lift a hand to smooth my hair or bite my lips for color. For God's sake, at least I was dressed.

"Goddammit, Ava, this isn't funny." Jack strode to a chaise, tossing a robe in his cousin's direction.

"Of course it's funny." Ignoring the robe, Ava stood at the pool's edge, twisting her long hair into a coil, water streaming in sinuous rivulets along her skin as if reluctant to let go. "It's hilarious. You should only see your face, Jack. It's an absolute study in moral outrage and fury."

I honestly tried not to stare—attempted to shift my attention to the fiercely scowling masks on the wall or the view beyond the windows—but it was as if Ava was a magnet, drawing all energy toward her, demanding that one's gaze remain focused on her. *Dios mío*, but she was almost inhumanly beautiful. Full breasted, wasp-waisted, with a delicate porcelain doll's face framed by a fall of strawberry-blonde hair. And even that, as unrealistically perfect as it seemed, was definitely natural as the only slightly darker-hued triangle between her legs attested. Idly, I wondered if that was what had been behind her choice of this house. Spectacular as it was, it was nevertheless exquisitely simple. The perfect backdrop against which she could shine with no effort.

"What the hell are you doing here? You were supposed to have been in Palm Springs before meeting us in L.A."

"I changed my mind." Nudging the robe aside with her foot, she gracefully dropped onto the chaise, reaching for a towel that she used to blot her hair. "Diana called and offered me a spread in Vogue. A shoot in Baja—winter fashions against a beach landscape. They let me frolic in the surf in a full Blackglama mink and nothing else. Doesn't that sound terrific? And much more fun than stuffy old Palm Springs. The Racquet Club would have never let me get away with wearing nothing but a mink on the courts."

"Of course. How Puritan of them." Undeterred, Jack retrieved the robe and tossed it over Ava's torso. "Did Diana understand that by spiriting you off to Baja you'd be in breach of contract with Harper's?" Equally undeterred, Ava rolled to her side, propping herself up on an elbow, the robe once again sliding to the floor.

"Don't be such a stick in the mud, Jack. It's just one stupid little contract. You can fix it. You always do." She smiled up at him, goddess transforming to winsome girl for just as long as she imagined it would take for her to get her way before the goddess reasserted herself.

"Now tell me, what do you think of the house? Just built. One of the other models on the shoot told me no sooner had the last screw been turned, the owner decided he wanted to live full-time in Monte Carlo for the time being. Some boring tax thing." She wrinkled her nose. "He put it up for lease so I called our real estate man right away and had him secure it for the next two years." Her eyes widened. "Do Mother and Daddy know yet? Are they furious?"

Without waiting for an answer, she rolled to her back, stretching her arms above her head with a satisfied sigh. "Anyway, it's so beautifully groovy. I adore being out here. Everything's new and modern with no tiresome history dragging it down. I do think I'll buy it. Eventually. The thought of Mother and Daddy stewing over the idea of leasing is simply too delicious to let go right away. So *nouveau*."

A dark shadow briefly marred the perfect features as she rose from the chaise and finally reached for the robe. Rather than putting it on, however, she very carefully folded the garment, the tip of her tongue peeking just beyond straight white teeth as she lined up the seams, even taking care that each cuff was precisely folded back the same amount on each side. Just as carefully, she laid it across the back of the chaise, a mocking banner as she sauntered toward a paneled door at the far end of the room. Peering back around the edge of the doorway she tossed out, "Take care of it, Jack," before the door closed on a charming, melodic giggle that was no doubt a potent weapon in an already loaded arsenal.

Jack turned, our gazes meeting—his weary and imploring, the sudden shadows that had appeared beneath his eyes throwing the normally muted green in them into stark relief.

You see now, what I meant?

I could only begin to imagine what might be reflected in my eyes if the clenched fists I took care to hide behind my back were any indication.

I had a job here, I reminded myself. To ghostwrite an accurate, sympathetic autobiography of a woman who was a member of one of this country's most celebrated families. A woman who, according to every article I'd read, every note I'd been given, every photograph I'd seen of her socializing with the rich, the famous, and the very well-connected, put her in a rarified class. She was for all intents and purposes, American royalty.

And I hated her.

FIFTEEN

"So what now, Natalia?"

We were seated on the patio of the Colony Shores Inn, a Malibu landmark situated well off the highway on a picture-postcard bluff overlooking the ocean. Cozy, understated, and undeniably private, it was ideal for everything from high-powered business meetings to discreet affairs to, in our case, discussing the foibles of eccentric, flighty relatives. I had to imagine, however, that convenience rather than privacy had been the driving force behind Jack's choice. Given that it was a mere five-minute drive from Ava's and according to Jack, served the best margaritas north of the border.

He hadn't lied.

"You're asking me?"

A short laugh escaped as he set his empty glass down and waved for another. "Why not? I'm at a loss."

"What would you like me to say?"

He slouched against the curved wicker back of his chair, shoulders sloped in exhaustion. "What I would like you to say is 'Jack, this is ridiculous, let's just get drunk and forget the whole thing.'"

"Tempting, but not precisely what I was thinking." Tequila and something about this man and all I'd learned this afternoon demanded honesty. "Although I can't deny part of me desperately wants to get on the first plane back to New York."

"And the other part?"

No answer needed, really. We both knew what the other option was. Regardless, I answered. I wanted to make certain there would be no misconceptions or misunderstandings. "The other part demands that I stay and see this through. Despite every reservation I have, and believe me, there are many."

"I was afraid you'd say that." He grimaced as he rubbed at the bridge of his nose. "Although I can't imagine why you'd stay."

"Because I made a promise."

"One you're being paid for."

Seagulls shrieked as they circled and swooped low over the beach, searching for scraps. I strained to see them in the rapidly fading light, brief flashes of white against the oncoming dark.

The silence was finally broken by the metallic snick of a lighter followed by a long sigh. "I'm sorry. I can't ever seem to say the right thing around you."

My gaze drifted upwards, picking out the emerging stars, marveling at the fact that they were the same ones he'd shown me through the telescopes at the Observatory. Was it possible it had only been earlier today? Right now, it seemed a lifetime ago and as distant as every other good memory I possessed. "Do you see this as just another form of whoring?"

He went so still only the glowing tip of his cigarette showed movement. "If it is, then I have to cast myself as a pimp, given my role in facilitating this."

I glanced down toward the beach. Unable to see the waves, I concentrated on the sound—the smooth, soothing rush intermittently broken as the water crashed against the rocks. "I don't think of you as a pimp."

Again, that stillness from Jack—more sensed than seen, since I was resolutely keeping my gaze focused toward the beach, imagining the cool waves washing over my heated skin.

"And I certainly don't think of you as a whore."

Just then, our waiter arrived, bearing Jack's drink and asking if we cared for anything to eat. While unintentional, it served to provide a necessary respite—a further break in the tension that allowed us to revert to some semblance of normality.

After asking my tolerance for spicy food as well as permission to choose for both of us, Jack placed an order, adding yet another piece to the enigma that was this man. The fresh tortilla chips and spicy *queso blanco* were the epitome of humble, but as I well knew both from the foods of my childhood and my years eating Remy's creations, humble did not automatically equate to lack of quality.

"Good, isn't it?"

I nodded, puffing quick breaths around the growing heat. I fanned my face, silently cursing that I'd just finished my margarita.

"This is the kind of food that feeds the soul," he added, reaching across the small table to hold his drink to my lips. "Helps me think."

Placing my hand over his to steady the glass, I took a grateful sip, studying him yet again over the rim. Imagine—someone like Jack appreciating the visceral connection between simple foods and comfort. The very antithesis of his type. Of that bitch currently lounging in the spectacular house perched on the cliff.

Reverse snobbery? From you? Really?

My conscience administered its chide in a gentle tone. As much as I'd accused him of not knowing anything about me, it was beyond presumptuous for me to make similar assumptions based on what little I knew of him.

"You're very good at masking what you're thinking. But not the action. I can practically see the wheels turning." He drew the glass back, taking a sip, the tip of his tongue emerging to lick salt crystals from his lower lip. "So, what are you thinking?"

The tequila burned warm through my veins. "That I don't like her much."

"Some days, neither do I," he said with a laugh that prompted a relieved sigh from me. "But she's my cousin and I love the sweet, adventurous girl I grew up with. The one I hope someday makes a reappearance. And I owe it to her to stick with her."

Owed her? How curious. But judging by the shuttered expression on his face, not an avenue for questioning. Just a statement of fact. I toyed with the stem of the fresh salt-rimmed glass the waiter placed before me along with the tapas platter of vegetables, cold cuts, and chilled shrimp Jack had ordered for us to share.

"Are you sure you don't want to run?"

"No."

"No, you're not sure or no, you're not going to run?"

"I'm … not sure?" Despite the indecision and slight hint of panic, I found myself laughing along with him, enjoying the wordplay and repartee.

He propped his forearms on the table, leaning forward slightly. "May I ask you something?"

"Of course."

"Why aren't you running?"

I'd asked myself the same thing. More than once, actually. Now, perhaps with an assist from tequila, I found the answer came rather easily. "Because I'm curious."

"About?"

"What could make a life so interesting it would be worth writing about by the age of thirty." I ran my thumb along the rim of the glass, salt crystals rasping pleasantly against my skin. "Maybe … I'm even a bit curious to see what *my* life might have been."

His sharp intake of breath had me glancing up to meet his gaze. "Even if your family still had their fortune, I suspect your life would be very different from Ava's."

"Are WASPs and Cubans that very different?"

He snorted and reached for a fresh cigarette. "More like Ava's that different."

"Hence the need for an autobiography?"

He picked a stray tobacco flake from the tip of his tongue before blowing out a thin stream of smoke. "I suppose."

"You don't sound entirely certain."

"I know the general public tends to be curious—" he inclined his head acknowledging my own term, "—about families like ours. About secrets and scandals both real and imagined. But Ava couldn't care less about the family or the public's interest in it. If she even imagined for a moment that could potentially be a driving force in generating interest in this book, she'd drop the idea like the proverbial hot potato."

"So why haven't you mentioned it as a possibility?"

He snorted. "You're assuming I could get her to believe that."

Selecting a fork, he began picking at the food on the platter between us. "But I couldn't. Her ego just won't accept it."

Skewering a fat shrimp with my fork, I took care to keep my gaze focused squarely down as I squeezed fresh lime over the shellfish.

"What ?"

I shouldn't have bothered. And the tequila struck again, accented with a healthy note of pique.

"Why do you put up with it? That ..." *That craziness*, I almost blurted. "That ... willfulness," I settled on. "Honestly, if she was Cuban—"

"But she's not." The statement was mild and all the more definitive for it. I'd forgotten. For a fleeting moment, I'd forgotten who he was.

"Of course. My apologies." I set the half-eaten shrimp down and reached again for my glass. Even though more alcohol was probably not the wisest idea.

"Not good to be drinking quite that much on an empty stomach." Clearly he was in agreement, even if his reasoning had a somewhat different basis. I silently watched as he transferred avocado and ham to my small plate. In the midst of adding another pair of shrimp, he casually asked, "What would have happened to her if she was Cuban?"

I toyed with my fork, finally spearing a bite of avocado. "She would have been turned over her father's knee and spanked until she couldn't walk, and if that didn't work, sent off to a convent until she'd learned her lesson or was of marriageable age. Then, at least, she'd be her husband's problem."

"Hm." I glanced up to find the edges of his mouth quirking. "Pity we're not Catholic. The convent idea doesn't sound half bad. Although I'm not sure there's a convent that could hold Ava."

"She's never met a Dominican sister."

"If only we'd known." The quirking developed into a fleeting grin, there and gone. "God knows, nothing else, including the husbands, ever worked." A shadow passed across his face, eerily similar to the one that had darkened his cousin's face earlier.

Ironically, showing for the first time, a clear familial resemblance.

After eating quietly for a while he asked, "So were you ever spanked until you couldn't walk?"

I glanced up. "Once. And believe me, it was enough."

"What was your crime?"

"Nico and I liberated a tank full of lobsters from the kitchens of the Yacht Club. Dropped them back into the ocean. What we didn't know was that they'd been imported from Spain and were worth several hundred dollars."

"Oh hell. Well, at least you had company in your discomfort."

"Not really. I was the only one who received a spanking."

Jack's mildly outraged "What?" drew a smile, even as the memory of the punishment had me shifting in my seat.

"Nico was a boy." I shrugged as I pushed at the discarded shrimp tails on my plate with a finger. "The escapade dismissed as typical boyish hijinks. I, on the other hand, was punished for blindly following on what was clearly a bad idea. I should have known better."

"Did you?"

I nodded. "I had tried to talk Nico out of it, but he swore if we were caught, he'd take the blame and any punishment. And oh, how he tried, arguing that since it had been his idea, he should be the one spanked, but to no avail. If anything, everyone was so proud, saying what a good family leader he would be with a bit more guidance in making better choices. In the end, he insisted that at the very least, he wanted to be there when I received my punishment. *Pobrecito*," I murmured, drifting further into the memory, recalling how he'd held my hand, his fingers convulsing with each crack of the belt against my skin, openly crying even though it might well have finally earned him his own spanking had my father told his. Which he hadn't. Nico told me much later, Papi had taken him aside and praised him for his strength of character. Said he knew he could trust him with me.

"I think that's when I knew for sure." My voice sounded slow and distant to my own ears, muffled by the past. "About us."

"How old were you?"

"Eight. He was eleven."

The clinking of china as the waiter reappeared and began clearing the table swept away the fog of memory and brought a heated rush to my cheeks over all I'd revealed. No more tequila, I silently swore. Ever. Clearly, it and I did not mix well.

Thankfully, Jack let the matter lie and instead, turned to outlining a new plan for our project over fragrant coffee and crispy cinnamon wafer cookies.

"It's too far for you to remain in Beverly Hills. Commuting out here could easily eat up half the day, and when you take into consideration that Ava doesn't exactly keep banker's hours—forget it. There are suites here at the Inn, so I'll see if they're available." Pausing from scribbling on the notepad he'd requested, he asked, "Do you drive?"

I recalled the pistachio green Thunderbird convertible that had been my sixteenth birthday present. Halcyon days spent driving to the beach and along the Malecon, reveling in the sun bathing my skin, the wind blowing through my hair as Elvis jousted with Orquesta Aragón and Tito Puente for dominance on the radio. Sweet, joyous freedom. Left behind, of course, like everything else.

"I used to."

"Good enough. We'll see about a car for you and get you back in practice. When you feel comfortable, you can drive yourself, but until then, I'll drive."

His brows drew together as he continued writing, occasionally muttering to himself as I seemed to fade into insignificance, which was ridiculous, really. This all had to do with me. In a manner of speaking.

"Jack?"

He looked up. "Yes?"

"So you're … planning on staying, then? Indefinitely?" A fact I had begun gathering from the glimpses of his lists that I'd been inadvertently privy to as he ripped the sheets off the pad and set them aside. Notes regarding communicating with the New York office and having files sent to him. I resolutely kept my gaze away from the sheets, a bit afraid of what else I might read.

"I think it's best, yes. At least until I'm reassured that things are going to go smoothly and she's going to behave." One eyebrow rose. "I hope that's all right."

Cursing the tongue that was running amok after so many years of restraint, I busied myself with pouring more coffee from the colorful stoneware coffeepot that had been left on the table. Jack had every right to be here. Clearly, his presence was needed. It had nothing to do with his estimation of my abilities. In the wake of this afternoon's myriad revelations, it was the one thing of which I was now certain.

"Of course it's all right. You have every reason to be concerned and to want to see the project successfully underway. I apologize. I don't know what got into me."

His hand grasped mine, stilling my agitated stirring. "Natalia." He waited for me to look up and meet his gaze. The friendly, undeniably concerned gaze of the man I'd first met, all those weeks ago. "I just want to make sure she doesn't leave you in the lurch or worse yet, pull you unsuspecting into the middle of some ridiculous stunt. But if you would rather I leave, I will. Or at the very least remain in Beverly Hills—stay at a remove."

He removed his hand, the evening breeze cool on my skin.

"It *is* better if you stay." Calmer now, I poured him more coffee. "Here. Not in Beverly Hills."

"I know it's better if I stay. That's not in question." He held my gaze. "But do you want me to?"

"Yes."

He smiled faintly as he added sugar to his cup. "Good," he said quietly. "We'll make our arrangements and then we can get started."

Much later, I lay in bed, listening to the welcome lullaby of the waves through the open windows of my new suite, wondering—when had this become "we?"

More importantly, when had "we" become not only fine, but welcome?

SIXTEEN

I studied the huge bronze door, focusing on its inset stained-glass window with the scrolled bars sternly protecting it, trying to shake off the prison-like image it evoked. My fingers curled around the edges of the leather portfolio with which Greg had gifted me on my departure from New York. Elegantly embossed with my initials, it was easily the loveliest thing I'd been given in a very long time.

"Relax. It'll be fine and if it's not, remember, you can walk away. I won't hold it against you. No one will."

"Stop saying that." My grip tightened in response to the dampness growing beneath my palms. "I already told you I won't." Oddly, every bit of his insecurity over this only strengthened my desire to succeed.

"Natalia, it's not you—you know tha—"

"Good morning."

Our heads turned in tandem to the suddenly open door where Ava posed against the doorjamb, impeccably turned out in a white beach casual caftan, large white teardrop hoops swinging from her ears, matching bangles at her wrists, and makeup dewy-fresh and as flawless as though for a photo shoot. In that uncomfortable moment in which our gazes met, I felt hideously lacking, fully aware of how conservative and no doubt dowdy I must have appeared to her, in my blue A-line sheath with the bracelet-length sleeves and flat bow at the empire waist, makeup limited to powder, mascara, and a subtle pink lipstick, no jewelry beyond a simple Lady Bulova and small pearl studs. But as her narrow-eyed assessment traveled from my low-heeled dark pumps to the simple French twist into which I'd pinned my hair, I stiffened. She was the socialite and model, not I.

My wardrobe, conservative and boring though it may have been, was more than appropriate for someone in my position.

The tense standoff was broken by Jack's amused, "You're awake."

Lush lips pursed in a disapproving moue. "When you called last night you were very specific about what time you expected to be here and also that you expected me to be awake and ready to go."

"Yes, but forgive me if I never know exactly when you're going to take me seriously."

"I always take you seriously, Jack. I just don't always choose to follow your directives." She lazily fluffed lustrous Breck Girl-worthy hair as a small smile played about her mouth. Gaze fixed on examining for nonexistent split ends, she said, "Doesn't do to let you think you're the boss all the time, darling."

Tossing her hair over her shoulder, she turned and retreated into the house, leaving Jack and I staring at each other in mutual bemusement. As he put a hand to my back he took the opportunity to lean in and murmur, "I wish I could be reassured."

So did I, but—and perhaps this was merely a product of overactive imagination and suspicion honed over the last several years—I could have sworn there was an odd glitter in those pale blue eyes during that intent inspection. I glanced at Jack, taking in the half smile and lowered brows that suggested he, too, was caught somewhere between hope and cautious suspicion.

"I'm sorry I don't have anything prepared. You know how terrible my coffee is and wanting to be sure that I was here to greet you, didn't even risk running into town. There's the most divine little bakery next door to the grocer—fabulous coffee and absolutely delectable French pastries, but perhaps another time." Again, Jack and I were left staring at each other as we followed her into the light-filled kitchen, a futuristic confection of angles and curves, blindingly white with glossy laminate counters and cabinets, and sleek appliances that looked as if they'd been selected straight from the pages of House Beautiful. The showpiece of the kitchen however, was yet another an immense window. Facing the ocean, it invited light into the room, long, graceful bands undulating along the walls in an otherworldly dance.

"I'm impressed, Ava, you really do seem ready to give this an honest go." With an obviously relieved smile, Jack placed the large reel-to-reel recorder he'd carried in from the car onto the round molded plastic table. "And if you'll tell me where everything is, I'll be happy to make coffee while you two get acquainted."

"Let her make it."

Half lost in wondering whether this would be the best place to work or if I should ask if there was a library or den, I barely heard the words. It was more Jack's reaction, the sudden sharp inhale and subsequent lack of movement leaving him frozen in a tangle of wires and a white-knuckled grip on the small microphone that had my brain finally registering not simply the words, but the cool calculated tone in which they'd been delivered. I watched his throat move, his Adam's apple shifting up, then down, with his hard swallow, every movement slow and sharply etched.

"Excuse me?"

Ignoring Jack's tense query, Ava turned to me, the glitter more pronounced in those remarkable eyes. Stupidly, in that strange, suspended animation moment, I noted Ava herself reflected her surroundings: in the snowy white of her caftan highlighting the brilliant blue of her eyes, their unnerving glitter mirroring the way the sun played off the waves. Only the fall of red-gold hair and the cherry-red lips stood out, fiery beacons amidst the cool blues and whites.

"Make the coffee. Then throw in a load of laundry. Just towels and sheets. I don't want you handling my clothes until I know your capabilities."

"What the hell, Ava?"

"Well, it's what these people *do*, no?" She studied her nails, perfectly manicured in cool silvery white. "I thought it be best to allow her to ease into this with simple tasks. Then we can progress to her English lessons. I refuse to have anyone working for me who can't be understood. The Professor Higgins I retained should be here at noon, so she'd best get to work. Chop, chop." She met my gaze, lips moving with exaggerated deliberation as she asked, "Do you understand?"

The sudden crash startled me from the trance of watching those red, red lips. From wondering how could such beautifully shaped lips make such ugly, twisted movements? Turning, I found Jack, hands flat against the table, the recorder on its side by his feet, spools spinning aimlessly.

"Jesus, Ava. You've pulled some embarrassing stunts, but I have never, until this moment, been *ashamed* of you." Slowly, he straightened, his gaze never leaving his cousin's face, slashes of red deepening along his cheekbones as he studied her mocking smile. His voice very quiet, he said, "Just as a refresher, cousin, our people were tradesmen. Hell, they may have been pirates and highwaymen for all I know. Our importance only grew along with this country's rise and you should thank God for it. Whereas Natalia's family can be traced back centuries and can claim scientists and explorers—men and women of arts and letters, not to mention, actual goddamned royalty. What our family has always pretended to be, with its airs and graces and faux gentility, hers actually *is*."

"Didn't stop her from becoming a whore."

Into the deathly still silence, a drawer slid open with an ominous metallic hiss. "Is that why you chose her, Jack?" she asked while idly leafing through the folder she'd withdrawn from the drawer. "God knows, you never bothered much with any of the other writers beyond vetting and hiring and packing them off to me, yet from what I've been hearing, you can't seem to get enough of her. And what I'm seeing appears to corroborate the rumors." She *tsked* and shook her head. "Fucking the help, darling? How gauche."

"Where did you get that?"

Once again, that mocking smile graced her face as she spared him a glance from beneath the thick black fan of false lashes. "The young man who clerks for you was all too eager to take me at my word earlier this week when I assured him you were staying here and in desperate need of this file." One shoulder rose beneath white voile. "Of course, the promise of an autographed photo didn't hurt either. I think he might have delivered the files himself, had I wanted. Regardless, he had it sent immediately and my, what riveting reading it's provided." The sidelong glance slid my way. "Pity about your husband."

My throat slammed shut, forcing out a gasp with a high-pitched whine. Oh no. *Madre de Dios, pero que no.* How could she? Even though I'd known, from the moment she withdrew the folder from the drawer and started rifling through it, what it had to have contained, a small, tiny part of me had hoped that she might have something approaching a shred of decency. And as much as I didn't want to react, to do anything more than just turn and leave with what little dignity I still retained, I *couldn't.* I stood frozen, unable to move or breathe or do anything other than curl my fingers, the nails cutting hard arcs into my palm.

Jack's hand closed around my upper arm, tremors vibrating through fabric and skin and down to my bones as his grasp tightened. Was he trying to hold me up? Or himself?

"We're going to leave now." His voice was very quiet—almost gentle. Dangerously so. "Your behavior has gone from embarrassing to loathsome. One, I can and have excused—for too goddamned long. The other, I can't." I took in the tight, pale lines of his face. "You have forty-eight hours."

"For what?" she retorted, the sneer as evident in her tone as it was in her face, yet Jack's voice, as he responded, remained even and soft.

"You can either choose to treat this woman with dignity and respect or, if you find that too difficult, this is over. Period. I won't contribute any further to this ridiculous exercise in vanity and I swear to God, if you try to do this on your own, I will throw up every conceivable roadblock and obstacles you can't even being to imagine. In other words, I will make it impossible." A surprising smile crossed his face. "I know you have no reason to believe me, but let me reassure you, I make a hell of an adversary."

His hold shifted from my arm to my waist, urging me to go. I was grateful for the assist, for as much as I longed to escape, I remained stunned into immobility.

"It's okay, Natalia," he murmured into my ear. "We can do this."

One foot, then the other, taking each step in tandem until he drew up at the kitchen's threshold. I followed his stare back to where Ava stood with her arms crossed, the sneer having given way to something caught somewhere between shock and bemusement. She *would* defy him—if only to see if he truly meant to carry out his threat.

Jack's lips momentarily thinned, as if trying to hold something back—words he desperately wanted to say. The planes of his face hardened, bringing to mind that night in Greg and Constance's library—the dark avenging angel. A shudder quaked through me, unbidden, at the memory. Oddly enough, it appeared that slight movement on my part was what ultimately broke his resolve. Almost as if he somehow shared my memory of that moment—reliving the terror as my past had been revealed.

"Natalia did the things she did to survive. What's your excuse?" He urged me along past the kitchen's threshold, down the airy hall and into the entryway. Almost there. Almost gone, thank God.

Just shy of a full escape, a sharp, brittle laugh startled us into pulling up short.

"Oh come on, Jack. Have you really becomes such a complete stick in the mud? What happened to that delicious sense of humor you used to have?"

No—Jack, please, don't listen to her. Let's go. Now.

Unable to hear my silent entreaties, he released me, turning slowly to face his cousin. As did I, against the better judgment that was urging me to *go*—to keep walking and leave. This was Jack's family. The latest act in what was clearly a long-standing drama. Not mine. I wanted no part of it.

"And what part, exactly, was supposed to appeal to my sense of humor?" he asked.

"The whole thing was a joke. Just a joke." She laughed again, the tail end of it edging ever higher, falling away in a breathy titter. "You understood that, right?" To my shock, she was directing the question at me. "You knew I was joking all along, didn't you, right? It was harmless. I was nervous."

My gaze met Jack's wondering what, exactly, he wanted me to say to this. Understanding there was nothing *to* say, I turned and wordlessly descended the bleached wood steps to the driveway, reassured to sense Jack close behind, helping me into the car before sliding into the driver's seat.

"Jack! Wait! I'm sorry! Jack!"

He glanced back to where she stood, clinging to the open door. "Maybe I should—"

"Do you honestly think she means it?"

"I—"

Whether protest or agreement, I'd never know, as his voice faded, lost beneath Ava's increasingly desperate, "Jack, no …"

No.

That word reverberated through my skull before settling into an insistent, painful throbbing behind my eyes.

No.

Supplanted immediately by an equally insistent *enough*. Enough. I had finally had enough. And for the first time in a very long time, I put my needs before someone else's.

"Please, Jack." I touched his arm, prompting him to look at me—to completely shift the focus of his attention solely to me.

Afraid that whatever that searching gaze might be seeing wouldn't be enough to convey how very much I wanted this, my fingers tightened on his forearm. Slipped on skin clammy with sweat. His or mine? I wasn't sure. "I can't stay here any longer. Please?"

His expression hardened as the car surged forward, the powerful engine roaring as if as desperate to get away as I was. As we turned onto the street, long past when I might have imagined we could possibly hear her, a shrill, *"Dammit, Jack … come back! I said I was sorry… You come back here, right now!"* echoed, sending shivers down my spine that I resolutely ignored.

SEVENTEEN

Noisy silence was a state I was well accustomed to. After all, New York was never truly silent. And back in the days of my childhood, silences had been filled with the waves and wind whispering their secrets, sharing them with the rustling palm fronds and shells crackling underfoot. With the slip of skin against skin as the innocent grasp of a boy's hand evolved from a young man's chaste kiss to a lover's possessive embrace. So very much said within those silences.

There were other noisy silences. Disappointment and recrimination gave silence sharp edges, and anger often simmered ominously. Bitterness tended toward a static finish, while suspicion and weariness brought with them heavy, basso overtones.

A truly still silence was rare. There was *always* something there. But from Jack, nothing save a void of quiet. Even the car's engine had subsided to little more than a docile hum, as if in deference.

It wasn't until we paused outside the door to my room that the first glimmer of emotion emerged. For all its quiet resignation, the sadness reflecting from within those faun's eyes was still powerful enough to strike a chord of recognition deep within me. But before I could say or do anything, he brushed the knuckles of one hand across my cheek and silently moved past me to disappear into his suite.

A touch that lingered long after his door had closed quietly behind him. That teased with unspoken questions and answers as I moved back and forth across my room, methodically repacking all that had been so recently unpacked and neatly arranged, calling the airline and filling in what had been an open return date on my ticket.

He'd known. It was at least part of what he'd acknowledged

with that look and its accompanying fleeting touch. He'd known I would go. That there was no longer any possible way I could stay—no apology or bribe that could entice me to remain, not knowing what cruelties that capricious bitch might conceive of for her own personal amusement. It was too similar to what I'd endured at Concord—always anticipating, never knowing, foolishly hoping. And above all else, that damnable feeling of helplessness. He knew there was no way I would ever willingly subject myself to that again.

So it would be a return to New York where the first thing on my agenda would be to confess to Greg Barnes face to face. I hated disappointing him and could only hope that he might understand. I suspected he would. I was also not above asking for another chance. Not with this project, obviously, but to ask if he had any openings as a proofreader or copyeditor or *something*. That it would mean starting at the bottom of the totem pole didn't matter. That it wouldn't necessarily be writing didn't matter. The world of books and publishing—so long dismissed as an innocent young girl's dream—was once again a possibility. Only a fool would dismiss such an opportunity.

Which left the question of Mercier's. My job was waiting there—that was a given. What was not a given was that without the cushion of time and distance on which I'd been counting, would I be able to return and behave as if all were normal? Could I possibly face Remy every day and live with the possibilities and might-have-beens swirling about us? I knew all too well what it felt like to have loved and lost, but to desire love—to have the promise of it dangled then snatched away—was a new sensation, leaving my silence throughout that night filled with a cacophony of questions and regrets.

Morning, however, brought a surprising respite to the noise in my head. But then again, solitary walks, with their particular brand of silence, had always had a calming effect. And with an endless stretch of beach at my disposal … I'd been quietly elated by Jack's decision to move our base of operations to this inn. Immediately, I'd begun weaving dreams of beginning each day with long walks, alone with nothing but the thoughts in my head. A vastly different tableau from the bridges or rain-slicked sidewalks lit by scrolled-iron lampposts of which I'd once dreamed, but the endless expanses of beach and water were nevertheless familiar—and soothing.

For the first time in years, I'd felt ready to face the thoughts in my head and heart. To look toward the future rather than simply exist. So foolish. One might think I would have known better, but it had seemed so ... *possible*.

Nevertheless, on this one day, it would be. I would walk barefoot for miles, feeling the cool, damp grittiness of the sand between my toes. Watch the waves build and swell and crash against the shore, the foam leaving behind abstract patterns, like some ethereal road map. I could sit on a large boulder and observe the early-morning surfers and the floppy-eared dogs splashing in the water as their owners laughed and tossed sticks and smiled and nodded as they walked by, inviting me, if only for that brief moment, to share in the beauty of the day with them.

As I walked, the warmth of the rising sun beckoned me to shed my sweater and leave my arms bare. So foreign yet so familiar at the same time—that prickle of heat and the breeze bathing my arms and shoulders, sharpening all my senses in turn. On impulse, I yanked my blouse free from my skirt, loosening several of the lower buttons and tying the fabric up under my breasts, leaving my back and abdomen bare. With each bit of skin revealed, I felt more weight fall away, each step growing lighter. I skipped along the sand and splashed in the shallows and laughed out loud, simply because I could. Finally out of breath, I sank down onto a giant, misshapen driftwood log, my fingers playing over the ridges and bumps of the ancient wood as I tilted my head toward the sun and allowed my mind to drift, weaving stories about the inhabitants of the houses perched on the dunes and hillsides. I was feeling so thoroughly lazy and content, I even allowed self-indulgence to extend to a leisurely breakfast at a thatch-roofed open air café, where the impossibly young waiters wore Hawaiian shirts with their tans and blindingly white smiles and obviously didn't care if you had sand grains dusting a bare midriff or carried the scent of the sea in your hair.

Finally returning to the inn, I continued my morning of hedonism, savoring a lengthy bath, taking the time to brush my hair dry as I hummed along to the strains of Etta James and Jerry Butler. It was only when the DJ announced a straight play through of one of the most influential albums of the last five years and stay tuned to listen to the entirety of *Time Out* by the Dave Brubeck Quartet, that a hint of tension returned.

There was no use putting it off for too much longer. Even if the car wasn't scheduled to arrive until late afternoon to transport me to the airport in time for my red-eye flight to New York. And while it wasn't strictly necessary, it seemed wrong to leave without saying anything. Of course, I could simply leave a note. But no, my overdeveloped conscience demanded I face him every bit as much as it demanded I face Greg Barnes. Leave no room for guesswork or misinterpretation.

However, knocking at his door and quietly calling his name returned no response beyond silence. Of course. I supposed it was possible he had stepped out. Even as my gut suggested that no … not likely. The last thing Jack would want to do in the wake of yesterday's events would be to go out. He would much prefer to hole up and close in on himself and try to forget the rest of the world existed.

Wouldn't he?

Or perhaps I was being an idiot, projecting my own experiences and how I'd reacted in the past.

"Mr. Roemer hasn't called the valet to bring his car around?"

"No, miss."

"Has he called for any car at all?"

The slight silver-haired concierge with the neat pencil mustache and elegant bearing shook his head as his eyes narrowed, forcing me to suppress an impatient sigh. "Thank you then."

I suppose even in somewhat free-spirited Malibu, a young woman asking after a gentleman's activities was cause for disapproval. I would simply have to wait and try knocking at his door again. I'd try until it was time to depart for the airport. All else failing, a note would have to suffice.

I'd not taken more than a step or two away from the polished wood-and-stone desk before I heard a tentative, "Miss Martin?"

Turning, I saw the concierge's brows had drawn together over still narrowed eyes, the look conveying a more obvious concern rather than the disapproval I'd assumed. "You're Mr. Roemer's guest, correct?"

Not precisely, but I wasn't about to quibble. Not with the skin along my arms rippling, the tiny hairs rising. "Yes."

"He seems a nice young man."

"Yes." I nodded slowly. "He is."

The man's mouth tightened, tiny white brackets appearing at the corners beneath his mustache. His gaze searching mine, he finally nodded, as if making up his mind. Beckoning me closer, he said in a hushed voice, "He remained at the patio bar for a considerable amount of time last night." He paused again, as if still trying to make up his mind, then, voice lowering even further, said, "Drinking steadily—remained a perfect gentleman," he added quickly at my questioning look. "However, after last call, he demanded that room service deliver two more bottles to his suite."

"And you *complied?*"

Two spots of color appeared beneath the man's smooth tan. "We are not in the habit of refusing requests from men of Mr. Roemer's station."

"I'll be needing the key to his suite." Not a polite question or gentle request, but a demand delivered in a voice dredged from my long-ago past. The type of voice to which this man would respond.

Perhaps later I would be embarrassed.

"Of course." He moved to the registration desk, selecting a key from a glass-fronted cabinet.

"And have room service deliver a pot of strong coffee and some dry toast."

"Very well, Miss Martin."

I started toward the elevator then paused and turned to meet the concierge's gaze. "Thank you."

He inclined his head, a gesture I caught only the briefest glimpse of as I hurried to catch the elevator, squeezing into the impossibly crowded car just as the doors slid closed. I shifted impatiently from foot to foot, silently cursing the mountain of luggage and two tiny, nervous snow-white poodles with their sparkling collars that skittered about my feet, yapping and growling at each other. Beside me, their similarly bejeweled and coiffed owner snapped as aggressively as her pets, demanding that the bellman slow down the car because couldn't he see how her babies were suffering?

"Oh for God's sake—"

I reached past the startled bellman and pushed the button for the next floor, shoving aside luggage, dogs, and yapping owner as soon as the doors opened, and leaving cries of outrage in my wake as one of the beasts escaped, tongue joyfully extended as it dashed past me. We parted ways at the stairs, the dog's nails clicking excitedly on the wooden treads as it raced down while I ran up the remaining two flights. At Jack's door, I knocked, twice, sharply, anxiously listening for something—anything—trying to hear over the sound of my heart pounding in my chest, echoing with a mocking chant of *Be careful … be careful…*

Too late.

Fumbling with the key, I finally shoved it into the lock and turned, pushing the door open, my breath catching at the sight of Jack slumped in a chair out on the balcony, head lolling to one side.

"Jack!"

Oh no … *Dios por favor, no.* I dropped to a crouch in front of him. "Jack!"

"Shh …"

My heart stuttered, then resumed racing again. "*What?*"

A crooked grin lifted one corner of his mouth as one bloodshot eye opened to stare at me blearily. Lifting one finger to his lips, he whispered, "Be vewwy vewwy quiet. I'm hunting wabbits."

"Be vewwy vewwy quiet. I'm hunting wabbits."

Startled, I jerked my head around, noticing for the first time the flickering screen of the large console television on which Saturday morning cartoons played, Elmer Fudd and Bugs Bunny engaging in their endless chase.

Attempting to steady my breathing, I turned back to Jack. "I would never have taken you for a Bugs Bunny fan."

"Why not? It's like watching *This is Your Life*. The drama's never ending and one's an eternal fool." Chuckling, Jack raised the bottle of bourbon to his lips and took a healthy pull without a single wince. Then again, how could he possibly feel anything, I noted, spying the empty bottle lying on the floor by the bed. At least the one he cradled so possessively was still reasonably full.

At the discreet knock, I stood, ordering, "Stay right there," and feeling ridiculous the moment I said it. He probably couldn't find his feet if asked. *Idiota.* I stepped into the hallway to take the tray of coffee and toast from the room service waiter, not wanting to allow prying eyes to see the condition Jack was in. Yes, we were far removed from New York, but experience and memory served as dual reminders that eyes were always watching and the last thing that needed to get out was that the young scion of an enormously wealthy and well-known family was falling down drunk in a hotel suite with a strange woman. Placing the tray on the small dining table, I poured a cup of coffee, hoping Jack would cooperate.

"Jack?" Again, I crouched in front of him, holding the steaming cup. "I think it's time you exchanged the bourbon for coffee."

Both bloodshot eyes opened, the same crooked grin curving his lips. "How 'bout the bourbon with the coffee?" he slurred. "Or I got a better idea. You have coffee, I'll keep the bourbon." He held the bottle close to his chest, one finger playing suggestively about the mouth while with the other he fumbled for a cigarette from the crushed box on the table beside him. Lighting it, he exhaled a stream of smoke, the edges of the plume just teasing my eyes and making them sting.

"I've had coffee, Jack." I tried to keep my voice calm and free of the urge to just tilt his head back and pour the brew straight down his throat. Or over his head.

His finger continued playing about the bottle's rim for another moment before he took another drink, his gaze focused on me the entire time, as if daring me to do something about it.

"This is accomplishing nothing."

"Not true. If I'm drunk, don't have to think."

"But you won't be drunk forever. And then you will have to think." My voice sharpened as he raised the bottle again. "And you'll feel foolish. Please, Jack, this isn't you."

"You don't know me." He laughed, a pained, rusty sound. "Isn't that what got you so upset? We didn't know you. We interfered. Should've just left you alone, working in that goddamned restaurant and letting those prep school brats fuck you whenever and however they wanted. Sucking out another piece of your soul every time they spread your legs and threw another dollar at you." He sank against the back of the chair, his chin dropping to his chest as he took another deep drag on the cigarette before abruptly crushing it out in an overflowing ashtray.

It was the liquor, I reminded myself. It had nothing to do with me. "This definitely isn't you, Jack," I said softly, ignoring the heat stinging the backs of my eyes.

"You don't know me," he repeated, sounding shockingly lucid. Setting the bottle aside, he leaned forward and ran one finger along my cheek, making me cringe at the overwhelming stink of bourbon and countless cigarettes and stale man. "What would it take, I wonder—" His eyes widened an instant before he jackknifed forward, a hot, pungent stream spewing from his mouth and splashing across my chest and lap. China shattered as I dropped the coffee and reached for him, one arm wrapped around his back as my hand supported his forehead, trying to keep him from pitching to the floor.

He retched and heaved for several long, interminable moments while I fought my own gag reflex and the memories flooding my mind. By the time he finally quieted, he was clutching me around the waist, his fingers digging painfully into my hip.

"Are you done?"

I felt, rather than saw his nod.

"Can you stand?"

Together, we struggled upright and headed in from the balcony, moving toward the suite's main door. Taking a quick look to make certain the coast was clear, I guided us the short distance between our rooms. Once inside mine, I led an unresisting Jack to the bathroom, leaving him swaying by the toilet while yanking the stool from beneath the vanity and shoving it behind his knees.

"Sit," I ordered, unceremoniously pushing him down onto the stool as I lifted the toilet lid. Leaning into the shower, I spun the taps open, not even waiting for the first wisps of steam to rise before stepping in, still fully dressed. I allowed the water to rinse the worst of the muck from my clothes before stripping and quickly showering, my tears flowing along with the water as I remembered. My hands slipped on the wet tile as I sank to my knees, scrabbling for something real to hold.

Desperately trying *not* to remember.

How I'd once held a boy, another family's young prince. Been his support and comfort through another wretched time. Wondering, when, *por todos los santos, when* would history stop repeating itself? Or was I destined to relive moments from my past, over and over, in various forms. Wondering, was this my punishment for having run?

Finally, with a shuddering breath, I rinsed my face, wrapped myself in a towel and pushed open the frosted glass door, leaving the water running.

"Jack, stand up."

He remained bent over the toilet, hands clenched in his hair, as if that pain could counteract what was going on inside his skull. "No."

"You're filthy and need to clean up."

"I don't care."

"You are not staying in here without showering."

"Fine. I'll go back to my room. Bourbon's there anyway."

I resisted the temptation to bludgeon him over the head with the heavy ceramic soap dish. "You can't."

"Why not?"

"I have your key."

He turned his head far enough to hit me with a malevolent glare but didn't say anything as he carefully rose, still cradling his head with one hand, as if afraid it would otherwise fall off. "You can leave now," he grumbled as he steadied himself with the other hand against the vanity.

"I'll leave once you're in the shower."

His eyes widened far enough to make him wince. "You're going to stand there and watch me strip?"

I shrugged.

With a grunt that was no doubt something uncomplimentary, he reached back over his head and yanked his stained, white cotton undershirt over his head, tossing it to the floor, before fumbling with the button and zipper of his khakis. Shoving them down past his hips, he kicked them free, his hands returning to the waistband of his boxers. His gaze held mine in a standoff that ended when his hands dropped away, leaving the shorts in place. He moved toward the shower, stumbling as he tried to step over the low rim, his shoulder crashing against the glass door's metal frame. "God*dammit*."

Part of me wanted to help. However, a larger part of me wanted to see him suffer. *Cabrón más estupido...* Splitting the difference, I waited only long enough for the door to slam shut and hear the string of curses that erupted as the scalding water hit his skin. Returning to the bedroom, I exchanged the bath towel for the heavy robe I'd left tossed across the bed earlier and picked up the phone.

"Concierge desk," a slightly formal, familiar voice intoned. "Mr. Gordon speaking."

"Mr. Gordon, this is Miss Martin."

"Miss Martin, is everything—"

"It's fine," I broke in, amending with, "more or less. However, I do need a bit more assistance."

"Of course."

"Housekeeping will need to attend to Mr. Roemer's suite. Discreetly," I added, knowing he'd understand what I meant. A good concierge always did.

"Consider it done. Will there be anything else?"

"I require another tray. Tea, I think, instead of coffee, as well as more toast. Sent to my suite this time, please."

There it was again. The subtle tones and inflections from my youth—the certainty that whatever I said would be responded to without question. How easily it had returned. What a seductive power.

"I'll have it sent up right away. And might I suggest some aspirin and a carafe of ice water as well?"

Plenty of water and two aspirin right before bedtime are the best cure for any potential hangovers.

Definitely came in handy during a collegiate bacchanal or two.

A silent, mirthless laugh escaped on a puff of air as I heard Jack's voice, as clearly as if he were walking alongside me down that elegant hallway. Back when he was just the nice young man inquiring after my welfare, and I was simply Natalie, sleepwalking in what I'd imagined to be my impenetrable little bubble.

"Miss Martin?"

I shook off the ghosts. Those people were gone. "That would be most appreciated, thank you."

As I replaced the receiver on the base, the door to the bathroom opened, Jack emerging from a cloud of steam, wearing the white terrycloth robe that was a twin to my own. He appeared far more sober, if still a bit green around the edges.

"I called for another tray. Tea, this time."

He nodded, then winced. "I borrowed your mouthwash. I hope you don't mind."

"Of course not." I gestured toward the bed. "Why don't you sit until the tea arrives?"

With the added measure of sobriety seemed to have come a certain acquiescence, as he gingerly nodded again and moved to the bed, carefully easing down to sit at the edge, his hands laced loosely together and hanging between his knees. I stood before the dresser, brushing the snarls from my hair, attempting to give him a measure of privacy, illusory though it was. In the mirror's reflection, I watched his chest rise and fall, as if he was preparing to speak, yet … nothing. As I continued brushing my hair, he continued to watch, his eyes following my movements.

"Natalia—" The quiet knock cut him off, almost as if in warning. His eyes clearly conveyed a tired resignation and something more that I only caught a hint of as I turned away from the mirror and went to answer the door. And by the time I maneuvered the tray into the room, he'd slumped over onto his side, one foot still on the floor, his breathing deep and even. Setting the tray aside, I gently eased his leg up to the mattress and shook a blanket over him. Just as well—he hadn't really been ready to speak, but had clearly felt some obligation. I stood beside him, taking in the bruised-looking circles beneath his eyes and the way his brows remained drawn together, as if protesting the daylight streaming into the room. Without benefit of the aspirin he was likely to suffer, as Abuela used to say, the devil crowing and pecking from the inside. *El pobre*—even as my rational mind protested that it was all of his own making and nothing less than he deserved.

After pulling the heavy drapes closed and leaving the room in much gentler shadow, I pushed a cushioned armchair closer to the bed and sat. As the murky half-light gradually gave way to full dark, I continued to sit, drinking tea and listening to the steady rise and fall of his breathing.

EIGHTEEN

"What time is it?"

The words emerged slow and heavily laced with sleep, but otherwise clear.

"Almost five. Sunday morning," I added, in case he wondered.

"Shit." A moment later, I heard the muffled thump of feet hitting the floor, the first few steps hesitant, then steadier as he approached the balcony. I'd been sitting out here for hours, lost in the hypnotic rhythm of the surf. Memories, thoughts, questions and more questions sweeping in with each wave, only to just as quickly retreat, leaving behind a trace of salt and a hint of their true depth.

He sat at the edge of the chaise beside mine. "Have you slept?"

"Off and on."

Still staring into the dark, I sensed, rather than actually saw his glance back toward the bed, only one pillow bearing an indentation, one side still neatly undisturbed. "You should get some real sleep. I'll go back to my room."

"The bourbon's gone."

The wind changed direction, rustling the leaves of the nearby palm trees. "Doesn't matter."

I nodded. "Your room key is on the table along with some water and aspirin. You should probably take some if you think your stomach can tolerate it. There are saltine crackers as well." A thoughtful addition for which I'd silently thanked the prescient Mr. Gordon.

Pushing himself to his feet, he stepped inside the French doors. "Thank you," he said quietly over the clink of the pitcher against a glass.

I rose from the chaise and sidled past him into the room. "It's only decent."

His lips pressed into a thin line at my carefully neutral response. "How bad?"

I inhaled sharply, swallowed past the tightness in my throat as I recalled his harsh barbs—wondered how much of it he'd really meant. Hours and hours of wondering how much he'd meant. What demons had driven him to behave the way he had.

"Never mind. What your face is saying—it's more than enough." He pinched the bridge of his nose, furrows marring his patrician forehead as he clearly tried to recall. "Natalia, I—"

"It's over, Jack. Just let it go. Please." I wanted nothing more than to let it go. It had been a very long afternoon and night, watching over him as he veered between a heavy, terrifying sleep that verged on unconscious to tossing and turning, his mutterings mostly unintelligible, but undeniably angry. Weariness swept over me, the floor feeling as if it were swaying underfoot.

His hand cupped my elbow, steadying me. But when he tried to lead me toward the bed, I pulled my arm free, shaking my head and regretting the motion as it brought on a fresh wave of lightheadedness.

Misunderstanding, he continued, "Look, Natalia, you've gone above and beyond the call. We can talk later. For now, get some rest. God knows, you've earned it."

"That's terribly considerate." Hopefully he was still hungover enough that the slight sarcasm wouldn't register. "However, I'm afraid I don't have time. The car will be here within the hour."

For the first time, his gaze took in the entirety of the room— cases neatly stacked by the door save for the train case sitting open on the dresser, waiting for the last of the incidentals. My traveling suit hanging in pale blue isolation within the open closet.

"You're really leaving."

"You knew I would."

He nodded slowly. "I suppose I did. I just—" His voice trailed off as he raised the glass and drained the rest of the water.

Don't ask. Let him drink his water and bid him goodbye.

Say you might run into each other in New York, both of you knowing it for an utter lie.

Because did I honestly want to know the conclusion to that truncated sentence? But even as my rational mind waged its argument, I heard my impulsive self ask, "You just what?"

Wandering back to the balcony, he gripped the railing, tension locking his arms in a straight line as he stared out into the dark. "I just hoped you might at least wait out the forty-eight hours. See what would happen."

"If it wasn't for you—" I stopped, reconsidered my words. "Rather, if it wasn't for what happened yesterday, I would have left last night. I had a seat on the red-eye."

"I see. Guess I can't blame you." Even in the low light, I could see the tendons in his forearms straining, as if trying to hold something back. "Did you call Greg and let him know you were coming home?"

"No."

"No?" His head turned slightly. "Why not?"

"Because he and Constance deserve more than what can be conveyed with a phone call. I'm planning on seeing them immediately upon my return."

With a deep breath, he pushed away from the balcony and reentered the room. He paused at the suite's door, fingers tapping a restless pattern on the jamb. "I'll wait to speak to him then. Seems only fair you get first crack at telling all of us how idiotic we were."

"I would hope if you've learned anything about me, that you know I wouldn't do that."

"I do know. But I still wouldn't blame you." A faint smile crossed his face. "Safe travels, Natalia."

I nodded and started to say thank you or something equally polite and innocuous. "When do you think you'll be returning to New York?"

His raised eyebrows conveyed his surprise at my question. Almost equal to my own surprise at asking it. "Not for several days at the very least, I'm afraid." The faint smile devolved to a mild grimace. "Have to clean up around here."

Of course. The promised forty-eight hour window was up and while he clearly desperately wanted to walk away from the whole mess, he just as clearly didn't feel as if he had that freedom.

I owe it to her.

That mysterious sense of obligation—even if I didn't understand or know its source, I recognized its demand. How family held one captive no matter how much the desire to break free existed. Helpless in the face of that recognition I glanced around. Needed to do something, no matter how useless it might appear on the surface. Because what he really needed I just *couldn't* bring myself to do. Nor would he expect me to. But after so many years of struggling alone, I had to think it would be *something*—just knowing there was someone else out there who … cared. I retrieved the bottle of aspirin from the table. "Here." I pressed it into his hand, curling his fingers over it. "You'll no doubt need more."

His free hand rose to cover mine as his gaze searched my face. I remained still beneath his scrutiny, hoping he could see what was truly being offered.

Finally he asked very quietly, "If I ever summon the nerve to ask, will you tell me what I said or did yesterday that hurt you?"

I glanced down, studying our joined hands. "You didn't hurt me."

"You're a terrible liar." As he had yesterday, he brushed the backs of his fingers gently across my cheek, this time lingering long enough to push a loose strand of hair back from my face and tuck it behind my ear. "And a very nice woman. You sure as hell didn't deserve to be dragged into this mess. Certainly not the way we—I— did it. I could spend a lifetime trying to make it up to you, Natalia, and it wouldn't begin to scratch the surface."

He'd already apologized once before. This, however, was subtly different. This was validation. This proud, stubborn man had finally yielded—taken full responsibility for a wrongdoing—and I felt nowhere near as vindicated or victorious as I should have.

In fact, gazing up into his face, I found myself … *laughing*. Rather than take offense, however, he merely stared, a furrow creasing his elegant brow.

"Interesting reaction."

"You'll think me crazy, but … I feel as if I should be thanking you."

"Thanking *me*?"

"Yes." My gaze shifted to look past his shoulder, so many things clarifying, leaving me shaking my head at how absurd life was. How I had once—not that long ago—longed to slap this man. Scratch, claw, kick, hit—anything to inflict a measure of the hurt I imagined he'd visited on me. "Thank you."

"I can't imagine what the hell for."

"It's just … don't you see? I needed *something*, Jack. Something to shock or break me out of the life I was living. Continuing indefinitely the way I was, I …" I took a deep breath. "It would have …"

Killed me.

"Not been good."

A shadow crossed his face. "Don't be a saint on my behalf, Natalia. I don't deserve it."

"Trust me, I am neither saint nor martyr."

"There's a difference?"

I cocked my head to the side and forced a lighter note to my voice. "Did they not teach you anything in your undoubtedly expensive education?"

"Clearly none of the good stuff." A smile briefly turned the corners of his mouth up then faded as his voice dropped. "Maybe one day …" He released a long breath. "Maybe we'll have the time for you to enlighten me." The hand that had remained holding mine this entire time tightened briefly before letting go.

A moment later, he was gone.

NINETEEN

Some time later, I sat in a sunny corner of the atrium-like lobby, handbag and gloves in my lap, one ankle primly tucked behind the other as I waited. Watched the ebb and flow of the hotel guests, playing my game of creating stories. Like that man—the one who appeared to be in his late thirties, wearing a not-quite-perfectly tailored suit, glancing about—neither obvious tourist nor in familiar surroundings. In from the suburbs then, to experience how the other half lived, or—

Well then. Judging by the cat-eyed brunette who had just joined him, wearing a scandalously short Mondrian-patterned A-line and high white boots, it was not so much seeing how the other half lived as choosing somewhere completely off the typically beaten path. At least for him, given the glint of gold on his ring finger. He was either not terribly wise or that was part of the thrill. The ability to get away with it.

I looked away as they walked past—away from the desperate hold she maintained on his arm, away from the features that beneath the teased and sharply angled bob, the heavy eyeliner and fashionably pale lipstick, were even younger than I'd assumed. There was no real mystery or magic to be created in that story.

Oddly disquieted now, I was grateful to hear the quiet hiss of the elevator doors opening, diverting my attention. An instant later, a familiar pair of white miniature poodles bounded out, rhinestone-studded turquoise collars sparkling as they yapped with excitement, dribbling urine as they dragged along a hapless bellman. As they made a beeline toward me, their white-haired owner snapped, "Do *not* allow them near her. She's that menace who nearly killed them yesterday. In fact, I wish to speak to someone about having her removed from the premises immediately."

"What the hell?"

I stood, turning my back on the dogs and their disagreeable owner who had poor Mr. Gordon cornered, and faced Jack. While still somewhat pale, he looked a great deal better than he had when he'd left my suite. At least one of us had managed more sleep.

"Natalia?" Grasping me by the arm, he led me to a nearby alcove. "What are you still doing here?"

"Waiting for you."

"What—why?"

I gripped my handbag tightly, the metal frame digging into my palms. "Because implicit in that forty-eight hour ultimatum you gave Ava, was that I would also be there. That was the whole point, was it not?" My voice rose slightly in pitch with each word. Taking a deep breath, I continued more steadily, "How can you give her another opportunity if I'm no longer around?"

"No. You have your out. You don't want to do this. Hell, *I* don't want you to do this."

"I have to."

He closed his eyes briefly, then opened them again, his stare hard and intent. "No. You don't. Go home, Natalia. Just … go home."

"No."

"Jesus *Christ*." The hand on my arm tightened as he said, "Look, I'll buy you a ticket to wherever the hell you want if you don't want to go back to New York. But for God's sake, Natalia, *go*. You're free."

I stood there silently, taking in the dark slashes of color painting the skin drawn tight across his cheekbones, the almost feral expression in his eyes as he spoke of freedom. He stood there, waiting, as did I. Wondering, who would break first? And the longer we stood there, the further his expression gradually evolved, from anger, to bemusement, to finally, something approaching acceptance. And overlying the acceptance, a distinct air of relief. My guess had been correct.

"Why?"

"I wish I knew." A lie. I did know. At least that it was something beyond pity. Jack had to sense that as well, because if he thought I was driven merely by pity, he would put up more of a fight or simply walk away without a backward glance.

"What I should do," he grumbled as he shifted his hand to my back to guide me through the lobby and outside to where the valet waited with the idling Jaguar, "is take you and put you on an airplane myself and wait until the damned thing's airborne."

"But you won't."

"No. I won't." After assisting me into the car, rather than close the door he leaned down, so close I could feel the heat from his body. "On one condition."

I paused in the midst of tying a scarf over my hair. "What's that?"

He waited until we'd pulled away from the hotel and turned onto the highway to answer. "Soon—not right now, but soon—I *am* going to ask you again what I said yesterday that hurt you." His fingers tightened on the gearshift as he accelerated, the wind rushing through the convertible with a high-pitched whine. But not so loud it masked his voice or the steel underlying each word. "And you're going to tell me, no evasion, no bullshit."

"But—"

"No. No questions or arguments or logical reasoning, Natalia. I don't want to hear it. Either you agree right now that you'll tell me or I'm turning around and taking you straight to the airport."

"Why?"

"Doesn't matter. Those are my conditions, take it or leave it."

"Fine." I sighed impatiently.

My terse agreement seemed to satisfy him, at least until we arrived at Ava's. Killing the engine, he leaned his head back against the seat and stared up into the trees. Patches of light penetrated the dense foliage, dappling his face and lending shadows to his profile that made it even more difficult than usual to read his expression.

"When I ask," he said, as if speaking to the trees, "and you tell me, then, I'll tell you why it's so important. I promise."

The shadows shifted as he turned his head. Sitting up, he removed his sunglasses, then reached across the short distance between us to remove mine, finding and holding my gaze. "I keep my promises, Natalia. No matter what happens, remember that."

I nodded, but wasn't sure if he even saw, since he'd already exited the car, swiftly rounding the hood to open my door. Together, we climbed the steps, pausing in front of the enormous bronze doors and exchanging a telling glance.

His hand hovering over the dome-shaped doorbell, he said, "Déjà vu all over again."

He waited for my nod before pressing down. From deep within the house, the Westminster chimes rang, once, then again, as Jack pressed the dome once more. And after waiting a minute or two, both of us listening for the sounds of footsteps or a voice, calling to come in or go away and hearing nothing, ringing a third time.

"Dammit," he sighed, slamming the flat of his hand against the door, stumbling as it swung open.

"Jack—" Instinctively, I reached out to steady him, my nails digging into his arm as suddenly it was me who needed his support, stunned into weak-kneed silence by what greeted us.

WHORE

Scrawled in menacing red across the once-pristine white walls of the foyer. Over and over, overlapping with other, even uglier, words.

Bitch … slut …

Words I'd first heard tittered in Spanish by the boys I'd known growing up, attempting to impress each other and shock the girls.

Cunt … cocksucker …

Words hissed in my ear by those loathsome Concord boys— titillating for them, humiliating for me as they lay over me or held my head, forcing—

"*Madre santisma.*" I swallowed hard, tried to blink away the heat and prickling sensation as those impossibly red letters blurred, then sharpened, then blurred again. Just words, I reminded myself. They weren't probing or groping or forcing me to their will. They were merely words. Nothing more than that.

Nothing more than that, I kept repeating to myself as Jack abruptly turned me away, his hand gripping the back of my neck as he held my head to his shoulder. A stunned, *"Jesus,"* emerged on the tail end of ragged breath, hovering above my head.

"Just words, Jack," I whispered against his shirt. Perhaps with saying it out loud I might be able to draw a full breath without feeling the suffocating pressure on my chest. Stupid words. Nevertheless, I kept my face buried against his shoulder, not quite ready to face them again.

"She could have called. Told me she wanted another writer. To go to hell. God knows, she's done it before." His voice had steadied, grown harder even as he rocked back and forth in a soothing motion. "There was no reason to do this. None." Pushing away from me, he snapped, "That's it. This is over."

"Jack—"

He pulled free from my grasp, pointing back to the front door as he charged down the floating staircase. "Wait for me in the car. I mean it."

Not an option. And now was not the time to explain I didn't need to be coddled. That at this point, we were in this together. I descended the stairs behind him, ignoring his warnings of, "Natalia, no—don't."

It was gallant, but what more could there possibly be? I was inured to more of the same. Was even able to breathe fairly naturally as I confronted more of the same filthy words scribbled across the white walls downstairs. Remained steady enough to disregard the graffiti in lieu of the unexpected sight of dozens of small silver lipstick cases lined up with a uniform precision along the long edge of the pool.

"Ava, wherever you're hiding, get the hell out here. "

Jack's voice echoed throughout the enormous room as he pushed open the various doors while I crouched down by the cases, picking them up, one by one. All of them identical, etched with delicate scrollwork and capped with tiny pearls and rhinestones. Memory warred with recognition as I traced the designs with a trembling fingertip. I knew these cases. Van Cleef & Arpels had made them for Revlon—an exclusive, highly sought-after item several years back, the glossy advertisements splashed across the pages of all the fashion magazines showing the numbered silver cases nestled inside red-velvet lined presentation boxes.

Fit for royalty, that spoiled, long-ago girl had daydreamed.

And adding to the appeal, the cases were so very *French*.

After listening to my endless burbling over how lovely they were, how special, how I wished and wanted and if *only*—Nico had arrived home from one of his trips to the States, greeting me with an indulgent smile as he presented me with a beautifully wrapped package. I could recall the thrill I'd experienced lifting the lid on the small box. So elegant—so unique. Something not everyone could have.

To see so many of them gathered in one place was unnerving. Verging on obscene. They sat there, pristine and polished, as if never handled, until removing the cap from one exposed the ravaged remains of a once-vibrant lipstick. The same dramatic red she'd worn the other day. The same shade as what was smeared across the walls. Slowly, I removed the caps from several more cases—all the same color—ground down to waxy nubs.

So immersed had I been in the mystery of the cases, that it only gradually dawned that the echo of Jack's voice had faded into an overwhelming silence. The tiny hairs on my arm prickled as gooseflesh rose along my skin.

"Jack?"

I began following the same path I'd seen him take, poking my head into the various open doors leading from the room. "Jack?"

"In here."

Not terribly loud, but spoken into the eerie silence, it was as effective as a shout. And despite the flat monotone, or perhaps because of it, it was clear to me there was something very wrong.

I pushed open the door at the far end of the room—the one behind which Ava had disappeared that first day, revealing a dazzling bedroom suite. Nearly two walls of spotless glass, overlooking that spectacular view, while in the center of the expansive space sat the perfectly made bed, sumptuously dressed in white and silver. Mirrored dressers played host to portraits of Ava—covers from Look and Photoplay that should have been vibrant with color, rendered instead in varying shades of black and white—polished silver frames artfully positioned on the immaculate surfaces. Even the closet, its mirrored doors folded open, revealed perfectly organized and aligned contents, the clothing in varying shades of white and ivory and silver hanging on identical white satin-padded hangers, the distances between them even and uniform. It was overwhelmingly sparkling and beautiful and very, very wrong. In this organic home perched above the wildness of the sea the almost militaristic uniformity hit a discordant note.

A shiver of unease skittered down my spine as I followed the trail of footsteps left in the deep plush of the white carpet, uncertain of what I would find as I crossed the threshold into the adjoining bathroom. Would it be more of the chaos that had initially greeted us or more of the sterile surroundings?

It was neither and both.

Another stunning white and silver room, the vanity and walls as immaculate and meticulously arranged as in the bedroom.

"*Dios mío ...*"

I crouched beside Jack, reaching for one of the dozens of photographs scattered about.

Ava. Wearing a mink coat and nothing else, cavorting in the surf, a long flash of leg, the generous curve of a breast revealed as she coyly glanced over a shoulder. The photo shoot she'd boasted of to Jack. Wild and free and unbound by any social conventions. Or so she'd claimed.

Those stunning, full-color photographs were strewn across the white floor like so much oversized confetti. Scrawled with the same words as on the walls, some of them so thickly scribbled over it was impossible to decipher what the image below was, slashes of red bleeding onto the marble where she'd lost control. More disturbing than those, even, were the ones that had been cut, sliced almost through in places, ravaging her face and body with angry slashes.

A sheet of heavy cream stationary stood out among the photographs with a single, elegantly scripted line.

Here are a set of proofs darling—you are, as always, a goddess. –D

Jack slumped heavily against the side of the tub, toppling several more of the silver lipstick cases she'd left lining its edge.

I sat beside him, moving another photograph—the mink spread on the sand like a luxurious blanket, Ava, lying face down, one leg swinging idly in the air, a lurid red *slut* written down her bare back and across her buttocks—out of the way. "What's going on?"

"More of the same. Except she's getting worse."

"What? What do you mean?" And where had she gone? Because it was abundantly clear she wasn't here. Not because she'd yet to appear, but because something in Jack's face, in the weariness evident in his tone and the curve of his neck as he looked back down at the ruined photos, spoke of a knowledge he'd rather not have.

"Jack, where *is* she?"

"Vegas. At least, that's where she'll have gone first. And here we fucking go again." He rose, toeing the pictures aside as he extended a hand to help me up. "Come on, let's go. I can make arrangements for you to catch a flight home before I leave."

"Don't be an idiot." I grasped his hand and allowed him to pull me to my feet. "Do you really think I would leave *now*? Leave you to deal with this by yourself?"

"I'm used to it."

Again, weariness dominated his voice, dulled the light in his eyes, reinforcing that sensation I'd tried to fight earlier this morning. That I'd finally had to give in to. That inescapable sensation of *wanting*...

I wanted to help. Knew that Jack Roemer, a man who wanted for nothing, needed something I could give.

"Jack, please."

"God!" The response was as unexpected as the sharp bark of laughter as he sank to the edge of the tub. He sent the remaining lipstick cases clattering across the floor with an angry swipe before he thrust both hands into his hair, cradling his forehead in his palms. "God," he repeated, so softly I more felt the word than actually heard it.

I crouched down in front of him. "What?"

His hands dropped away as he looked up. "You need to go home."

Studying his face as intently as he was studying mine, I chose my words carefully. "Earlier ... when you told me to leave, you said it was so I could be free." I held up a hand. "I know you meant of my obligations to my family. But Jack, you can't ask me to leave this behind and pretend it doesn't exist. I know it would be easier—for both of us—if I could. But I can't. Not knowing what I know."

"And what, exactly, do you know?" His voice was dull and flat.

"That whatever this is, you've done it alone for a very long time."

A gut instinct guess, but the right one, judging by the spark of recognition—faint, yet undeniably there—that lit those faun's eyes. "Please—" I stood and extended a hand. "Let me help you."

Staring at it as if mesmerized, he murmured, "You say please. And she never has."

"I'm not her."

"I know." Slowly, he took my hand and stood. "I know."

TWENTY

"Why Las Vegas?"

"Because that's where she always goes first." He spared me a glance as he shifted and accelerated past a ponderous farm truck loaded with crates of chickens, the Jaguar's powerful engine overwhelming their outraged squawking. My back molded itself to the leather seat at the sudden change in speed, my breath catching at the alien landscape unfurling before us as we broke free of the truck's shadow. A seemingly endless sweep interrupted only by patches of scrub or the occasional gnarled tree and washed in shades of gold and brown, this desert struck me with the same sense of unease as the urban jungle of New York. Extraordinary, beautiful in its own unique way, but not particularly comfortable and more than a little bit foreboding. Echoing my feelings since our hurried departure from Malibu. Other than heading toward Las Vegas, I had no idea what we were doing and Jack wasn't exactly being forthcoming. There was only the one question I wanted answered—I simply wanted to know *why?* Of course, there were infinite variations. Why Vegas? Why did she behave so erratically? Why was it not only condoned, but apparently encouraged? And *why* did Jack feel so compelled to come to her rescue, because that's exactly what this was. A mission to come to her rescue—one he'd so obviously done many times before.

What was I missing?

Two questions, then.

In a matter of moments, the snorting, backfiring truck was reduced to a dot in the sideview mirror, leaving us alone on the highway with only the growl of the car's engine and the rush of the wind as accompaniment. Both more than adequate excuses for avoiding further conversation which I expected Jack to take advantage of. But he surprised me, sending another sidelong glance my direction, accompanied by a soft, resigned laugh.

"The wheels in that head of yours—they're going fast and furious."

"I—" I ground my teeth as I looked away, aggravated at the continued transparency I couldn't seem to help around him, and resolutely focused my attention on the scenery.

"So fascinating to see your mind work—I wonder if maybe that's why I don't offer everything up right off the bat."

"I suspect it's more that you're not accustomed to being held accountable to anyone else."

"Not true. Although I understand how you might think that."

"Really?" I crossed my arms, aware that I no doubt looked—and sounded—like a petulant girl. "When was the last time anyone held you accountable? For anything?"

"Well, unless it was a liquor-soaked hallucination, I seem to recall you doing a fairly admirable job of doing just that. Telling me how much I was going to regret my actions." With the road a straight, unbroken ribbon ahead of us, he was able to turn and face me, head on, one questioning eyebrow raised.

"So you remember?"

"Bits and pieces are dribbling back." He returned his attention to the road, one hand casually propped on the spokes of the steering wheel. "Not enough to let you—or me—off the hook, however."

Sighing, I turned to stare out the window. Once again he'd seen right through me. Seen the momentary hope, imagining I wouldn't have to fulfill my end of our agreement and tell him what he'd said. Because I just wanted to forget. Wanted to push not simply Jack's words, but all of it—the boys, the money, the discovery that my secrets hadn't been quite so secret—as much to the back of my mind as possible. I had no illusions I'd ever be able to completely forget. But perhaps with time and distance, the humiliation and pain might at least fade to something manageable—the type of specter that only crept up on the occasional dark night. I could be satisfied with that.

"You've been holding me accountable almost since the moment we met."

I turned to study his profile, tried to see past the deepening twilight and the shadows it cast across the proud, set lines of his face—revealing no sign that he'd spoken. Clearly, I'd imagined those words. After all, I was exhausted. And if I'd slept more than three hours out of the previous twenty-four, that would be a generous estimation. I rubbed my eyes with the tips of thumb and forefinger, blinked them rapidly, trying to wash away the grittiness. But each blink felt heavier and slower, the dark behind my lids so seductive, drawing me further in. Tempting me with promises of calm and a sweet, all-encompassing warmth.

"Natalia, wake up. We're here."

"¿Qué—?" I blinked again, squinting against the brilliant glare piercing the dark. Who'd turned on the lights? I hated being shocked awake—needed to ease into consciousness. Nico knew that. "No. Dejame." I buried my head in my pillow.

"We're in Vegas, sweetheart." The low voice rumbled across my skin, ruffled the hair along my forehead. "You need to wake up."

Vegas? My eyes snapped open, taking in the stubbled underside of jaw, inhaled the distinctive male scents of deodorant overlaid with a hint of clean sweat, my sleep-fogged brain finally recognizing that my comfortable pillow was in fact, Jack's shoulder.

"Oh … I—"

I struggled to sit up, feeling as if I was slogging through molasses, slowly realizing it was at least in part because of the weight of Jack's arm across my shoulders.

His hand gently squeezed my upper arm. "It's all right. You just fell asleep for a while. You needed it."

"Yes, but—" My skin rippled with gooseflesh as I experienced more of the odd heightened awareness unique to those first moments of wakefulness—cotton, smooth and warm beneath my palm, the drag of his hand across my shoulders and the skin of my neck as his hold relaxed and I was able to straighten. "It had to have been uncomfortable."

"It was fine." A surprising grin chased the shadows from his face. "Do you know you talk in your sleep?"

I pretended nonchalance, smoothing stray wisps of hair away from my face, trying to tuck them into place. "Yes." Nico used to tease me, saying he'd one day unearth all my secrets. Knowing it for a joke. We both knew I had no secrets—not from him.

"Relax—you didn't say anything incriminating. I don't think." Rolling his shoulders, he stretched, straightening his arms against the steering wheel. "It was mostly Spanish."

Once again the lines between my two worlds blurred, becoming ever more indistinguishable between what had once been real from that which had been fashioned from a few key details and sheer imagination. Strangely fitting that we were headed into the heart of a place touted as the ultimate fantasyland, rising improbably from barren desert and spawning grandiose dreams. Where even the names—Riviera, Flamingo, Sands, Stardust—inspired images of vibrant, exotic locales. Where visitors could pretend to be anything—could *be* anyone. All it required was a favorable pull, a lucky roll, or a practiced bluff.

An illusion that could shatter just as quickly.

Jack glanced over. "Are you all right?"

"I'm fine." I hugged my elbows, trying to contain the tremors that shook my body, grateful that for once, he didn't seem to be noticing—wasn't looking straight through me. I wasn't up to explaining something I couldn't even comprehend beyond the refrains of *who are you, really?* and *what are you doing here?* Hearing endless variations on *why?* with its multitudes of meaning. As if the questions weren't ones I'd asked myself a thousand times already.

At the northernmost end of the Strip, just past the Sahara with its gaudy Arabian Nights-styled porte-cochère, Jack made a turn into a long circular driveway, its entrance simply marked by a pair of towering palms constructed completely from glass and white lights. The moment we rolled to a stop in front of the large, sprawling white building, a uniformed valet opened my door, offering a hand.

"Welcome to The Royal Palms, will you be staying with us or visiting the casino?"

"Not sure yet." Jack had already rounded the front of the car, cutting in front of the valet to help me himself. A supporting hand cupped my elbow as I subtly stretched, working out the kinks.

"Oh, Mr. Roemer, of course—we've been expecting you. Mr. Campisi will be alerted to your arrival and meet you in the penthouse shortly."

Jack nodded and handed the bellman who'd greeted us a couple of folded bills. Drawing my hand through his arm, he led us through the heavy iron and glass doors and into yet another new world—one that resonated with a shocking echo. The men, all sleek, pomaded hair and snowy dinner jackets, the women on their arms clad in lamé cocktail dresses and richly beaded gowns, capped by furs and jewels and elaborate lacquered updos. Exuding the air of exotic, privileged creatures as they strolled past vibrant hibiscus and bougainvillea, breathed in the heavy, jasmine-scented air while a sultry bossa nova wafted from hidden speakers. As if drawn by some unseen force, I drifted away from Jack, running a fingertip along a glossy leaf, a scrolled railing—taking the ambience in with a distant eye, such as one might observe an artistic masterpiece.

So surprising, this lush and elegant setting, defying both the arid desert and garish nightlife beyond its boundaries. So familiar.

Even with no intent of ever returning, the memories had lived within me. A whisper of the girl I'd been shadowing my movements among the concrete and metal and cold angles of New York, entreating me to remember home. To hold it close. Dancing with Jack on the dreamy, moonlit patio of the Beverly Hills Hotel had come close, draping itself around me with a melancholy sweetness, but this—

So close. As close to perfect as it could be, really, recapturing the tropical surroundings of my youth. And yet—

Completely, utterly alien.

It no longer fit.

Moreover, I no longer *wanted* it to fit.

"How unexpected," I said softly. And frightening.

"I know."

I understood Jack meant the unexpected quiet opulence surrounding us. Remarkably prescient though he might be where I was concerned, there was no way he could possibly know the magnitude of the thoughts tumbling one after another in my head. With one final glance over my shoulder, I allowed him to lead us into a gleaming mirrored elevator with tiny inset lights, reflecting like so many brilliant stars.

"Dante wanted to create something unique, even by Vegas standards. To be ... more." He nodded at the elevator operator, another man who obviously recognized him.

"What, beyond being Ava's ex-husband, does he have to do with all of this, Jack?" I replied in a quiet undertone as the operator removed a small brass key from his pocket and inserted it beside one of the three buttons marked PH. They'd been divorced for over five years, as I recalled from Ava's biographical information, but Dante was the first person Jack had called when she'd failed to show up in Beverly Hills and now, Vegas had been the first—the only—destination considered after she'd disappeared. Why?

"Just a few minutes more. I promise."

I looked away, but no matter where my gaze landed, I couldn't escape the doubts roiling through my mind, the mirrors lining the elevator car clearly reflecting the tension holding my shoulders rigid. Yet, those same mirrors just as clearly exposed hope. It flickered amidst the shadows cast by the soft gold light wavering across my face as my reflection appeared to sway toward him.

You want to trust him, the reflection seemed to say. *He's sworn he keeps his promises.*

Well then, he'd have opportunity to prove himself an honest man. And provided yet another moment for me to question my own folly in insisting on accompanying him.

After a smooth, swift ride, the doors silently slid open directly into a living area of spare elegance—cool marble and dark woods, the walls painted a deep, claret red. Wide, panoramic windows overlooked not the Strip, as one might have expected, but rather, the quieter lights of the city away from its signature thoroughfare.

Dante's apartment. For it made perfect sense that a man who created and lived the majority of his life against the decadence that defined the public spaces downstairs would desire something markedly different for his private quarters. Similar to Remy's appetite for simple foods after a day spent immersed in heavy cream sauces and rich ingredients.

Oh, Remy.

When was the last time I'd thought of him?

It took a moment to recall that it hadn't been since that lovely walk on the beach. My moment out of time, pretending at being young and carefree. Only yesterday morning, but with what felt like months' worth of experiences and events since then. I felt so removed from that girl. And ever more from the girl who'd departed New York a scant week before.

"I apologize it's not as spectacular as it would be from the other side, but a good owner always lets the guests believe they're getting the best we've got to offer."

Jack turned, a broad smile erasing miles of road and worry that had shadowed him since Malibu. "Dante."

"It's been too long, brother." The other man pulled Jack into a hard embrace that to my surprise, was not only welcomed, but returned. "You keep promising you'll come see me for an actual vacation."

Jack pulled back, still smiling, but with the light in his eyes dimmed. "Maybe one of these days I'll actually be able to take one."

"Hell, you know you're preaching to the choir," he replied. After a final affectionate pat to Jack's cheek, he shifted his attention to me. "Dante Campisi," he said simply, taking my hand in both of his. Exceptionally warm and pleasantly rough with calluses that even regular manicures couldn't completely eradicate, the rest of the man appeared to be a study of similar contrasts. A rugged man's man in his forties, clad in a tailored dinner jacket that couldn't quite disguise a burly body that spoke of the same hard, physical labor that had created the calluses. And while his voice was smooth and cultured, it was underscored with a definite New York flavor I suspected he went to no particular pains to mask. Dark blond hair touched with the beginnings of silver at the temples, green eyes and deep dimples bracketing a full mouth spoke to a conventional handsomeness—at least, until one noticed the crooked bridge of the nose, the thin scar bisecting one eyebrow, and the tiny chip in a tooth glimpsed during a smile that was equal parts welcoming and appraising.

At first glance, it was obvious what Ava would have seen in him. Equally as obvious as what would have driven them apart. And once again begged the question, what, exactly, continued to draw them together?

Patience.

Those cool green eyes studied me, his hands remaining loosely clasped around mine as if everything he was unable to see, he could somehow physically absorb via that simple touch. Finally releasing my hand he said, "So—you're Natalia San Martín."

Stunned, I turned to Jack who shrugged and smiled apologetically. "I should have asked which you preferred."

"It's all right," I said slowly, searching Jack's gaze. "It is my name."

What else had Jack told him? What had Ava told him? Because clearly, contained within that loose grasp, behind that long, considered stare, I could tell ... he knew. He knew *everything.*

Jack closed the distance between us, leaning in until his forehead nearly touched mine. "I can't think of you as anyone else now. But tell me if I overstep my bounds again."

As I nodded, Dante's voice broke in, piercing the bubble that had so quickly formed around us. "Well, hell. No wonder Ava's so hot under the collar." He stood beside a sleek curved mahogany credenza, dropping ice into cut-crystal tumblers and pouring a generous measure of Scotch into each. His sharp gaze rested briefly on my face as he handed me a glass before shifting to Jack, studying him as intently as he'd studied me.

"She's still here?" Jack sounded oddly surprised as he accepted the glass from Dante, glancing down as if tempted before setting it aside on a small chrome and glass table. If he hadn't expected to find her, then what were we doing here?

Patience...

"Nah—took off this morning. Predictably. And what I mean is that she was good and furious, my friend." Raising his glass slightly, he murmured, "*Cent'anni,*" before taking a sip and continuing. "On the surface, it was all about your having hired Natalia. Said you were mocking her ambitions—bringing in someone with barely a high school education. How dare you consider someone so supremely unqualified." His voice rose in an uncanny impersonation before dropping back to its normal register. "Along with some commentary about the true nature of your relationship, delivered in language that, out of respect for our guest, I won't repeat here."

"Appreciated, but not necessary." Giving up, Jack reached for his abandoned glass and tossed back its contents in one swallow. "She made herself perfectly clear when we last saw her."

"In other words, typical Ava."

"Yes and no," Jack replied as he crossed to the bar and refilled his glass. "She's getting worse, Dante, and I'm not going to stand for it anymore. She can't keep treating people like they're just so much garbage and expect there not to be consequences. She can't expect that I'll fix it every goddamned time. I'm tired of it."

"Sounds then, like we need to have a talk, brother." Dante's gaze shifted from Jack to me, then back to Jack once again. "Starting with what you're obviously not seeing."

Jack's eyebrows lifted as he paused with the glass halfway to his lips. "Come again?"

Dante's smile was a disarming flash of dimples and very white teeth that had no doubt lulled more than one opponent into a false sense of complacency. Just as quickly, that expression evolved into something far more shrewd and calculating.

"Whatever relationship you two do or don't have, it still stands that for the first time in your life you put yourself ahead of Ava.

Worse still, as far as she's concerned, you put another woman ahead of her."

The ice in the glass shifted with the visible tremor of Jack's hand though his voice remained steady. "So I did."

Dante's smile deepened. "I gotta tell you, it's about damned time."

TWENTY-ONE

"The hotel business—she's a harsh mistress, you know? Demands everything, blood and bone and soul, and Ava, she won't come second to nothing or no one." With a casual nod, Dante dismissed the waiter who'd delivered our meal and had remained, discreetly serving each course as we'd leisurely eaten, Jack and Dante catching up in that way men had, with anecdotes exchanged in the verbal shorthand of long acquaintance, only the central theme wasn't sporting events or common business ventures.

Even lacking a physical presence, Ava managed to be the undisputed center of attention.

Reverting to form, I'd attempted to remain silent and listen, to file the facts gleaned for later incorporation into this odd tapestry, except Jack wouldn't allow it. Over and over again, he deferred to me for corroboration of facts or asking my opinion or interpretation of the situation, as if seeking reassurance that the whole debacle had unfolded as he recalled and wasn't just some twisted figment of his imagination. Or Ava's.

As the waiter silently retreated to the apartment's kitchen, Dante took over the task of pouring coffee himself, his large, work-roughened hands deft and sure with the china. "Worked my way in this business from the ground up," he commented with a smile as he handed me a delicate platinum-edged cup balanced on a matching saucer. "There's nothing in this industry I haven't done. Best way to be a boss, my pop always said. How could I tell people what to do if I didn't know how to do it myself? Generally served with a slap upside the back of my stubborn head as I complained about another shift washing dishes at our diner."

He crossed to the large window overlooking the expansive nighttime vista of the "real Las Vegas" as he'd not-so-off-handedly mentioned over dinner. The Vegas where the fantasy ended. A fascinating man, this Dante Campisi, devoting his entire life to building dreams and fantasies, while simultaneously turning his back on the façade he was so adept at creating. Remaining attached to a woman who was the embodiment of every man's fantasy—not for the façade she presented to the world, but for the real woman lurking beneath, well aware of the insecurities and issues that clearly transcended mere idiosyncrasy.

As Jack led me from the dining table to one of the long sofas facing the view, Dante remained by the window, thoughtfully sipping his coffee. "With Ava, you've got to give her all of you and even then, it's a crap shoot. But I live in Vegas for a reason, right?" His shoulder lifted in a casual shrug at odds with the stark expression reflecting back from the window. "I would've devoted everything to her and let the business go to hell if I thought I had a shot at winning it all."

He turned away from the window, his face smoothed into the practiced lines of the genial hotelier. "But her folks, they would've backed me into a corner, bled me dry, and Ava—" His gaze met Jack's. "She would've been Ava and I would've ended up with nothing."

Beside me, Jack tensed. "I'm sorry I didn't know more about that when it was happening."

"I've never once held you responsible for it, Jack, you know that."

"I know, but if I'd *known*—"

"You'd have done what?" Dante withdrew a silver case from his inside pocket and removed a thin, dark cigar. Smoothly lighting up and blowing out a stream of fragrant smoke he continued, "What *could* you have done? You were still a kid, in law school, living your life for once, fighting for your own causes."

I remained very still, fighting the urge to remove the delicate coffee cup from Jack's white-knuckled grip before it shattered.

"Jack."

It took a moment before I realized that while Dante had addressed Jack, his intent gaze was fixed on me.

Following his gaze, Jack made a visible effort at relaxing, shaking his head and presumably, shaking himself free of memories. "I'm sorry, Natalia—old history. Has a way of still getting to me."

"Perhaps I should—" Leave, I was about to say. Let them talk and figure out what the next step should be without having to be circumspect on my behalf. But where could I go? Hours since we'd arrived and I *still* had no idea what we were doing here.

"You should have another coffee, then we'll get you settled in for the night." Ever the practiced host, Dante had brought the coffee service over to the low mahogany table positioned before the sofa. "Forgive my bluntness, but you two look like hammered shit and it's clear your nerves are shot. Hitting the road tonight isn't likely to gain you any real ground, so staying's the best option, don't you think?" Offered as a question, begging an opinion, but not. Pulling a recessed drawer from the table, he pressed a button; an instant later, our waiter appeared from the kitchen.

"Call down to valet, have them send the young lady and gentleman's bags up here." A man accustomed to calling the shots, albeit in a polished, urbane, and oh-so-understated way. So similar, he and Jack.

"Yes sir."

After the waiter had disappeared as quietly and efficiently as he'd appeared, Dante continued refilling the coffee cups while resuming the thread of conversation. Clarifying the "old history" for the newcomer.

"Ava's parents thought I was trash. Just some guinea wiseguy. I wasn't, at least not the wiseguy part," he clarified. "But in the neighborhood I grew up in, almost everyone was connected to someone who knew someone or was someone and maybe every now and again, you ran an errand for one of the guys in order to pick up a nickel or a dime tip. That's all. But for her folks, that was more than enough to tar me with the same brush as if I took guys' kneecaps out every Sunday after Mass. Definitely not good enough for Ava. Or rather, not good enough to be associated with the family. They've never given a rat's ass whether anything was good for Ava or not—just how it reflected on the family."

Relaxing back into the sofa cushions, he casually crossed one leg over the other, the light playing across the toe of his polished dress shoe with nervous intensity. "In that way, they're just as bad as the people they accused me of rolling in the gutter with."

"They threatened Dante." Jack's voice was tight and strained with the tension that Dante's relaxed pose attempted to mask. "Threatened his business. Divorce Ava and any obstacles he'd been encountering would mysteriously disappear."

Recognizing their telling me this was tantamount to invitation, I finally succumbed. "So what happened?"

"I told them to go to hell. This is my world, not theirs. And just because I'm not in bed with any of the families back east doesn't mean I'm not willing to play just as dirty as they do to protect what's mine. At the same time, by that point I also knew there was something wrong—not just with our marriage, but with Ava. Something dark I couldn't fix or make better. There wasn't a jewel or fur or car fancy or expensive enough—nothing I could say or do. It didn't have a damned thing to do with how I felt and everything to do with something broken inside her."

Dante studied the column of ash balanced on the edge of his cigar before leaning forward and flicking it into the cut crystal dish on the table. "I've always been pretty good at knowing when to cut bait, so I let myself get absorbed in work, fighting the wolves scratching at the door, and let her think she was coming second. Let her decide to leave in that way she's got. That it's sad and tragic, but she just needed more than I could possibly give her and maybe someday, I could understand and we could end up friends."

He held his hands up in a gesture of surrender, yet the tip of the cigar balanced between two fingers glowed red and defiant. "It did let us stay friends in the end. Her thinking it was all her idea." A wistful half-smile crossed his face. "And because we're still friends, I always hoped that maybe … someday, she'd be better and we could—"

The slow shaking of Jack's head only served to deepen Dante's smile. "I know, brother. I know. But a man's got to have dreams. It's what's gotten me this far."

"Dreams." Jack's head jerked involuntarily with the harsh bark of laughter that escaped. "I don't even know what those are anymore."

Dante's steady, appraising gaze studied Jack. "I wouldn't be so sure about that."

• • •

"So what now?"

Jack paced the length of the elegantly appointed guest room to which Dante had escorted me, picking up framed photographs and decorative baubles and putting them down without even glancing at them. "What now should be my getting you on a plane first thing tomorrow and off to the destination of your choice. How do you feel about Tahiti?"

I busied myself removing pins from my hair, loosening it from the confines of the French twist in which it had remained for far too many hours. "This has an all-too-familiar ring to it."

"Natalia, it's not that I don't want you—"

At Jack's pause, our gazes met in the mirror. "It's not that I don't want your help," he clarified, the distinction subtle, but pointed. "It's just ... I don't want for you to have to deal with this any longer. It's dark and ugly as hell, and you don't need to be dragged further into this. I should have never let it get this far, you don't deserve it—"

"Shut up, Jack." I lowered my head, breaking the hold of his gaze with its lingering pain that I so intimately understood. That haunted us both. I rubbed the back of my neck, trying to loosen the tense knots gripping the base.

"You are so goddamned stubborn, Natalia."

My downcast gaze traced the intricate chrome scrollwork that framed the mirrored vanity tray, attempting to find where it began or ended. "I believe this is what has historically been referred to as the pot calling the kettle black."

"You don't say?"

"I do." I tensed, then relaxed as his hand pushed mine aside, gently massaging the knotted muscles, his sure touch doing a far more effective job than my agitated fumblings. His free hand grasped my waist, holding me steady as the motion of his fingers grew more purposeful, eliciting a deep groan as they dug into a particularly painful spot.

Cool air bathed the skin of my neck as the heavy mass of my hair was moved aside, threads of heightened sensation winding down my spine as Jack's mouth replaced his fingers.

"Jack—"

His hands fisted on my hips, twisting in the fabric of my skirt. "You should tell me to stop." His breath fanned across my neck and teased the rim of my ear, soft as the brush of goose down. He was right—I should tell him to stop. Ignore the tension coiling deep within, making my body grow more languid and soft, molding itself to his.

"What if I don't want to?" My voice sounded distant, but with an underlying certainty, echoing the war going on between mind and body. The mind whispering urgently—*run*. The body wanting nothing more than to stay.

I'd followed the dictates of both mind and heart in the past. Never had my body's demands taken precedence.

"You shouldn't say things like that if you don't mean them."

I reached back, his stubble abrading the sensitive skin of my palm. Another layer of awareness awakening long dormant sensations. "I know exactly what I'm saying."

"You're a smart woman, Natalia. You know you should tell me to stop."

"Do I?"

"You should." His hands opened and closed, releasing my skirt only to refasten more firmly on my hips, his fingers splayed wide. His thumbs dug into my lower back, twin points of pressure, hard enough to leave marks.

"Why do you keep trying to push me away?"

The air thrummed with quiet anticipation. Somewhere in the distance, a phone rang, footsteps echoed down the marbled-floored hallways, hushed voices conferred, the rest of the world going on while I waited as if we had endless amounts of time.

"I don't know," he finally said. "I wonder if it's because I'm trying to protect you. Or maybe myself." Even as the words vibrated against my jaw, his lips explored the sensitive hollow beneath my ear and his hold relaxed. I turned, looking up into Jack's face, seeing the doubts, the questions—and the acceptance.

"No matter how hard I push, you won't go." His hands rose to frame my face, his fingers threading through my hair. "Such tremendous loyalty, Natalia."

"If you think this is about loyalty, then you're even more out of practice at this than I am."

Perhaps loyalty might have played a role at one point. Or a sense of obligation, but neither of those sentiments had anything to do with what I was currently feeling.

"Oh, I'll grant you out of practice," he murmured as his head lowered, "but not completely stupid." He stopped with his mouth a hair's breadth away from mine, close enough so I could feel the occasional brush of his lips against mine as he said. "Or maybe I'm exceptionally stupid."

I leaned a fraction of an inch closer, my breath mingling with his. "Shut up, Jack," I whispered a scant second before he finally answered my demands, his fingers tightening once more in my hair as he tilted my head to a better angle, his mouth taking full possession of mine.

Another first kiss, another new experience, another revelation. Where Nico's kisses had been the sweetness of first love and Remy's a finely-honed sensuality, Jack's kisses were raw passion finessed with a heavy sense of want. Passion had him biting into the flesh of my lower lip—want had him soothing the sting with the tip of his tongue, leisurely tasting and exploring. A contrast of emotions that

I recognized and answered with a slow path of kisses along the line of his jaw while my nails dug into his chest.

His hands moved to the front of my suit, smoothly sliding the oversized brocade buttons through their holes, while I worked at the much smaller buttons on his seersucker shirt, fumbling to free his undershirt from his waistband.

"Shh ..." His lips teased my ear as his hands traveled a sensual path along my abdomen and up to my breasts, heating the thin nylon of my slip and making the heavy structure of my bra feel like a torture device. "Slow down. We have all night."

Gradually, he walked me backwards toward the bed, pushing the jacket from my shoulders and shrugging his shirt off along the way. In the room's low light, shadows played across the angular planes of his face, masking his thoughts one moment, revealing much more than I imagine he intended in the next.

"How could I have ever thought you cold?" I murmured as I traced the lines of jaw and mouth, my fingertips drawing a portrait I knew I'd hold close.

He eased us down to the bed, using one hand to brace his body over mine while the other traveled a slow, maddening path up my midsection. "There's a difference between cold and self-control." Reaching the edge of my slip, the tips of his fingers drew idle circles on my skin and hooked into the fabric of slip and bra both, pulling it down a scant inch, revealing a new sliver of skin he christened with a light, fleeting kiss, there and gone and making me want more. "I'd think you, of all people, would understand that."

"I do." Much to my regret. I pulled him to lie completely over me, relishing his weight pressing me into the mattress. "You keep your promises."

He propped himself on an elbow. "I do."

"So promise me."

"What?"

"No control tonight, Jack. Whatever you want, give into it. What I want, you give to me."

"I—"

Whatever he might have said was lost in the sharp knock. "Jack, you in there?"

"*Jesus.*" He leaned his forehead against mine, breathing heavily. "I'm going to kill the son of a bitch, I swear."

I forced one hand to unclench and stroke the tense line of his jaw as a second, more urgent knock rapped against the wood.

"Jack, it's Ava. She just called."

Because what—or who—else could it be?

"*Shit.*" He pushed himself up but before leaving the bed completely, leaned down to press a lingering kiss to my lips. A slice of light briefly illuminated the room, sharply etching his silhouette as he slipped out into the hallway. Turning to my side, I contemplated the carelessly abandoned mass of his shirt and my suit jacket, tangled together on the plush carpet, before rising. Slipping out of my skirt and slip, I pulled a robe on over my remaining undergarments. False propriety was a useless vanity at this point.

However, before I could act on the impulse to follow, the door burst open. Light flooded the room once more, illuminating a weariness and resignation on Jack's face that eradicated the heat and passion so recently revealed.

He took my hands in his, his hold tight and feeling of desperation. My fingers tightened in return, trying to provide the anchor he appeared to need.

"She's in New Orleans."

"I've called the airfield—" Looking past Jack's shoulder I saw Dante's backlit silhouette framed in the doorway. "They're prepping the plane—be ready to leave within the hour."

Confused, I searched Jack's face.

"This is what she does, Natalia." Anger bled through his words, underscoring the weariness that went hand in hand with any mention of Ava. "It's a goddamned stupid game she plays. Needing to know someone cares. That someone will chase after and come rescue her."

"Someone? Or you?"

"I—" His eyes widened slightly. "I'm family," he said, somewhat helplessly.

That much I'd gathered. However, in getting to know Jack—getting to know the man he really was—I suspected it went far deeper than mere familial or legal obligation. This was an obligation with nearly unbreakable strings attached.

"But this is the last time. I can't do this anymore—" His voice tapered off on the final word, anger and exhaustion clearly warring for dominance. "Please come with me?"

"Of course." My response was immediate, unhesitating. "I promised."

"No—" He shook his head. "Not because you promised. The hell with promises and obligations. If that's all it is, then you can stay here. Dante'll make certain you're well taken care of, then after this is over, we—"

"Jack, stop. Just ... *stop*." I took his face in my hands, stilling him, forcing him to look at me. "I *want* to, you idiot."

What was it about this man—the sight of him closing his eyes in such obvious relief, the almost imperceptible shudder that ran through him as he released a breath—that provoked such intense feeling? Not since Carlito had I felt anything approaching this deep-seated urge to protect, this ferocity, except ... what I felt for Jack could hardly be described as sisterly.

It wasn't until after the door closed behind him and I was pulling a fresh change of clothes from my case that I realized—

Throughout the course of this surreal journey he'd been by turns, demanding and imperious. I had pushed and cajoled and argued. But for the first time, he asked.

For the first time, Jack needed me.

TWENTY-TWO

I had to hand it to the woman. Even in flight, running away from or toward whatever demons drove her, no one could deny Ava possessed style. This rumored haunt of hers, the Hotel Monteleone was a grande dame much in the vein of the Paris Ritz or the Dorchester in London, rich with history and no doubt hiding many a high society secret amidst her elegant layers of marble and crystal and brass. Even the chimes of the imperious grandfather clock rang with the weight of all it had observed in its many years overseeing the lobby. Hopefully, Ava's exact whereabouts were a secret with which it would be willing to part.

"How can you be so certain she's here?"

Jack tiredly rolled his head on his neck. "Here, the hotel or here, New Orleans?"

"Both, I suppose."

Outwardly, he was the picture of relaxation as we waited to speak with the hotel's manager, but his narrow-eyed gaze remained alert, constantly skimming the lobby, taking inventory. Observing the early-morning risers eagerly heading toward the intoxicating scents of beignets and chicory-laced coffee weaving their way through the revelers returning after a late night of Big Easy debauchery. So easy to tell apart—one group bright and chattering, sharply dressed in crisp khakis and Madras-plaid Bermudas, the women, chic in colorful headscarves and oversized, white-framed sunglasses, while members of the other group staggered past, wrinkled and reeking, even from a distance, of smoke and alcohol and to my exhausted mind, desperation mingled with regret. Whatever dreams and expectations with which they'd headed out into the night, it would appear, judging by the lined, weary faces passing by, that very few had been met, regardless of whether the search had taken them to brightly lit bars and clubs or the corners of dark, fetid alleyways.

They'd convince themselves otherwise of course. They'd sleep it off and when they awoke, would tell themselves it had been a hell of a night. What could be recalled would be embellished upon, filling in the larger dark holes and spaces. Weaving answers to those lingering questions and doubts. It would become a tale that would leave friends and acquaintances envious and desiring their very own adventure garnished with a paper umbrella and a maraschino cherry.

"She loves New Orleans. The heat and history. The dissolute greatness that's slightly shabby and decaying around the edges. It's relentless and primal and everything hedonistic that she's always wanted to be."

"I rather thought she already was all of those things."

His gaze turned inward, as if examining a truth long held close. "No," he finally said. "Not really. In a way, she's bound by restrictions that are more unyielding than anything society ever tried to impose on her."

He continued studying each individual coming and going through the massive lobby doors, clearly hoping that for once, we would catch a break. Growing perceptibly more tense with each person who wasn't Ava. "As for the hotel—it's beautiful, it's got history, and most importantly if you're Ava, it's got notoriety. Immortalized by the likes of Hemingway and Williams. Faulkner and Capote."

A revelation that should have come as a surprise, yet somehow, didn't. Just another piece of the intricate puzzle that was Ava Roemer. "It would seem to go hand-in-hand with her desire to be immortalized on the page."

"I suppose it does."

"Yet she's never actually written herself."

"It requires actual work." He took my hand in his, turning it palm up and tracing the lines. "And putting more than a bit of yourself on the page. I don't think Ava's capable of that. So she admires people who can. Who can provide other worlds into which she can escape. Almost as much as she envies them."

Gently, he returned my hand to my lap and lifted the demitasse of strong black coffee the receptionist had served along with admiring glances for Jack and honey sweet assurances that her boss would be joining us directly.

"Mr. Roemer. How good to see you again." The tall man with the deep drawl greeted Jack with the same level of familiarity as the employees of Dante's hotel. Exhausted and half-drifting within my own thoughts, I listened idly as it was ascertained that yes, Ava had arrived the day before, had rested a bit before going out for the evening. An evening from which she'd yet to return.

"All we can do at this point is wait her out," Jack said as soon as the door closed on the suite Dante had reserved for us while we were en route from Las Vegas. "See if she comes back."

"If she comes back?" My legs feeling watery and insubstantial, I dropped onto the pale blue raw silk sofa. My fingertips played along the subtle nubs and ridges of the fabric. "Are you saying this might be another dead end?"

"Well, we know she's been here. The question remains, however, whether she'll come back before traipsing off to her next stop." He sat beside me, his head falling back to rest against the sofa's ornate Victorian frame. Despite our hurried departure from Las Vegas, he was as impeccably turned out as ever, his dark blue suit miraculously unwrinkled, his shirt crisp, the cuffs with their elegant gold-and-onyx links showing a precise half-inch past the edges of the jacket's sleeves. Yet, exhaustion also clearly marked him. It was there, in the unfastened top button, the loosened knot of his tie—in the ashen tone to his normally even complexion and the bruising beneath his eyes.

My fingers curled into my palms, restraining myself from reaching out. Regardless of what had—or rather, *almost* had—happened last night, I had no idea where I stood with him. If it was destined to remain nothing more than a moment—there and gone and never to be recaptured.

"What happens next?"

He rubbed tiredly at his eyes, before scrubbing a hand along the side of his face, the sound of his palm rasping against early morning stubble loud in the quiet room. "If she shows up, I deal with her. If she doesn't, I wait until she sends up a flare or a goddamned smoke signal or whatever the hell she's going to use as her royal summons. Then I'll go chasing after her some more until she decides she wants to end this particular round of cat-and-mouse. And then I'll deal with her. And then, that's it. I wasn't kidding when I told Dante I was done. I'll deal with her this one last time, but that's it."

"We."

His eyes slowly opened, their painful redness yet another measure of his exhaustion.

"You asked me to come with you, Jack."

"I did."

"Are you regretting that now?"

He shook his head, his gaze resolutely holding mine. "I regret this whole goddamned mess. But not that you're here with me." My skin prickled with awareness as he took one of my hands and painstakingly uncurled each finger, until finally, his palm lay flush with mine. One moment our fingers would be interlocked, the next, teasing, exploring the play of bone and muscle.

"The suite … it has two bedrooms. I think Dante was trying to make sure your reputation was protected."

I closed my eyes as Jack drew my hand to his mouth, lips and tongue following the same path his fingers had just been taking, exploring every ridge, tracing every subtle line.

"That was thoughtful," I managed on a breathy sigh that should have been embarrassing, but wasn't. He pressed a series of kisses from my hand to my wrist, his teeth dragging lightly along the extraordinarily sensitive skin. "Pity it's not necessary."

His mouth stilled. "Don't do this," he murmured, each word a small, damp puff against my skin. "Not because you think your past somehow makes this easy or meaningless. Not because you think you're a—" He turned my hand over, resting his forehead on the back of my wrist.

"I'm not them, Natalia. Do *not* paint me with that brush."

Slowly, almost of its own volition, my free hand rose. Gently stroked his tawny head—over and over, a touch meant to soothe myself as much as him. Took my time learning the coarse texture of his hair, explored the delicate whorls of an ear, traced the strong curve of his neck. My fingers skimmed along the tense cords before coming to rest against his pulse, its rapid throb exposing anticipation. Through all that, he never moved, his shallow breaths feathering across my skin the only caress he allowed himself as I touched. Never spoke. Just allowed me unrestrained freedom. And choice.

"You're nothing like them."

It was so easy after that. Taking his outstretched hand. Kneeling across from each other on the bed, picking up the threads of all those interrupted moments and weaving them into this one moment. Into this need that had been growing, yet pushed aside time and again—stoked by secrets and missed opportunities and realities that forced us both to hide behind carefully constructed façades. Masks we were finally able to cast aside.

The first languorous caresses gradually ceded to that need—clothes shed, desires revealed with a glance and assented to with hands and lips, skin brushing against skin, a leg hooking over a hip, fingers twisting in hair, teeth digging into the flesh of a shoulder salty with sweat. Only once did he speak, holding himself poised over me, teasing us both for one long suspended moment, a single finger tracing a line down my sternum and around each breast. Concentric circles that left goose bumps in their wake and drew my nipples tighter and heightened every nerve-ending into something fiercely bright and extraordinarily sensitive.

"You're so lovely."

Reverent, yet overlaid with an almost wry wonder that this was finally happening.

And as he lowered himself more fully over me and ever so slowly and carefully into me, reverence gave way to urgency, more words whispered into my ear, layered between his long hissed-out breath and my welcoming sigh. Words I couldn't quite comprehend, other than somewhere deep in the most primitive part of my brain, where they would lie dormant until I was ready to hear them, because now was not the moment. Now was about the movement of our bodies, tentative at first, then surer, each thrust met with an answering parry of *yes* and entreaties of *more*. Admissions of how deeply this had been wanted and assurances that neither of us would break if it went faster and was harder and bordered on pain that broke on a wave of release so long denied.

Over and over, as the sun climbed higher in the sky, shifting the angle of the shadows in the room, we learned the secrets of each other's bodies. The lowering of his voice and rasp of his breath becoming as familiar as my own heartbeat. The tastes and smells of him, salt and tang and clean sweat, and most of all, the feel of him— over me, under me, beside and behind, I spent that day wrapped in him the way I'd once spent entire days wrapped in the warmth and buoyancy of the sea—a feeling I'd long since ceased hoping I'd ever experience again.

But what I treasured most during the endless hours and minutes of that day, were the quiet moments of after. Nonsensical murmurs and fleeting touches giving way to quiet and stillness broken only by the sound of our breathing slowly falling into synchronized rhythm, deep and even and perfectly matched.

TWENTY-THREE

"You promised you'd tell me."

I wanted to pretend I didn't understand what Jack was asking. But we were past those kinds of ruses, he and I. We'd come too far and fought too hard for this one stolen day and the price was that we now knew each other almost too well. But I had no desire to revisit the past hurts and injustices, regardless of how instrumental they'd been in bringing us to this place. All I wanted was to enjoy lying in his arms and believe for just a while longer that this day out of time was real.

"Jack, do we have to—"

"Yes. Because I promised, too. And I don't want us reneging on promises—not to each other."

How I wanted to believe this was real.

"You were drunk," I began, hoping to defer some of the guilt or anger or whatever it was that drove him to know exactly what he'd said that night.

"Yes, and I was a complete bastard." The finely etched curve of his mouth thinned into a straight line as he stared up at the ceiling. "That much I remember. I just can't remember the specifics."

"And I don't *want* to remember this. I just ... I don't."

Except I couldn't forget either.

I hadn't realized I'd closed my eyes against the memories of that night until I felt Jack's touch, cupping my cheek in his hand as his thumb traced the curve of my lashes. I opened my eyes, but after so many hours spent fearlessly lost within the depths of those changeable faun's eyes, learning so much of him, I was terrified at what I might find now. Looking past him, I focused on the Tiffany blue and gold scrolls of the rococo-inspired wallpaper, the frosted wall sconces glowing softly and casting odd, disjointed shadows across the room.

"You were so angry that I was trying to help ..." I released a shaky breath. "You lashed out." The soft light reflected off the glass doorknobs, undulating in crystalline waves across the thick, pale blue carpet. If I listened very hard, I could almost hear the pounding of the surf, the relentless chorus that had underscored those bitter words.

"You told me I lost a piece of my soul every time they ... they—" The words remained trapped in my chest, a hard, painful knot as I twisted the sheet in my fists, unable to continue, though it ultimately proved unnecessary as his sharply indrawn breath attested.

"Every time they spread your legs and threw another dollar at you. And then I wondered what it would take for you to—*Jesus*." His voice faltered, each word emerging more slowly than the one before as he clearly recalled both what was said and what remained unsaid. But we both knew what had been implied. "I wanted you so badly that night. Needed you. And I was so goddamned angry about it, because—"

A heavy breath escaped as he buried his hands in his hair. "What does it matter why I was so angry? I took it out on you in the worst possible way. And here I am, insisting I'm nothing like them. *Fuck*."

I stiffened, resisting his attempts to pull me close, to comfort, to assuage the guilt deepening the fine lines at the corners of his eyes. Rolling from the bed, I pulled the sheet around myself. "I told you—you're nothing like them. And I meant it. I wouldn't be here if I didn't. But that night ..." I stared at his haunted expression, feeling more naked and exposed than ever before. "It's the only time I ever actually *felt* like a whore, Jack."

I retreated to the bathroom just shy of a full run, barely managing to close the door behind myself before I sank to the floor—and proceeded to break. All the slights and insults, the bodies invading mine—the terror and sheer aloneness of the past five years. All the restraints I'd so carefully constructed—shattered into jagged pieces.

Rocking back and forth, soundless, choking sobs clawed at the inside of my chest, leaving huge, burning gashes in their wake, my luxurious surroundings surrendering to that other reality, the individual horrors crowding together and overlapping. Repeating, over and over, like a broken record.

Wood, cool at first, then growing warmer beneath palms and cheek as I was bent over and used, time and again, their voices, filthy with privilege and entitlement, reducing me to nothing more than a cheap commodity—there to satisfy a momentary urge—assuaging the darkness just enough for them to present a smooth, unblemished face to society. Until the next time.

Harsh laughter echoing as Nico's disbelieving eyes widened, dark red blooming across his chest—pinpoints of light in the distance as cold water closed over my head, even colder winds buffeting my body as I gazed out over the city where I lived but where I could never make a life.

I tasted salt, felt black nothingness closing over my head as I rocked and fought against the current threatening to pull me under, against the winds attempting to lure me out into an endless void, heard the splash as my shoe fell and was swallowed by the water, disappearing like the dreams it had once represented. Dreams blown away by harsh winter winds and a shotgun's blast.

I felt myself lifted and cradled, pressed against warmth and solidity, soothed and molded into something limp and boneless.

"Let go, Natalia. Just let it go. I'll be here."

And with those words, the sobs took substance, transforming into keening cries accompanied by the tears I'd battled and defeated so many times before. But I was *so* tired of fighting. I just ... I couldn't any longer ... no more ... *no más, no puedo más ... Dios, no puedo soportar este dolor ... no puedo ... no puedo ...*

I beat my fists, whipped my head back and forth, ignoring the sudden sharp pain spearing the back of my skull. But no matter how much I hit and scratched and cried, he remained true to his word, never letting go, never fighting back. He simply cradled me close, catching each piece as I fell apart, putting me back together with gentle strokes and even gentler words filling in the fractures and smoothing over the cracks.

Tucking the sheet more securely about me, he left me curled on the floor with a fleeting kiss and quiet assurances that he wasn't leaving—that he would take care of me. Through watery, blurred vision, I watched as he spun the taps, testing the water. Only when the tub was nearly filled, wisps of steam rising from the water's surface, the lights dimmed to something that wouldn't aggravate swollen, sensitive eyes, did he return, unwrapping the sheet and lifting me easily.

In the tub, he sat behind me, pouring water from a crystal pitcher over my hair before massaging in a handful of shampoo. Fragrant suds spilled over my shoulders and the slopes of my breasts as his fingers massaged my scalp and neck, taking care to avoid the tender spot that elicited a sharp hiss after his fingers glanced over it with a bit too much pressure.

After rinsing my hair, he soaped a washcloth, taking his time running it over every inch of my body he could easily reach, my arms, beneath each breast, along my thighs and even a careful foray between my legs. There was nothing sexual or seductive in what he was doing, yet it was an unabashedly, wholly intimate task. One requiring complete trust.

Finally, he released the washcloth, waiting for it to bubble up with air and sink to the bottom of the tub before drawing me back against his chest, his arms wrapped loosely around my waist. Exhausted, I lay against him and waited.

"Once upon a time," he began, his voice raspy and uneven, "there was a very young boy and a very young girl. Cousins, born less than a year apart, which fostered a natural closeness, but beyond the bonds of family, they were also best friends."

"Jack—" My voice emerged hoarse and nearly as raw as his. "You don't have to do this."

His response was a single damp finger against my lips, held there for a moment before he leaned down and replaced that finger with his mouth, a brief, almost chaste kiss. His eyes, as he drew back, pleaded with me to not say anything more. Exposed in the amber and green depths, more fully than before, his quiet desperation. He needed to do this and I might be his sole opportunity.

With a nod, I resettled myself, shifting to my side so I could rest my head against his shoulder, my hand over the steady beat that sped up as he took a deep breath.

"To the world, these cousins were blessed with immense good fortune. Because the war raged during a large part of their early childhood, the European vacations their parents preferred were limited, but still, there were the homes in New York and Palm Beach and the Cape with endless parties and gatherings where they could run free, associating with other children from families of similar, exalted means. The best of everything because for this family, nothing less than the best was to be expected. Even so, it was a lonely childhood. Nannies and governesses when they were young, boarding schools as they grew older. The boy was shy, preferring books to most people and the girl—" His chest rose again.

"As a very young girl, she was viewed by the family as precocious—perhaps a bit too precocious. She certainly knew more than any child her age should and never hesitated to let others know. The adults, they would have preferred if she took on some of the boy's reticence, while he would have been well-served to adopt a measure of her exuberance. I don't know," he said quietly, breaking the storytelling spell, "maybe that's why we were thrown together more often than we might have been otherwise."

One corner of his mouth twitched—from my perspective I couldn't quite tell if it was meant as grimace or smile. "Honestly, the more likely explanation is that it was convenient. Our parents were occupied with their civic duty in the form of social engagements, political strategy meetings, and of course, the all-important philanthropic war efforts. Fashion shows for war bonds, teas for military hospital support, of course, the endless cocktail parties to celebrate sending our boys overseas to become heroes and protect the American Way before more often than not returning in plain wooden coffins. Much easier to let nannies and governesses take care of our social lives. Except Ava couldn't stand the children deemed suitable as playmates and developed a nasty habit of running off, dragging me along, with some outrageous adventure in mind. And I usually didn't mind. Everything Ava cooked up—it was like the adventures in my books coming to life. Worth every grounding and punishment we endured."

One hand rose to play along the water's surface, light touches expanding into small ripples that grew and broke against our bodies and lapped against the sides of the tub in hypnotic splashes. "It couldn't last, of course. In keeping with family tradition, Ava was sent to Miss Porter's, I was packed off to Farraday. Childhood's end and the beginning of separate lives as was right and proper."

He reached past me to release the drain then stood, water sluicing from his body in a warm fall against my back. Stepping from the tub, he briskly dried himself off, then held a fresh towel open, enveloping me in its thick folds. Sensing that what he'd told me was merely prologue to the main story, that he needed these moments to gather himself for the next round, I submitted to his ministrations—standing quietly as he ran the towel over my body, blotted my hair dry, and even brushed a generous dusting of fragrant jasmine powder across my skin. Then, rather than simply lead me back to the bedroom, he took me in his arms, carrying me to the bed, his lips brushing kisses against my hair, my cheeks, my lips. Lying there, wrapped in the sheets and blankets and twilight shadows that carried our combined scent, his lips moved against my skin—words I couldn't quite make out, that I didn't strain to understand or ask to be repeated because I understood that the words themselves weren't what mattered.

With a shuddering breath, Jack drew away and propped himself up against the headboard, while I once again curled myself against him, head on his shoulder. Somewhere in the distance, a saxophone wailed, a trumpet offering an answering call that cut off abruptly, leaving an echoing silence in its wake.

"I loved Farraday," he finally said. "Loved my teachers, my classes, loved that my interests and opinions were encouraged and valued. They even called me by my given name rather than my nickname which allowed me to feel like a completely different person. No expectations, no baggage—I was permitted to simply … be."

Without warning, his initial self-introduction poked through layers of memory and time.

John Roemer. Although most people just call me Jack.

A second memory, chasing the first—the odd, irrational thought that had occurred to me in that moment of introduction that the more classic and elegant John really suited him better. And that he then became the first person in nearly four years to use my given name. How ironic. Exposing my true self that night, but also in a manner of speaking, his own.

"I'd finally found somewhere I belonged," he continued. "Ava, on the other hand, hated Porter's. To her, it was like a prison. And for someone like her—it was. Even then, she had her own way of doing things—rituals, I guess you could call them, but they didn't fall in line with the way things were done at Porter's. The more they tried to make her adhere, the more she rebelled. By that first Christmas break, she'd been expelled."

I could feel the tension gathering in the clenched muscles beneath my hand, in the subtle tremors that ran through his legs and made the covers twitch. He took my hand in his, gripping it lightly, his fingers restlessly playing along mine. "The expulsion was somewhat humiliating but hardly a tragedy—plenty of schools would be more than happy to take a Roemer, especially accompanied by a generous endowment—so after a lecture on expectations, both our families traveled to Palm Beach for the holidays, everything as usual, which suited Ava just fine."

Beneath my cheek, his chest rose and fell in rapid, shallow breaths, the low light in the room reflecting off the thin sheen of sweat glazing his skin.

"She loves the ocean, you know. Anywhere she can swim, actually—pool, lake, but the ocean … there's something about it that's always called to her. It wasn't unusual for her to sneak over to my house and talk me into going for a midnight swim. Just another adventure—we'd pretend to look for pirate ships or mermaids. But one night, she came over and … she didn't want to swim—"

As his breathing grew faster and more erratic, mine ceased, a sick feeling settling deep in the pit of my stomach.

"She'd been so damned lonely," he said, his normally patrician tones stripped down to bare clipped syllables. "I'd missed her too, but not like that. I'd never thought of her like that. She was just Ava. My cousin. My best friend. But never that. But I didn't know how to say no."

"*Madre de Dios.*" Not shock. I was beyond shock. More … invocation—a prayer for that confused long-ago boy who'd cared so much. "How old were you?"

"I'd just turned fourteen. She was almost fifteen." His fingers tightened around mine, his nails digging arcs into my skin. "I knew it was wrong. But I couldn't say no. Every night she'd come to me and no matter how sick and guilty I felt, I was fascinated by the things she did—what she did to me. And as the weeks went on, it went from every night to even during the day. It was like she was tempting fate, waiting to be caught and the longer we went undiscovered, the more reckless she got. Day after day … and I could never say no."

His eyes closed and his hold relaxed, as if he was giving me permission to leave, now that I knew. Not just permission, I realized, studying the slumped lines of his shoulders and bowed curve to his neck. Resignation. Expecting that I would recoil in horror or revulsion. But this story was far from over. He had still more to tell. I stroked his cheek, waiting for him to open his eyes.

"You should know me well enough by now to know I don't frighten so easily."

Amazingly, a smile crossed his face, softening the tense, austere lines into the younger features—the *real* features—of the man I'd grown to like very much.

"Might've been better if you did."

"For who?" I asked gently.

Pulling me close against him, he pressed his lips to my hair. "There you go again, holding me accountable."

The rest of the story unfolded like the plot of a gothic novel. How they'd finally been discovered on the deck of the family sailboat by friends of their parents, out on their own sailing excursion. The hushed, icy confrontation that followed. Ava's cool defiance in the face of their shock and disgust, pointing out both of her parents' many dalliances and indiscretions, including the affair her father had had with his sister-in-law—Jack's mother.

"The next day, I was sent back to New York to finish out the break before returning to Farraday. Thank God. I'm not sure what I would've done if they'd taken that away from me."

"And Ava?"

"Sent away." He studied our joined hands, his thumb restlessly playing across the tops of my knuckles. "They didn't tell me where, of course, but eventually I found out she'd been sent to a Swiss clinic to … be fixed. Electroshock therapy. After the operation."

"Operation?"

For the first time, his voice trembled, verged on breaking as he said, "They had her sterilized. The family didn't want to risk any potential … mistakes if the electroshock didn't 'settle her down.'"

True horror finally caught up, winding its way through stomach and chest and up into my throat. "*Madre santisima*, Jack, was she—"

"I don't know. I don't want to know."

I thought he was done then. I hoped he was, for his sake, because this was something no one should ever have to revisit. Why he'd felt it so important—

"When I turned fifteen, my father procured a companion for me. A … girlfriend of sorts. Had to make certain I hadn't been permanently damaged by my youthful transgression, after all." A bark of laughter echoed throughout the room—as if on cue, the distant saxophone and trumpet resumed their point and counterpoint, mournful dissonance painting the melodic wails with anger and a sharp edge of black humor.

"That's what he called it. 'Youthful transgression,' as if it was nothing more than getting caught taking the Aston for a joyride." He laughed again. "But I had to be certified fit to carry on the family name. Deemed … normal, especially since it was an open secret within my parents' circle, what had happened with me and Ava. And I went along with it, because I wanted nothing more than to prove I was normal, if only to myself."

He sighed. "What I said to you—I had no right. It's not as if I'm any better than those little Concord bastards. I had no—"

I pressed my fingers to his lips, replacing them a moment later with my mouth, swallowing his apology and guilt. Gradually, his arms rose to embrace me, pull me closer until I was draped over him like a comforting blanket. Our lovemaking this time was quiet, washing away a multitude of sins and hurts—a coming together of two people borne of extraordinary circumstances, but who, in the end, were really nothing more than two ordinary people.

Just Jack and Natalia.

How I wished we could remain that way.

TWENTY-FOUR

At some point, a drum had joined the duet of trumpet and saxophone—adding a militant, insistent beat at odds with the mournful blues-tinged lullabies that had continued as soundtrack to my fitful sleep. It took more than a few moments of blinking into the darkness—of a final note dissipating into the humid night air while the drumming continued, insistent and urgent—to recognize the tapping's true origins.

The care I took sliding from beneath Jack's arm proved unnecessary, as he did nothing more than burrow further into the bedclothes, one hand reaching out then stilling as it latched onto my recently occupied pillow. Sleeping the heavy, motionless sleep of the emotionally drained.

Regardless, I moved hurriedly through the room, pausing only to retrieve Jack's discarded shirt before closing the bedroom door behind myself. Thrusting my arms through the sleeves, I fastened a few buttons, enough for decency's sake, but beyond caring about decorum. All I cared about was making that infernal knocking stop. Maintaining the peace and quiet—however temporary or illusory it might be. I eased the suite's door open a crack, revealing the hotel manager in the sliver of doorway, his features elongated and distorted into something that might have appeared comical, had it not been for the pinched strain clearly evident.

"Yes?"

"Pardon the intrusion, ma'am, but I need to speak with Mr. Roemer."

"He's not available."

Predictably, the man's gaze took a subtle, yet thorough

inventory: the tousled hair, the masculine shirt, the bare legs. To his credit, however, his features remained professionally impassive as he insisted in the clipped drawl so evocative of Remy's, "I'm afraid, ma'am, that this is a matter of some urgency."

"With respect to Miss Roemer, I presume?" I asked, my own aristocratic tone making a timely reappearance. Thank God, because it served to keep my voice steady and cool in the face of sudden nerves and an unexpected flare of anger.

While his carefully schooled features never so much as flickered, his chest rose and fell with an obviously relieved breath.

"May I?" he asked, gesturing at the door. "I'll be but a moment, but I'm sure you understand the need for discretion?" A ghost of a smile crossed his face. "The halls of the Monteleone are well-known to be haunted. Always have to be aware of the walls having ears and telling tales."

Almost against my will, an answering smile touched my lips, even as a thread of unease began winding its way down my spine. "Of course."

Long after I'd closed the door on the manager, obviously relieved to have passed the responsibility of his knowledge on to another party, I sat on the bed, studying Jack's sleeping features. Reluctant as I was to disturb him, I couldn't help but trace a fingertip over his eyebrows and along the straight, prominent line of his nose before pausing just above the lower lip that relaxed in sleep was surprisingly full, the sharply etched edges of the upper lip providing balance. The two sides of the man clearly illustrated in this one small bit of anatomy if one cared to look closely enough. Even during waking hours, his mouth as a whole tended to appear thinner, more severe, the practice of holding himself in check such a force of habit, it permeated every aspect of his bearing.

What would it be like, I wondered, to let him remain this way for a while longer? Limbs relaxed and sprawled across the expanse of the king-sized bed, each breath deep and easy. Hair disheveled and falling over his brow, emphasizing the sharp patrician angles of his bone structure, marred only by an irregular purplish bruise spread high across one cheekbone. Ruefully, I rubbed at the still-tender spot on the back of my head, recalling how tightly he'd held on. Refusing to let go, allowing the rage to run its course and absorbing all my fury.

I wanted nothing more than to crawl beneath the covers and allow his body to warm mine. To sink into blissful unawareness if only to enjoy the delicious feeling of waking in bed beside another. Experience the magic of sharing those first, quiet moments, that truest self, with someone else. A desire so intense it was as if I could see it, shimmering, drawing me closer still with seductive whispers and promises of soothing the ache that went so much deeper than mere physical want.

If I chose not to wake him—chose not to say anything—we could continue, for just a while longer, to exist in this idyllic state. What harm could come of it, after all?

What harm, really?

My surroundings faded, replaced by sharp winds and the mind-numbing bleakness I'd experienced not so long ago—the city spread out before me, the fairy lights teasing and beckoning me to join them. Too easily, I could recall the temptation, the desire to let go—what it had taken to throw my hands up and back away. To run from the illusion of peace and tranquility, so high above the noisy, frantic earth. To save myself, even if I wasn't entirely certain how.

The one thing I had that Ava lacked. The sense of self-preservation. Among all the dark moments I'd endured, to be able to say no. Eighty-four stories up, when all appeared lost with no chance of ever reclaiming the girl I'd once been, I had still been able to recognize that regardless of everything that had happened, somewhere deep within, there still burned a tiny flicker of hope. Enough to allow me to experience fear. To draw me back from the edge.

Did Ava have anything like that? My arms wrapped around my legs, chin resting on upraised knees, I pondered Jack's sleeping form.

No. She didn't. She'd spent a lifetime relying on Jack, and more peripherally, Dante, and the other men who flitted in and out of her life to provide her with that hope. And in their constant effort to reassure her that she mattered, to give her life meaning, they'd also provided her with a buffer against reality.

Jack's confession had gone a long way toward explaining why he'd chosen to shoulder so much of this particular burden, and if there remained a slight niggling sense there was more still to the story, it was for the moment, inconsequential. The choice had long since been made, the patterns set. Until now. He said he was done. And for a myriad of reasons, including one or two selfish ones of my own that I didn't care to examine too closely, I hoped, after this adventure reached whatever conclusion it was destined for, it would truly be over.

We stared at each other in the shadowed room, his gaze sleepy and relaxed, a small smile playing about the edges of his mouth as he lazily trailed a finger up my calf. Capturing his hand in mine, I leaned down, pressing my mouth to his fingers.

"We have to talk."

• • •

"I do hope, Mr. Roemer, that you'll accept my sincerest apologies—"

"It's fine. You did your best," Jack cut the manager off, each syllable clipped and harsh, betraying the frustration lacing his magnanimous words. "Is the car on its way?"

"Yes sir. It's being brought round directly."

A few steps away, I nursed the coffee the manager had oh-so-solicitously served us, darkly amused by the power and influence obscene amounts of money could wield. How easily I'd forgotten the miracles it could make happen. Once apprised of the situation, the first thing Jack had done was phone down for a car—never mind that the close of business hours had long since passed. Less than thirty minutes later, we were packed, dressed, and downstairs waiting for its imminent arrival, driven over, apparently, by the owner himself of New Orleans' leading rental agency. For all I knew, it could well be the man's personal car.

"And you're certain that's all she said?"

"Yes sir, according to the desk clerk, those were her exact words—that she was going to catch a bus." The manager was relaying the same information he'd delivered to me—Jack making absolutely certain that it was true. That the fragile bubble had burst and our stolen time together was well and truly over.

"Struck me as mighty odd, she'd say such a thing, considering she left in the car she arrived here in. First thing I checked, after I found out she'd up and gone—seeing whether her car was still here or not. And no offense, sir, but Miss Ava's never seemed like one to take something as common as a bus."

"Shit." The purple bruise stood out livid and angry against skin faded to an anxious pallor. He stared through the lobby windows, seemingly looking past Royal Street and off into some imagined distance. "How the hell did she find out?"

"Beg pardon, sir?"

"Never mind." He shook his head, his gaze capturing mine for a brief moment. I answered his unspoken request, stepping close and putting a reassuring hand to his back as he shook out the map he held. "Can you help me figure out the best route to Montgomery?"

"Certainly."

Less than fifteen minutes later, our luggage was stored in the spacious trunk of the baby blue Lincoln with suicide doors that had rolled to a stop before the hotel doors, a hastily packed picnic basket placed on the backseat within easy reach. With any luck, the only things we'd have to stop for were gasoline and cold drinks.

With the lights of New Orleans dwindling behind us, I finally spoke. "Why Montgomery?"

"Because she *can*." He slammed his hand against the steering wheel, eliciting a sharp blare as his palm connected with the horn. Luckily, at this hour, there was no one to hear beyond drowsing birds and whatever prowled the silent waters of Lake Pontchartrain.

I stared out into the blue-black night, watching as the clouds thickened, backlit into silver, fairytale masses by the full moon. The knowledge that I'd been right—that there remained still more to this story—brought with it no relief. Not with the way we were racing through swamps and bayous toward yet another destination. I breathed deeply of the humid air, thick with the sickly-sweetness of decaying vegetation and the sharp bitterness of Jack's cigarette.

"She has no idea how lucky she is."

"Has no one ever chased you?"

I automatically began to respond no, but before the word had even fully formed, recognized it for a lie. "Once. A very long time ago." Unrealized dreams of adventure and Paris and boundless young love crystallized for a brief, wondrous moment before just as quickly dissipating and floating out to join the mass of clouds. "I didn't recognize it or appreciate it for the gift it was," I admitted quietly.

"But you do now."

"Yes."

"See, that's the difference between the two of you. You're capable of learning from your experiences. While she just keeps repeating them because it's the only thing she knows. The only thing she's capable of."

"I don't understand."

"I'm not sure I do either." He pulled deeply from his cigarette, the tip glowing a fierce red in the darkness. "It's just that, after Switzerland, she was ... different," he said, exhaling a narrow plume of smoke through the partially cracked window. "Worse in a lot of ways. Her little rituals and quirks became ... more. Things she was compelled to do. Repeating them over and over. And it extended to the bigger things in her life. Like she was trying to get it right for lack of a better description. If it wasn't perfect—to her way of thinking, at least—she'd destroy that attempt and start over."

Immediately, I envisioned those silver lipstick cases, lined up with uniform precision, the pristine white and silver expanse of her bedroom. The once spotless walls and tiles and photographs marred by a violent, fiery red. The illusion of cool perfection destroyed.

"How long was she there?"

"Nearly three years." The red tip of the cigarette arced out the window as he tossed it with an impatient flick of his fingers.

"Conveniently keeping her locked away until she turned eighteen."

"Then what?"

"They couldn't keep her any longer. And she turned up in New York, first husband—a French movie producer in his fifties who was going to make her a *star*—in tow." He spared me a quick glance. "At the time, I didn't see the differences. I was too deep into my own life—getting ready to graduate, go off to Stanford. Different coast, different world … putting what had happened even further behind me." He sighed. "Frankly, I'd been relieved she stayed away for so long. Even convinced myself that she'd forged a new existence for herself, going to school, socializing—doing the same thing I'd done."

"What was expected."

"Exactly." He snorted. "That's how self-absorbed I was—that I could believe Ava would ever conform. Then I found out."

"About what happened?"

"Yes." His fingers opened and closed around the steering wheel. "Once I got to college, she started sending postcards—one every day. At first, they just recounted every time we'd been … together—in exacting detail. Then they evolved into describing exactly what had been done to her in Switzerland. And at the end of every postcard asking why I hadn't helped."

"Oh, my God," I breathed. Shoving the armrest back up between the seatbacks, I slid across the wide front seat, resting my hand on the rigid muscles of his thigh. Trying to transmit comfort. Absolution. "It wasn't your fault, Jack. It wasn't. It's obvious she was never well. You were just a boy. You didn't even know where they'd taken her, let alone what had been done."

"I know," he sighed. "In my right mind, I know that. But those damned postcards … she taunted me with them, especially after she began changing the message at the end from asking why I hadn't helped, to saying I needed to help her. Needed to fix things. Make them perfect."

Twisting the knife just a bit further. I was torn between sympathy for such a sick woman and fury that she'd insisted on dragging Jack into her twisted machinations.

"What about her husband?"

"He was a means to an end—only lasted eight months. And her parents had more or less disowned her. She'd come into her own money when she turned eighteen, so they basically washed their hands of anything to do with her." He paused and added, "Unless, of course, the family reputation was at stake."

"Which left only you."

"Afraid so."

"You could have washed your hands of her as well and no one would have blamed you in the slightest. Why didn't you?"

Miles passed, the silence weighty and oppressive, compelling him to lean forward and turn on the radio, spinning the dial past crackling static and hard driving rock-and-roll and the twangy, too-strident strains of lovelorn country ballads until he found some faraway station he liked. Beneath quiet piano, muted sax and trumpet, and the hushed, intimate vocals that melded into an aching, plaintive jazz ballad his equally hushed, "Because if I'd only said no, none of it would have ever happened," could barely be heard.

"Oh, Jack." A sinking helplessness wound through me at his heartbreaking confession. So many years spent with this burden—a burden that should never have been his. "Oh … Jack," I repeated, incapable of more. Taking his hand in mine, I leaned my head against his shoulder, allowing night and music and the steady drone of rubber against asphalt to shroud us within its protective cocoon. It wasn't the idyllic escape of our luxurious hotel room, but for now, it would do.

TWENTY-FIVE

"There's more, you know."

We were parked at a rest stop off the highway, dawn beginning to shed watery light across the landscape, painting it in muted shades of grays and blues. A diner glowed at the far end of the expansive parking lot, a nimbus of neon and fluorescence cutting through the early morning gloom, inviting the weary to come and rest, but we'd eschewed the inevitable droning chatter and the scrape and clatter of silverware and ceramic plates in favor of sitting on the Lincoln's broad trunk. The contents of the hotel picnic basket spread between us on a cloth, anchored by condensation-drenched Coca-Colas that Jack had purchased at the service station end of the rest stop when he had the car filled up for the last leg of the journey.

Considering the hurry with which we'd departed New Orleans, we appeared to be slowing the closer we got to Montgomery. There still remained urgency and tension: in his white-knuckled grip on the steering wheel, in the rigid muscles of shoulder and thigh, where I rested against him for the majority of the drive, but our pace had undeniably slowed the closer we drew to Montgomery, until finally, he'd pulled into the rest stop. Ostensibly, for gas, but to my mind, it was almost as if he viewed it as his final line of defense—a point of no return. It was as if here, choice remained an option.

"There always is," I said quietly.

Cellophane crackled loudly as he unwrapped a fresh box of Marlboros, followed by the distinctive metallic *snick* of his lighter. When the expected sweet-acrid smell of burning tobacco didn't follow, I turned my head to find him staring off into the distance, the unlit cigarette dangling between two fingers.

Rolling the curved glass bottle between my palms I spoke slowly. "But this is your story. To keep or to tell. You've already revealed a great deal—certainly enough for me to understand why we're here. To understand … us. If you need to keep the rest close—keep it hidden away or protected—" My thumb played around the bottle's mouth, an infinite series of tiny circles. "I'm certainly in no position to judge."

The bottle was suddenly jerked from my hands, weak rays of emerging sunlight following its path, winking off the glass and giving it the appearance of a treasure hidden within the high grass where it ultimately landed. Jack's hands took possession of mine, damp and beseeching. "Tell me to turn around, Natalia. Tell me to take you—us—away and I will. Just tell me and we'll go."

Birds called to each other as the world around us continued to awaken, massive trucks chugging into the lot, spewing diesel fumes, engines screeching and sighing as they ground to a halt, their drivers tiredly heading into the diner, sparing us brief, disinterested glances as Jack pulled me close, desperation and defeat in his embrace.

"How I wish I could, Jack. How I wish you could." My forehead rested against his chest, my words emerging in the small space between us and floating off on the humid air. "But we both know you can't."

• • •

The sun blazed high overhead before we resumed our journey. We'd remained reclined on the car's trunk, holding each other, until the day was fully underway. Waiting for Jack to make up his mind. And until the moment we turned onto the road heading toward Montgomery rather than away, I wasn't at all certain he would complete the journey. I wasn't entirely certain he knew himself until he made that turn and began speaking.

"So, Montgomery."

"You don't need to do this."

"I do." His chest rose and fell, sweat darkening the pale blue chambray beneath his arms. "I need to keep talking, otherwise, I don't know … I'll turn around, head the hell away from this sick madness even though I can't outrun it, no matter how hard I try."

Part of me wishing he would turn around, knowing he'd hate himself if he did, I gently urged, "Then tell me."

The big car ate away the miles as he spoke—recalling the privileged, sheltered young man he'd been, exposed at Farraday for the first time to students from different cultures and walks of life. The headmaster there, a remarkably forward thinking man, encouraging that same openness of thought among the young men whose lives he was entrusted with shaping.

"Reverend Beckett and his wife inspired not only trust, but fostered an intense desire to change things. Made us aware that any world we desired to live in had to be of our own making. That if we remained static bystanders, we had no right to complain. They opened our previously narrow and defined worlds and spread it out like a treasure map. We just had to choose our paths."

"And what was your path?" Because if I knew nothing else, his chosen path had been anything but becoming Ava's caretaker.

"Path?" A trace of bitterness laced his short laugh. "There wasn't a single path for me. No, I was going to follow as many as I possibly could. As many places as I possibly could. Changing the world, one column inch at a time."

"Really?"

A corner of his mouth rose. "Nice to know I can still surprise you."

"I suspect, Jack, there's quite a lot about you that could still surprise me."

Writing. Of all things.

I studied him through new eyes, the doggedness and single-minded determination sharpening into something that made greater sense. Providing a more complete, more … *right* picture of the man. "On second thought," I said slowly, "not so surprising at all."

Again, the corners of his mouth twitched. "Well, my family was shocked. And predictably, horrified—such a vulgar pursuit, you know—but I didn't care. I went off to Stanford, full of fire and righteousness and eager to learn everything I could to become a damn crack reporter. I wanted the Pulitzer. Preferably before I was thirty."

"Ambitious."

"Family trait." He shrugged. "But I was outspoken about it. Considered every bit as vulgar as my chosen career."

So—the man who'd walked the visibly straight and narrow path of family respectability was in truth the rebel Ava had so desperately tried to be. And she obviously had no idea, thinking herself some sort of irresistible Pied Piper. Then, something more of what he'd said registered and I rapidly did the math. "You'll turn thirty this year, won't you?"

Outwardly, his expression never changed, but the air about him altered almost imperceptibly. "In December."

More miles disappeared as he lapsed into silence once again, clearly struggling with the effort of condensing a lifetime of drama into the miles that remained. As if in response, the car slowed yet again, buying more time.

"Then those fucking postcards started. Day after day, each chapter detailing her nightmare—but still, I was able to shove them to the back of my mind, determined to live my life, even though the guilt did start wearing at me." His thumb rubbed small circles on the steering wheel, smudged whorls, as if trying to obscure memories.

"Finally, a couple years later, a card came from New Orleans saying I needed to find her, now. That I needed to help her, now—before they took her away again. Like she somehow knew it was the one thing I wouldn't be able to ignore. I flew down and found her holed up at the Monteleone with three men, one of them some deadbeat musician claiming he'd married her. They were on their honeymoon and the other two were his gift to her." He spared me a sardonic glance.

"I cleaned up the mess, put the fear of God, the law, and the power of our family in those bastards, and got her straightened up. At least, momentarily. She was contrite, swearing up and down it would never happen again, until, of course, it did. And so, the pattern was set. After the first time, she stopped apologizing. We both knew it was a lie. She was trying to fix things to her satisfaction—find that elusive person who would make things right. Give her the fairytale ending. I suppose it came as a bonus, that when the fairytale fractured and I had to come riding to the rescue, she was exacting revenge for the one time I didn't come. Frankly, I'm not even sure which drives her more these days—the fairytale or the revenge."

"And no one would help?" He'd been a *boy*. The thought kept returning, rolling through my body with the force of a hurricane—that had my fists clenching against my thighs, desperately wishing I'd worn a skirt rather than the polished cotton capris, the fabric slick and too close-fitting to grasp. Never mind that he'd been older than I'd been, when I made my desperate swim to land—older even, than when I had struck out on my own. Yet it didn't negate the fact that I desperately wanted to protect the boy he should have been. Perhaps wanting to protect the girl I should have been as well.

"Who was going to help?" Tiny bones in his neck cracked and popped as he rolled his head. "And I wouldn't accept that my attempts were in all likelihood futile. I was too damned guilty—and arrogant. Convinced it was my responsibility to make things right. So I figured best thing I could do was put myself in a position of unquestionable power. I came back east, thrilled the family by finally following expectations all the way to Yale Law, learned the business, and put myself in charge of Ava's affairs."

"Jack—" I was on the verge of telling him to turn the car around—to take us somewhere we could disappear. Never be found again. Never to take on demands that should never have been ours to begin with.

"And even after all that, I was naïve enough to still hold out hope."

"For?"

"For me." His fingers thrummed against the steering wheel, an agitated tattoo. "What do you know of the Freedom Rides?"

Vague, grainy images—of buses, of bloodied young men

and women, some white, most of them black, of uniformed men, all of them white, wielding their weapons and their rage in equal measure—flashed through my mind. Images I'd instinctively shied away from if I happened across them in newspapers or on the television, reaching instead for Molière or Austen or Wodehouse. Retreating into worlds of manner and discourse, where differences of opinion were settled with sharp wit and gentle humor, rather than angry words and fists and so much blood it was difficult to discern the features beneath.

"I know of them, but not much more."

Jack nodded, understanding evident in his quick glance. "When they happened, I thought … maybe I could have both."

I shook my head, confused, yet knowing he would explain. Terrified, at this point, of what new nightmare would emerge.

"Reverend Beckett contacted me. Asked if I wanted to participate. Write about it. Ava and Dante were married, she was settled—actually seemed happy. Certainly happier than I'd ever seen her. And I let myself be sucked into the fantasy. Thinking it was finally over. And I knew the Ride had the potential to be one of those defining moments—the kind that would not only change lives but history. I wanted nothing more than to be there. Record it for posterity." He snorted. "I was so damned sure it was finally my shot. That maybe, I could return to the path I'd been meant for."

"What happened?"

"Never even made it onto the damned bus."

A sinking feeling took hold in my stomach. "What did she do?"

"Does it really matter?" He braced his arms against the steering wheel, the tendons standing out in stark relief—ropes drawn tight, holding him together. I knew, from experience, he welcomed that tension as much as he resented its necessity. That if I reached out, his skin would be cold to the touch even as his heart raced and anger simmered beneath the surface. Rage directed at everything he had to do to maintain order and a life not of his choosing.

"I missed the first bus in order to deal with her. But I was determined to fulfill my promise to Reverend Beckett and do something that was just for me, you know?"

I nodded, even though his attention was resolutely focused on the road ahead. "As soon as I could, I came down to try to catch up with one of the other buses."

The car lurched as he abruptly pulled it over to the shoulder, shuddering as a large tractor-trailer sped past.

"The things I saw, Natalia. What those bastards did—"

His gaze was haunted, clouded with the memories that refused to fade. Both hands firm on either side of his face, I forced him to keep looking at me. "It's all right, Jack. I know." Even without explicit knowledge of the details, I knew. All I had to do was recall Lazaro's maniacal laughter, the feral viciousness of his so-called comrades as they'd paraded through the streets, attacking anyone guilty of nothing more than being in the wrong place at the wrong time. "I know what you saw. You don't have to say anything more."

But this was it—the final piece of his story—the memories unfolding behind the opaque, shuttered depths of his eyes, scrolling like scenes from a horror film, endlessly repeating. "The bus I was supposed to be on? Stopped and set on fire by the Klan. Other buses, under police escort, made it into Montgomery, only to see those escorts mysteriously disappear and more Klansmen waiting with their bats and iron pipes and chains."

His jaw worked in a silent scream. "The photographer I was going to work with had gone on ahead without me. They smashed his camera against the side of his head—beat him to within an inch of his life. And people stood by and watched. No one stepping forward to help." His chest heaved with barely restrained emotion. "He's blind now. And I guess this is where I'm supposed to say at least the poor son of a bitch got out alive. Was one of the lucky ones."

His hands gripped mine, urgency in his voice as he asked, "How did you do it? Forget?"

"I didn't." The words emerged without hesitation or thought. An absolute truth. I may have thought I'd succeeded, I may have been able to push it to the furthest recesses of my mind, hidden in a dark corner where I'd imagined it rotting away to dust that would eventually blow away, but when brought out into the light of day, had emerged as sharp-edged and fully realized as if it had just occurred. "I tried, but no matter how much I wanted to, I could never really forget."

I wished I had some magic formula to eradicate his nightmares—and mine. To wipe the proverbial slate clean.

He stared, unseeing past me. "I can't keep doing this. I have to find some way to make it stop."

Did he mean the memories? Or Ava?

Did it even matter?

TWENTY-SIX

The powerful rumbling ceased, giving way to clicks and rattles as the engine settled, a pleasant counterpoint to the sharp staccato of rain against the windshield and the sibilant rush of tires on wet asphalt. A nearby traffic signal flashed its sequence of green to yellow to red, the lights piercing the eerie, storm-shrouded gloom with authority. People strolled briskly beneath the sheltering domes of umbrellas or, if caught unprepared by the sudden storm, dashed past with greater purpose, newspapers and handbags held aloft.

On the sidewalk beside where Jack had parked, a well-dressed Negro woman, slowed by an armful of shopping bags and the young child whose hand she held in a firm grip, paused beneath an awning's shelter, shifting her packages and blinking rainwater from her eyes. The moment was infinitesimal, barely long enough for her to catch her breath, but it was more than long enough to pull a florid-faced man to an abrupt stop. With the rain thrumming steadily against the car and the windows closed tight, we could hear nothing, but it wasn't necessary. It was like an old-fashioned silent movie, all large eyes and exaggerated gestures, his mouth drawn back in a rictus evocative of an angry child as he pointed to the prominently displayed *Whites Only* sign and she nodded, her gaze cast resolutely downward, shoulders hunched forward, her white-gloved hand cupped around the child's head.

"The more things change—"

I shifted my attention to Jack, whose gaze remained focused on the ugly scene, one hand curled around the door handle. Only when that white-knuckled grip relaxed, his hand sliding to rest on his thigh, did I glance back to the sidewalk, where the woman was nowhere to be found and the man remained, thumbs hooked in his waistband, a smile wreathing his fat face as if he'd been solely responsible for putting down an insurrection. Unease shuddered along my spine as my mind superimposed olive drab and rifles and cries of "*¡Viva Cuba Libre!*" over the man's self-satisfied posturing.

Change, regardless of reason, always seemed to be heralded with blood and violence and men playing at soldier even when they had no real understanding of why they fought. Maybe especially so.

"There will be more bloodshed before it's over, won't there?"

"I'm afraid so. If it can ever really be over." He scrubbed a tired hand over his face, rubbing at bloodshot eyes with thumb and forefinger. "But that's a fight for another day. Or maybe for someone else who still has the idealism and energy." He took several deep breaths; with each, he appeared to sit straighter, exhaustion ceding to resolve, his gaze cool and calculating.

"Well, at least we're in the right place." He pointed out a sleek white convertible parked in front of the station, neatly situated between two lines, the neon lights from the Greyhound sign painting the car's shimmering surface with wavering, imperfect waves of blue and red. "Time to see what the hell she wants now."

"Should I remain here?" Suddenly uncertain over what he might want. He'd needed me to this point, but would he want a witness to this final chapter? "I understand if this is something you need to do by yourself." Even though I was experiencing a deep-seated reluctance to his leaving the car. Temptation washing over me once more—near overwhelming in its intensity—to beg him to just turn the car back on and go. Anywhere. Away from this.

He sat, silently staring out at the sheets of rain. Long enough for the storm to subside to a gentle shower, faint slashes of blue bleeding through the gray morass of clouds. "I know I should tell you to stay here. That this is my battle and I need to finish it by myself, but I don't want to. I need to know that someone's beside me for once." He took my hand, his hold light, yet conveying a wealth of emotion. "I suppose I can add selfish bastard to my list of sins."

It was my turn to sit quietly, studying the rivulets of water as they trickled down the slope of the windshield. "I think … even if you told me to stay, I might not listen." I turned my hand so we were palm to palm. "I stood and watched the man I loved die, helpless to do anything. Watching as no one would do anything. I've spent too much of my life since then little more than a passive spectator—watching life go by, afraid to become involved with anyone or anything. I can't do that any longer."

My voice dropped. "Has anyone ever chased you, Jack?" Each word emerging slow and hesitant into the hushed silence of the abating storm. Asking, even though we both knew the answer.

He leaned in, his forehead coming to rest against mine. "As soon as this is over, we're going to start over, Natalia. I promise." His breath ghosted against my cheek, prompting me to shiver and clutch his hand, my voice trapped in my throat. Squeezing my hand, he brushed a gentle kiss across my temple, putting an effective seal on the words that were struggling to escape.

Emerging from the safety of the car, we crossed the street, pausing just outside the spotless glass door. From our vantage point, we could see her, swathed in white, from the magnificent fur coat to the broad-brimmed hat, to the framed sunglasses. As if sensing her very alienness, everyone walking through the terminal gave her a wide berth, but for curious glances and whispers while she sat, isolated like a queen surveying her subjects, steadily smoking.

The only indication that she noticed our entrance was a slight cock of the head, as if listening to voices only she could hear.

"Stay behind me," Jack said quietly, just before pushing open the door. Approaching slowly, he spoke in a steady voice. "Okay, Ava, here I am. I found you. Again."

"Of course you did, darling. A child could have found me." A narrow plume of smoke wound itself about her head, an obscene halo.

"Why here, Ava? How did you even—"

"You really thought I wouldn't find out?" Peering around his shoulder, I watched as she bent slightly and slid a magazine across the floor. The glossy paper slid against the tile with an ominous hiss before coming to a stop just shy of Jack's shoes, the simple block title *Reflections* facing up. A heraldic crest blazed from the cover, a rearing horse silhouetted against a pair of crossed swords, the motto, "*Cui servire est regnare*" imprinted on a banner unfurling from the rider's upraised arm.

"Whom to serve is to reign," I murmured almost absent-mindedly, drawing from another lifetime of Sunday Masses and long afternoons spent in tedious study of an ancient language.

"Or the interpretation we used, 'whose service is perfect freedom,'" Jack responded, his hand reaching back for mine, although his gaze remained trained on Ava.

"What is it?" I asked quietly.

"The alumni magazine. I wrote an article." A deep, shuddering breath wracked his body so thoroughly, I put a hand to his back, a steadying touch.

"About Montgomery?"

He nodded. "It was stupid. Just feeding my own vanity."

No. An attempt to hold on to a piece of himself. An act for which he hated himself, only because of *her*. And like a shark scenting blood, every time he attempted to break free, to live his life, the closer she circled, attempting to keep him trapped. My fingers curled, bunching into the material of his shirt within.

"You were a fool to think I'd never find out."

"I wasn't trying to hide it, Ava. I just can't imagine why you would care. You've never given a damn about anything but yourself."

"I care if it takes you away from me. Who else is going to fix things? I need you to fix things." Her voice rose, tinged with a hysterical edge. Looking around, I noticed that all motion had stopped, all attention focused on the unfolding drama. Ava at center stage, finally holding an audience rapt. Her voice steadier, she said, "Now tell her goodbye," the last word almost lost amidst gasps and cries and the sounds of toppling chairs and rapid footsteps and pleas to call the police.

"Christ, Ava, have you completely lost your mind?"

Hearing the tremor in his voice, I grew frantic, trying to look past him, clawing at the arm he had barring my way, his hissed, *"Don't,"* fueling my panic. Turning my head, I saw our reflections in the large plate glass window—Jack, positioned between me and Ava, one arm thrust protectively back around my body, the other outstretched, placating, his gaze focused on the gun held in a steady hand.

"You can't go, Jack." Her voice rose and fell in a dreamy, childlike sing-song. "Don't you understand? You can't leave."

"Ava, I'm here, I'm not going until we have this figured out."

My grip tightened in his shirt, my forehead tucked against his back, trying to hold on, terrified to let go.

"There's nothing to figure out. You just need to fix it. Like always."

His back rose and fell beneath me in a shuddering breath. "You need help, Ava—can't you see that?" His voice remained steady and gentle even as his back shuddered beneath my forehead. "More than what I can give."

"I don't need help. I just need things to be … fixed. And you can't do that if you're out playing at these stupid games." Another peek at our reflections revealed her waving the hand holding the gun at the magazine still resting by Jack's feet. "Trying to rescue worthless niggers and whores and God knows what other kinds of trash. You not allowed to help them—you're supposed to help *me.*" Her voice grew more bitter and shrill with each word. "And you certainly can't fix anything if you're busy fucking her. You're not supposed to be with *her.*"

"Leave her out of this. This is between you and me."

"Exactly." The dreamy quality of her voice intensified, a siren's ethereal call. "It's always going to be between you and me, Jack. Always."

The world tilted, the ground shifting and going out from beneath my feet, as I went tumbling, clutching my hands to my head, trying to block out the thundering roar that was so close … so much more deafening than the echo of memory it had been for all these years. Slowly, almost gracefully, Jack fell, pain and fear clouding those beautiful, haunted faun's eyes as he reached for me, brilliant scarlet blooming across his chest.

No. No. Not again. Dios mío, no, no, no...

Amidst the screams and sounds of shattering glass, I scrambled across the floor, throwing myself over him, blanketing his body.

"Get away from him!"

I looked up at her, still so perfect amidst the chaos, perfect but for the wild shaking of her hands as they attempted to hold the gun steady.

"Get away! He needs to get up. Jack, come on, Jack ... it was just a joke. Get up, Jack. Get up, get up, get *up*. Stop playing. It's not funny, Jack! It's not, it's not funny, it's *not!*"

"Shut up!"

With jerky motions, I yanked off my cardigan, balling it up and pressing it to Jack's chest. "Stay with me, please. Please don't go, Jack. Please." A tiny, isolated corner of my brain echoed with laughter tinged with more than a little hysteria at the fact that I was using Ava's very words, begging him not to leave me. Peals of laughter that turned to pained cries as I released everything I'd held locked away for so very long, every word I wished I could have said to Nico. Reverting to Spanish as I implored him to stay with me, that I couldn't let him go, couldn't bear to lose him—

"Get up, Jack, or I'll ... I'll shoot myself. I mean it this time. I'll really do it. I swear."

Ava stood with the gun to her temple, twisting it back and forth, the barrel tangling with the glorious red-gold strands of her hair in an obscene embrace.

"Do it," I spat. "Do you really think anyone would care?"

Wild-eyed, she looked around, taking in the near-deserted surroundings, only a few brave or unlucky souls left crouched behind ticket counters and peering around the edges of doors.

"Jack?"

Sirens wailed, growing closer as she repeated, "Jack?"

Damp fingers curled around my wrist. He met my gaze, his

hand moving from my wrist to my face, cupping my cheek. As I turned my head, kissing his palm, he spoke, his voice faint, yet every word clear.

"I can't fix things anymore. I never could."

An admission to me. A dismissal of her. Finally done—as he'd promised. But at what cost?

The gun lowered, almost as if of its own volition, as she continued to stare at Jack, head cocked. Her ocean blue eyes glittered brilliantly, endlessly empty and lost beyond their beautiful façade.

The approaching sirens grew impossibly loud, bullhorn amplified voices booming with orders to surrender competing with calls for medical help, and almost, but not quite, managing to drown out the screams.

TWENTY-SEVEN

Please don't go, Jack. Please. Stay with me.
    Please, Jack ... don't go ... don't go—
    Don't leave...

Blurred, wavering outlines gradually took shape and substance as I slowly blinked—the bullet-shaped metal shade of a gooseneck lamp, a white window frame, the unfurled petals of a large flower arrangement, their vibrant yellows and creamy ivories competing with the silver and gray of steadily falling rain and heavy clouds, the completely unexpected rumpled visage of Dante Campisi, collar open, shirtsleeves rolled to the elbow, slumped in a nearby chair.

"Dante?"

He straightened, a slow smiled crossing his face, but even in my muzzy state, I could see it didn't quite reach his eyes. "There you are, doll. We've been worried about you."

"We?" More indistinguishable croak than actual word, but Dante was clearly able to decipher its meaning, answering as he rose to pour a glass of water from a nearby plastic pitcher.

"Greg and Constance. They're with Jack right now."

"*Jack—*" I struggled to sit up, memories returning in a terrifying rush. Rain. Confrontation. Rose-gold hair tangling with the barrel of a gun. Thunder and burnt-metal combining with a rush of red and the hot scent of fresh blood. "I need to see him—" It was suddenly the most important thing in the world that I see him. Right *now*. Didn't Dante understand? I needed to see him. To make sure—

Pain shot from my hand up my arm as I inadvertently jostled the needle connecting a long tube to a bottle of IV fluid, the glass rattling against its metal stand.

"Hey, enough of that—" The mattress sank as Dante blocked my body with his, murmuring, "Enough, doll … enough. You need to stop. He's fine. I swear on my mother's grave, he's going to be fine." Big hands gripped my shoulders, their hold gentle, but firm as they eased me back to the pillows.

A wave of exhaustion suddenly overwhelmed me, draining what little fight remained. Sinking into the pillows, I asked, "What am I doing here?"

An unexpected grin crossed his face as he eased back. "Apparently, you went after Ava like a bat out of hell when she tried to make a move toward Jack." Inserting a straw into the plastic cup, he held it to my lips. "Wouldn't calm down even after the cops split you up, so the medics finally had to knock you out with a shot. Doc said you've been hysterical off and on, so they've been keeping you sedated."

Pulling a tray table over the bed, he placed the cup within easy reach. "I figured the reason you were so hysterical was because you needed to know about Jack, so I told them to lay off the sauce and I'd stay with you until you woke up. I wanted to tell you what you needed to know myself."

"He's really fine?" I managed, grateful to hear my voice sounding more like itself, albeit a bit hoarse.

My fingers traced the cup's edges, heart in my throat, even as I kept hearing Dante's reassurances. Jack was fine. He would be fine.

"About as fine as someone who's survived a bullet to the chest can be."

Before I even realized what had happened, he was leaning over me again, righting the overturned cup and throwing a towel over the water. "You can see him soon, if you want." His hand covered my shaking one. "He's been asking for you," he added before I could even form the words, much less speak them aloud.

"But … how?" I croaked, so much more to the question than the two words could convey, frustrated that my battered throat seemed to be incapable of producing more than a few words at a time. Luckily, Dante didn't appear to need more than a word or two, understanding the depths of my confusion and curiosity over what was clearly many lost hours. Perhaps even days.

"The nurses found my card in Jack's effects and called me." He pulled a slim engraved gold case from his pocket and extracted a thin, dark cigar, rolling it between the fingers of one hand while the other toyed with a matching gold lighter. "I called Greg and Constance and we all got here as soon as we could."

"And Ava?"

He leaned back in his chair, his posture ostensibly relaxed, but with a visible thread of tension lining him with sharply defined edges. "Locked away in the psychiatric ward until Jack and Greg can arrange for her to be transferred to a long-term home." He flicked the cap of the gold lighter open and closed, the metallic clicking ominously loud and foreboding.

"She's not going to get better." The words were flat, colored with an accepting matter-of-factness, but his gaze was distant and perhaps even a bit wistful, revealing that even he, too, had continued to hold out hope. Hope that had finally dissipated with the pull of a trigger. "She never was."

Rain continued steadily drumming against the windows, nearly drowning out the sounds of the door opening and the murmured conversation between a uniformed nurse and Dante which preceded his absenting himself as she approached with a whisper of white stockings and crêpe-soled shoes, her easy southern charm and kind eyes barely masking curiosity. After all, it wasn't as if there was anything physically wrong with me. However, her efficient manner never faltered, starched black-ribboned cap bobbing as she bustled about, fluffing pillows and adjusting the bed so I could sit more readily. Two fingers firm against my wrist, she stared at her plain, serviceable watch—worn with the face resting against the inside of the wrist, I idly noted before shifting my gaze back to the window and the brilliant flowers. Who had brought them?

"How do you feel about him?"

I turned my head away from the window to discover that Dante had silently returned and resumed his former post in the chair. How long had he been there, I wondered, studying me with that sharp, green gaze that saw so much?

"Excuse me?"

"I need to know how you feel about him."

"Why?"

"Because I love that man like a brother and he's got a hell of a road ahead of him."

My pulse, so recently praised by the nurse as steady and downright normal, skittered erratically before accelerating, drumming heavily at the base of my throat. "I thought you said he would be fine."

"Physically, sure." The toothpick resting in one corner of his mouth smoothly shifted to the other. "But after a lifetime of Ava's shit—after what just happened—do you really think he's going to be okay up here?" He touched a finger to his temple. "I guarantee you, he's not okay. Not right now. Maybe not for a long time. Maybe not ever."

My gaze followed the almost meditative motion of the toothpick as it shifted once again.

"I ..." I stopped, swallowed hard. I knew without a doubt, I hadn't wanted to lose him. Couldn't bear the thought of losing him. But was that because it was him? Or simply the idea of losing again? "I care about him," I admitted quietly, staring down, my fingers twisting the satin binding of the blanket the nurse had so solicitously tucked about me. "But ... I don't know."

"Caring's not good enough, Natalia." Pulling the toothpick from his mouth, Dante leaned forward in the chair, his expression set in harsh lines. The scent of fresh tobacco clung to him, adding a subtle edge of something dark and potentially unforgiving. Here, then, was the hardnosed man behind the genial façade he presented to the public. Not a man anyone with sense wanted to cross.

"Just a few years of Ava left me ass-end up and praying to the Holy Mother for salvation. So how do you think Jack must feel right now? With everything that's happened between them?"

His eyes narrowed as he leaned further forward, propping his forearms on the mattress. "Truth is, even if you loved him to the ends of the earth, I'm not sure either of you are good for each other right now. He needs to figure out what's next for him. Needs to figure out how to live a life where he's not constantly waiting for the other shoe to drop." I flinched as his hand came to rest over mine, bringing a momentary halt to my restless fidgeting. "And unless I'm completely off the mark, you, doll, have unfinished business of your own you got to make peace with."

"What makes you say that?" I would have congratulated myself on how cool and neutral my voice sounded except for the telltale prickles of heat beneath my skin—the uneasy twitching of my fingers that caused Dante's hand to further tighten over mine.

"Because—" His voice held an extraordinarily gentle note. A note that gave more weight to his words than if he'd shouted them. "People like you and me and Jack—we tend to have unfinished business. It's what drives us. Trying to outrun the devil."

"Like Ava?"

"Like Ava." He leaned back once more, his gaze shifting to the window, staring out past the rain. "So tell me, doll—what's your unfinished business?"

· · ·

I hovered in the doorway, swaying back and forth, as if to some rhythm understood only by my body. Fear did that to a person, I supposed. But there would be no turning and running. No longer. I'd made that promise to myself, what seemed like several lifetimes ago. Finally done running away. If there was any running to be done, it would be toward something. Toward new beginnings Toward what *I* wanted. Except I had no idea what I wanted. But at least I now had some inkling what was needed to begin the journey toward that discovery.

Or to quote Dante—clean slates were a necessary bitch.

"Courage, doll," the man himself whispered in my ear, his hand against the small of my back as much gentle urging as firm hold, keeping me from bolting. Dante was no one's fool. He knew just how torn I remained.

With a final deep breath, I crossed fully into the room, reassured by the warm presence of Greg and Constance, seated by Jack's bed. We'd already visited—they knew of my plans and agreed with Dante that it was the only real viable choice—for both of us.

"We'll be out in the hall, Natalia, if you need anything."

I registered Greg's quiet words and even managed a smile at the comforting squeeze of Constance's hand around mine as they passed by on their way out, but all else was a blur, my attention resolutely focused on Jack, still and unmoving as he stared out the window. His expression remained perfectly blank, seemingly oblivious to the movement and conversation around him, yet the minute twitching of his fingers against the blanket gave lie to the illusion.

With the room finally clear, I allowed myself to simply drink in the sight of him. Pale, his hair tumbling over his forehead and a slight glitter heightening the amber hues within his eyes and highlighting the two red splotches along his cheekbones, evidence of the slight fever he'd been running off and on. Not at all threatening, as Greg and Constance had reassured me during their visit. Just his body righting itself. And despite the frightening tangle of wires and tubes connected to him, the steady beeping of the monitor served as evidence that he was fine.

At the very least, alive.

"When are you leaving?"

His voice was pitched low, with ragged edges, ravaged by anesthesia and the tube which had fed him oxygen during those first terrifying hours.

"Soon."

He nodded and held out his hand. Closing the distance between us, I clung to it like a stranded swimmer clinging to a buoy. Warm and strong, his fingers closed over mine, his thumb stroking the erratic jackhammer of my pulse—even now, trying to soothe.

"I wish I could ask you to stay." A corner of his mouth twitched. "Again."

"I wish I could stay." Sinking into the bedside chair, I lowered my forehead to our joined hands. "Again."

"Did Dante give you the unfinished business lecture?"

Against my will, I found myself smiling, even as a lone tear trickled from the corner of my eye to bathe the back of his hand. "Yes."

"I hate admitting he's right."

"Oh, Jack—" I wished I had the strength to battle the tears, but I simply couldn't. Not any longer. I had come to love so much about him, but I didn't love him. I couldn't. There was too much standing between us. And he didn't love me either. The surety of that knowledge filled me with an indescribable sadness I couldn't begin to understand. How could I mourn for something I hadn't sought or wanted—that, in fact, didn't actually exist?

"Christ, if only things had been different."

The fantasy his words conjured flitted in and out of my mind, sweet and tempting before reality reasserted itself. "We most likely would never have met."

"Ever the pragmatist." His hand released mine, but only to cradle my cheek in his palm—maintaining contact until the bitter end. "So what are you going to do now?" The corner of his mouth quirked slightly before he gave up pretense that this was all right. That it was truly what either of us really wanted.

"Jack …" My voice trailed helplessly. Why was he making this so hard?

"Ah." His hand fell from my face to the blankets as his gaze shifted once again to the window. Looking for answers? Escape?

"Dante gave you the clean break for your own good treatise as well, I'm presuming." His speech, for the first time in recent memory, reverting to the clipped syllables and rounded patrician tones of our earliest meetings.

"Constance, actually." My hands recaptured his, desperate to hold on for just a moment longer. "Is it a mistake, Jack?"

"What?"

"Allowing others to determine what our choices should be? What direction our lives should take? Are we making an enormous mistake?" My hold tightened, committing his touch to memory and praying, for the first time in a very long time, for divine guidance.

"It's not as if either of us has a stellar track record in decision making. Our intentions might have been for the good, but at what cost?"

"We're still here. We've survived."

"True." He finally looked away from the window and met my gaze, his eyes as clear as I'd ever seen them, for once lacking the turmoil that had too often dulled their brilliant colors. "But is surviving the same as living?"

Several moments, pregnant with the words of a thousand unspoken conversations elapsed until, finally, he inclined his head toward the closed door.

"No—"

"You need to, because I can't. I'm on the verge of being the biggest selfish bastard imaginable, so you need to go. Go live and I'll do my damnedest to do the same and then maybe someday …" A cough masked the faltering of his voice, providing an excuse for him to turn away.

Knowing this was my last chance—that I *had* to let go, or else I wouldn't be able to at all—I released his hand and backed away.

"Maybe someday," I repeated, taking another step back, and another, the growing distance desperately needed. My heart broke anew, realizing that my last sight of him for the foreseeable future would be through a watery, blurry scrim, but there was no alternative. I simply couldn't take the necessary time to gather myself—to be an adult and leave calmly and rationally, with careful guarded goodbyes and an impersonal take care of yourself, secure in the knowledge that we were doing the right thing. How could I be at all certain this was the right thing? As many mistakes as I'd made in my life, could this be the biggest?

I lurched into the hallway and into Constance's waiting arms which closed around me as much to comfort as to keep me from running straight back into Jack's room.

"You're going to be fine, darling." She drew away, her free

hand smoothing my hair back with an elegant hand, soft brown eyes bright with emotion. "You're a strong girl and you're going to be fine." I had no idea how she knew with such certainty, but she knew—knew that I wanted nothing more than to retreat. To lock the door against an outside world I was terrified to face without benefit of the protective armor with which I'd shielded myself for so long.

Which, for the first time made me think, perhaps, just perhaps … what Dante and Greg and Constance were urging might, after all, be the right thing.

Go live and I'll do my damnedest to do the same and then maybe someday…

If Jack could come face to face with himself—confront his demons in order to move forward and whatever the future might bring—then maybe, just maybe—so could I.

TWENTY-EIGHT

I lifted the latch on the chain link fence gate, the metallic squeak like a ghost's wail, thin and lonely. What if no one was here? What if they'd left—moved away? My gaze scanned the yard and faded stucco exterior looking for any indication of either their continued residence or signs that someone new now inhabited this small shabby box.

I remained still, balanced between two of the round paving stones marking the path to the front door, imagining them much like Hansel and Gretel's trail of breadcrumbs.

Nothing prevents happiness like the memory of happiness.

The words floated through the transom of my mind, a teasing whisper recalled from a book, read during another lifetime and near-forgotten until this moment. It's not that I had ever been happy here. Living here had been a constant, concrete reminder of all I'd lost. I would never have been completely happy here. I could never be happy here.

But I *could* make peace—could reconcile past and present. Depending on what I'd find at the end of the path, I could at least reassure myself that I'd tried. And in the act of trying, I could finally move forward.

One measured step after another, I followed the stones until I stood in front of the door, my hand hovering just above the peeling brass knocker. I hesitated for another moment, doing nothing more than listening—to the distant traffic sounds from Calle Ocho, the insistent beat of a Tito Puente song drifting from a nearby radio. I even imagined I could hear the pop and sizzle of the onions and garlic being stirred in hot olive oil whose scent wafted from the cracked-open jalousies of a neighboring window.

I could even swear—beneath all of those noises—that I could discern the cultured voices of Mr. and Mrs. Cleaver, gently admonishing Beaver for some mischief or another. So even and well-modulated, every hurt and injury addressed and solved with nothing more than a few well-placed words.

Was it real? Or simply my imagination, returning to the final night I'd spent in this house? My injuries and hurts too deep-seated and overwhelming for good intentions and well-meaning words.

Taking a deep breath, I lifted the knocker and let it drop once. Then again. The sound of approaching footsteps echoed the heavy pounding of my heart. As they drew closer, I shut my eyes—unwilling to see. So afraid to be disappointed.

"Talia? Oh my God … *Talia?*"

The voice held but an echo of what it had once been, but it was enough. I opened my eyes.

"Carlito."

I said it again, my voice muffled against the front of his shirt as he hugged me close—my baby brother who now towered over me.

"Carlito."

MEN WALK ON MOON
VOICE FROM MOON: 'EAGLE HAS LANDED'

THE NEW YORK TIMES
JULY 21, 1969

EPILOGUE

JULY 1969

Everything and nothing had changed.

The roads still twisted and turned, hugging the mountain curves like a lover's embrace. The setting sun still bathed the uniquely California landscape in shimmering gold and white, accented at this time of year with radiant fingers of red and orange, beckoning twilight closer. The endless expanse of beach remained familiar and welcoming, knots of people scattered across its surface while surfers still paddled far out into the Pacific, ever in search of the perfect wave. And the salt and brine on the air still spoke of an exhilarating freedom.

Yet so very much else was different—the world having succumbed to changes no one could have possibly predicted. There had been cultural revolutions and riots and heartbreaking losses— from the brutal, seemingly endless conflict half a world away in Vietnam, to the ones closer to home. The lost including young men whether willing or not sent to fight a war not our own, to the fine minds and noble hearts taken too soon by the whims of madmen.

There was, as of yesterday evening, a man, standing on the moon's surface at the hopefully named Tranquility Base, looking back toward a peaceful blue and green and white sphere, literally a world removed from the turmoil that rocked humanity in ways both large and small.

But perhaps nothing had changed so much in the last tumultuous four years as the solitary man, easily balanced on the promontory separating two segments of sandy beach. Wearing loose dark pants and a shirt that the incoming breezes molded closely to a body rendered perhaps too thin—a sharp contrast to the business suits and preppy khakis and starched button-downs he'd once worn like impenetrable armor. The hair, too, was longer, brushing past his collar and falling across his forehead, no more razor-cut and sharp angles, slicked back as if to reveal all, but in reality, as much a mask as the former young lawyer's wardrobe had been a costume. For a role he had played for far too long and in which he'd very nearly lost himself.

Took one to know one, after all.

And it wasn't as if I hadn't undergone my fair share of changes as well. The dark structured sheath dresses and ladylike pumps exchanged for light, flowing dresses and airy sandals in the rainbow hues which I'd denied myself in my attempts to blend in.

To hide.

My hair, too, worn loose rather than imprisoned in the chignons and French twists that had served as much as armor as Jack's Savile Row suits and engraved cufflinks. The one anomaly to my seemingly Bohemian wardrobe was the diamond pendant worn on a thin platinum chain around my neck. The past had finally been delegated to its rightful place, but that stone would remain with me always. My touchstone.

"Ready, doll?"

Hugging my elbows close, I kept my stare fixed on Jack, drinking in all the changes. As solitary and aloof as ever, yet at the same time projecting a certain vulnerability he wore as comfortably as the new wardrobe and hair.

"You're absolutely certain he wants me here?" I murmured to Dante as we stepped from the parking lot's asphalt surface to the sand.

"You think I would screw with you about this?"

"No. Not really." I shook my head as I put a hand to his shoulder for balance, slipping off one sandal, then the other. "As manipulative a bastard as you can be, this is the one thing I'm certain you wouldn't play with." I sighed and toyed with the thin leather straps of the sandals, twisting them around my fingers.

His brows drew together as his sharp gaze raked over me with a fond—and familiar—exasperation. "You know, I think I liked it better when you used to be all reserved and proper. This outspokenness of yours still takes me by surprise every now and again. And you know I don't like surprises."

"You would prefer boring?"

"Doll, the one thing you have never been is boring." The corners of his mouth quirked briefly before his expression settled back into somber lines. "Look—he had only two requests—that it be here and that I bring you."

The late-afternoon heat of the sand soaked into the soles of my feet, the grittiness heightening awareness to a razor-sharp point. "I admit, I wondered if this day would ever come."

"It was inevitable." His response was clipped, yet resigned. "Come on—let's get it over with." Taking Dante's proffered arm, we traversed the short distance to where Jack stood, seemingly lost in thought and unaware of our approach. A deception that was revealed as his voice drifted back while we were still several steps away.

"I'm glad you came, Natalia."

Reserve and uncertainty dissipated like the mist splashing over the rocks from the incoming waves. Dropping my shoes to the sand and releasing Dante's arm, I crossed the final few feet on my own, reaching out to grasp Jack's outstretched hand as he pulled me up onto rocks worn smooth by millennia of waves. Up close, I noted more changes—the beginnings of gray at his temples that lent a new gravity to his features and a fine webbing of lines radiating from the corners of his eyes, as if evidence of many days spent staring into the distance. Overall, however, there was a far more settled air about him. Settled, that is, but for the shadows lurking in his eyes, shadows that were nevertheless accompanied by a smile as he grasped both of my hands—a hold I returned with a squeeze of my own. This moment *had* been inevitable.

"I couldn't say no. Even if I'd wanted to. Which I didn't."

His smile deepened as my voice drifted off on the ocean breeze.

"Like I said—I'm glad. I can't imagine doing this without either of you." He glanced past my shoulder to acknowledge Dante's presence. Releasing my hands, he turned to pick up the small silver urn that had been resting on the rocks by his feet.

"How did it happen?" I asked quietly as he turned the urn in his hands, studying the play of light and waves across the warm burnished surface.

"The way she would have wanted," he replied, looking out toward the horizon. "You know we'd found that facility for her outside Monterey—" The smile he exchanged with Dante who'd joined us on the promontory was wistful and tinged with more than a bit of irony, sending a cold finger of a chill down my spine despite the day's lingering warmth. "We thought she'd like being near the ocean, you know?"

From an outcropping of rocks further down the beach a lone seal barked, as if in understanding. "Short story is, she somehow managed to escape the building one night and make her way to the beach. They found her the next day, just … floating."

"Not your fault, brother," Dante interjected as Jack's voice tapered off. "You know her doctors all said it was likely more a matter of when than if."

Jack nodded, his thumb toying over the simple engraved name and dates etched on the smooth metal. "I know."

"When was the last time you saw her?" I asked, mesmerized by the dance a pair of seagulls were performing against the lavender-hued twilight sky.

"The bus station."

Shocked, I looked from Jack to Dante for confirmation. "Yeah." Dante shrugged, hands thrust deep into the pockets of his linen slacks. "None of us. Not Jack or me or Greg or Constance. Sent back every damned letter anyone tried writing. Her doctors said we were better off just letting it be. Like I said—they told us it was a matter of when, not if, so I figure their reasoning was it was best for her to have what peace she could. If any."

"I hope so," Jack murmured beside me. "I hope so," he repeated, as he began unscrewing the urn's lid. Stepping forward, he drew his arm back then forward in a graceful arc, fine gray ash following the same trajectory until it was picked up by the wind and carried out to sea. Without a word, he handed the urn to Dante and stepped back, and it seemed like the most natural thing to reach out and take his hand, the feel of his fingers around mine intimately familiar, even after all this time. Silently we watched as Dante tossed the remaining ashes into the wind before pressing a kiss to the urn and flinging it far out into the surf where it bobbed for a few moments, capturing the seagulls' attention, until it was swallowed by the blue-gray waves. As the setting sun captured the final glints of silver, a measure of weightlessness overtook me, a profound sense of gratefulness.

"*Vaya con Dios*," I whispered into the oncoming night.

With a deep breath, Dante turned his back to the ocean. "Well, if you two don't mind, I'm gonna take myself off for a bit. Jack?"

Releasing my hand with a crooked half-smile, Jack followed Dante a few steps away where they had a quick, hushed exchange before Dante pulled Jack close for a quick embrace and the type of kiss on the cheek that only the most confident and masculine of men could exchange without hesitation or embarrassment.

"I'm to get you back to the hotel," Jack said as he returned to my side. Rather than take my hand again, he stood, arms crossed, his restless gaze playing across the water, the families slowly packing up after a long day on the shore, the surfers determined to grab that one last perfect wave.

"I presumed as much."

"You appear to have made a hell of an impression on him the last few years."

"Dante and I, we understand each other." A statement conveyed in a tone that I hoped expressed the nature of our understanding.

"So I've gathered." Like Dante, he turned his back to the ocean, shifting his focus completely to me. This close, I could discern the individual greens and ambers and golds in the eyes I'd so long ago likened to those of the mythical faun. And as remarkable and otherworldly as they remained, they also carried within them a calm, centered feel, to borrow the vernacular of the yogi whose book I'd most recently worked on. Whether Ava had ultimately found peace or not, Jack clearly had. At some point, he had finally let go.

What did he see, looking into my eyes, I wondered?

"I heard your father works for him now."

I nodded. "Dante decided it would be a wise move to build an oceanfront hotel north of Miami Beach. He sees that as the next big area of growth and tourism in the city. And he thought hiring someone who was bilingual and had a wealth of business experience would be to his benefit. Allow him to keep his primary focus in Las Vegas while expanding his empire."

Jack's head went back as a full-bodied laugh exploded. "Goddamned sneaky bastard."

"Indeed." I had tried, so often, to be annoyed with what I'd seen as his meddling—had let him know in no uncertain terms what he provided was unasked for interference and skirted dangerously close to pity.

He'd told me to shut up.

Dante Campisi was not the sort of man who did things simply out of the kindness of his heart. He had made a wise decision— for all parties involved. A fact of which he reminded me at every possible opportunity, as if to reinforce understanding that it was not and never would be pity.

As I said, we understood each other.

"So you've reunited with your family?"

"Consider it more ... a work in progress. They still don't

completely understand me, but I think we've come to a mutual agreement that they don't necessarily have to understand me to love me."

As I'd come to the understanding that I needed their love.

The lone exception had been Abuela. To her dying breath, she had never forgiven me for the shame she insisted I'd visited on the San Martín name. Simply because I refused to conform. Still refused to get married for propriety's sake—to preserve the integrity of a name which no longer carried any import. However, I could no more control her feelings than I could make her understand how little the San Martín name mattered any longer. My one regret was that she'd been unable to find it in herself to unbend enough to accept me as the woman I'd become. But that would have meant acknowledging that she had been wrong, all those years ago, trying to force her vision of a future on me. That misguided belief that Cuba—our Cuba—would one day be returned to us. More and more, it was obvious that would never be the case.

"I think we all understand the important thing is we not lose each other again—especially now."

I turned away from Jack and stared intently over the water—attempting to visualize that imaginary line where west became east.

"Carlito's in Vietnam."

"Oh, Christ."

"Stupid little fool had a deferment—was attending medical school when he up and decided to join the Army. Couldn't stand the thought of anyone needing medical attention and there not being enough people over there to give it to them. And if that's not enough, he volunteered to become a helicopter medic. Flying right into the teeth of danger."

I swallowed hard. "I'm so proud of him, but *Dios mío*, how I hate it."

"And your parents?"

"Mamá lights a lot of candles. Papi doesn't say much, but he makes a point to hire returning veterans. He's good to them when so few others are."

Silence fell, not the awkward pause of acquaintances having run out of things to say, but rather a respite—a gathering of energy and strength to forge ahead and confront that which had remained unspoken between us for all these years. The only question would be who would be brave enough to breach the stillness first.

"What about you, Natalia?"

"Me?" I shrugged, my hands toying with the gauzy folds of my skirt. "I work. I attended the Sorbonne for a year." I offered the last almost shyly.

The long breath he released wove together with the light breeze. "You finally went to Paris."

"I did." Suddenly restless, I eased down to sit on the rocks, hoping their residual warmth would soothe the urge to run and hide. It wasn't often it overtook me anymore, but every now and then, when it seemed as if my world was about to undergo a seismic shift, the impulse reappeared, making its demands in sly, insidious whispers.

"Was it everything you expected?"

"No," I answered flatly. "But I am glad I went."

His noncommittal, "Hm," lingered briefly before floating away on the breeze. Taking a seat on the rocks beside me, he tilted his head back, allowing the last rays of daylight to bathe his face in an otherworldly glow, gilding his tawny head with fiery streaks.

"What happened?"

"Nothing. I've just come to the understanding there are some questions that will never have answers."

"So you're making it a point to address the ones you can." The beginnings of a smile emerged, nothing more than a deepening of the lines around his eyes.

"I prefer to think of it as living with no regrets. As someone I respect a great deal once exhorted me to do."

The faint smile faded. "And have you lived, Natalia? Are you happy?"

Another silence fell—one that waited for me to pierce its veil. "I think so," I finally said.

"You think?"

"There are things about my life that make me very happy." I mirrored his pose, tilting my head back, allowing the wind to play through my hair like a lover's caress. "Having a relationship, however tenuous, with my family, is good. Working with Greg and Constance makes me very happy."

"They say you've turned into a really fine editor. And an even better writer."

A smile tugged at the corners of my mouth. "I suppose I shouldn't be surprised that you know."

"Greg's downright smug about the whole thing."

"Let's see if I have a second one in me before he gets too smug."

"You do."

A quiet confidence underscored his words, beating back, at least for the moment, the secret fears I'd harbored since shyly offering Greg and Constance the manuscript that had come pouring out during a long, Paris winter.

A lengthy pause, pregnant with expectation, stretched between us. Whatever weighed on his mind, I understood he wouldn't ask unless I provided him with an opening.

"You can ask, Jack."

"Can I? Even after all this time?"

"Of course."

"Why would you say that with such certainty?"

"Because we promised," I replied gently.

A grateful half-smile lightened his expression, the brief touch of his hand to mine a sign that he, too, remembered our pact. "Have you found love?"

"I did."

"Did?" He paused, then asked, "Is the past tense an accident?"

"No."

"What happened?"

I brushed a wayward strand of hair from my eyes, staring up into the early evening sky with its shades of deep blues and grays bleeding into the last hints of rose gold painting the horizon. This time of day might always remind me of him, but in a wistful and bittersweet sort of way. Small mercies, I supposed.

"It was very good for a long while. It seemed as if we were perfect for each other. Despite many differences in our backgrounds, we had a remarkable compatibility."

"But?"

"But we were too frightened. There was trust, but the basic foundation wasn't sound. I think we were each scared the differences might drive one or the other to leave. Finally, one of us did."

"Which one?"

I answered with a shrug. My final act of running away, the devil on my shoulder had whispered, but that was a fear I was able to wrestle into submission with relative ease. There had been no running, no sneaking off, no fights or recriminations or misunderstandings. Remy and I had both gone into our relationship understanding it was a risk—we had both hurt each other and had responded in ways long conditioned into us—but we both decided being together was a risk worth taking.

No regrets or unanswered questions.

"Do you think it's possible to ever find it again?"

The tiny hairs along the base of my neck prickled, inherently understanding he meant not what I'd had with Remy, but rather, with Nico. The sense of inevitable.

Of forever.

"I think—" I paused, carefully choosing my next words. "It couldn't ever be exactly the same."

"But does it have to be?"

"No."

"Good." He took a deep breath and released it slowly. "Good."

"What about you, Jack? What about your life?"

"Have you ever been to Hawaii?" On the surface an odd non sequitur rather than an answer, yet obvious in its meaning. At least, to me.

"No. I haven't."

"It's amazing. Green mountains and white beaches and an

endless blue expanse of water that extends to forever."

His description teased a memory from deep within—of similar mountains and beaches and warm waters that defied description. And prodded deep-seated longing to the surface. "It sounds beautiful."

"It is. The islands—they have a life of their own. As if something greater is lying in wait, just beneath the surface."

"I believe they call those volcanoes."

I grinned as he chuckled. "Touché. Volcanoes aside, however, it's a good place to stop running. To just ... be." The web of lines about his eyes deepened once again, but this time, rather than looking out over the seascape, his gaze turned inward. "I did what I needed to do. I traveled. Began writing again. Felt good."

"I saw your byline a few places." An admission I felt safe making without revealing how anxiously I'd perused newspapers and periodicals once Greg had alerted me to the first of Jack's articles, beating back terror when a story posted from a particularly dangerous corner of the world, attempting to read between the lines to see if he was really all right. Attempting to reassure myself that we had both made the right decision. That these were the lives we had to live, before—

Taking a deep breath, I rose and carefully picked my way down the rocks to the sand, leaving him staring out over the water—saying his goodbyes. Taking time for myself to confront the questions that had plagued me since the middle of the night phone call from Dante summoning me to California. To this moment.

I had lived. I had answered all the questions that could conceivably be answered. I had no regrets.

But one.

I sensed him standing beside me. "What are you waiting for?" His voice was soft.

"You."

"You sure?"

"About waiting for you?"

He shook his head as his hand rose to my face, brushing that errant strand of hair back. "About the rest of it." His gaze bored into mine, open and clear and without any guile. "I have good days and bad days."

My hand covered his, my heart beating with the rapid tattoo of hummingbird wings against my chest. "Who doesn't? So long as you let me help with your bad days and I promise to let you do the same when I have them—and I *do* have them. Just so long as there's no more hiding—or running."

What we'd been doing, under the guise of living, I understood. We'd had to, in order to heal. And so when the right moment finally presented itself, we'd know. We'd be open to new possibilities.

What a hopelessly tangled web, this business of living and loving with its inherent deceptions and inadvertently inflicted wounds. But worth it, in the end.

"You sure?" he repeated, giving me one last chance to retreat, to run—but no. Not again.

"I'm sure, Jack." I stepped close, my arms going around his waist as I closed my eyes.

Under starlit skies and to the music of the waves ... coming home.

ACKNOWLEDGMENTS

To *mon capitan*, Adrienne Rosado—whither thou goest, I go too, dude. As ever, you are the best.

Many thanks to my very patient editor, Randall Klein, and to everyone on the team at Diversion Books. You all have made this particular dream a reality for which I will be forever grateful.

To my twinling—onward to new adventures.

To my Writer Girls—hang on for the ride.

For my online families—thank you so much for the laughs and the support and the bright moments when all seems dark.

And as always, many, many, many thanks to my husband Lewis—you keep me from winding up in a clock tower far more than you might even imagine. I wouldn't be able to do this without you.

Both Sides Now
is available now!

In grief,
they find each other.

Through loss,
they find love.

They meet in a hospital corridor. Libby is there for Ethan, her mentor, her best friend, her husband. He's dying, and she's struggling to survive. Nick is there for Katharine, his reason for living, the love of his life, his wife. She's dying, and he holds on all the tighter as she slips away from him.

They can't do this alone. But maybe they don't have to.

From that chance meeting grows a fast friendship, one of gallows humor, of life in South Florida, of shared experiences in their marriages—the fights, the quirks, the love. Libby and Nick become for each other what no one else can: the person who understands, who hears with the same ears, who sees with the same eyes. In stunning prose, Barbara Ferrer maps the sacred terrain of Libby and Nick's connection as it develops from one of necessity, to one of possibility.

Deep and powerful, this nuanced, elegiac portrait of two marriages, of sickness and survival, and of the healing power of human connection will resonate with readers for years, and showcases Ferrer in all of her brilliant insightfulness.

CPSIA information can be obtained at www.ICGtesting.com
Printed in the USA
BVOW08s2055101215

429949BV00003B/13/P